Angel's Rebellion

Estelle Maher

Angel's Rebellion

First published in 2018
Estelle Maher

Copyright © Estelle Maher 2018

The rights of the author have been asserted in accordance with Sections 77 and 78 of the Copyright Designs and Patents Act, 1988.

All rights reserved.
No part of this book may be reproduced (including photocopying or storing in any medium by electronic means and whether or not transiently or incidentally to some other use of this publication) without the written permission of the copyright holder except in accordance with the provisions of the Copyright, design and Patents Act 1988. Applications for the Copyright holder's written permission to reproduce any part of this publication should be addresses to the publishers.

ISBN: 978-1723292651

This book is a work of fiction. Names, characters, businesses, organisations, places and events other than those clearly in the public domain, are either the product of the author's imagination or are used fictitiously. Any resemblance to actual persons, living or dead, events or locales is entirely coincidental.

DEDICATION

For my babies.
They're older now, but the name stuck.

It was pride that changed angels into devils; it is humility that makes men as angels.
　　　　　　　　　　　　　　　　　Saint Augustine

ACKNOWLEDGEMENTS

I'd like to thank Sue Miller my editor, who is Canadian. She can do everything, and I mean everything. She edits, she writes, she advises, she mentors, she promotes, she organises a lot of people's lives and she makes dreams come true.
But she can't say Wirral.

I'd like to thank Alan Jones for another fabulous cover. Some of my earlier suggestions were only fit for the 'top shelf'. He put his foot down, went somewhere in his house to swear about me and then created that beautiful picture on the front that your greasy fingers are now marking.

I have to give a big thanks to the TeamAuthorUK team for their support, humour and friendship,
especially Lorna McCann.

I'd like to thank Tom Baker. No, he's not a 1970's Time Lord with a penchant for an exaggerated scarf. He actually works…well I'm not sure where he works…but he must get paid well as he has a fair amount of chocolate in his fridge. I'd like to not only thank him for his advice on poker and helping me write a scene in this book, but for being one of its first readers and telling me it was good. I would also like to thank him for putting me in countless taxis when he knew my liver could take no more.

I'd like to thank another Allan Jones. I feel it necessary to say he has a good job too. Again, not sure what it is but he goes to France a lot and walks around like he knows something the rest of us don't. Even I'm not sure what it is but I keep him close in case he spills. I thought he might when I asked him to 'test' this book. He was very complimentary and gave me the confidence to change things and taught me to listen to my gut. But I still don't know why he smiles all the time.

I'd like to thank Helen Payne. Not only for all her design work, not only for her printing, not only for her help in making a lot of my promotional material but for her ice cream. After a hard day's work, she gives me ice cream and not crap stuff either. Proper posh stuff with swirly bits. She's been there for me always and is the biggest giver I know.

Finally, my family. My children, Chloé & Zack, to know you are proud of me is one of the reasons I keep writing. That and the money, of course!

And to Mr M, he's not only kept my glass full but my heart as well. And I know you think I mean with love but that was always there. He fills it with hope and ambition when I feel like I'm a fraud and I should find a job as a lint picker in the local charity shop. Thank you, my darling, for keeping the house quiet when I needed it, for bringing me wine when I needed it and for giving me hugs whether
I needed them or not.

I'd like to thank the tree in helping me create this book (unless it's on Kindle, yay for you, Sting will be proud).
But most of all, thank you, the reader of this book. Enjoy!

CHAPTER 1

'BRACE! BRACE! BRACE!'
As Sean threw his head between his knees his whole body flooded with pins and needles piercing every nerve and fibre in his body. His mind was racing with thoughts of his mum, his friends and whether he should try and phone someone. He even thought for a split second of whether he should put his shoes back on. He knew it was an absurd thought, but if he was going to die he wanted it to be in his new Jimmy Choo's. The thought of being found with his socked feet sticking out like the Wicked Witch of the East filled him with horror and humour at the same time. He could see them between his feet, but he felt he couldn't move any more than he had been told to.

He could hear banging all around the plane especially from underneath and thought that maybe they had landed but the lurch upwards told him not. The banging became more violent and the plane was heaving and shaking too much for it to be near the ground. He could feel the stinging of tears in his eyes and wished he'd done more. He wasn't sure what 'more' meant. Only that he wished he'd done something more. He was only thirty.

He had flown back from New York on a row of three seats, with only him occupying the row. He was pleased when the flight had started, and he was alone. He had kicked off his shoes early on, spread himself out like an opening cabbage and slowly drank a bottle of wine through the flight while licking his lips as he watched Hugh Jackman's rippling muscles as Wolverine played on the small screen in front of him.

It all changed on the descent. The atmosphere within the cabin was as dark as the rainclouds outside and concerned attendants whispered grim secrets amongst themselves, unwilling to share with the rest of the airborne population. Sean, being at the rear of the plane could hear the strains in Sheila's, the lead attendant's, voice. Then Sean became aware of the ride feeling different, it sounded different, it was the different we all fear, and we don't know why. It was the 'different' our guts tell us to stay away from. Unfortunately, flying high in the sky in a metal tube didn't allow Sean the luxury of staying away. He was stuck with this 'different' and now he knew what is was.

Sean could hear people starting to scream. With his head between his knees he wondered if they could see something that he couldn't. Should he look? The buffeting of the plane was increasing and that's when Sean realised there was no engine noise. He knew he was going to die and immediately, of all the things he should have thought, or indeed felt, he was strangely first struck with disappointment that he never went to watch *Wicked* with his friend Grace while in New York.

He raised his head slightly to his right as he wanted to see the passengers on the far side of the cabin. He wanted some last human contact before the end, but his view was blocked by a man standing in the aisle. He could tell from the lower part of the man's body that he was facing Sean. While still curled, Sean craned his neck and looked at the face of a man in his forties. With his soft brown curls and slight tan, his blue eyes stared straight at Sean.

'Move to this seat.' The man pointed to the aisle seat, two seats away from where Sean was sitting by the window. The plane continued to shudder more violently, and Sean noticed the man had not stumbled or even reached for an object to steady him.

'NOW!' he commanded.

In a split second, Sean knew he must do as he was told, something deep inside him was screaming for him to move. He fumbled for his seatbelt clasp, desperately trying to open it and as soon as he felt the release he slid over to the aisle seat, found the straps to the seatbelt, wrapped them around his waist, clicked them in place and pulled with all his might.

The noise was deafening.

The screaming of people.

The screeching of abused metal.

The thunderous atmosphere and then black.

CHAPTER 2

Sean sat staring at the television craned over his hospital bed. He had seen the news numerous times, but still obsessed listening to all the various bulletins, analysation and the varying reasons as to what had made his plane crash. Most reports had all stated that there had been a complete engine failure, a flameout, during the descent after flying through a severe thunderstorm. With the engines failing to reignite, the plane had glided during the last few thousand feet. It had crash landed into a field and some woods. It had missed the runway by just over a mile.

Sean was one of the lucky ones. Some had died, and some wished they had. To accompany various bruises and grazes to his face, Sean was fortunate to have only suffered a herniated disc in his neck. Tablets, a recommendation of physiotherapy and hospital discharge were swiftly administered after 16 hours. He knew 15 people had not made it and according to the news, the hospital he was in had confirmed the fatality number was likely to rise.

He remembered very little from the crash. In fact, he didn't remember when the plane stopped and for that he was grateful. As Sean watched the videos on the news it was a miracle that anyone had walked away from the plane at all, but apparently, some did. Some had walked out of the wreckage, no more jelly-legged as if they had been on the waltzers. They had already been interviewed and news channels were periodically running key details from their stories. The plane had not only ripped apart, but trees caused further damage to the plane as it punched and battered its path through a wood.

Sean had been found unconscious in the back half of the broken plane, his upper body covered in tree debris. A huge tree stump was imbedded in the seat nearest the window and he was told that if he had been sitting there instead of the aisle he would never had made it to a hospital bed.

The live video footage was still running on the news, delivering graphic images of the crash site while peppering the reports with photographs of the dead when his mum walked in with his step-dad.

Sean's mum, now in her fifties, looked older today. The worry of her son had clearly temporarily aged her overnight. The relief felt from all of them once together was palpable.

'Oh, my boy,' Maggie cried as she bent forward to hug her son and then hesitated.

'It's okay Mum, give us a hug,' he croaked.

'Oh, Sean,' she gently scooped him to her chest. 'Your beautiful face,' she caressed his chin softly.

'I know, I've got more scratches than your old ABBA albums. I know I said I needed a good exfoliating, but I might have taken it to the extreme,' he chuckled. Maggie sat down at the bedside clutching Sean's hand while Charlie pulled up another chair he retrieved from the far side of the room.

'So, when can we take you home then?' pushed Maggie.

'I've been dressed for ages. All I'm waiting for is the discharge nurse to give me a prescription and some tablets and then I think I can go,' he replied.

'Don't you need a neck brace, son,' asked Charlie.

'No, I'm gonna phone a physio once I get back to Lanson.'

'I thought you were staying with us for a bit,' cried Maggie.

'Only for a few days Mum, then I need to get back. If I stay at yours any longer I'll end up with a gut like Charlie's,' he sniggered. Charlie glanced down at his rotund frame spilling out over his thighs. With only Charlie at home, Maggie liked to indulge him with food and good wine. While Charlie reciprocated with small gifts, bear hugs, and surprise weekends away, when he could get cover at his butcher's shop.

Maggie and Charlie had met later in life than usual and had only been married for twelve years. Charlie had slowly fallen in love with Maggie when she occasionally came in for some slices of pork and egg and the odd bag of mince. He had mustered the courage to ask her for a drink after he had chatted to her at the town carnival. They had sat in the sunshine outside the beer tent on the local common and talked until it was dark and a fifteen-year-old Sean complained that he wanted to go home. Three years later they were married, and Sean finally had a permanent dad at the age of eighteen.

Sean's real dad had not so much run for the hills but took a casual stroll out of her life as soon as Maggie had said she was pregnant. She was twenty-three and still living at home when she told Chris about the baby. He said he would look after her. So much so, he managed to get himself a job on a rig off the coast of Aberdeen. He would visit during his time off but then the visits became infrequent and his excuses became more elaborate for needing to stay in Scotland during his time off. By the time Maggie was eight months pregnant, he declared that he would be moving to Scotland permanently. Chris was never seen again, or any of his maintenance money.

Maggie was not broken-hearted, she was just scared more than anything. But the arrival of a healthy Sean made all her fears disappear as soon as he was born. But then that could have been the diamorphine.

When Sean was a few months old, Maggie couldn't bear her mother's moaning about lack of money, space and sleep so she moved to Clune where she still lived. Her house with Charlie is a far cry from the little two-bedroomed flat they had above an old antique shop, but Maggie and Sean have always agreed that they were happy, poor but happy.

Sean used to wonder about his real dad a lot when he was younger. He sometimes entertained the thought of taking a train to Scotland to find him. But once he questioned why to himself, he couldn't think of a good reason. He didn't need to know why Chris left them. He didn't need to know why he didn't send money to him. He didn't need to know why he never sent a birthday or Christmas card. He knew the answer already, his dad simply didn't care. So why should Sean. Then Charlie came into their lives and his mum had never been happier. She finally had someone she could look after until the end of her days. Charlie and Sean hit it off immediately. Maybe because there was no 'Dad' to replace, maybe it was because he made his mum happy or maybe it was because he bought him a Blu-ray player the first Christmas they were together. It all helped.

But Sean really fell in love with Charlie when he came

'out'. Sean had told his step-dad before he told his mum. It was easier to tell Charlie first, and Charlie had been amazingly supportive as he held Sean's hand under the kitchen table when he told his mum. She wasn't surprised, of course. Maggie had always known, she was simply relieved that it was now out in the open and they could all acknowledge it and talk freely about his feelings and relationships.

Today was one of those days when he was glad they were all there. Sean needed his mum, and his mum needed Charlie, and Sean needed Charlie to support his mum.

'Well, your room is all ready for you and you can stay for as long as you want. Charlie brought some nice steak from the shop for you to get your strength up, didn't you Charlie?' she smiled.

'Maybe I should have brought some extra for his face,' he tittered.

'They'll soon heal,' Maggie rubbed Sean's hand, 'at least we have him to nurse. Some are not so lucky,' she glanced at the TV screen hanging over the bed. They all stared at it in uncomfortable silence until the point that Sean could bear to listen to it no more and he swiftly turned it off. He swung his legs to the side of the bed and glanced at his socked feet. His memory took him to staring at his new shoes before the blackness.

'Did you bring me any shoes, Mum?' Sean asked softly. She rummaged into a calico tote bag and produced an old pair of trainers that Sean had left in his mum's years ago. She walked around the bed to where Sean was seated while Charlie vacated the chair. She silently slipped them onto his dangling feet and tied the laces like he was five-years-old. When she finished, she stood in front of him, raised her hand to stroke his face and weakly smiled. It wasn't long before a young nurse arrived with Sean's bag of medication and various forms to give to his GP.

'There's a lot of press at the front of the hospital,' she sighed. 'However, if you want to avoid them I can take you out through the maternity side door. There's no one around there.' The nurse walked over to the window and peered down to the main hospital entrance. Even from the third floor the sight was overwhelming. Hundreds of people with cameras, pads and microphones were jostling beneath, while the car park was rammed with media trucks.

'They're like vultures out there,' she sneered. 'I know they want a story but even still, could they not wait until people are psychically and mentally ready to talk about it? They're even pouncing on people who weren't involved in the crash. Some poor bugger practically got mauled this morning when he walked out. They thought he'd been in the plane crash 'cos he was walking a bit gingerly. You'd walk a bit gingerly if you'd just had a haemorrhoid operation. Apparently, his wife was screaming at reporters to back off ' *'as 'er 'usband 'ad a sore arse'.*'

'Oh, that's hilarious,' sniggered Sean.

'Quite,' sniffed Maggie.

'I think the maternity exit may be best then, love,' said Charlie, nodding to the nurse. The nurse and Charlie helped Sean off the bed and after they left the side ward they followed the nurse silently through the warren of corridors until they reached the big wide world. They thanked the nurse for all her help and then Charlie left quickly to get the car to pick them up from the discreet entrance.

Maggie just stood silently next to Sean holding his hand. She wouldn't be happy until she had him safely home. Her mind started to wander to a dark place, but she stopped herself when Charlie's old Range Rover pulled up beside them.

'Here we go love, you jump in the front and I'll take your bag with me in the back,' Maggie said softly. After they had piled in, Charlie had no choice but to drive through the wall of reporters that were spilling out onto the narrow exit road in front of the main entrance.

'Look at that bloody car park!' Charlie shouted looking to his right. 'Patients have a hard enough time trying to get bloody parked here and look at it, filled with bloody news vans and flashy motors. That nurse was right, they're like parasites, feeding off the unfortunates.'

Sean stayed silent. In fact, he stayed silent throughout most of the hour's journey back to Clune. He relaxed a little when the familiarity of the streets he grew up in started to cocoon his vision.

He had loved Clune until his mid-teens. Clune suffocated all the teenagers at some point, but Sean's ordeal was harder than most. Any other gay people had stayed firmly in the closet and when Sean eventually admitted that he was, he really did feel like the only gay in the village. People he went to school with started to treat him differently. He never encountered anything violent or even mild verbal abuse but Clune wasn't like that anyway. The population of Clune would talk about it behind closed doors or at the next Round Table Meeting, no doubt. For Sean, he was silently sent to Coventry. The lads he had hung around with started to blame another person in his group if Sean had heard of a night out he wasn't included on. Holidays to Ibiza were booked and paid for before Sean got wind of it, then there would be theatrical disappointment from them all if Sean couldn't get a flight. He took the hint; it took nearly two years but eventually he realised they would never come around. It was then that he decided to move to Lanson, a larger town, twenty minutes' drive through the countryside and a higher population of homosexuals than 1.

Maggie and Charlie had been saddened with his decision to leave. Not disappointment with him, but with the village. They even contemplated moving to Lanson themselves, but Sean made it clear that this was something he needed to do on his own and besides, moving-house was one thing but moving the business as well was quite another.

As he continued to look out of the window at the passing rows of small shops, Sean's eye was caught by two young men walking in the opposite direction holding hands.

'Were those two holding hands?' he cried. Charlie glanced through his rear-view mirror.

'Oh yeah, they come in the shop a lot. They've been living here for about a year now,' he replied.

'May's daughter,' Maggie said leaning forward from the back seat, 'Gabby. Not sure if you remember her, Sean. Well, they say she's shacked up with Lorna from the local nursery. I'm not so sure though, I think she just likes wearing checked shirts as it hides the kiddie stains better. And Graham who divorced Karen last year and went to London, well they say that marriage broke up because he was found in bed with his best man.'

'Was it his best man? I never knew that. Someone told me it was the pizza delivery guy,' shouted Charlie.

'No,' replied Maggie settling back into the seat. 'He just walks funny from sitting on that motorbike all day.'

Sean burst out laughing. 'They'll be having Gay Pride here soon.'

'Oh, I do hope so,' Maggie said excitedly, 'the Clune Summer Carnival is shit.'

'You don't think it's shit when you add up the takings

from the burger and sausage order for the carnival barbecue,' bellowed Charlie.

'Gay people like burgers too, Charlie….and a bit of sausage,' she sniggered. They all burst out laughing until Sean asked them to stop as it was making his neck worse. They sniffed their laughing tears back until they pulled up onto the gravel drive of number 1 Clune Court. The red bricked house was built in the seventies and Maggie and Charlie were the second owners of the property. Clune Court was probably the nicest cul-de-sac in the village and even though the house looked a little dated it was still regarded as a lovely home.

Maggie rushed to open the front door while Charlie collected Sean's bag and helped him out. Sean felt a little stiff after the journey and was glad of the stretch as he walked into the house.

The house had not changed much since his parents had moved in. The stairs were still an open tread which seemed to be coming back into fashion. The open plan kitchen and family room was at the bottom of the wide hall and was the area of the house that most people gravitated toward.

'I'll put the kettle on.' Maggie threw her handbag down on to the breakfast bar and moved to the other side toward the sink. 'Charlie, will you run Sean a nice bath and make sure his room is warm. I'll make some tea and then maybe something to eat.' Maggie was starting to fuss. It was the kind of fussing mums do to keep busy and to make things seem normal.

'A bath would be lovely, thanks Charlie. But don't be putting your best Blue Stratos bubble bath in there. Be wasted on a tart like me,' he chortled. Charlie disappeared shaking his head.

'He's upped his game now, Sean. Likes a bit of Lynx

now, he thinks he's all manly when he wears it. Mind you, it does take the smell of meat off him a treat.'

Maggie walked around to the far side of the breakfast bar to where Sean was seated. She gave him a gentle hug and then instructed him to go to the bathroom and she would bring his tea up to him. As Sean ascended the stairs the smell of black pepper and limes drifted down the stairs from the steamy bathroom. Charlie was busying himself in there when Sean walked in.

'There are some fresh towels on the radiator and I've hung a clean bathrobe on the back of the door. Now, if you want anything else just shout.' He stared at Sean for a moment and smiled softly which Sean reciprocated as Charlie left.

In the steamy bathroom, Sean slowly began to undress. It was only when his clothes were on the floor he realised how filthy they were. As he looked down at his naked body he was a little shocked to see his entire body was covered in bruises. Huge blossoming cushions of purple and blue decorated his tender body. His mind could hear the ripping body of the plane.

He stepped into the hot steaming water and slowly immersed himself into a seating position. As he splashed the water over his shoulders his mum appeared from behind the door with his tea and a small plate of bourbon biscuits.

'Mum! I'm a bit old for you to be helping me in the bath now!' He raised his knees to his chin and wrapped his arms around his shins feeling a little self-conscious. Sean could see the distress in her face as she caught sight of his body. Maggie placed the mug and plate on top of the window sill and turned her back to him.

'I thought you might need a hand, son,' she whispered. 'What with your sore neck and all. You might do more damage straining your head to wash your hair. I can get Charlie to come up instead if that's more comfortable for you?'

She had a point, Sean thought. He would struggle to wash himself properly and this was his mum. Even though he felt he was too old, too exposed he also felt a little silly. She needed to mother him, and he understood that.

'You're right as always, Mum,' he said softly. 'And I rather you helped me, if you don't mind?' Maggie turned, and Sean caught a moment of relief in her face.

'Let me get that shower attachment and I'll wash your hair for you eh?' her voice wobbled at the end. She gently ran the shower water through her hand and when satisfied she gently pushed the water through Sean's jet-black hair away from his face. She silently began to massage the shampoo through while Sean kept his eyes closed.

'You always did have beautiful hair,' Maggie murmured. Sean kept his eyes closed and let his mum rinse his hair like she did when he was small, taking care that the soap didn't go into his eyes. 'There. Now pass me that flannel and I'll wash your back for you,' she instructed. Maggie slowly swathed the soap cloth over her son's back. The bruising wasn't so bad on his back as it was on his front.

When she finished, she passed him the tea and placed the biscuits on the edge of the bath for him to reach with ease. She turned to walk out silently when Sean said, 'I thought I was gonna die, Mum.' Maggie, still in the bathroom, shut the door and closed her eyes before turning. It was as if she was praying before facing her son and hear what he had been through. She walked over to the radiator, picked up the towel and rolled it as if she was about to go the swimming pool. But instead, she placed it on the floor beside the bath and sat down on it like a cushion. Once she was comfortable she sought for Sean's hand that was gripping the side of the bath and then waited for him to start.

'It's not like in the movies when they say your whole life flashes before your eyes. Well, not for me anyway. I just kept thinking that I should have done more and I dunno what.' He paused for a moment to try and make sense and explain seconds of his life that had absorbed a lifetime of feelings. 'I thought about you and Charlie of course, but no more than I thought about my new pair of shoes. I know that's awful, isn't it?' Maggie just smiled. There was more to the story and there was more to Sean. 'I didn't feel regret as such, or pity for myself. All I felt was…. disappointed, I s'pose. Yeah, disappointed that I hadn't done enough and not because I'm only thirty but simply because I've done nothing with my life. My best friend has upped sticks and moved her whole life to New York and I am so happy for her, but I always think that things like that don't happen to people like me. And I don't know what I'm supposed to do. All I do know is that when my time really does come, I don't want to feel like that again. I want to know that my life or even my death meant something. I can't explain it Mum, I'm sorry.'

'Sweetheart, we all feel like that at some point or another. God forgive me Sean, but when you were little I used to cry about my life. Thinking who was going to look at me with a kid on my own? Why would anyone want to love me? And yes, I eventually met Charlie and life got better and as much as I loved you Sean I still had deep moments of dissatisfaction.'

He knew his mum didn't understand. He couldn't really put it into words himself. But all he knew was at the moment he thought he was going to die there was also a feeling of not only unfinished business but business that hadn't even started yet. He wasn't sure if all people felt like this when they had a near-death experience but from what he had read or watched on dodgy Channel Five documentaries, people only ever talked about fear, pain and panic. He felt some fear and certainly panic but looking back it was over his lack of life not his impending death.

'I guess you're right. All I know for certain though, is once I'm back on my feet I'm going to sort my life out. Long term! I'm not waiting for Bradley Cooper to sweep me off my feet anymore. I just need to figure out what I want and go for it.'

'There's my boy,' she smiled and passed him a biscuit to dunk in his tea. The door opened, and Charlie poked his head in.

'Sorry Sean, but the phone went before. A man called Mr Armstrong from the AAIB wants to come over and talk to you about the accident. I said he could come later this evening but if you were too tired then I would call him back and arrange for another day.'

'They must be the crash investigating people,' said Sean, 'I might as well get it over and done with. No point putting it off is there?' he shrugged his shoulders. Maggie raised her head to Charlie and gave him a reassuring smile as he left the room and shut the door. She sat watching her son wash the rest of his body with the face cloth she had just used.

'When I heard about the crash I just thought, 'those poor people', you know as you do when you see something on the news. Then when they said the airline and it was a flight from JFK, I just knew it was yours. Charlie realised straight away too, and he started to talk to me. I could see his mouth moving but I couldn't hear the words. I couldn't even hear the man on the telly talking. I just kept looking at the pictures until Charlie grabbed me. Charlie kept saying we needed to phone the helpline number, but I kept saying 'no'. If you were dead Sean, I would know, I would *feel* it and I kept saying this to Charlie. He must have thought I was mad. He called the number in the end and they just took his details and said they would call back when they had more information. Then the phone never stopped with every Tom, Dick and Harry from the village wanting to know if you were on the plane and if you were dead or alive and we couldn't ignore the phone as we were waiting on the sodding helpline people! Anyway, they finally called and told us that you were one of the lucky ones, like you'd just got picked to go to the X-Factor boot camp!'

'Well, I am one of the lucky ones. A bit of physio and a spray tan and I'll be as good as new.' Maggie smiled at her son and felt nothing but overwhelming pride. Through all his pain and nightmare ordeal he still found humour. Whether that was to make him cope or to calm her, she wasn't sure, and she didn't care. All she cared about was the fact he was alive and sitting in her bath.

'Right, my little Oompa Loompa, are you going to be okay getting out of the bath on your own?'

'You go on down Mum, I'll be there in a bit.'

Maggie took herself down to the kitchen and once Sean was out of the bath and dried he padded to his old room and closed the door behind him. His room was still the same from the day he left except his old posters had been taken down revealing more of the dark green paint he had chosen when he was 18-years-old. Interior design programmes of the last decade had had a lot of influence on Sean's colour choices including what compass point his bed should be pointing at.

He stood in front of his mirrored wardrobe and looked at his reflection, telling himself he was lucky to be alive and to be standing in the depressing bedroom at all. He thought about making a few phone calls to his friends, but then decided it was best to speak to the investigator first. He figured that the whole story could be told to them and then he could edit the bits he wanted when he spoke to his friends. He didn't want to have to regale the same story over and over again.

He dried his hair with his old hairdryer that stank of dust and old electricity and silently wished for a bit of wax. Instead of sporting a gravity defying quiff, his reflection reminded him of his sixth form school photograph.

His wardrobe still housed some old clothes and some new ones he kept for times when he simply wanted to hang out with his parents. He marvelled at the smell of fabric conditioner as he slid open the door. He was sure his mum periodically washed his clothes every now and again to keep them fresh. He pulled on a pair of grey tracksuit bottoms and figured pulling a t-shirt over his head might be painful so opted for an old denim shirt that reeked of magnolia and ylang ylang. He felt homely, smiled to himself and headed downstairs to be made a fuss of.

They had watched TV on and off during the day and Sean would occasionally nap, as would Charlie. When it came to the evening Maggie cooked steak and chips and when they were all in the kitchen tidying away the dishes, the doorbell rang.

'That'll be that fella from the BBI or BBC, wherever he's from,' Maggie was starting to slightly panic. 'Sean, go through to the lounge and I'll make some coffee. Charlie, you get the door seeing as he spoke to you on the phone.' Charlie nodded and walked down the hall while Sean made his way to the lounge. He dithered about whether to sit or to stay standing while he waited for the investigator. But before he made up his mind, Charlie stepped in. He was followed by a small man with shocking red hair that reminded Sean of Ron Weasley.

'Mr Allister?' the small man held out his hand.

'Please, call me Sean.' Sean shook the hand that felt very small in his own.

'Tea? Coffee?' asked Charlie.

'May I just have a glass of water please?' Charlie nodded at his request and disappeared into the kitchen while Sean and Mr Armstrong sat down.

'I'm sure your dad explained who I am from my telephone conversation with him earlier, but anyway, I work for the Air Accidents Investigation Branch. It's my job to speak to you about the accident, what you remember, if you saw anything and what happened afterwards. I know this is very upsetting for you, but your recollection of events can help our investigations immensely and I'm sure you would like to know what happened up there as much, if not more, than we do.' The small man smiled, and Sean nodded. As the man rooted in his bag, Sean sat transfixed by the colour of his hair and wondered if it was naturally that red.

'Do you mind if I use a Dictaphone? I tend to find that it puts people off if I ask them to slow down as I write and they forget some details or shorten the story as they lose their patience with me,' he confessed.

'No, not at all,' replied Sean. Maggie appeared in the room with a tray carrying a jug of water, 2 glasses and a plate of chocolate digestives.

'Mrs Allister, I presume?' he stood to shake her hand.

'No. It's Mrs Jensen…. remarried,' she slightly giggled with nerves, 'erm…should I stay?'

'By all means…'

'I rather you didn't, Mum. Sorry.' Maggie looked awkward and tried to smile. Sean could see she was disappointed, but he wanted to spare his mum the story of what he actually went through. All she needed to know was that he was alive and, in her lounge, eating her biscuits. She didn't need to know any more than that.

'Okay, sweetheart,' she said meekly. Everyone felt slightly embarrassed and when she left the room Mr Armstrong glanced at Sean who then seated himself again and waited for the investigator to follow suit.

Maggie walked back into the kitchen where she found Charlie seated in the family room area. She plonked herself down next to him and waited for him to raise his arm, so she could bury herself into him. It was her safe place.

They waited for what seemed like a very long time and Maggie was starting to feel twitchy. She pulled herself out of Charlie's hug and said she was going to check that they had enough water. She knocked before entering only to find that Mr Armstrong was packing his things back into the bag.

'Oh, you've nearly finished,' concluded Maggie.

'Yes, just a couple of more things and then we are done. Can I ask you Mr Allister what your seat number was?'

'28A.' Mr Armstrong shuffled through some papers.

'28A is a window seat. You were found on the aisle seat.'

'Yeah, I moved. All three seats were empty so I kind of used all of them.' confessed Sean.

'Well, my boy. It was lucky you did.' Mr Armstrong raised his eyebrows. Maggie cocked her head for him to reveal more.

'Row 28 was where the plane broke in two. As the front of the plane…well…shifted to the right and twisted away from the rear of the craft it exposed row 28 to the trees. The injuries your son has to the front of his body is no doubt caused by severe lashings from the branches as the plane skidded to a halt. However, I do know that a large stump from a tree or even several trees completely destroyed all the seats that were next to the window, in other words the 'A' seats. You were very, very lucky Mr Allister.' He turned to face Sean who stared at him blankly.

The silence fell as they absorbed the enormity of Sean switching seats until Mr Armstrong felt it was time to go. He quickly gathered up his things while he advised Sean to contact him if he could remember anything else. Sean stood and allowed Mr Armstrong to walk into the hall first and then opened the front door quickly before the small man reached it. Mr Armstrong again offered his hand to Sean as he stood on the threshold.

'Thank you, Mr Armstrong. I will contact you, if I remember anything but I'm sure that's it.' Sean just wanted him to go. He felt like he needed another bath.

'Good luck, Mr Allister. Not that you will need it as you clearly have someone looking out for you,' he sniffed and smiled and the same time and scurried out of the house. Sean shut the door and breathed a sigh of relief.

'You okay, son?' Charlie was stood with his mum in the hall looking concerned.

'I'm going to bed, if that's okay? I'm really tired all of a sudden, and I just want to close my eyes.' Sean felt like he wanted to cry, alone.

'Of course,' his parents both stepped forward and embraced him in a group hug.

'Love you two,' he whispered.

'Love us three,' Charlie and Maggie said in unison. Sean broke away and his parents watched him walk upstairs as he said goodnight.

Sean headed straight for the bed. He switched on his bedside lamp, climbed on top of the single bed and stared at the ceiling for a long time. He knew he was lucky before the investigator came but he didn't know how lucky he had been. What if the plane had broken beneath him instead of front of him? Where were the people sitting that had lost their lives? Were they all in 'A' seats? Was someone in the row in front of him? Yes, there was a black woman! She was on her own as well. Did she move? Was she in the other half of the plane or did she fall out when the plane ripped? Oh God, that poor woman! She was in front of him when he was by the window. Why was he in an aisle seat? He hated the aisle seat. You always had people pushing past you or even worse stopping by your seat so all you could see was their arse! Why was he there?

Sean started to remember trying to undo his seat belt when he was by the window. He could remember it was when the plane was about to crash that he was struggling to open the clasp. Sean remembered him. The man. He told him to move. The man. He was so calm and wasn't moving from the force of the plane. He shouted at him to change his seats and Sean knew he was right. Sean sat up in bed with a start.

Who was the man?

CHAPTER 3

'Congratulations, to you all on a successful first assignment, observing a Protector.' The man on the podium, Bathisma, looked on his new recruits with an air of pride and superiority. He was dressed as if he was about to go into a board meeting and discuss the latest on Wall Street and the current global economy, not very celestial at all. 'You have all absorbed the lessons and teachings of Guardianship and I have to say, some are showing great skill and promise. Some of your talent in suggestion and gentle manipulation has really shone through and the feedback I have been receiving from your appointed angels has been promising; I applaud you all.' The white room was filled with various beings nodding and smiling in a self-congratulatory manner. It wasn't too dissimilar to a Slimming World meeting.

'Now, Rucelle has asked me to remind you all that any interaction with our earthly-bound subjects is still to be authorised by his division and your presence is still only limited to 5 Earth bound minutes, so use them wisely. So, until our next reception, good luck.' Bathisma raised his hands to conclude. The whole room began to glow as if a million stars were on fire that faded as soon as they came, then the room was empty. All except for one man, his name was Crowley. Bathisma's face turned a little sour as he looked down on Crowley who seemed a little dumbfounded that he had not 'become' elsewhere. Elsewhere being at a bar with a crisp, cool Dom Perignon.

'Rucelle would like to see you, Crowley. Come with me, please?' Bathisma's tone spoke more than his actual words. Before he had time to contemplate the request Crowley was standing before a seated Rucelle. He was dressed in white, of course, white tunic and white tailored trousers. The fact that he was white identified his angel hierarchy. Until you reached Rucelle's level, which could take about two thousand years give or take a century or two, you could dress in whatever you wanted, as long as it was a tunic and as long as it was black. Crowley's choice was a black tuxedo (tie optional) with a pair of platinum cufflinks that his wife had given him on their wedding day. He could wear whatever he wanted, being a soul not an angel, and most days he was found in a tux.

Rucelle was seated, and even when Crowley came, he still did not look up from his engrossing report. Behind the white desk in the white glowing room stood Bathisma with his hands clasped in front of him. Crowley wondered if he had ever worked for the US Secret Service.

'Crowley, Crowley, Crowley,' sighed Rucelle. He eventually looked up from his desk and directed his piercing blue eyes deep into Crowley's soul. Rucelle rose from the desk. He was around the same height as Bathisma but a little smaller than Crowley. He was slim, and his blond curls sat tight to his scalp and as he walked around his desk, Crowley could smell Parma Violets.

'You do know why you are in here, don't you?' asked

Rucelle perching his bottom on the front edge of his desk. Crowley thought for a moment. Should he act dumb? What was the point? They would know that he was lying straight away. *Honesty is the best policy, especially here*, he thought. Crowley silently and reluctantly nodded.

'You not only visited your earthly subject without an appointed angel, you not only spoke to your earthly subject without an appointed angel, but you appeared!' Even though Rucelle's tone was soft, the assertiveness was unmistakable. 'I have been here for over two millennia and never have I known a soul, still in training, to not only arrive without an appointed angel, but to manifest themselves! Something even an angel is not permitted to do!'

'What about the three men that appeared before Abraham?' questioned Crowley.

'The three MEN that appeared to Abraham were archangels. And since you are neither man nor angel and have clearly not listened to Bathisma's teachings, I wonder if we made the right decision in pursuing with you in your training.' Rucelle's eyes were no longer the perfect blue that penetrated Crowley when he arrived; they were now the colour of cold, grey steel. 'Your first relations with your living soul should be subtle, veiled and most certainly questionable by the recipient of your inconspicuous manipulation.'

'To be fair, my living soul was about to hit the Earth at 500 miles an hour and at most I had ten seconds to 'manipulate' the situation. Discreet and low key would have been a little lost amongst the screaming of 200 people and a metal plane being whipped and ripped as it smashed into the dirt. No sooner had I learned that Sean Allister was my charge to be protected I was quickly informed by…. what was his name…. oh…' Crowley began to click his fingers as if to speed up his memory, it failed. 'The man who looks like Charlton Heston.... anyway, he told me that my charge was about to die, and it wasn't his time, so I had better put my skates on...or words to that affect. I presumed whoever his Protector was would...well...meet me there, I guess,' Crowley muttered. 'Look, the point is I'm not sure what else I could have done and I'm not sure a Protector, who clearly has trouble reading a map, could have done any better. Maybe, this job was for someone who was at 'A' level or something, not for a novice like me. But at the end of the day, Sean Allister is still walking Earth and he probably doesn't remember me,' he concluded. Rucelle walked around his desk, back to his chair and sat back down. He opened the file he was originally reading when Crowley 'became'.

'But he does remember you, Crowley.'

'Oh.'

'Yes, indeed 'oh'. We must now assess how we move forward with this particular and rather unique situation we have.'

'Is it unique? People on Earth are always saying they saw angels and things.'

'An angel has never been seen on Earth. I'm not sure what they have seen but be assured it is not anyone from this Heavenly plain.' This news disappointed Crowley. Clearly any sightings of heavenly bodies on Earth had not been angels, just simple souls like him.

Crowley had only been in Heaven for less than a year. He had made it through the transitional plane, a sort of half-way house between the living and the dead and completed his task with aplomb. It was then he was told of his 'promotion' which led him to the Protectors' Division. He was initially pleased as this advancement had allowed him to be reunited with his wife and son who had left the earthly plane years before him.

'Crowley, I will need to deliberate further on your case before I can come to a decision,' said Rucelle.

'What more do you need to know, I've told you everything.' replied Crowley.

'I need to monitor Mr Allister; I may also need to speak to John who appointed such an urgent case to a novice like yourself…'

'John!' interrupted Crowley, 'the Charlton Heston guy!'

'That's because he is Charlton Heston, or was,' Rucelle looked slightly bored. Crowley tried to hide his surprise. 'I also need to reassess your suitability for this Division. Until I make a decision you will not be appointed any further duties. In the meantime, you may fill your time as you see fit,' Rucelle looked up and smiled sarcastically, 'after all this is Heaven.' Before Crowley could speak Rucelle announced he was dismissed and Crowley was swathed in a feeling of warmth and contentment as he 'became' on a bar stool.

'What can I get you, Crowley?' asked Benito laying a coaster in front of his guest.

'I'll have a whisky please. A Macallan 1926,' he sighed. Benito quickly found the bottle and poured a generous measure into a cut crystal glass and placed the drink on the coaster.

Crowley liked Benito's bar. It looked like it had been decorated in the 1950's but once it had reached its perfect lived-in look it hadn't deteriorated anymore. There were plenty of places to drink in Heaven. Some bars you could go in and merely think of the drink and it would appear in your hand. But Crowley still liked to be served. He liked to be attended to. He liked to interact with people who were also like-minded. Only a certain clientele patronised Benito's bar. Usually older men of the late 19th and 20th centuries who remembered bars like this on Earth.

Benito had run a bar in Venice until 1956 where he dropped dead during an inventory. His family all agreed it was the way he wanted to go, in the beloved bar that he had lived in all his life. Benito had recreated the bar in Heaven and started serving immediately. Over the years his wife, brother and his brother's wife had joined him and now Benito truly was in Heaven and he wouldn't change a thing.

Crowley absent-mindedly watched his Italian barman busy himself as he sliced a bag of lemons when he became aware of a customer appearing on the bar stool next to him. The silver-haired man raised a finger to Benito who nodded in acknowledgement and abandoned his lemons. Within seconds a 1937 Glenfiddich was placed in front of Benito's latest patron. Crowley noted the choice.

'May I say, what excellent taste you have in whisky?' Crowley raised his glass to the gentleman. The man, dressed in a black turtleneck and black pants, smiled gently and also raised his glass. He did not speak.

'Have you been here long?' asked Crowley trying to be friendly.

'I've just arrived.' Crowley noted his neighbour was English. He was around sixty-years-old, fit, extremely good looking and no doubt if he had walked the Earth he would have left a string of broken-hearted women behind; he just had that air about him.

'No, I mean…up here, in general,' Crowley clarified. The man let out a slightly exasperated sigh.

'I take it you have been here less than a year?' he raised an eyebrow and looked at Crowley who meekly nodded.

'The new ones always still measure time. How long for this and how long for that? Eventually, you will lose your hankering for time frames and the constant question of 'when' and just learn to accept the 'now'.

'Well, how do you plan anything?' asked Crowley. The man burst out laughing.

'What the hell do you need to plan? A holiday with the Mrs? A day out? Tonight's supper?' Crowley mused for a moment. He was beginning to realise that he hadn't planned anything since he died. If he wanted to do something, he simply did it. He didn't have to think any further than the moment he was in. He also realised he had no idea what month it was, never mind the day.

'I suppose, you're right,' Crowley chuckled. 'Crowley's the name,' and he extended his hand toward the stranger.

'Jack.' He shook Crowley's hand and smiled.

The men sat in silence while they gently sipped their drinks. A few more men 'became' much to Benito's delight. Crowley found himself listening to conversations throughout the oak panelled room of people being reunited with loved ones and a friendly debate about which car was the best on Earth. An overweight man was dismissing the Aston Martin DB5 for the DB6 to which his friend laughed and said the only reason he liked the DB6 was because it was flabby as he was. They both laughed at the retort. To counteract his eavesdropping Crowley wished for music and he could soon hear Debussy ringing in his ears.

'Ah, Debussy,' sighed a contented Crowley.

'Debussy eh?' asked Jack. 'I'm currently listening to the Rolling Stones.' They both slightly sniggered at their opposing tastes in music. 'Another?' asked Jack.

'Why not? If your theory regarding time is true, then my wife will have no need to say I'm late!' Jack caught Benito's attention and as quick as a flash another round of fresh drinks was placed in front of them.

'So, Crowley, tell me, what division do you work for?'

'Protectors,' replied Crowley. 'Just had my first assignment.'

'And how did it go?' enquired Jack.

'Well, I thought it went well. Saved my appointed and thought I saved the day.'

'But Rucelle had a different opinion?' asked Jack still looking at a busy Benito.

'Indeed.' Crowley was intrigued as how his new acquaintance had guessed. 'You know Rucelle?'

'Rucelle and I go back a long way.'

'Oh, so you're in the Protector Division too. Maybe, you could give me some pointers. I fear I failed miserably at the first hurdle.'

'What did you do?' asked Jack.

'Appeared,' he said reluctantly.

'Ooooh,' Jack drawled.

'Without the Protector,' he finished.

'Ooooh,' Jack said in a lower tone.

'Yes, oh indeed. They are now assessing my suitability to such a post. Half of me is hoping they send me to another Division.'

'Don't say that! You could end up anywhere! You don't want to end up in somewhere like the War Division.'

'They have a War Division?' spat Crowley. 'What on earth do they do?'

'They call it population control. There's an ongoing battle between them and the Birth Division. The Birth Division are stating they work too hard in mapping individual destinies for the War Division to simply take it on themselves to cut the lifelines short. The War Division say if the Birth Division didn't go around blessing everyone with babies then Earth wouldn't have a population problem. And who is stuck in the middle of it all. Us lot!! The Protectors! Running around like headless chickens trying to guide men away from landmines, bullets and men with bulging rucksacks.' Crowley was taken aback by Jack's outburst. Even though he had whispered most of it, there was no mistaking that Jack was harbouring a heap of frustration. 'Trust me,' Jack continued, 'with things the way they are at the moment, the Protectors' Division is one that…' Jack caught himself and stopped speaking. Crowley turned to face him, confused.

'One that what?' Jack lifted his glass to his lips and slowly drank the remaining contents.

'One that will look on your blunder with more sympathy than others.' Jack tried to smile but Crowley noted there was a slight nervous tic to his lips. He had only just met this gentleman and felt it was good manners to leave it as it stood and not probe any further. Jack, who also felt the conversation had come to a natural end, stood and held out his hand.

'I take it you are leaving. I hope I see you in here soon to debate our wide taste in music over some of Benito's finest offerings,' said Crowley. Jack took Crowley's hand and shook it and as he did Crowley felt that his new acquaintance was reading his soul. He then turned and with a slow confident stride walked out of the bar. Crowley watched him until the huge oak door shut.

Crowley looked to his left through a far window that had no view, just a white glow diffusing into the room. There was still a lot to learn about his new home. He had been in a transitional Heaven for a few weeks after his death and could only move on to his final place when it had been earned. This last plane had allowed him to still have contact with one living person on Earth and together they helped him move on.

Now assigned to the Protectors' Division, his spiritual mission was to help angels with the living and keep them on the path that had been recorded within the Birth Division. A simple objective, he thought, until you throw an out of control plane in the mix. His mind was taken back to his meeting with Rucelle. *Maybe, I should have been more repentant*, he thought. Would that have made a difference?

Crowley finished his drink and decided to go home. Maybe, his wife Jennifer could offer some advice or comfort. He placed his empty glass down on the bar and slipped from the bar stool, thanking Benito as he walked towards the oak doors. As he pushed the door he entered his study from his ancestral home on Earth, De Mondford Hall. The room was quintessentially English with its antique furniture including his old desk in the window and the battered burgundy velvet couches that sat in front of the roaring open fire. The far end of the room was referred to as The Snug. It was reached through an open archway and housed hundreds of Crowley's treasured books and his two favourite armchairs that were placed beneath a tall slim arched window which looked out onto the manicured gardens of the Hall.

He walked over to the fire and turned his back on the flames to consider what was going to happen to him. As he pondered, Jennifer walked in. Crowley felt immediate relief at seeing his beautiful wife.

'Darling!' Her face lit up as she sped up her step to greet her husband with a kiss. He opened his arms and she immediately found her place against his body. After a short embrace, Jennifer pulled away slightly to look on her husband's face. She noted he looked distracted.

'Max has gone to bed and I've just finished preparing supper. Why don't we eat in here in front of the fire and you can tell me what's bothering you.' He looked down on her sweet face. Her blonde wavy hair was sitting perfectly against her pink cheeks and he couldn't resist in touching it.

'That obvious, eh?' he said as he gently brushed her hair from her face.

'Only to me,' she replied. 'Pull the small tables over to the sofa and I'll bring the food through.' She pulled away and as she left the room shouted, 'There's a lovely red in the decanter as well.' Crowley immediately pulled two tables from the wall and placed them in front of the sofa. He then poured two large glasses of wine while Jennifer entered the room with two steaming plates of Beef Bourguignon. They placed their meals on each of the tables and settled with a napkin on their lap. Jennifer began to tuck in.

'So, how did your first day go?'

'Well, the good news is I have completed my first mission.' Jennifer continued to chew. She knew there was more to the story and found Crowley was more talkative if she adopted a slightly unfocused approach. Whenever she listened intently she found her husband would become self-conscious and start to edit his stories and wrap them up before she was ready. She nodded to acknowledge his opening. 'The bad news is, I failed at it miserably.' He slid a piece of beef from the fork into his mouth.

'According to who?' asked Jennifer.

'Rucelle. I was summoned to his office by MI5 agent, Bathisma.'

'And do you think you failed?' she stopped chewing and casually moved food around her plate.

'I showed myself and spoke to the living soul before the Protector arrived,' he sighed.

'I see.' She placed her fork on the plate. This was serious. She had been in Heaven a lot longer than Crowley and knew that he had broken the number one rule.

'The circumstances, darling, were somewhat extreme. A plane was about to crash, and I had to save my subject. How am I supposed to do that discreetly? His angel hadn't arrived, so I felt I had no choice but to take matters into my own hands. I appeared in front of the boy and told him to move seats and he did.'

'Maybe the boy won't remember you?'

'Apparently, he does,' he groaned. Crowley began to stare at the fire and Jennifer collected her thoughts.

'Eat your dinner before it gets cold,' she pushed softly. Crowley did as he was bid and continued to eat his meal. Jennifer continued to mull over his news and how Rucelle would deal with him. 'Am I right in thinking that souls can sometimes fail at their first mission?' asked Jennifer.

'Not that I'm aware of. I mean technically I didn't fail, it's just my execution that has caused the issue,' Crowley sulked. 'Surely, they won't just judge me on isolated facts. They have to see the bigger picture otherwise people like Alexander Fleming would simply be remembered as someone who had an aversion to washing his dishes!'

'I don't think that's quite the same.'

'You know what I mean, darling. It's the end result that they should be looking at.'

'Did they offer any advice as to how you should have done it?' Crowley thought for a moment.

'Come to think of it, no. I will raise that at my next meeting with them.'

'No, I didn't mean it like that. I don't know. It's just in my time here I always thought that souls were given more challenging cases after they had some experience. Plane crashes and other huge disasters are usually given to Protectors who work closely with the Transitional Division and they only ever send angels to them. They don't usually make them part of your training.'

'Really?' Crowley placed his fork on his plate and raised his napkin to wipe his mouth. 'Then why give an assignment like that to someone like me?'

'I'm not sure, darling. Are you sure you went to the right person?'

'Of course, I'm sure. They even said his name when I was called to the office. Plus, I met the boy before when I was waiting to cross over to you.'

'Do you mean you knew him when you were alive?'

'No, my dear, I knew him when I was completing my task to enter Heaven. He was Grace's best friend, Sean Allister,' he clarified.

'So, you were allocated a living soul to you that you already knew?' she pushed.

'Yes,' he was wondering where this was going. 'Is there a problem with that? I'm sure they knew that I knew him.'

'I'm sure they did,' she added.

'But?' he pushed.

'I've never known a soul to be appointed a living person that they know. It just seems odd to me, that's all.'

'What? Never?'

'No.' They both sat in silence for a while with their thoughts. Then Jennifer picked up her fork and indicated to Crowley for him to do the same. 'When you go to your meeting with them, whenever that is, can I suggest you let them do all the talking? Pushing for answers as to why your first assignment was so challenging might only rile Rucelle and he may push you on a Division that is more demanding, shall we say.' Crowley remembered Jack's comments about the War Division and concluded that his wife may be talking sense.

'I will, Dear. I shall try and charm the socks off Rucelle and be back in his good books before you know it.' Jennifer smiled at her husband. One thing he did possess was a warm personality that won everyone over. His laid-back style and unassuming wisdom earned him respect and love.

They finished their dinner and talked of times on Earth and how they would visit some gardens after they had eaten their dessert. Jennifer insisted Crowley refill their glasses while she cleared their plates and went off to fetch some plum pudding. As he was refilling the glasses he was aware that someone had 'became' behind him. As he turned, there stood Bathisma, like a nightclub bouncer.

'Rucelle wishes to see you,' he said flatly.

'Now?'

'Yes, now.' Jennifer walked back into the room and gasped at Bathisma's presence.

'Darling, I have to go. I have been summoned,' he placed the glasses back on the silver tray next to the decanter. Jennifer put the dishes down and walked over to Crowley.

'Remember what I said,' she whispered. He nodded at his wife, looked at Bathisma and then disappeared leaving Jennifer in an empty room and her mind bursting with questions.

CHAPTER 4

Sean was packing a few items in a small bag when he heard a knock on the bedroom door. His mum appeared with a cup of tea and placed it on his bedside table.

'Thought you might like a quick cuppa before you go,' she said as she sat on the bed.

'Cheers, Mum.' Sean started to gather some of his tablets in various places in the room.

'You sure you're ready to go? You can stay a bit longer. It's only been a week,' she pleaded.

'I'm fine. The pain isn't that bad anymore, but I should start my physio in Lanson as soon as.'

Maggie sighed. 'Yes, I know, but even still, you may not be able to manage cooking and cleaning.' Sean took the bag off the bed and sat beside her.

'I have a sore neck, that's all. I can manage a washing machine and chucking a can of soup in a pan.' Maggie went to interrupt but Sean stopped her. 'I know you want to take care of me, but I'm a big boy now. And besides, you need to get back to normal yourself, don't think I didn't hear you and Charlie arguing about you helping in the shop.' Maggie had insisted that Sean still needed taking care of while Charlie could see that she was becoming too attached and that road always led to tears.

'He's got Eddie in there all the time now. I don't know why he needs another pair of hands. Eddie's belly's bigger than Charlie's. It's like refereeing two sumo wrestlers behind that counter,' she snapped.

'Well, maybe he thinks a pretty lady will make his queues grow longer,' he nudged his mum.

'What if, you know, you start to think and then something happens?' she asked.

'What? Like I realise I was in a plane crash and start frothing at the mouth with stress. If you knew about some of the trauma I've been through with boyfriends recently you'd know I'm made of sterner stuff.'

'Tell me,' she whispered.

'No, Mum! If I told you half of it, you would only be able to wear Aladdin's slippers 'cos your toes will have curled that much. Trust me, I'll be fine.' He threw his arms around his mum and gave her a reassuring squeeze. 'Now, do us a favour? Take that tea back down and I'll drink it downstairs with you. I'm finished up here. I just need to get my phone and then we can make a move.'

'Okay, son.' Maggie picked herself up and collected the cup of tea as Sean zipped up his bag and followed her down the stairs.

He had mixed feelings about going back to his flat. He would miss his mum and Charlie and that had started the deliberation of going home. If he stayed much longer he would have become used to being waited on hand and foot. But he also missed silly things, like his own bed, being able to eat on the couch and his TV programmes. There was only so much news, current affairs and detective dramas he could stomach. Charlie was reading the paper at the breakfast bar when Sean walked in.

'You should have shouted me, Son, I would've carried your bag,' he gently scolded. Maggie put Sean's tea down while he took a seat next to Charlie. They all sat in awkward silence while they drank their tea. They all knew that Sean had to leave but each had their own mixed feelings about it. Once Sean had finished his tea, Charlie climbed down off the bar stool and made his way to Sean's bag. Maggie simply walked over to her son and silently hugged him. When Sean pulled away he could see his mum's eyes were starting to fill up.

'I'll phone you tonight, Mum.' He started to walk to the open front door to where Charlie was stowing his bag in the boot. 'I'll call before nine, so you don't miss finding out who killed Mary with the mullet,' he joked. 'She deserved to die anyway with that haircut.' After one final hug he walked to the car and by the time he had put his seatbelt on she was staring at him through the passenger window. Charlie started the car and gave his wife a wave and pulled away.

'Why are Mum's goodbyes more dramatic than Dorothy Gale's?' quipped Sean.

'Because "there's no place like home",' Charlie joked. They talked all the way to Lanson about how Maggie would be fine once she was busy in the shop and that Sean would make sure he called her often to keep her mind at peace. They also talked of Sean's future since he had jacked in his job at the haulage firm when he left for New York.

'I earned quite a bit while I was over there, and Grace gave me some money to start my beauty course, but I'm not so sure now,' he confessed.

'I thought that's what you always wanted to do.' Charlie was surprised.

'I did, and I still do in a way. It's just,' he paused for a moment and wondered how he could word a multitude of feelings into a simple sentence, 'it's just... I'm not sure if it's something I want to do anymore. The last couple of weeks have made me think differently.'

'I can understand that, lad. Having a near-death experience is bound to make you take stock,' said Charlie.

'I dunno. I just feel like I've spent my whole life making one bad decision after another, and I'm not sure if I can trust myself anymore. What if I spend all this money on the course and I hate it? I mean, I've dreamed about doing it for so long and I've created this image in my head of where I'm gonna be the next Max Factor, when the truth of the matter is I'll be on some old lady counter in Palmers selling sacks full of face powder and lipstick in Barbara Cartland Pink. I just want to make sure that what I do next is the right thing for me and I'm good at it.' Sean began staring out of the window. The thought of failing terrified him and he wasn't sure if that was why he was reluctant to sign on to the course or if it was because it wasn't his dream anymore.

Charlie stayed silent for the remainder of the journey and they were soon pulling into the courtyard of the flats where Sean lived. The twenty flats were in a horseshoe shape and Sean lived in the top corner flat above the bin house. Charlie collected Sean's bag while Sean climbed the short flight of steps to his front door. As they walked in, Sean stooped to collect his post off the mat and then walked down the hall into the lounge where he threw it on top of his side table.

'Stuffy in here isn't it?' announced Sean as he flung open the French doors on the opposite side of the room.

'I'll make you a cuppa Charlie, if you can drink it black. I've got no milk,' he offered.

'I'm fine. I'm not stopping. I need to get back, so Eddie

can do the deliveries this afternoon.' Sean nodded. 'Sit down though a minute, Son.' Sean was slightly taken aback by Charlie's request. It felt like a telling off was coming his way. Even though he couldn't think of what he had done wrong, he knew Charlie would have no problem in pointing something out. He sat down, and Charlie did the same on the other sofa.

'I want to tell you something about me and my dad,' began Charlie. Sean felt some relief knowing this wasn't about him and relaxed a little. 'My dad ran the butcher's shop for years and was great at it. Everyone knew him and loved him, and I always knew that one day the shop would be mine and that terrified me. And as the time got nearer to him retiring he could see that I wasn't happy. He asked me what it was, and I couldn't explain it to him because I didn't understand at the time why I was scared. He then said that if I wanted I could sell the shop and do whatever I wanted with my life. He wasn't going to force me to take over something just because it was expected. Well, once he said that it made me realise that I did want the shop, but the fear was still there. And then he said to me, "it's ok to be scared, our fear is not just about failing it's about wondering if you have the courage to try. The people who are unhappy are the ones that didn't try, not the ones that failed while fighting". And it's true; you just need to give it your best shot. If you don't do what is in your heart, then you will always feel like a failure. Now, I don't know if beauty and make-up is the thing that will make you happy, only you know that. But take the fear of failure away and really look in your heart as to what will make you happy. For some people, it can be becoming a pop star or winning the lottery but for some folk it's making sausages and going home to a woman called Maggie.' Sean could feel a lump in his throat and tried to swallow. 'Take your time Sean;

you've been given a second chance, so there's no rush.' Charlie let out a big sigh and stood up. Sean stood and stepped forward for Charlie to hug him.

'Love you, Charlie. You're the best,' he sniffed.

'Love you too.' He pulled away and started to stride to the front door. 'Now, there's a bag in your bag that will need to go in the fridge. Text your mum and tell her I'm on my way and remind her I'm going straight to the shop.' Charlie started to descend the metal steps to the car park. 'And chase the physio for an appointment.' He climbed into his car and started the engine. He then opened his window and waved as he pulled away.

'See ya, Charlie,' shouted Sean over the safety railing. The car disappeared, and Sean made his way back to the flat. There was a sense of relief that he was finally home and he immediately felt less 'sick'. He went over to his bag and unzipped it to find a large bag of shopping, including milk. Sean smiled to himself. His parents thought of everything.

He busied himself around the flat, opening some cards from well-wishers and changed his bed. While he unpacked the shopping, his phone rang. He assumed it was his mum, but the screen showed that it was Faye, his friend and neighbour in one of the flats below.

'Hey, Faye,' greeted Sean.

'Sean! Are you home? I thought I saw Charlie's car pull away,' Faye sounded bright down the phone.

'Yeah, got home a couple of hours ago,' he replied.

'Can I come up?'

'Sure, I'll put the kettle on.' He hung up the phone and walked over to the kitchen at the far end of his lounge. Faye was one of his neighbours and an occasional drinking buddy. She lived alone with her seven-year-old son, Josh and even though she had been with Aiden for the last three years she didn't want him to move in properly, so he stayed a couple of nights a week. Faye worked from home as a children's book illustrator. While not well-known in the industry, she had a steady stream of work that came in from her small client list. She was happy as she could revolve her work around Josh, school and hangovers.

Sean could hear her running up the metal steps to his floor and as he opened the front door, there she stood. She had clearly been working from the paint dabbled shirt she wore with black leggings. Her fresh face had a streak of green paint across the cheek which made her look even more cute.

'Sean!' she squealed and threw her arms around him.

'Steady, girl,' said Sean wincing slightly as she pulled on his neck.

'Oh, God, I'm so stupid! Did I hurt you? I'm so sorry,' she looked worried.

'It's a good job you're built like a fairy otherwise I'd have lamped you one,' he chuckled. 'Come in, the kettle's on.' Faye ran through and immediately started to busy herself with cups and tea bags while Sean sat down and watched her.

'Oh, Sean I was worried sick about you. Did your mum tell you I called?'

'She did.'

'Bet she's gutted that you're home. Loads of the neighbours have been asking after you and everyone in The Fox keep asking when you are coming home. Even my mum has been going on about wanting to see you.'

'Jesus, make sure I've had a few wines and co-codamol before you subject Psychic Sue on me, eh?' laughed Sean.

'She reckons she's getting messages from Princess Di now. She called the other day to say she was only going to eat organic as Diana had revealed it was the secret to her beautiful hair.'

'Behave! We'd all have beautiful hair if Nicky Clarke was blow drying it every morning while we ate our Coco Pops,' Sean scoffed. Faye finished making the tea and joined Sean on the sofa.

'She's proper batty. Josh is the only one who can get away with telling her she's nuts. She told him the other day she could see the future and one day we'll all be living in a big house in the country. He just looked at her and said that was never going to happen as Aiden had said she was going to end up in a place called Loony Bin. Sean, I didn't know where to put my face.' Sean was laughing hard trying to imagine the scene. 'I had to tell him off saying Loony Bin wasn't a nice place for her to go and he just looked at me and said, "then why did she tell Aiden that she was?". So, Aiden and I are now talking in code in front of Josh, so he doesn't understand what we are saying but half the time Aiden and I don't know what we are saying either. Anyway, I'm rabbiting on and not even asked about you? You okay?'

'I'm fine, but I'm gonna tell you straight. I don't want to talk about the crash. It's bad enough watching it on the news and no doubt I'm going to have to put up with sympathetic stares around Lanson. If I want to talk about it believe me you'll be the first on my list, but for now I just need to focus on something else, like sorting my life out,' he finished.

'Would you not ask Bill for your job back?'

'Oh, dear God, no! No, I need to think about whether I'm going to do this beauty course or do something else?'

'Like what?'

'I dunno. Something with people though. I like helping people. Working in the gallery in New York made me realise that I like being around lots of people. I can't go back to an office; I'd be dead in a month from the monotony of it all. I just need to think about it for a few days now I'm back in my own space.'

'Well, I still think you would make an amazing make-up artist,' said Faye.

'If I do it, I don't just want to do make-up. I want to open a salon where you go in and you get your hair done, your face done, your tan, your nails, get all your bits waxed from eyebrows to bikinis and then all you need to do is go home and get changed. I want people to walk out feeling a million dollars all over, not just bits of them.'

'There's plenty of ugly, hairy women in Lanson to take advantage of a package like that. What you gonna call it?' Faye asked.

'I dunno. How about Lashes and Gashes?' he shouted, streaking his hand in the air. The pair of them burst out laughing and said it would have to be done now just to see people's faces when the sign was unveiled. They calmed themselves down and started to sip their tea.

'Josh has missed you. He drew a picture for you with a crown on your head because he said you told him you were the biggest Queen in Lanson,' she giggled.

'Well that's true as well.' As they drank their tea Sean told Faye all about his trip to New York and Faye eventually agreed that some time out might be good for him to make sure he made the right decision. Faye looked at her watch and realised she needed to collect Josh from school.

'I have to go. Listen, my mum is in The Fox tonight doing a psychic night. I wasn't going to go but you know how she goes on. Why don't you come along and see if she can see your future? It will no doubt involve organic vegetables as she's trying to convert everyone,' said Faye.

Sean mulled the idea over for a moment. While he couldn't drink with all the painkillers he was on he thought it might be a good idea to get everyone's reaction to him being home in one fell swoop. The thought of being stopped on the street for weeks on end was not a more appealing alternative.

'Yeah, all right. I'll pop down to yours and we can walk over together,' suggested Sean.

'Pick me up at seven then.' Faye walked to the door to let herself out. He then kissed her goodbye and watched her leave. As he returned to his lounge he started to become a little excited about the psychic night. While Sue was a lot more *miss* than *hit* with her predictions, she could be amusing, and the distraction would be good for him.

Sean's afternoon was spent with a bottle of fake tan. He was tired of looking in the mirror and seeing his dad looking back at him. He couldn't remember Chris, but Maggie had kept a photograph of him in an old box in the airing cupboard. Sean had never told her that he had discovered it in the box marked: OLD LINEN. He hadn't been rooting, he had stayed in his parents' house one weekend and didn't want to get tan on her good sheets so went searching for something old. That's when he found it. It was amongst a number of old photos when Maggie was younger. In the photo his mum was pregnant and his dad, Chris, was smiling with his arm around her. They looked happy, but Sean always looked at the photo with a degree of scepticism. He wasn't sure if Chris was just pretending or if he truly was happy. He also felt sorry for the woman in the picture as she had no idea what lay ahead.

Later that evening when it was time to leave, Sean felt more normal when he looked at his reflection. He popped his blazer on over his shirt and jeans and headed out into the warm evening to meet Faye in the cobbled courtyard.

She was already waiting for Sean and she had lit a cigarette for a quick smoke before they reached the pub. Sean too reached for his cigarettes and they began to walk through the arch in the courtyard onto the High Street. It was fairly quiet at this time of night with all the commuter traffic gone. Most of the shops were shut and the only people walking in the streets were dog walkers, people with take-aways and little clusters of teenagers. Lanson was one of the larger towns in the area but it still only had a population of around 4,000 people and that increased to around 5,500 during working hours. Most people, disappointingly to Sean, were straight.

They reached the pub and finished their cigarettes. Sean was feeling a little nervous and wasn't sure what he was going to say to people if they asked him about the accident. Faye noticed his apprehension.

'You okay?'

'Yeah, I'm fine,' he said dismissively and tried to smile.

'Any time you want to go, just say and we'll go, okay?' she took his hand and Sean nodded silently.

The Fox was busy, especially for this time of night. There were posters all over the yellowing walls advertising the psychic night with local resident Psychic Sue. The photo used of Sue looked like it had been taken in 1985 judging by the bubble perm and bright blue eyeshadow. Faye kept a hold of Sean's hand as they walked to the bar and ordered the drinks.

'Oh, my word, look what the cat dragged in!' Sean swung around to see Sue, Faye's mother, beaming at him with her arms open wide. Sean stepped forward and was soon rocking side to side in a bear hug.

' 'Ello Ducky, how are you? You look like you've been the Caribbean!' Sue squawked.

'Just a bit of gear, Sue. You know me, can't go out

looking like a bleeding vampire.' Sue roared laughing…she roared laughing at everything. She was a big lady with a big presence.

'Faye, I've saved you a table in the corner over here. Come on sit down,' she pushed Sean into the corner seat while Faye placed the drinks down.

'You want a drink, Mum?'

'No, dear. I need a clear head tonight for all these readings. I've already had three gins and that's my limit. Look, I'd love to stay and have a chat but the sooner I start the better.' She bent down to a seated Faye and whispered, 'If you see me give you the eye though, just get me another small one. Sometimes all the talking can make one's palette very dry, very dry indeed.'

Sue walked off to the far end of the pub where a table had been set up in the corner. Some washing line had been strung across the corner and old sheets had been pegged to it to ensure privacy during the readings. It was only private from the deaf and lip readers as Sue was not known for her ability to whisper.

'I forgot to say, Mum said you can go in any time. She doesn't want you waiting, so just let me know and I'll go and kno…well, flap her sheet or something,' shrugged Faye.

'Oh, I dunno now. I might just leave it,' Sean grumbled.

'Don't be daft! She's been going around telling people she predicted your crash. Why do you think this place is so busy tonight? Plus, you turning up just makes people think that you believe what she says,' exclaimed Faye.

'What? Well, you can tell that soppy cow I want commission on her takings tonight! Predicting the crash? She couldn't predict the weather in the Sahara bleeding Desert!' Sean pretended he was cross and Faye gave a chuckle.

As the night wore on, various people came to speak to Sean and all were polite enough not to mention the crash. They just asked if he was okay and a few sent a drink over to his table with love. He was glad he came out in the end and once he felt suitably gassed-up on Diet Coke he decided to get Sue over and done with.

'I'll go and tell her,' said Faye jumping to her feet. Sean walked a little slower through the pub and could see Faye peering over the washing line to tell Sue that Sean was up next. By the time Sean got there he could hear Sue telling her customer that it had 'all gone dark and she could see no more.' The fat woman complained that she had spent a tenner and had only been in there two minutes.

'Well, it's not my fault no one wants to talk to you. Maybe that's a message in itself, now shift!' The woman snatched back the fitted sheet on the line which sent a shower of pegs pinging across the floor.

'What a load of shite! She couldn't read the alphabet never mind the future!' The woman stomped off in a huff while Sean pegged the sheet back on the line.

'You all right, Sue?' Sean took a seat in the makeshift den.

'I feel like telling the fat cow that her husband is having it off with the girl from the travel agent's and no one needs to be psychic to see that.' Sean muffled a chuckle under his breath. 'Right, ducky, let's have a look, shall we?' She pulled Sean towards her. 'Now hold my hands and close your eyes.' Sue closed hers once she was sure Sean had and tried to talk softly. 'Now think of white light. Bathe yourself in it; let it wrap itself all around you. Feel its warmth.' Sean tried his best to focus on the light but all he could hear was the various conversations in the pub, glasses being collected and the occasional thump from darts being thrown at the board. Sean could hear Sue's breathing becoming deeper and he played along until she whispered to him. 'You're not concentrating Sean, I can tell. Stop listening to the pub and try and listen to your own heartbeat. The light will come.' Sean tried again but only out of respect for Sue. He sat for a moment still holding Sue's hands when the noise in the pub became quieter and he could faintly hear his heart. As the pub became quieter, his heartbeat became louder and he could see the light. The light became brighter and brighter and just when he thought he would be blinded he found himself back on the plane. He was looking at a man that was telling him to move seats. He could hear the screeching of the metal and then with a yank on his hands he was back in the pub. Sue was staring at him trying to catch her breath. Her face was white, and she was starting to sweat.

'Bloody hell Sue, you all right love?' Sean started to become concerned. She looked like she was about to have a heart attack.

'I saw it, Sean. I saw you!' she babbled. She wiped her face with the bottom of her voluminous blouse and stared at Sean.

'What do you mean, you saw it?' asked Sean.

'You! On the plane! I saw you on the plane,' she stuttered. Did Sue just see what had flashed through his mind? Surely not. She could have just said that as it was the most eventful thing that had happened in his life, ever! 'And I saw him,' she whispered, her eyes becoming wide. 'I saw the man who told you to move seats. The man who saved your life. I saw your guardian angel.'

CHAPTER 5

Crowley stood in Rucelle's office in front of his desk. It hadn't seemed that long since he was here and as there was no concept of time he realised it was pointless trying to guess. Bathisma was in his usual place and Crowley found himself staring at him. He half expected Bathisma to raise his wrist to his mouth and start whispering something to whoever was listening.

'Take a seat please, Crowley,' asked Rucelle who was sat back in his chair looking very relaxed. His demeanour made Crowley nervous and he half expected an evil white cat to jump on Rucelle's lap. Crowley stepped forward and sat in the white chair in front of Rucelle's desk. 'Let me start by saying your case has been discussed at length with various people in and outside of this room. And I can honestly say that the only thing we all agreed on is just how unique your case, or should I say dilemma, is.' Rucelle pressed his fingertips together as if he was about to pray. 'Your action has had a far wider implication than you can imagine and that is why we have graced this 'dilemma' with lengthy discussions, which some might call debates, and huge effort into finding a solution that will suit all Divisions.' Rucelle's manner had stayed calm throughout his delivery but his unnerving stare was enough to illustrate his anger. 'Is there anything you would like to say before I conclude?' Rucelle raised his eyebrows expectantly while maintaining his death stare. Crowley shifted uncomfortably in his chair.

'Only that I am truly sorry.' He bowed his head as he felt it was appropriate and awaited Rucelle's response. It felt like a long time before Rucelle spoke and Crowley wasn't sure if he should say more.

'The Angel Council, by a majority vote, have decided to re-appoint you as a spiritual guide. You'll be happy to learn that it is still under the Protectors' Division, which means you will still be answerable to me. Bathisma will be liaising with your new head and be reporting back anything and *everything*. You are to start immediately, and your new head will explain the intricacies of your new position.'

'Spiritual guide, eh?' said Crowley, not sure what it actually meant. However, he did pick up the fact he would still be under Rucelle and he wasn't sure if this was a good thing or a bad thing. At this moment in time it felt like a bad thing.

'Indeed,' Rucelle continued with his death stare which made Crowley feel he should be saying a lot more. Should he ask what had been debated in the meeting? Should he ask why his actions had caused so much fuss? After a brief deliberation, he concluded that Rucelle would give nothing away so what was the point. 'I'll be keeping a close eye on you, Crowley. In fact, a number of people will be monitoring your actions. Please do not put the spotlight on the Protectors' Division again. Do I make myself clear?'

Clear about what? You've told me nothing. You're as clear as an inebriated DJ, thought Crowley. All he knew was what his new position was.

'Mmm,' muttered Crowley. He felt it was best to be just as ambiguous. There was a small pause when Crowley realised that they were expecting him to leave. 'I'll go now then, shall I?' Crowley rose from the chair.

'I'm sure you have a more pressing engagement,' said Rucelle sarcastically.

'Thank you, Rucelle,' Crowley cast his glance behind Rucelle. 'At ease, Bathisma,' he said with a smile and he disappeared before he could see their reaction.

Crowley found himself in a white corridor with various closed white doors. The area reminded him of the Death Star in Star Wars. The door in front of him was the only one in the corridor with a plaque. In fancy script, it read SPIRITUAL GUIDES. He stood for a moment to collect himself. He had no idea what to expect, who he was about to meet or what lay behind the door. He toyed with the idea of going home but then he remembered he was being monitored, probably even while he was stood there. He took a deep breath, stepped forward and knocked on the door. He waited to hear someone beckon him in so was surprised when the door opened.

He was greeted by a man, Native American and in his forties. His hair was long and carbon black and his skin was deep brown. His brown eyes were wise, and he wore a black jacket that was buttoned to his Adam's apple, and black pants. The man stood for a moment as if drinking Crowley in and then his face began to brighten with a large smile. Crowley found himself smiling back.

'You must be Crowley,' said the gentle man.

'I suppose, I must be,' smiled Crowley. The man stood to one side and waved his arm to beckon Crowley in. The room was surprisingly dark with only a small desk lamp and some light diffusing from a small window. A huge desk dominated most of the floor space in the small room while the walls were littered with shelves of books. Crowley noticed there was no order to the books unlike his own library. These books looked like they had been thrown and wherever and however they landed was good enough.

'I was about to make tea. Please, come.' The man walked over to an empty tray that looked quite lonely on a small table. Crowley approached the table next to the man. 'I want you to make your tea. You can make whatever tea you desire. I only ask that you make it yourself. Okay?' he smiled at Crowley and then waved his hand gently to the tray to indicate to Crowley to begin. Crowley looked at the tray and knew in his heart what he wanted. Within a moment, a teapot, strainer, milk jug, and a perfect white china cup complete with saucer appeared. Crowley cast the man a sideward glance who smiled approvingly. Crowley picked up the teapot and started to swirl the contents.

'I don't like to use a teaspoon. I find the leaves diffuse much more gently with an encouraging swish,' he smiled as if the man had waited all his life for this top tip. 'And I'm a "milk first" man.' Crowley splashed the white liquid in the bottom of the teacup. He then proceeded to pour his tea into the remainder of the cup. Once he had finished he turned to his host. 'There. Did I pass the test?'

'Please take a seat,' offered the man. Crowley could see 2 small armchairs near the door he had just come in with a small table between them. He made his way over and sat down. The man had his back to him making his own tea. Crowley's items had disappeared and a small black metal teapot with a wooden handle had taken its place. Crowley watched the man pour his tea into a pottery mug that was cupped in his hand; he then took hold of the small protruding pan handle and walked over to the vacant chair to join Crowley who found the whole spectacle fascinating.

'My name is Nazriel, and I shall be your guide and teacher for however long our journey is. Welcome,' he said gently.

'Thank you, Nazriel.' Crowley placed his cup down on the table and looked at his new guide. Crowley felt that he was going to like him and his new position. 'To be honest, Nazriel, I'm not sure what my new position is. Rucelle said very little, and what he did say, was well, rather cryptic,' explained Crowley. Nazriel drank from his crude cup and Crowley caught the smell of the contents which reminded him of cut grass and burning wood.

'You have been offered a position of great privilege, my friend. Spiritual guides walk among the living and yet are only seen by few,' Nazriel began.

'Like ghosts?' asked Crowley. Nazriel chuckled.

'Not quite. We walk among the living and are only seen in the mind's eye of the few. The few that believe and understand our existence. The few that use this knowledge for good, guidance, strength and courage. The few that are respectful to our influence.' Crowley was listening intently to Nazriel's soft and velvety voice.

'Influence?' asked Crowley. 'Is that not like a Protector?'

'A little. A living soul should never be aware of the Protector. The soul should always feel they have made a choice and that choice was based on instinct. However, instinct is most always an influence by the Protector.' Nazriel drained his cup and stood to make another. While Crowley looked at the long black plait that trailed down Nazriel's back he continued to listen. 'Only a soul can be a Spiritual Guide, not an angel. And Guides are a little more obvious than Protectors. We can directly help living souls with those that can hear us.'

'You mean like mediums?' questioned Crowley. Nazriel chuckled again and with his refilled cup walked back to his seat.

'I suppose,' said Nazriel.

'So basically, you can see a Guide but not a Protector, but they do the same thing?'

'A spiritual guide will not need to show himself as such. The appointed living soul will be able to see you with their own soul. I think they call it a sixth sense. A Guide can directly speak to the soul.' Crowley was beginning to understand.

'So, a Guide can tell a living soul to buy a lottery ticket, but a Protector may make them drop their money on the way to the shop to make sure they don't get killed by the out-of-control bus that would have hit them if they had been a couple of seconds earlier?' asked Crowley. Nazriel let out a hearty laugh. He was glad Crowley was in his division.

'A very human way of looking at it, but you are correct.'

'So, how do I know what to say?'

'A Guide is ruled by instinct. Some Guides are used for rituals, some are used to simply guide one person's path but most like to influence greater numbers through their appointed soul. Such as mediumship that you referred to before.'

'But, I still won't know how to guide them for the best,' protested Crowley.

'You will know if you follow your heart. If you believe what you do is for the good and trust your own choices, you and your appointed soul will find spiritual satisfaction. Using your instinct is something you do all the time without realising it. You knew by following your heart, listening to your soul and allowing instinct to take over that you would make a perfect cup of tea.'

'It's hardly the same,' protested Crowley.

'Ah, but it is. Our whole lives are dictated by the choices that we make, and those choices are based on instinct. The problem for most people is to trust it. Instinct is always right.' Crowley mulled over his last statement and wasn't sure he agreed with it. He had made a lot of decisions while he was alive and had followed his gut and it turned out he had made some bad choices.

'You are no doubt thinking of all the times where you felt instinct let you down.' Nazriel was sipping from his cup. 'Just because the decision you made did not fulfil your expectations, does not mean that it was the wrong decision. It will simply be a piece of a larger puzzle that you were still yet to complete.' Crowley sat in silence and analysed decisions he had made and how they had contributed to a bigger picture but after a couple of minutes he found his life was too complicated and confusing to fathom.

'You make something that's clearly complex sound very simple,' said Crowley.

'People complicate life, not the other way around,' smiled Nazriel. Crowley shrugged his shoulders in agreement to this point.

'I understand you have already met your appointed, Sean Allister,' asked Nazriel.

'Oh, you heard about that, did you?'

'I make no judgement on your actions. But once you have decided what your role is, then you must make contact with his soul.'

'But how do I know what my role is?'

'Have we not just discussed this?' Nazriel said gently. Crowley sat confused for a moment and then realised.

'Instinct?' Nazriel smiled and stood to put his cup back

on the tray. He turned to face Crowley who also stood up.

'Come back when you have contacted him. I should like to hear about your first steps on the path that you have chosen.' Nazriel walked to the door and opened it for Crowley to walk through. The corridor was no longer outside; it was Crowley's study where Jennifer was sat by the fire. Crowley stepped into the room and his wife looked up immediately.

'Darling! Where did you come from?' She walked over to embrace him and looked behind her husband. 'Was that an Indian I just saw you with?' Crowley looked behind him, but the door had gone.

'A Native American,' he corrected. 'Yes, Nazriel. He's my new …erm…boss, I suppose.'

'You're a spiritual guide! Under Nazriel? Oh, that's wonderful,' she cried.

'I hope so, and I hope Sean Allister thinks so too.'

CHAPTER 6

Sean hadn't been able to sleep all night. Sue's revelation of seeing what had happened on the plane was whirring through his mind. He had only told Mr Armstrong from the AAIB what had happened in the last few moments on the plane, but he had not told anyone about the man asking him to move. He couldn't stop thinking about him having a Guardian Angel. He had never given any thought to his spiritual beliefs. Coping with life was tough enough without considering there could be more. But what if there was? He immediately thought that surely it should be someone he would have known from his past, but he hadn't recognised the man on the plane. *It had been quick*, he thought, *and I was distracted by my new shoes. Maybe the image was too quick to see if it was some long-lost relative.*

Sean plugged in his laptop and aided with a strong coffee began to research Guardian Angels. He spent most of the day looking at various websites that all offered their own opinion on angels. After some time, he concluded that no one really knew anything. There were some stories he read that he could loosely relate to, people saying they felt someone at times of trouble, but he struggled to find information on people who had actually seen an angel. The only thing that most of them agreed on was you didn't have to have known them and there was no reason why some had one and some didn't, that's if they existed at all.

Sean only stopped his research now and again to take some tablets, and as the day wore on he replaced his coffee with herbal tea. He watched his TV programmes and checked in with his mum before he decided to go to bed. He was glad he was tired after the bad night before and as soon as his head hit the pillow, he fell asleep.

His dreams began early in the night. It was the plane dream again and even though it was flying fine, the feeling of dread was still there. He knew what was about to come and couldn't move from his seat to tell anyone. He felt paralysed in the seat and could only move his eyes. His conscious brain was telling him to wake up before the inevitable crash and while he was shouting his name to wake himself up he could see the man, the man from the plane.

He was stood in the aisle but in front of him as opposed to his side where he had actually been and was looking straight at Sean. As Sean shouted his own name he could see the man's mouth moving as if he was saying it too. Sean stopped shouting his name and soon the plane began to shudder.

'Would you like a cup of tea?' said the man in the aisle. Sean silently nodded his head and, in a blink, was sat on his couch in his lounge next to the man. Sean looked around the room and then back at the man who was now passing him a steaming cup of tea. 'I made you chamomile. There is a used bag still in the sink, so I made the presumption of thinking you drink that,' the man smiled. 'However, I exercised some decadence and made your tea with a fresh bag. You should discard your bags in the bin, tea stains in the sink are such a chore to remove, don't you think?' Sean silently nodded. 'Do you remember me at all?' asked Crowley.

'You're the fella off the plane. You told me to move,' Sean said flatly. The research earlier in the evening was obviously still playing on his mind and this dream was the result.

'I am, and I did. I got into a bit of trouble about that,' he sniffed, 'but then that's nothing for you to worry about.' Sean, feeling a little more alert, continued to look at the man. He was wearing the same suit as he wore on the plane and this time he could smell him. He smelled of whisky and Imperial Leather soap and surprisingly, it made Sean feel comfortable.

'Well Sean, my name is Hugh, but everyone calls me Crowley.'

'Why?'

'Because that's my name.'

'Oh!' Sean continued to stare, and Crowley began to feel a little nervous.

'I'm new at this, but I've been told to trust my instinct, so here I am,' he smiled.

'Here you are, what?' asked Sean.

'With you,' replied Crowley.

'Oh!'

Crowley wasn't sure what he was supposed to do. He hadn't really thought this through properly. His wife wanted to discuss how he was going to introduce himself and how he could interact with Sean, but the discussion alone was confusing him, so he decided to wing it with instinct as Nazriel had advised and here he was.

'Are you my Guardian Angel?' asked Sean.

'Not exactly, I'm more of a spiritual guide. I can read your soul,' he whispered.

'Jesus,' snorted Sean, 'you don't want to delve in there, mate unless you've got an NVQ in finding your way around confusion, bad choices and why I'm addicted to Holby City.'

Crowley laughed. 'Holby City eh? I'm more of a cop show man myself. Although, I did particularly enjoy The South Bank Show.' Crowley looked at Sean expectantly and was disappointed by the lack of recognition to his TV choices. 'Anyway, you know there is more to you than that,' continued Crowley. Sean knew he wasn't bad, but he felt that looking around his soul would not only be quick but a boring exercise as well. 'I see a man that is very comfortable in his skin, painted or not,' Crowley cocked his head towards Sean. 'I see a man of courage and conviction. I see a man of loyalty, humour and wit. But most of all, there is a lot of love in your life.'

Sean tutted when he heard that. He hadn't had a bloke in some time and he had never had a partner that had stayed. 'Yes, I agree you are yet to find your soul mate or your life partner or whatever it is they call it these days. But love is measured in so many other ways. Be grateful for what you have.' Crowley caught Sean rolling his eyes and felt a twinge of disappointment. 'I have learned the happiest people are those that say thank you today, not the ones that still await another gift.'

'You sound like a cross between Merlin, Yoda and Lord Charles,' sniggered Sean.

'Lord Charles? Lord Charles? Did he have Lunberry Hall?' asked Crowley.

'No, he had some fella with his hand stuck up his wooden arse last time he was on at the Palladium,' laughed Sean.

'Oh, the puppet! Yes, of course!' Crowley joined in the laughter. 'I wonder what happened to him.'

'Dunno, probably contracted woodworm and saw out the rest of his days in Costa Del Attic.' They both laughed again, and Crowley began to relax a bit more. Sean took a sideward glance and studied his guest.

'My mate had a friend called Crowley,' Sean recalled. 'Never met him, mind. She's in New York at the moment. She'll probably stay there, lucky cow.'

'Grace,' Crowley whispered.

'Yeah, how did you know that?' Sean was puzzled. Crowley realised he had said too much. He didn't want Sean to know about how he knew Grace. Grace had never said who Crowley was and he wanted to respect her wishes.

'I can read souls, remember?' Crowley quickly offered.

'Oh yeah.' Sean was satisfied and accepted the answer as true. 'So, is that your job then? To go around and tell people stuff they already know?' Sean heard himself and realised that he had been rude. 'I don't mean that to sound the way it did. I just mean...well, I don't know actually what I mean.' That was the good thing about dreams; they didn't need to make sense.

'I suppose I am part of your soul now, Sean. I will help you and those you love, and we shall see where our journey takes us, for there is one thing I have learned from living and dying and that is there is no point in planning.'

'I like to think I'm a planner, but I'm not. I'm like Will-O-The-Wisp. Floating around when really I should be getting my act together.'

'I feel that's how most people live their life, so I wouldn't worry too much about it,' Crowley offered reassuringly. Sean sat for a moment and looked at the floor and then back to Crowley beside him.

'This has to be one of the funkiest dreams I've ever

had,' smiled Sean. Crowley stood up and Sean naturally followed suit.

'Then I take it you are not a whisky drinker?' Crowley raised an amused eyebrow. 'Anyway, back to bed. I'm sure you value your beauty sleep.' Sean automatically turned toward the bedroom and without any emotion simply bid Crowley good night. He didn't need to see his guest out or make sure the front door was shut properly. Sean climbed into bed and hoped his continued sleep didn't send him back to the plane.

The rest of the night was uneventful, but as he woke he became aware of the pain from his neck. He opened his eyes and stayed still for a few moments. He knew the slightest movement would send the pain shooting to all four corners of his body. He thought of his dreams. The plane and the man named Crowley. He smiled at the way the dream had brought him to his lounge drinking tea. He smacked his lips and he could still taste the ghost of tea in his mouth from the evening before. No wonder he had dreamed he was drinking it. It was funny how he had named the man Crowley, the same as one of Grace's friends whom he had never met. Watching 'Friends' the night before must have triggered some buried thoughts about New York. Sean tried to figure out the strangeness of his dream and once he was satisfied that he had accounted for every weird and wonderful detail, he slowly raised his head from the pillow and braced for the pain. The pain did come but not as bad as previous mornings and he took it as a sign he was on the mend.

As he stood, his feet found the slippers by the bedside from the night before and his toes began to munch their way to the top. His plan today was to pop to the shops and then see Faye back at her flat for a coffee. Sean, bleary-eyed, headed for the kitchen through the lounge, and as he turned the tap on and reached for a glass he noticed the old tea bag from last night sitting in the sink. He stared at it for a moment, filled his glass and placed the glass on the counter. He carried on staring at it and remembered his dream. He only frowned a little when he fished it out and walked to the pedal bin to throw it away but as he stood on the pedal to lift the lid he could see the coffee table. Two white mugs, one with a tea dribble down one side stared at him. The sight made Sean jolt and he took a sharp breath.

There he stood in his kitchen complete in his pink dressing gown holding a used tea bag and the only thing he could hear was his hammering heart in his chest. His mind was blank. His head began to tell him that he should think something, but his brain was shouting back that it didn't know what to think, so he continued to stand and stare until his brain kicked in and shouted, 'Why are there two cups?! Who had a cup of tea last night?! Why are there two cups?!' Then his head kicked in shouting, 'Go and pick them up!' Then his brain shouted, 'What for?! It's not like you can tell what happened by just picking it up!' Then Sean's mouth joined in.

'What the fuck….?'

Still holding the tea bag out to one side, he slowly shuffled his way to the coffee table. Clutching the front of his dressing gown close to his body with his other hand, he moved forward and peered into the cups. His body jolted back to reality and as he swung around, the tea bag flew out of his hand and hit a picture on his fridge that Josh had painted for him. Sean could see the wetness devouring what was supposed to be a horse on the paper.

'Shit!' He quickly snatched the paper from the magnet, placed the painting on the counter and started to dab at the blob with the pink belt from his dressing gown. 'It can't be real...it can't be real....it can't be real.' Still pressing on the picture, he turned his head to look at the mugs again on the table. 'It's fucking real...it's fucking real,' he gabbled, now dabbing harder at the splodge. His breath was quickening, and he could feel the panic rising in him. It started to rush through his guts and then he became aware of the pain in his neck, then he felt like his whole scalp exploded in pure terror. He swung around and pinned his back to the counter top, so he could see the whole kitchen and lounge in one go.

'So, are you there?' he shouted wishing he hadn't, but he couldn't stop. 'I mean...well, are you? Don't go jumping out of me fridge and pulling a Jackie Chan on me.' He was still shouting and now felt he was hyper-ventilating. He waited for a response but there was nothing.

The whole night came back to him as he stood in the silence. It wasn't a dream. All of that was real. That meant seeing him on the plane was real and this man, Crowley, had saved his life. So why was he frightened? Sean started to calm a little and tried to steady his breathing. After what felt like an age, he eventually got his breathing normal and quelled his thunderous heartbeat. He remembered Crowley had said they could help the people he loved. He hoped that was true. He wanted Faye to get her big break, he wanted Josh to grow into a respectful man, he wanted his mum and Charlie to be healthy for as long as possible and yes, he wanted happiness for himself in whatever shape or form.

Sean tried to busy himself in an attempt to extinguish the enormity of what had happened the night before. He spent the whole morning bustling around the flat, cleaning every surface and straightening anything that could move, but his head was still swimming and the answers to all his questions did not come. He needed to get out. He needed some fresh air to cleanse his mind. He continued to think and pick at the detail of the night with Crowley and by the time he left his flat he was grateful he could light up a cigarette. He took a long drag and closed his eyes at the instant relief it gave him.

'You really shouldn't,' heard Sean in his head. But Sean found it strange as the voice was not his own subconscious, it was Crowley's. Sean stood like a startled rabbit not sure what to do or even where to look. He stayed silent for a moment to see if he could hear the voice again, but nothing. He took another drag on his cigarette and looked over his shoulder. Even though he couldn't see anyone he knew someone was with him. He took a deep breath and closed his eyes,

'Are you there?' asked Sean in his mind.

'I am,' came an echoed voice. Sean quickly opened his eyes and spun around. There was still no one there and he knew he was not controlling the voice in his head. The voice was not the same as he had had with his own thoughts. He started to feel scared and could feel his heart thumping in his chest.

'Are you inside me? Like a possession thingy?'

'No, not like that,' came the voice. In fear, Sean decided to walk across the cobbled courtyard, through the arch and onto the High Street. For some reason, Sean felt that he may be safer in a more populated area. He stopped outside a shop and pressed his back against the brick wall and watched the passers-by run around Lanson.

'Then what, then?' There was a silence. Crowley was thinking of what he could say, and Sean wasn't sure if he had lost a signal or something by turning into a busier street. Had he gone? Was he just imagining the voice? Maybe, the crash had given him brain damage? Maybe, he was suffering from post-traumatic stress? 'You still there, mate? Can you hear me?' Sean felt like he was losing his mind.

'I'm still here,' responded Crowley from within. Sean shot off the wall and started hurrying through the street. His mind was racing about the night before, about drinking tea and about a journey. Just like a dream, he couldn't remember the finer details. Had he sold his soul? He couldn't remember. But one was for certain that last night when he spoke to Crowley, he could see him.

'I'm not sure if my mind is playing tricks or I'm traumatised or if I've got a brain tumour.'

'You are quite well.' How could he tell if he was well? Even if he was mad his brain would tell him he was well. You only had to watch One Flew Over the Cuckoo's Nest to know that.

'Is that better?' The voice was no longer in his head, it was beside him. Sean turned to see a happy Crowley. As he went to speak, Crowley raised his hand to stop him. 'No one else can see me Sean, so I suggest you continue to speak to me as you were, unless you want to invite some strange looks.' Sean discreetly nodded, and Crowley indicated to keep walking.

'I take it you are now convinced that last night was not a dream?' asked Crowley. Sean wasn't sure how he was supposed to react. How could he carry on walking to the shops with a man that no one could see? Why was this happening to him now? Was it because of the accident? Did having a near-death experience make him more receptive to things like this? What was this anyway? Could he turn him off? Sean thought for a moment to all the paranormal shows he had watched when psychics said they had a guide. He had always taken it with a pinch of scepticism and a large degree of showmanship. *Maybe if I just talk to him I can find out why this is happening? Maybe I am just going doolally,* Sean said to himself.

'I'm not gonna lie, I nearly had a heart attack this morning when I saw those cups,' he said in his head. 'Jesus Christ, is this for real? I am seriously talking to you?'

'Mind the pram.'

'What?' Sean looked at Crowley.

'The pram!' Crowley pointed to just in front of Sean. Sean stumbled when he noticed the pram at his feet. The child seemed quite happy with his box of raisins, but his mother looked cross.

'Are you blind? You nearly fell on him you stupid idiot!'

'I'm so sorry, I was talking,' Sean went to nod to his companion and realised, 'I mean, I was in a world of my own. Seriously, I'm sorry.' The woman tutted and stormed passed Sean in a huff, clearly unimpressed with his apology.

'I thought you were here to help me with people. I nearly killed a baby 'cos of you! I can't do this in the bleeding street. I only came out for a fag and I'm walking around the town like friggin' Derek Acorah.'

'Do you want me to go?' asked Crowley. Sean noted that he looked a little sorry for himself.

'I'm sorry, but yes!' No sooner was the word out, Crowley had disappeared. Sean was left alone in the street. He looked no different to passers-by but as Sean stood there, he felt very vulnerable. He turned on his heel and was walking back towards his flat when he heard his name being called.

'Sean!' He knew the voice and when he turned, Sue was running to catch up with him.

'All right, Sue? I'm just going home,' he tried to be dismissive. He was in no mood for her.

'Good, I'll walk back with you and then you can put the kettle on. I need to speak to you.'

'I'm not being funny, Sue; I think I need a lie down.

The pain and all that,' he lied.

'I won't be long,' she carried on walking beside him, 'plus, you can't avoid me forever, Sean. You ran out of the pub last night and I need to talk to you about it.'

'Sue...'

'It was a big thing for me as well, Sean. Please?' she insisted. Sean mulled for a moment. Sue was always so bubbly but could sometime be quite frankly, annoying. But this was a side he had never seen in her, she was serious.

'Come on then.' They walked in silence back to the flat and Sean immediately put the kettle on.

'I've never been in your flat before. I like the way your kitchen and lounge are open plan. Very sociable.' Sean could tell she was making polite chit chat and noted that she seemed a little nervous. She continued to babble on about how she was thinking of joining the local diet group when Sean placed a cup of tea in front of her and sat beside her on the couch. The silence fell, and Sean felt he should start.

'Look Sue, I'm really sorry I ran out on you like that.'

'Oh, it's okay sweetie. A few in the pub seem to think I told you of your impending death and you got scared,' she chuckled.

'Oh, I'm sorry.'

'On the contrary, more people wanted to see me after that; they probably just want a bit of drama in their own lives. So, I'd appreciate it if you kept your reading all a bit vague if anyone asks you. Add to the intrigue and all that. Plus, it doesn't do any harm to my purse,' she chuckled. 'The reason I need to talk to you is...' she hesitated, 'I saw your last conscious moments on that plane, yes?' Sean nodded. 'And I remember the lovely gentleman that asked you to move. He was in a suit, wasn't he?' Sean nodded again. 'Sean, I'm not sure if you were aware. But this man, this person, he erm…' she paused again and then took a gulp, '…he wasn't of this world.' Sean continued to stare at her. 'I can't explain it,' she continued, 'but when I saw him, apart from being calm of the impending crash, it was the fact …well… he had a light around him, like an angel.' Sean went to speak, and Sue raised her hand. She wanted to say it all in one go as she knew she might not find the courage again. 'I know it sounds daft, and I thought I could be wrong and maybe have read my vision wrong. I've never seen an angel in a vision before and no one has ever told me what they look like. But I know I'm right, and I know that they don't have wings or a harp or a long white dress. I've been up all night thinking about it and I can still see his face clearly but by the time the morning came I thought maybe I had conjured up the image in my head from things that Faye had told me when you were in hospital. I thought that the man was there, but he was actually a passenger, and the light around him was just some weird thing. So, I had a little nap, got up, and felt better. Then I decided to go to the cake shop, buy us some Danishes and pop over for a cup of tea to make sure you were all right and that I hadn't frightened you or anything. But when I came out of the bakers, there you were. Walking down the street and who was beside you? But the man from my vision. Chattering away to you he was and then you looked cross and he disappeared.' Sean could feel all the colour draining from his face. 'I didn't imagine that, did I Sean?'

'Fucking hell, Sue,' Sean's cup began to tremble in his hand and he placed it on the table in front of them. 'You could see him? Seriously?'

'Can you see him, Sean?'

'See him? I can hear him! He came here last night and had a cup of tea with me. I thought I was dreaming until I got up and saw the cups still on the table.'

'Do you remember him in the crash?'

'Yeah, but at the time, I mean I didn't think he was an angel or anything. I just did as I was told.'

'Do you know who he is?'

'He told me his name is Crowley, and that he is my spiritual guide and erm… oh jeez, I can't think.'

'A spiritual guide!! Oh Sean, you are so lucky!' she squealed.

'Am I?' Sean couldn't see what was so great about being permanently haunted.

'Sean, you have been given a wonderful gift. I have the odd vision but not direct messages from a guide. Only a lucky few have genuine guides. This is something you should embrace.'

'Really? What? Being permanently watched by a spook?'

'There's more to it than that.'

'Like what?'

'Haven't you asked him?'

Sean thought for a moment. He hadn't felt he should ask what all this was about. He was just about getting his head around the fact that he could see him and now Sue had dropped the bombshell that she could see him too.

'No, I haven't.'

'Why don't you see if you can contact him now? Get some answers.'

'How do I do that?'

'Maybe you should go to spiritual instruction. I used to go a few years back and they do these wonderful…'

'Oh, I haven't got time for that. Going to some bleeding church telling me how to speak to 'the other side'. Just tell me what you know, Sue. If he turns up, then I'll ask him how to do it properly or whatever.'

Sue could see that Sean was winding himself up. She had had a few visions herself but not all of them came true. But she always acted on any strong feelings she had. When Faye was born, she read tarot cards in her house to make a few pounds and keep the fridge full. But she knew what Sean was experiencing was in a different league to her and she had to help him.

'Okay, this is something they told me that you should always do so no bad spirits come through, okay?' She took Sean's hands and asked him to close his eyes. 'I want you to empty your mind completely. Listen only to your breathing and concentrate on that. Once you feel your mind is empty, I want you to imagine a white light. Make it small. And with each breath make the light bigger and keep making it bigger until it completely surrounds you. Tell yourself that this is the light of protection, this is good light, this is good energy and, in this light, nothing can harm you. Once you can feel the warmth of the light, imagine Crowley and ask him to come to you.' Sue stopped speaking. She could hear Sean breathing and a ticking clock from the wall in his kitchen. She wondered if the incessant ticking ever annoyed him and her mind began to wander to a more appealing and silent digital clock. Sean continued to hold her hands and she kept her eyes closed hoping that Sean was able to empty his mind. Time passed, and Sue began to wonder if Sean had fell asleep.

'She doesn't seem your type, Sean.' Sean opened his eyes and could see Crowley sat in his armchair like King Tut.

'Sue,' Sean whispered. Sue opened her eyes and gasped at the sight of Crowley looking very relaxed. 'She's my mate's mum. She can see you, you know,' said Sean.

'Oh, I know she can see me. But she can't hear me,' said Crowley.

Sean turned to Sue, 'Can you hear him?'

'No dear, is he talking?'

'Why can't she hear you?'

'Well, I'm your guide not hers. She can only see me because she has... well, I suppose you could say a slightly heightened psychic ability.' Sean looked confused. 'Let's imagine most people are analogue, the regular person who is not aware or can pick up 'extra waves'. Then there are people who have Freeview, they can see a lot more and are aware that there are other things out there but cannot receive them as they are not on broadband. People on broadband can see, hear and interact with just about anything. Sue only has the Freeview subscription I'm afraid.'

'While I'm the one with a stonking satellite dish in my head?'

'Exactly!' Crowley was pleased he understood.

'What the bleeding hell is he saying?' said Sue. Sean repeated Crowley's analogy back to Sue who seemed satisfied but tried not to show her disappointment at only having Freeview.

"Anyway, you called young man, in a rather dramatic fashion I hasten to add.'

'So, how do I call you then?' asked Sean

'A combination of thought and want is usually pretty sufficient. You can leave the bathing yourself in the white light for when you next go to the tanning shop.' Sean shifted a little in his chair. 'What can I do for you? Have you had any thoughts about how we can start our journey together?'

'No, I haven't! You only left me half an hour ago! I can take three hours deciding whether to journey to the toilet for a crap.'

'Sean!' shouted Sue.

'Sorry Sue, but he's asking what we should do. How the hell do I know? Shouldn't you be telling me?' he asked. Crowley sat for a moment. He supposed it was a little presumptuous to think that Sean would have all the answers. Nazriel had said follow his instinct but his instinct was unfortunately shy at the moment. It wasn't long, however, before Crowley could see a couple becoming in the far corner of the room. He stared at them and once they were clear he could see it was a large woman and a smaller man and they both looked very happy.

'My name is Stan.'

'And mine is Doris. We're Susan's parents. Can you tell her that we are together and are waiting for her? But we don't want to see her too soon,' they laughed together. 'Tell her we love what she did with the roses on the gazebo. Lovely idea, wasn't it, Stan?' Stan nodded approvingly and then they were gone. Crowley turned to Sean and Sue who were looking expectantly at him.

'Sean, could you tell Sue that her parents were here. They are happy and will be there when her time has come. Tell her that they love the roses on the gazebo.'

Sean looked at Crowley, completely confused, but did as he was bid and turned to Sue to tell her. When he had finished, he could see her eyes were welling up and becoming tinged with red.

'Oh, God Sean, really? I planted a climbing rose at the side of the gazebo when my mum died. My dad followed her a few months later; he probably pined for her. So, I planted another one on the other side. One side is yellow and the other is pink. They're all intertwined now, and I always think that it's like them, their memories all mingled together.' Sean was starting to sniff as he listened to the story. Sue turned to Crowley and said thank you to which he bowed his head. 'This is it Sean! This is what you should do!'

'What? Get a gazebo and plant some roses?'

'No! You should be a medium! Passing on all these lovely messages.'

THE FOLLOWING YEAR

~ ~ ~

CHAPTER 7

Crowley found himself in front of Nazriel's door and gave it a gentle knock. Almost instantly the door was opened by a happy looking Nazriel.

'Crowley, come in.' He stepped into the room and as Crowley took his usual position in the armchair, Nazriel busied himself making them tea. Soon they were seated together and enjoyed their hot refreshment for a moment. 'It's been a while since I last saw you and I hear you have been busy, Crowley. These last months you have spent with Sean have certainly brought him a lot of attention.'

'I'll say. It's been a bit of a rollercoaster, but we seem to be finding our feet now. Sean is certainly going from strength to strength. He's had a sell-out national tour and has been on every TV show you can think of. He's the new sensation and he's in talks with an American network about doing a celebrity chat show slash reading but I'm not sure about that.' Nazriel chuckled.

'Why ever not?'

'American TV! It's one thing picking people out of an audience and relaying bits and bobs but to do it one to one on a chat show, it seems too exposed.'

'They won't be able to see you any more on American television than they do on British TV.'

'No, it's not that. I mean what if someone comes through and says something that could ruin the person's career, like they killed someone or pushed drugs or something. You know what these celebrities are like.'

Nazriel continued to laugh. 'Are you enjoying your role? There is talk all over Heaven about the impression that Sean is having on a number of souls, living and passed. You should be very proud of all the comfort you are both giving to them.'

'I suppose,' sniffed Crowley. While he sipped his tea Nazriel could see that his friend was troubled.

'Tell me Crowley, what is it that makes the puzzle so hard to finish?' Crowley was a little taken aback by the question. He understood it completely but didn't realise that his thoughts were so transparent to others. Or maybe it was only Nazriel that could see he was troubled. He often thought of Nazriel. He only knew that he was a spirit that few Native American tribes would dance to or pow wow. The people of the tribe would hope to connect with Nazriel and for him to bring peace. Nazriel was one of the few angels who had the power to allow his essence to descend to Earth, not that it happened much these days. But in the days when he was prayed to a lot, he learned the fragility of the human soul and the strength of human spirit.

'I feel there has to be more than this,' admitted Crowley.

'This?'

'I can't explain it, Nazriel. This friendship, partnership, whatever you want to call it between Sean and I, it doesn't seem enough.'

'What more do you want?'

'I don't know. Yes, he has fame and fortune and I am very happy that he is deemed a success, but is this it?'

'You have helped make a lot of people very happy and let us not forget you were only originally sent to help Sean. And yet you have gifted to Sean a marvellous career. It wasn't that long ago you said you were playing to a dozen or so people in church halls and look at you both now. And I know you are going to say that his friend Sue has helped, and I believe she has but only to raise his profile. His gift is his and his alone and you have provided the nourishment to allow that gift to grow into something that everyone can enjoy.'

'I know. But I just have a feeling that Sean and I aren't doing enough, and I think Sean feels like that as well.' Nazriel stood and silently walked to the small table to top up his cup.

'Have you ever been lost my friend?' asked Nazriel. Crowley recalled a time when he had not long passed his driving test and was driving his friend Charles, a uni chum at the time, to Charles' parents' house. The journey was supposed to take an hour at most but after a couple of hours, doubt set in if they were on the right road. With every unfamiliar mile behind them their tempers rose with Charles blaming Crowley for not planning the journey, and Crowley blaming Charles for not knowing where he actually lived. The sign that said *Welcome to Wales* was the final indicator that they were nowhere near Oxford.

'Yes, I've been lost,' admitted Crowley.

'And when you knew you were lost did you immediately turn around or wait for a sign that told you which direction you should be in?' The *Welcome to Wales* sign popped back into his memory.

'I suppose I waited so I could get my bearings before I decided which way I should go.'

Nazriel sat himself down in his armchair and before his lips touched his cup he said, 'Life is much the same, my friend.' Crowley mulled over the veiled lesson that had taken place. His experience with Sean so far did indeed feel as if their journey had begun, but they both were not sure if this was the right road to be on. He felt a little more at peace knowing that eventually a sign would come that would show them where they should be. He hoped the sign was as obvious as when they were in Abergavenny. Crowley drained his cup and stood to place it on the tea tray.

'Are you leaving already?' asked Nazriel.

'I am. I know it was short and sweet and I will come again soon, but I promised my friend Jack that I would meet him for a nightcap in Benito's.'

Nazriel stood and smiled, 'Ah, Benito's. Your second home I do believe.'

'My dear Nazriel, you do yourself an injustice! Your study is by far more welcoming than my favourite watering hole. However, I am a slave to the refreshment that has a little more kick than your tea. Which is delicious, I hasten to add!' Nazriel opened the door for Crowley to exit and as he did, Crowley noted his friend's smile had slipped a little.

'Only let the firewater ignite your passion. Do not let it dampen your beliefs.' Nazriel nodded to Crowley and gently shut the door, leaving him stood in the white corridor. Crowley turned and stared at the closed door and wondered if there was a lesson imbedded in that last statement or was it simply a more eloquent way of saying 'don't get pissed'.

Crowley soon found himself in Benito's and after being served a whisky he took a seat in an old buttoned leather Captain's chair. It had become the usual spot for him and

Jack to converse and within minutes Jack was also seated in the matching chair opposite. The small low table that stood between them housed a large glass ashtray ready for the burnt memories from a pair of good cigars.

'So, Jack, tell me what you have been up to? I do believe last time we met you let me witter on about Sean's BBC special and I failed to ask about your own adventures,' he apologised. Jack silently smiled as he delved into his pocket and produced two Gurkha HMR cigars and passed one to his friend. Crowley inspected the cigar within its clear casing and glanced toward Jack to show his appreciation of his fine choice. Within minutes they were both sat in a satisfying billowing cloud.

'How is Sean these days?' enquired Jack.

'After eight months, I think he is finally coming to terms with the trappings of his new lifestyle. I think he especially loves his new car and being able to treat his parents and friends.'

'He sounds like a good boy,' Jack pulled on his cigar and scrutinised the rising glow from the tip as he did. 'Tell me, how does Sean feel about the whole thing?'

'The whole thing?'

'I mean, how does he feel about guides and angels influencing matters of the living world, our interventions, messages and spiritual advice?' Crowley quickly assessed Sean's changing attitude the last few months and concluded that Sean had simply accepted his new-found gift.

'I feel that Sean deems himself very lucky to be have been given this ability. He sees now that it is his destiny to pass these messages on and bring comfort to those who need it. However, I do know that deep down it bothers him when people call him a fraud and say he is only in it to make a quick buck. I think that's why he gives a lot of his earnings away or spends them on others. There is a self-inflicted guilt with him and by doing that I think he finds temporary exoneration. But as far as divine intervention goes, I'm not sure. But to be fair a lot of humankind accept that there is more than their simple existence on Earth. In whatever religion, there are teachings of a higher plane.'

'Yes, but most of these teachings define it as that, a higher but different plane. What is truly happening is a collision of the two and there are very few who are aware of this let alone become a part of it.'

'Then maybe Sean was chosen because they knew he would be able to accept his part and still be happy within the overlap.'

'Maybe. But tell me this, how would Sean react if he could see and hear not only you but maybe dozens of other Heavenly beings?' Crowley gave a hearty laugh.

'I think the shock would turn him straight for a start. He just about accepts me and that's only because I allow him to find as much humour as he can in my accent, my demeanour, my clothes and well, just about anything he can home in on and completely take the piss out of. Aside from furthering his career, of course,' he concluded. Crowley took a drag on the cigar and found he was being studied by Jack. While he enjoyed his company, there was a side to Jack that Crowley felt uneasy with and he was never sure why, but it was always there behind that stare.

'And as a newbie yourself in this, what you call 'overlap', how do you feel about our unacknowledged intervention, especially angels? Souls can be seen but angels do as much work if not more.'

'But Sean always explains that I am there as his spiritual guide,' disputed Crowley.

'That may be. But they thank Sean for the messages, not you. They never introduce you and Sean together before you walk on the stage or a TV set, they only introduce Sean.'

'But they only see Sean!' stated Crowley.

'Exactly!'

'I'm sorry, Jack. I have no idea where you are going with this. Are you saying that I should be visible to all when Sean has a gig at the Winter Gardens or on the set of Loose Women?'

'What's the worst that could happen?' Jack casually reverted his gaze to his cigar and gently twirled between his finger and thumb.

'Are you serious?' asked Crowley.

'Humour me,' Jack said in a low voice. Crowley took a deep breath and continued to watch Jack and his casual manner. He wasn't convinced Jack was as relaxed as he was trying to project.

'Are you talking about a minority of humans being able to see a majority of us or a majority of humans being able to see a minority of us?'

'Let's try all humans being able to see all of us: angels and souls,' said Jack slowly and softly.

'Apart from causing widespread panic, I think irrevocable damage would be caused to the foundations of global religious and spiritual beliefs.'

'But surely after a while we would be accepted like any new creature found on Earth?'

Crowley sniffed at the absurdity and naivety of Jack's comment. 'This is not the same as the discovery of a new tropical fish or the creation of a Labradoodle!'

'I think you underestimate the tolerance for change within the living,' sneered Jack.

'For all its strength, there is always a vein of delicacy in the human spirit. I am not sure a revelation such as that would allow the soul to recover to its former glory.'

Silence fell between them and Crowley tried his best to keep his temper under control even though he wasn't sure why he was angry in the first place. After all, this was a hypothetical argument but somehow Jack had the knack of making a perfectly healthy debate into a battle of the senses and right now Crowley's felt like they had taken a slight beating. Jack seemed to snap himself out of his self-induced trance and brightly asked if Crowley would like another drink. After noting there was still half a cigar left to smoke, he accepted and hoped that the conversation would turn to a lighter subject.

The rest of the evening indeed became more pleasant as they discussed varying subjects from concerts Crowley attended while alive to who's poster was pinned to the teenage Crowley's bedroom wall. Their filthy laughing drew smiles from various corners of the bar and Crowley was relieved that the night had ended with them in a far brighter mood than the earlier hours had suggested would follow.

Eventually, Jack bade Crowley good night and scooped up his few belongings. With a promise to see each other soon Jack walked through the doors of Benito's and found himself in a familiar room. The room was not his home.

This room was far too grand for Jack. He stood still on the same spot on the velvety Persian rug. To his right, an unlit fireplace dominated the pale-yellow wall. The whiteness of the marble surround suggested a fire had never been lit, but Jack knew the contrary. The gold over mantle mirror was too high for Jack to see his reflection. However, he could see the huge crystal chandelier that hung above his head in it. To his left, stood a marble topped, oak side table where a small but highly decorated clock stood proud. Jack suspected it was Fabergé and the fact that nothing else stood on the table raised his suspicions further. In front of him the wall was dominated with ceiling high glass doors that were softened with billowing lengths of gauzy white silk. The ends reached out to the huge oak desk that sat like a bully amongst all the beauty around it. The chair that partnered the desk was turned toward the view. Jack knew he was there.

'It's been a while, Jack,' came the English voice that Jack knew well. He cleared his throat to answer.

'I've been taking it gently. He's going to be a hard one to get on side. He's still very...' Jack stayed rooted to the spot he became on.

'Very what?!' Jack wanted to fidget but he knew that would show a sign of weakness. He had spent too long convincing this man he was up to the task.

'I guess the word is...human, sir.' The chair bounced slightly but did not turn.

'And the boy?'

'They still continue to perform the 'psychic shows' as Crowley likes to call them. But he has revealed that they are both dissatisfied with this current arrangement. I feel I may know more upon my next encounter with Crowley…'

'ENOUGH!'

Jack stopped mid-sentence, but his mouth remained open.

'You have had plenty of opportunity to gather information on Sean and it was you who said that Crowley was our best man to get Sean to co-operate. But it seems to me that the only information you have acquired is his taste in whisky, women and the fact he used to fancy Princess Margaret,' he hissed.

'You've been watching me?' whispered Jack.

'If you like,' the man smiled but Jack couldn't see. 'I prefer to use the word, appraising.' There was a long pause.

In his mind's eye Jack started to scan Benito's. It could have been anyone. It could have been everyone. 'This plan is moving too slow, Jack. And if I have to throw more manpower at it, souls, angels, I don't care, then I shall. Indeed, if I have to make some changes with leadership, I'm not adverse to that idea either. One more chance Jack, get Crowley on side and get him to talk to the boy. Otherwise, who knows what will happen in that happy place called Earth. But if it all goes belly up, rest assured it will be your fault, Jack.' The chair bounced slightly again as its occupant crossed his legs. 'Now run along Jack and play with your cars, there's a good lad.'

Jack could feel his skin prickle with rage and embarrassment as he became back on the stool in Benito's. A large whisky was placed in front of him and in the blink of an eye, it was drunk. Another soon replaced it and while Jack gently caressed the glass he slowly began to look around at the rest of the patrons in the bar. A table of four men were playing cards and didn't look like they had noticed Jack had even arrived, never mind watching him, while another man was waving to Benito as he left. If he wanted to become part of the new plan, then he had to step up now and show he was capable. In the scheme of things, the request made was not that big. He just realised that he had to be a lot cleverer than he had been.

* * *

Crowley sat down at the table for two within the bay window of his drawing room. Jennifer came with a large tray balancing 2 bowls of steaming soup. Crowley remained seated and poured two large glasses of wine from the bottle in the ice bucket to his left. They began to sip their soup in silence. Crowley was distracted as he thought of Jack and their previous meeting in Benito's and thought of his probing questions about Sean. Was he reading too much into it? Maybe. Or maybe it was simply that Crowley felt very protective of Sean. Crowley's thoughts turned to tonight's performance and Jennifer began to ask her husband about the show. She knew this was a major date in their calendar.

'Is he nervous?'

'Nervous? Wouldn't you be nervous performing to 5,000 people? I'm nervous and they can't bloody see me. Still, the first night is always the worst; he'll be fine by the third and final night.'

'His life has changed so much this last year. You start to understand why they turn to drinks and drugs,' said Jennifer.

'The only things Sean is addicted to are fake tan, designer shoes and something called 'Twitter'. Mind you, Sue keeps him grounded even though she's an absolute fruit cake. But I suppose that's a blessing.'

'A blessing?'

'People expect Sean to be batty but he looks positively sane once they meet her. She doesn't realise but she actually does wonders for his credibility.'

'She sounds trippy!'

'Oh, darling, you'd love her, for a whole five minutes and then you'd want to stuff your socks into her mouth.' They both laughed, finished their soup, polished off the wine and then Crowley announced it was time to leave. He walked over to the mirror that hung over the fire and rubbed the palm of his hands across the sides of his hair. 'If I could be seen, as Jack suggested, I think I would have to entertain a haircut. Sean once asked if I modelled my hair on a mound of potato peelings,' he sighed.

'Oh, take no notice of him. At least your skin

is...well...skin-coloured and your teeth don't look like they were made by Wedgewood.' She brushed non-existent lint from his shoulders.

'Later, darling.' He kissed her gently and disappeared.

Crowley became in a dressing room, much bigger and smarter than their last gig, to find Sean with his head resting on his folded arms over his dressing table. Sue was standing over him with her hands on her hips. She noticed Crowley sitting on a small couch in the corner of the room.

'Casper's arrived, maybe he can talk some sense in to you.' She walked over towards Crowley and sharply pointed at Sean for him to take his turn. Crowley stood and walked over to the spot Sue had just vacated.

'Tell your manager or 'Agent to the Gifted Stars' as she is now calling herself, that I am not a ghost, I am a spiritual guide.'

'Tell her yourself,' came the muffled reply.

'Tell me what?' spat Sue.

Sean raised his head. 'He said your new job title is wanky.'

'I did no such thing!! Even though it is!' Crowley's eyes were wide, and he looked at Sue trying to look innocent.

'Just sort the little bugger out! He's doing his usual, saying he can't go on and he feels a fraud, blah blah.' Sue was clearly fed up and frustrated in equal measure.

'It's the flamin' Royal Hall! I was working in an office this time two years ago.'

'Yeah, but you wasn't tuned into Radio bleeding Dead People then!' spat Sue.

'I can't do it. It's too big. What if no one talks to you?' he moaned to Crowley. Crowley looked around the room. He could see at least thirty people patiently waiting for the show to start.

'Believe me Sean, this room alone has enough material to keep us going until Christmas.'

'Really, you're not just saying that? Don't have me walking out and have me stood there like one of those dickheads on Britain's Got Talent.'

'Sean, trust me.' Crowley gave him an encouraging smile. 'Now, if you've finished Cuprinolling your face, let's get this over with.' Sue stood up, even though she couldn't hear what Crowley was saying she could tell that he had managed to get through to him. He always could.

'Thanks Crowley. You're like valium in human form or spirit form, whatever. I dunno what I would do without you,' sighed Sean.

'Not have a show for a start,' Crowley pointed out. Sean began to laugh, stepped forward and hugged his friend.

'Right then,' started Sue, 'let me go and tell them that you're ready. And where's Ambrose? I told him to fetch some bottled water ages ago. I swear that boy takes the piss.' She then marched over to the door and after disappearing they could both hear her in the corridor shouting for someone called Dicky and screaming at Ambrose to put the water on the stage.

Sean stood and checked himself in the full-length mirror. His suit was sharp, and the whiteness of his shirt was only rivalled by his teeth.

'You look marvellous,' Crowley beamed. 'So, are you ready?'

'Ready.'

They both walked into the corridor and immediately could feel the electric atmosphere that was building in the hall. As they strode toward the backstage, passing Sue and Ambrose, a large man noted Sean's arrival and nodded for him to join him. In what felt like a blink of an eye, Sean was stood in the middle of an empty stage looking out onto a black canvas which was pierced with flashing stars. He smiled, took a graceful bow while the picture taking continued and fed off the applause. Crowley stood to the side like a proud dad. Even though he was nervous, Sean never let it show once he was on stage. His personality won an audience over in seconds with his cheeky humour, and gentle jokes at some of the messages he delivered.

After the usual script of how he liked to do things and calling out to his parents who had made the journey to see him, he began to talk of Crowley. Always, with affection he would say how he could not do what he did without his guide, even if he did dress like a mannequin from Moss Bros. Crowley began the night picking a man from the side of the stage dressed in a Gladiator outfit, complete with helmet and sandals.

'I have a man named Alan. He's dressed like a Gladiator for some bizarre reason and he has a message for his brother and his wife,' Crowley told Sean, trying not to laugh.

'Okay, ladies and gentlemen. Is there anyone here who had a brother, or a husband called Alan who fancies himself as a bit of a Russell Crowe?' The dimly lit room fell silent until Sean could see a cluster of heads look in one direction toward the back. A stout man in his sixties was on his feet and as he drew breath, a microphone was shoved in his face by an enthusiastic fleece-wearing teen.

'What's your name, sir?' asked Sean.

'Richy. Alan's me bruvver and this was 'is wife, Tina.'

'Well, Richy, I've been asked to tell you that Alan says he always knew about the two of you.'

A low 'ooo' came from the audience. 'He says he doesn't mind though. He knows Tina was only ever happy with you and she simply married the wrong brother. He gives his blessing as he knows the pair of you were never at peace even after he died and you two got married. He's telling me to tell you that it's okay. He's telling me you have earned the right for his grandkids to call you Grandad.' Alan could be heard sniffing copious amounts of snot up his nostrils while the ill-prepared Tina made good use of her sleeve. 'Before I send him on his way, can you tell me why he's dressed like Spartacus?' The mic picked up an "Oh my God" from Tina while the audience gave a titter. Tina stood and leaned toward the microphone.

'He liked dressing up...you know...he died...you know.' The audience burst into laughter, including Alan and Tina.

'Jesus Christ! Every man's dream eh? To die with your sandals on. Well, I don't think he will be able to find the ticket to take it back to the fancy dress shop, so you can kiss your £5 deposit goodbye. Thank you both and God Bless.' This was Sean's way of saying: *Sit down…Next!*

As the night passed, the audience became more enthralled and amazed at Sean's messages. Sue liked to stand in the lobby as they all filed out for "instant feedback" as she called it. She would stand and listen to people talk about the show and get a buzz from all the positive comments she could hear. As she walked back into the dressing room she could see Crowley back on the couch talking to Sean as he took his make-up off. While Ambrose, Sean's assistant, busied himself hanging up clothes.

'All good, I take it?' asked Sean.

'Ten out of ten, young man. Great night. Tomorrow will be even better. Are your mum and Charlie coming back stage?'

'No. I told them to go straight to the hotel. I'll meet up with them later for a drink.'

'They must be so proud of you, Sean. The Royal Hall!' said Crowley.

'Is Crowley staying long?' Sue turned and looked at Crowley. 'Did you hear me?' she exaggeratedly mouthed.

'Why does she talk to me like I'm deaf? Does she not get this at all? I am the only one who can hear everybody and yet she still talks to me like I'm a deaf foreigner. I wish she could hear me. I'm dying to tell her that she needs to go up a dress size and that chocolate oranges are not a healthy snack.'

'Crowley says you're fat,' said Sean dismissively. Sue swung round, her mouth tighter than a knotted balloon but he was gone. Ambrose could be heard laughing behind a wall of swinging shirts.

'Cheeky, snooty bastard!' she spat. 'And what the hell are you laughing at Ambrose Tully?'

'Well, that cheeky, snooty bastard helps us pay the rent. To be fair though, you give as you good as you get,' said Ambrose.

'Do I? How the hell do I know? I can't hear what he's saying. But I know he doesn't like me. I don't need to hear him, I can see enough.' Sue was snatching things up and tidying away.

'Does it matter if he likes you?'

'Mmm, I think he's jealous. I mean we are so close now Sean. Maybe, he sees me as a threat.' Sean burst out laughing.

'Believe me, Crowley is not jealous. He's in bleeding Heaven for God's sake! Look, put all that stuff down and go back to the hotel and have a drink with Maggie and Charlie. Just tell Michael to come back for me and Ambrose after he has dropped you off.'

Sue looked slightly reluctant to go but with Crowley gone and Ambrose finishing everything off, she realised there was not much point to her staying.

'Okay, I'll see you back at the hotel. If I'm not in the

bar, then presume I've been picked up by George Clooney for a night of frolicking and...'

'Oh, okay! Enough!' Sean interrupted quickly, raising his hand for her to stop. As Sue chuckled, she turned and said goodbye and then left the room.

'I feel sick. The thought of her and George,' Sean shuddered.

'I can't bring myself to imagine her without her jacket on, never mind...well...you know,' smiled Ambrose. He sat himself down on the couch. All his work was done, and he was simply waiting for his boss to finish and for a call from Michael, Sean's driver, to say he was back to collect them.

'I've never known Sue to have a fella. Her first husband scarpered years ago. Faye never talks about him much. You'd like Faye. Not a bit like her ma.'

'Well, if she's not like her now then she is bound to change into her. Daughters and mothers always overlap somewhere in their lifetimes.' Sean shifted slightly on his stool and looked at Ambrose as if to remind himself of who he was.

'For someone who is twenty-three-years-old you seem very wise sometimes.'

'I suppose I'm an old soul, whatever that means. I think I'm just perceptive. I like watching people and observing habits. I'm amazed at how people convince themselves of their own uniqueness, when in actual fact we are all pretty much the same,' Ambrose finished.

'I don't think there is many like me out there,' smirked Sean.

'I think I'd have to agree with that. There's not many like you at all, thank God.' They both laughed. Sean liked Ambrose and was glad he had offered him the job as his assistant. He had met Ambrose a few months back. He had been working in a hotel where Sean was staying following a show. Ambrose had been very attentive, making sure that he had everything he required and seemed to know what Sean needed before he did. After a couple of days of him being at his beck and call he offered him a job as his PA. To Sean's surprise he accepted on the spot and he had been at his side ever since. He now relied on Ambrose heavily and even though he was on the payroll, Sean classed him as a friend.

'Are you still happy working for me?' Sean tried to sound casual and he could hear Ambrose sit up on the couch. Instinct told him to look at his assistant. Ambrose was sat upright and staring intently at Sean. His face was still soft, but his eyes were harder. They showed determination.

'As long as you need me Sean Allister, I will always be here. And yes, I am very happy working for you,' Ambrose smiled and Sean was relieved.

'Well, look. Seeing as this is turning into a bit of a one-to-one meeting, I just want to say that as long as you are happy, and Sue keeps getting me the gigs then there will always be a job for you. And if there is anything I can do for you, then just tell me. We're a team, remember? You, me, Sue, Michael and old Crowley. A weird team admittedly but even still. I hope that, if not already, we all start to feel like a family. So, if there is anything, then just ask.'

'I will,' said Ambrose. Sean began popping his make-up back into his vanity case. After, Ambrose helped Sean on with his coat and busied himself collecting a few things to take back to the hotel. They continued to chit chat until Ambrose's phone bleeped.

'Michael is outside.' After being assisted by Dicky to the back of the hall, they soon spotted the black Mercedes with

Michael waiting behind the wheel. Not that anyone could see but Sean blushed a little. He and Ambrose climbed in the back while Michael pulled away.

'How did it go?' asked the piercing blue eyes in the rear-view mirror.

'Didn't Sue regale you?'

'She did, but you know Sue, she's coming from the angle of customer satisfaction. It's like talking to Trip Advisor. She never says how the show was.'

Sean and Ambrose gave Michael the edited highlights which he found very entertaining, judging by his genuine laugh. Sean liked to make Michael laugh, the sound of it made him feel good. Sean also liked to watch Michael's eyes screw up in the mirror when he was laughing. He liked the way his shoulders moved, well his left one anyway as that was the only one he could see from the back, when he laughed.

When Sean offered the job to Michael, he was wearing a black shirt (two unopened buttons) and black slim fitting trousers with a black leather jacket. Sean had insisted that this was to be his uniform which Michael seemed pleased about, but not as much as Sean. With his short jet-black hair, pale skin and closely trimmed beard it was the only look on Michael that Sean ever wanted to see him in.

They continued to talk about the night and Michael and Ambrose congratulated Sean on a great achievement of making the night a success. Sean was still giddy when the car pulled up outside the brightly lit hotel and a portly commissionaire opened the car door.

'Mr Allister, welcome back.' Sean climbed from the back of the car, quickly followed by Ambrose. They soon stepped into the lobby and headed for the open lift and after riding in the lift to the 40th floor, they bid each other good night with Ambrose promising to join Sean and Sue for breakfast in Sean's suite the following morning.

Sean made his way to the end of the corridor to his rooms. This was the best hotel he had stayed in yet. It had been a treat for all of them, but he had insisted as his mum and Charlie were up to see him playing the Royal Hall. His own suite with separate bedroom, lounge, dining area and a bathroom as big as Lanson Town Hall came complete with butler services. Sean was not comfortable with having a butler. If he wanted anything he would simply ask Ambrose. However, he had asked for the service at breakfast tomorrow.

Sean sat on the end of the bed and marvelled at the view before him. To his right was Tower Bridge and the Thames snaked beyond and to his left, his gaze was drawn to St Paul's Cathedral. He wished he could take a moment and spot the landmarks, but his tiredness began to beat him into submission and before he knew it he was slipping between the Egyptian cotton sheets and was out like a light.

The dark suspense of slumber didn't feel like it had held Sean for long. He found himself walking around London in the brightness, but he could feel no heat. He wasn't sure where he was heading but his determined stride seemed to be taking him somewhere. As he walked passed the Museum of London he noticed that the city was quiet. Not just quiet in the sense of traffic and general noises of the city but quiet of people. As he spun on the spot he realised that he was the only person on the street and he suspected the whole city as well and his initial confusion began to grow into panic. He wasn't sure why he was scared but he knew he had to keep moving. Then the rumbling started. The ground began to shake but he kept running and straight ahead he could see St Paul's Cathedral. The nearer he got the louder the rumbling became and then he stopped in the street as he saw the cathedral crumbling and burying itself into a mountainous cloud of varying grey. Then more thunderous noises could be heard and as he ran to try and escape, the street became filled with synagogues, mosques, churches all collapsing into identical dusty clouds. He kept running but the scene was at every turn and the more he ran the more they fell. He could feel himself crying and wanted to shout. He didn't. Who would hear him? Who could stop this? As he coughed he could hear someone calling his name. He could hear his mum. Her voice became more urgent and he could hear pounding.

'Sean!' The knocking on the door sounded impatient. He realised he was in his hotel bed, it was clearly morning and his mum was trying to get in. As he sat up he glanced at the pillow and noticed the small damp patch from his tears. 'Sean! Are you awake?' He threw his legs out of the bed and shuffled his way to the door. His mum greeted him with a scowl. 'I've been banging on that door like bleeding Rigsby looking for rent.'

'What time is it?' Sean began to make his way back to the bedroom.

'Oh no, young man. You get yourself showered before that butler arrives.'

'What?' Sean looked at his mum with a screwed-up face.

'The butler…coming to do breakfast. I want this place tidy before he comes, and I want you washed and dressed. Charlie will be up here soon, so he can give me a hand.'

'A hand to do what?'

'Well I don't know,' she sounded exasperated, 'I just want us ready, that's all.'

'For God's sake, Mum. He's coming to throw some milk on me Weetabix. He's here to serve us.'

'SHOWER! NOW!'

As Sean disappeared in the bathroom, Maggie made the bed and picked up last night's clothes off the floor. She made them both a coffee and soon Sean was back rubbing a towel through his hair.

'Right, son. You make yourself all gorgeous and I'll wait for Charlie in the other room.' She caught Sean's look. He looked worried. A look she hadn't seen since Sean took his GCSE's. 'You okay, Sean? You sleep all right?' Sean was still thinking about his dream.

'Just still a bit tired. I'm all right. Stay in here for a bit while I get ready.' Maggie knew that voice. Her son sounded scared and she started to try and figure out why. Sure, he had a lot on his plate, especially now he had people working for him and felt responsible, but it wasn't that. He looked fearful. She wasn't sure what to ask him. Since he had discovered his gift she felt that there had been a shift in their relationship and as this side of him became more prominent, the Sean she knew disappeared into a place where she felt she couldn't reach him sometimes. She decided not to say anything and by the time he was dressed, Charlie had already arrived and was quite happily sat on the couch reading the paper. He only shifted slightly when a knock was heard at the door.

A small team silently came into the room and made their way to the dining area of the suite. Within a few minutes, the table was set, and the food was ready to be served. While the dining team whispered, Maggie could be heard in the background trying to be posh on her mobile phone as she told various people to get to Sean's suite right away.

Sean was already helping himself when his friends started to trickle through with stories about how they all slept. Sean lied and agreed with all of them that it was the best night's sleep he had ever had. Sue held court for a while as she repeated the comments that she heard from the audience as they filed out of the hall, while Ambrose agreed it was a successful show.

'I mean you can't just think of the money made from last night's show, it's the success of this that will generate more work and of course, more money,' Sue said gleefully to the PA.

'I was talking about success in regard to healing people.' Even though Ambrose had said it quietly, no one missed the forcefulness of his delivery. Sue sniffed and piled more eggs on her plate. She then looked up at Ambrose as if she was telling him off.

'He's a psychic medium, not a healer!' she pointed the eggy spoon in Sean's direction.

'He brings them peace. Is that not a form of healing? After all, grief is an invisible wound,' pushed Ambrose. Sue put her knife and fork down and looked squarely at Ambrose across the table.

'Listen here, young man. My job is to look after this lad and his family by getting him the best gigs, with plenty of bums on seats, worldwide exposure, positive reviews and most of all a few quid in his pocket. Your job is to make sure that pocket looks good on him and if it does then you can have some of the money in that pocket that I put in there!'

The table went quiet. People stopped chewing and began to look at Sue who had locked her gaze on Ambrose. Maggie caught one of the waitresses stood at the side give an uneasy glance at her colleague.

'I think you will find,' Maggie had now dropped the posh accent and Sean recognised the 'Mum' voice, 'that Sean would be able to fill his pockets, as you so eloquently put it, with or without you! Managers are ten a penny Sue, but there is only one boy like mine. Nobody is denying you do a good job, but don't you dare forget there are plenty of other people that love him too! Ambrose, you do a sterling job in looking after him and no one knows more than me what a demanding little shit he can be. But Sean and Charlie will both tell you that I will not have cross words over breakfast. It simply ruins the rest of the day. Being in this posh hotel makes no difference so please, let's remember what a joyous night last night was and finish this lovely breakfast.' Maggie locked her gaze on Sue who now looked in a thunderous mood.

Michael broke out into a huge grin and grabbed the large spoon handle protruding from the silver pot in front of him. 'Well, can anyone tell me what these green bits are in the eggs?' Michael plopped a huge pile onto his plate.

'Spinach, sir,' smiled the butler.

'Spinach! Good for muscles, I heard.' Michael began to eat enthusiastically and eventually they all slowly began to continue with their breakfast. Maggie gave Sean's knee a squeeze under the table and Sean acknowledged with a grateful smile and caught Charlie giving his wife a wink.

Throughout the meal, Sean remained quiet and occasionally noticed that Michael was watching him. He noted that it was more out of concern than anything and felt slightly grateful that Michael recognised that the whole scene had made him feel uneasy. Sean spent most of the meal pushing his food around his plate, his thoughts elsewhere as the table discussed what they were all doing that day. His parents were planning to leave for Lanson after breakfast while others were sightseeing or shopping. After wiping his mouth, Sean placed the napkin back on the table and stood up.

'I'm popping out now if you all don't mind.' Maggie looked surprised.

'Well, when will you be back?'

'I'm not sure, so I'll say my goodbyes now in case I'm not back by the time you check out.' Maggie looked at Charlie who shrugged his shoulders as he continued to chew his sausage. She stood up and gave her son a huge hug and whispered to him.

'You were wonderful last night. Charlie and I are very proud of you, but me more.' Maggie could feel a little chuckle in Sean's body as she embraced him. Charlie then stood and joined in the hug.

'Love you two,' said Sean.

'Love us three,' said Maggie and Charlie.

'Call me when you are home,' he instructed his parents as he released them from his clutches. As he began to walk out of the room, Michael stood and threw his napkin down. Sean stopped and turned.

'If you don't mind, I'd like to be on my own for a bit.'

'And I know just the place to take you.' He walked passed Sean without waiting for his protestations and collected his jacket from the adjoining room. Sean watched him and realised there was no point in insisting he wanted to stay in the hotel. He turned back to the remaining diners and told them to play nice and that he would be back later.

Sean found Michael in the corridor using his hand to hold the lift doors open and he sped up his step to enter the lift. They both stood in silence as the lift went down and continued not to speak as they walked across the underground car park to the Mercedes.

'I'll ride up front, if you don't mind Michael.' Michael opened the passenger door and Sean climbed in and waited for Michael to join him.

They were soon out of the car park and into the busy streets of London. Sean mentally noted how calm Michael was as he drove around the busy streets amongst the angry, frustrated, impatient and hesitant. He wondered if his driver had ever had road rage. He couldn't imagine Michael losing his temper. Sean looked out of the window and silently let Michael take him to wherever he was driving. He only hoped that he would not have to ask Michael to leave him alone. He always felt awkward asking anyone to leave him with his thoughts as he didn't want the other person to think he was annoyed with them. Michael soon began to slow as he entered a narrow one-way street and then eventually stopped outside a pub called the Rising Sun.

'Here we are, text me when you need collecting.' Sean looked at the tiny pub, clearly not impressed with Michael's choice of venue for some alone time.

'Bit early for the sauce isn't it? Mind you, if Crowley was here, he wouldn't argue with you.' Sean strained to get a better view through the windscreen.

'Not there, you idiot. There!' and he pointed to the other side of the road. Sean switched his gaze and looked at the old building nestled amongst some trees.

'Whenever I have troubles, I always find a good old-fashioned church clears my mind.'

CHAPTER 8

Sean couldn't decide if he was more shocked at Michael's choice or the fact that Michael had ever entered a church.

'I didn't know you were religious,' he whispered. Michael smiled and then glanced over his shoulder.

'Mate, I have a three-car pile-up of pissed off drivers waiting for me to get out of the road. Go on, get gone!' Michael pressed the button and released Sean's seat belt.

'But it's a church,' his voice was monotone, and he searched for the door handle while still looking out of his window.

'Text me.' The van behind impatiently beeped and Sean raised his hand apologetically as he shut the passenger door. No sooner was it shut, the car pulled away and Sean was left standing at the side of the road.

He began to slowly walk toward the open gate where he saw a sign. It read: *The Priory Church of St Bartholomew the Great*. He stood for a moment confused. He had not told Michael of his dream where the churches were crumbling but then most people did come to church for quiet contemplation. He stood in the street, looking down the courtyard path and concluded it was simply a coincidence, unless Michael was a mind reader. He walked toward the large wooden entrance of the church and as he entered, he immediately felt safe. A woman could be seen ahead taking money from a small group of tourists. Sean approached her and felt for his wallet.

'Hi, I…um…,' he looked around to see if he could find the answer, 'erm…where is the quietest place in the church?' he whispered.

'Go through the church and make your way to the left. You will find Lady Chapel through the iron gates.' She smiled as she took Sean's money and pointed in the general direction for him to follow.

As he walked through the large church and marvelled at the vaulted ceilings and the huge organ in front of him, he could feel the age of the building deep within him and although he had never set foot in there it felt familiar and welcoming. He soon found the chapel and was grateful to find it empty. He took a seat on the second row and stared upward to gaze at the picture above the altar. As he sat staring, a man walked in, took a seat beside him and began to look at the picture. Sean gave him a sideward glance. *Of all the seats in the chapel, why did he have to sit right next to him*, he thought.

'It is the Madonna with her child, painted by a Spaniard named Alfredo Roldán,' the Irish voice said quietly. The man leant forward and rested his large arms over the back of the chair in front of him. Sean could see from his back that the man had probably once sported a head full of ginger hair but now only a few gentle copper hairs that nestled amongst the grey and white hinted at what was before. The breadth of the man's back suggested the front was probably just as big if not bigger yet Sean could tell the man was dressed smart as he spied the black blazer and matching trousers.

'Doesn't it look like it could have been here for hundreds of years? But if the truth be told, I have underpants that are older than that,' he chuckled. Sean continued to look at the painting and agreed with the stranger that it did look old. The man sat back, and Sean noted the black blazer would have struggled to button over the large belly. He felt a little odd to be sat in such close proximity to the stranger when every other seat was empty within the chapel and decided to leave.

'I come here to think sometimes,' started the man. 'I find that looking at this painting clears my mind,' he sighed. 'I don't have many troubles in my life. No wife. No children. No huge family decisions to partake in or give my opinion on. The only thing that belongs to me is the rest of the day. And yet, I still feel the need sometimes to come and look at her,' he nodded toward the Madonna, 'and reinforce my sense of purpose. Does that make sense?' The man shifted in his chair and turned to Sean. Straight away he saw the flash of the white dog collar sitting in the shadow of the man's double chin. 'Ah yes, priests more than most need time of contemplation. Father O'Carroll,' he extended his hand, 'and you are?'

'Sean. Sean Allister.'

'Great to meet you, Sean,' he shook Sean's hand with an inappropriate amount of enthusiasm. 'Now tell me, what do you think of the painting?' Sean gazed upon the face again.

'I don't know much about art. I once worked at a gallery in New York, but it wasn't this kind of art. It was all photos, old stuff. But this, I dunno. Is it wrong to say I think she's pretty?'

'Jeez, and why wouldn't she be pretty? She's the mother

of us all and everyone knows that their mum is the prettiest lass in the whole wide world, don't you agree?' he laughed.

'I do,' Sean chuckled. He thought again about leaving and then quickly dismissed the idea. He realised he was quite conformable in the priest's company. He wondered if it was because he was a priest or simply because he was friendly. *It's probably because he's Irish*, Sean thought. His soft spot had remained for Irish men since he saw Liam Neeson in Love Actually.

'Do you normally come here for peace?' asked the priest.

'I've never been in here before. My drive…my friend thought it would be a good place for me to spend some time alone.'

'Well, if you don't mind the odd tourist poking their head round, then it's as good a place as any.' Father O'Carroll looked at Sean and Sean knew he was being studied.

'So, what's troubling you then?' The priest asked the question in a manner that told Sean the priest expected an answer. There was no question as to whether he wanted to talk about it or not. So, within the next few minutes Sean found himself telling the perfect stranger of his dream and how he had woken crying and that he hadn't done that since he was a child.

'Well, as you can see, as you sit here in the oldest church in London that all is well. Tell me, why has this dream resonated with you?'

'I don't know. I just woke up feeling so helpless and I couldn't shake the feeling off and even sitting in here hasn't made it go away.'

'Some dreams make a bigger impression on us than others. The dreams about someone we love dying have a profound effect on our emotions for hours, sometimes even days afterwards. Why not look on it as a fortunate dream? The dream brought you here to this beautiful building to gaze at the face of the mother of our Lord. It also brought you a new friend in me for if we see each other again you wouldn't walk past me, would you?' Sean shook his head and smiled.

'Course you wouldn't! I would hope you would have the good grace to buy me a pint of Guinness at the very least.'

'Do you work here?' asked Sean.

'Ah no, I've never had the pleasure with old St. Bart's. My parish isn't too far from here though. No, I like to come here and look at her,' he nodded at the painting. Sean turned to look as well.

'What? You just come and stare at the picture? Why?'

'She helps me sometimes. Helps me make decisions.' Sean raised his eyebrows and sat for a moment. Did the priest hear his answers here? Did he just feel them in his heart?

'What kind of decisions?'

'Oh, all kinds. Should I tell someone that a husband is acting the maggot and has confessed he's beating on his wife? Should I have fish fingers or sausages for my supper? Should I confess to stealing money?' The priest heard the small gasp from Sean.

'Ah, it's when I play Monopoly, but stealing is stealing all the same,' he chuckled and watched Sean's relief flood his face.

'I have people work for me,' Sean picked at his fingernails. 'They tend to do a lot of the decision making for me.'

'Well, aren't you the lucky one? I thought people were employed to do your grouting or mow the lawn. How did you advertise that job? Person wanted to take away my free will and render me a total eejit to the point where I can't decide how many sheets to use when I wipe me arse,' he snorted.

'I'm not that bad, but I see what you are saying. When you think about it I was dropped off here with no idea where I was or what I was supposed to do because someone else decided that I should come here.'

'And here we are making friends. But just make sure whatever's being decided for you is just the small stuff. The big stuff...well, that's down to you and the harder the decision the more alone you feel. No one said life was easy including those who cheat a bit, like you.' Father O'Carroll took one last glance at the painting and then stood up. 'It was great to meet you, Sean.' Sean stood and shook the priest's hand and watched the large frame leave the chapel. 'And don't forget now, next time I see you make sure you get that Guinness in for me.' He didn't turn but still gave a wave as he stepped through the iron gates.

Sean stood for a moment and again, felt very alone. He looked over again at the painting and decided to leave and even though he had not done it when he arrived, he felt the need to perform the sign of the cross upon himself. He walked out, saying thanks to the lady on the desk again and stepped out on to the street. The day was cold but not cold enough to make him want to go back to the hotel. He decided he would take advantage of this time and began to walk toward a main road that he could see in the distance. It didn't matter that he didn't really know where he was or the fact that he didn't know where he was heading. All he knew was he could do whatever he wanted, and it was up to him to decide which direction looked best.

* * *

Crowley was sat on a bench that was perched on top of a cliff. The cliffs reminded him of the ones at Dover, except at these ones he was alone and happy with a fine bottle of red wine and a copy of A Christmas Carol by Charles Dickens. He was nearing the part when Bob Cratchit requests Christmas Day off when he was aware that someone was walking behind him. He turned, expecting to see Jennifer but instead Jack, dressed in his familiar black turtleneck and pants, strode towards him. Jack gave a smile, but it wasn't lost on Crowley that it seemed a bit forced.

'Crowley, you're a hard man to find. Nazriel pointed me in the right direction and said you like to come here to read. The man clearly knows you well.' Jack sat beside Crowley on the park bench and admired the view. 'Well, this is a splendid spot you have picked for yourself,' He leant forward and spotted the wine and without waiting for an answer produced a glass in his hand and reached for the bottle. 'Don't mind if I join you do you, old chap?' Crowley still had not spoken but continued to watch the spectacle in wonderment as to why Jack was here. 'A very good vintage,' Jack inspected the label. 'But then again, I would expect little else from you. A man with such good taste.' He spun on the bench to look at what Crowley was still clutching in his hand. 'Dickens! Now I had you down more as a Fleming sort of man. Spies and secrets and women,' Jack nodded and chuckled at his own joke even though he nor his audience found it funny.

'What are you doing here, Jack?' Crowley slowly shut his book and placed it gently on his lap.

'Well, I wondered if you would like to come to a card evening later. After your little show, of course. Some of my friends and I meet up and play a few hands. They're souls like you so we play with money, so it keeps the thrill for them,' Jack looked at Crowley expectantly.

'You asked around as to my whereabouts and called on Nazriel to simply find me and ask me if I want to play cards?' Crowley raised an eyebrow and Jack felt his story was falling apart.

'Okay, I admit, I went to your home and Benito's to find you. The simple truth is…well…you see…. well, one of the men we play with, Ed, is nothing short of a shark and I figured if any man was going to beat him then it would be you. I told my buddies about you and we were all in agreement to ask you into the group. It's not even about winning for us anymore it's just about him losing. Just bloody once! I know it's childish but the satisfaction of seeing that smug look being wiped off his face…well…it's enough to make me dance. So, can I tell the boys that you are the man for the job?'

'Well, it's been a whi…'

'Oh, it'll come back to you! Like riding a bike.' Jack stood up without giving Crowley another opportunity to refuse. 'We'll see you after the show at my house.' Then he was gone.

Crowley sat for a moment a little dumbfounded. It wasn't the fact that Jack had just turned up out of the blue. Or even the great lengths he went to find him. It was just the way he had insisted he come. He thought of the reason Jack had offered as to why it was so important he be there, and Crowley understood that. He too had been part of games where some players seemed to have all the luck, and yes, it could be frustrating. In the end, Crowley convinced himself it was nothing more than a frustrated friend needing help and if he was the man to do it then how could he refuse, he may even enjoy it, he told himself.

It was the second night at the Hall for Sean tonight. Crowley hoped that his friend would feel a little calmer tonight before he went on. He suspected that Sue didn't help matters and unwittingly wound Sean up. Crowley decided that it may be a good idea to join Sean a bit earlier and hoped that it would make some difference.

* * *

Jack became and found he was sitting on the couch within the yellow room. He could hear his master's voice from the adjoining room. The voice was low, but the tone was unmistakable. Whoever he was speaking to was not allowed to disappoint him, that much he could gather. The footsteps approached, and Jack stayed rooted to the spot.

'Ah, Jack.' His master appeared before him and paused slightly to eye Jack from head to foot. Jack caught the stare from the deep brown, nearly black eyes that sat beneath a headful of grey hair that ended at the white collar of the familiar tunic. His master's tunic and white trousers always looked like they were brand new and had never even been sat in. The pale brown, soft leather shoes carried the large frame of their owner to his usual place behind his desk.

'What brings you here, Jack?'

'It's just to report that Crowley will be joining me and some of the boys later.'

'Do you mean 'my boys'?'

'Er...yes,' Jack tried to disguise his stutter with a failed smile. 'Ed, Joe and Sam will be there.'

'Yes, I know,' he sneered. Jack was taken aback by this response. Not that Jack ever felt comfortable in this room but at the moment he was praying that he would be dismissed sooner rather than later. 'Don't let me down, Jack. I've not come this far for it to fall apart because of you. Remember what is at stake here.' He was almost whispering. Jack lowered his gaze. He could bear the penetrating stare no longer. 'The next time you see me it'll be to tell me that it's done. Do you understand?'

'Yes, sir.'

'Then get out.' The man leaned back in his chair and swung around, leaving Jack in no uncertainty that he had now been dismissed.

* * *

Crowley became at the front of the Mercedes and was seated next to Michael who was driving. Sean and Ambrose were sitting quietly in the back until Sean jumped at the sight of their new passenger.

'Fuckin' 'ell!!' shouted Sean. Ambrose and Michael simultaneously began to look panicked and started looking around the car and outside to see what had startled their boss.

'What?!' shouted Michael.

'Crowley! Just turned up and is sitting next to you. What the bleeding hell are you doing here? You are supposed to meet us at the Hall when I've rubbed your magic lamp.' Michael shifted his gaze to the passenger seat and then to his rear-view mirror to make sure Sean was okay.

'I wanted to chat to you before the show,' said Crowley in a calm tone. Sean looked at him suspiciously.

'What about?' Then fear crept into his mind. 'Oh, you've upset the big fella ain't ya? What is it this time? Is he sending you to Hell? Is this what the chat is about to tell me that my career is over? Well, you can tell him from me that the factor 50 will have to stay on your shelf until this bloody tour is finished.' Crowley sat, silently amused. 'And you can take that bloody stupid smile off your face. It's not funny! What did you do? Insult him about what wine he should be drinking or what music he should be listening to? Well, you've got no room to talk! I saw you the other day swinging your creaky hips to Showaddywaddy in the interval.' Sean was interrupted by Michael and Ambrose's sniggering and he closed his mouth and stared out of the window like a petulant teenager.

'My God, you ramble with the ferocity of a prison letter,' Crowley said eventually. He turned in his seat, so he could look at Sean directly. 'I simply wanted to talk to you, before the nerves got the better of you and Sue starts winding you up as if you are about to set foot in a boxing ring.' Sean continued to look out of the window and refused to acknowledge Crowley at all. Crowley shifted back around to watch the world rush toward him through the windscreen. 'You are your own worst enemy, Mr Allister,' muttered Crowley.

The rest of the journey continued in silence until they reached the back of the Royal Hall. Michael, as usual, opened the door for Sean while Ambrose climbed out. Ambrose immediately went to find Sue as Sean walked to the dressing room where Crowley was already waiting for him. Sean sat down at the dressing table stool. He felt deflated and for some reason was ready for a telling-off. He hung his head and waited for Crowley to speak.

'Sean, son, what is it?' Sean didn't expect this question, or the kind, concerned tone in which it was asked. He looked up slightly and it was clear to both of them that Sean didn't know what to say. 'You've not been yourself lately. And I know some of it is down to the pressures of...well...holding gigs like these. Plus, the pressures of looking after everybody and making sure everyone is happy.' Sean hung his head again. 'But I just want you to know that you can talk to me. I'm not just here to tell you what everyone is saying, I was hoping that you could just talk to me every now and again.'

Sean felt a lump growing in his throat as he realised that he was not alone in these strange times. Crowley was not only his friend, he was his best friend and he needed him more than ever right now. Who else did he have to talk to? He didn't like to worry his mum and Charlie so that only left Crowley, who on reflection, gained nothing from this set up at all.

'I'm sorry, Crowley. And you are right, I should talk to you more.' Sean started to empty the contents of his vanity case on to the dressing table. 'When I worked at Bill's there was a little lad who worked in the accounts department with us. His job was to put all the invoices on the computer. My job was to pay them. I couldn't have done my job without him doing his and yet he seemed so insignificant when I worked there. And I've just realised I am being exactly the same with you.' He turned to face Crowley, sitting on the couch, took a deep breath and told him about his dream and his trip to St Bart's church and meeting Father O'Carroll. He then talked of how he felt overwhelmed by all the attention he received and how he felt responsible for everyone's happiness, including strangers.

'I'm sorry I haven't told you how much I appreciate you. I should be talking to you more, after all you are probably the only one who knows what I am going through because…well… you're there aren't you?' Sean chuckled.

'Indeed I am. I will be here whenever you want me. Now promise me you will talk to me in future?' Crowley pushed.

'I will.'

'Answer me one question, though. Why do you think this dream upset you so much? People have bad dreams all the time.'

'It was how I felt when I woke up that upset me more,' confessed Sean.

'And how did you feel?'

Sean let out a big sigh. 'Helpless.'

CHAPTER 9

Crowley became in a dark room that smelled of whisky, cigar smoke and corned beef. Four men were sat at a table that was covered in a green cloth, and the whisky and ashtray were lit from the one bulb above the table itself. Crowley was surprised as to how shabby it all felt.

'Crowley!' Jack jumped to his feet and looked genuinely happy to see him.

'So glad you made it. Boys, this is Crowley,' he said enthusiastically. 'Crowley, this is Joe.' Crowley stepped forward and shook the hand of a small framed man with a large 1950's quiff. He was dressed in a black suit with a white shirt buttoned to his Adam's apple.

'So, you're Crowley, huh? Great to meet you.' The little man seemed a little excited to meet him.

'New York Italian, I do believe,' said Crowley extending his hand to shake. Joe looked impressed.

'Wow! What were you? Like some kind of professor of languages or something?'

'No,' chuckled Crowley, 'just a fan of Goodfellas.'

'This is Sam. His real name is James, but we call him Sam,' said Jack.

'Oh, really? Why?'

'Because I prefer Sam to James,' he sounded bored.

'And this is Ed.' Jack presented a man that was reluctant to be presented. He was around fifty and looked a little flabby. Crowley looked over his non-descript blue shirt which looked clean enough, *'cleaner than his hair'* Crowley thought. Ed did not rise from his seat and barely gave Crowley a look as he continued to shuffle the cards in a relaxed, almost menacing fashion.

'Pleased to meet you.' Crowley made no attempt to shake his hand. Instead, he moved towards the table and took the empty seat while everyone else sat down. Crowley noticed that Jack looked a little off. Nervous was not the word. He supposed that if he had to describe his behaviour he would call it 'observant'.

'Whisky, old chap?' asked Jack as he began to pour before Crowley could answer him. Crowley had already partaken in a few before he arrived here. Joe, sat to Crowley's left, passed the glass over to him. Joe began to probe Crowley about how he died and who was here waiting for him and what he thought of Heaven. As Crowley began to tell them of his surprise as to how Heaven worked but how happy he was, he noted that the other men listened in silence. But the silence was unnerving, and Crowley wasn't sure if they simply didn't agree with his thoughts regarding Heaven or if they were simply not interested. Either way, Crowley found his small audience slightly menacing.

'So, you work for Rucelle then?' asked Joe.

'I do. He doesn't like me very much. I think we are the Bette Davis and Joan Crawford of the Protectors' Division.' Crowley joked but no one laughed. Crowley knocked back his whisky which was promptly topped up by Joe. Joe made no attempt to look at anyone else's glass.

'Rucelle is a ball-breaker,' started Joe, 'the guy thinks he's running the joint but he's in for a few surprises.' With this comment, Crowley could feel a sense of change around the table. It was as if they all gave out an invisible cloud of reaction and to Crowley it felt like trouble. Jack, still looking at Crowley, told Joe to start the evening.

'Okay, boys, let's get this thing started,' began Joe. 'First off, I wanna say welcome to the new guy and you lot for coming, even though I know some of you don't like the room.' He waved his hand around to unnecessarily illustrate what he meant. 'But it's what I like and it was my turn to choose. I don't moan when it's your turn and you pick all these fancy joints with the girls with the tits walking around. Which I find very distracting, I wanna say. And that other one you picked,' he pointed to Sam, 'some fucking gold-plated joint that looked like it should have been in China somewhere. So, I don't wanna hear about how dark it is or about the smell. I like it, okay.'

'No one is moaning, Joe,' hissed Ed.

'It smells like corned beef. I like corned beef,' said Crowley encouragingly.

'Corned beef? Corned beef? Are you outta your fucking mind? My mom is cooking for us out the back,' Joe snapped.

'I'm so sorry!' he apologised, 'I'm not the best judge. But please believe me when I say it smells delicious.'

'Of course, it does!' said Joe.

'He gets very tetchy about his mom,' moaned Sam.

'I do not get tetchy!' snapped Joe.

'Yes, you do.' Sam turned to Crowley. 'This man once went bat shit crazy at me for deviating from the regular lasagne recipe.' Crowley raised an amused eyebrow and glanced at Joe who was nodding emphatically. He was about to interject but as Sam raised his hand, Joe lowered his gaze and began fidgeting in his chair. 'Everyone has their own take on lasagne, some put wine in it.' Crowley could see that Sam was enjoying the telling of this story if only to watch his friend squirm. He continued in his laid-back fashion. 'Some mess around with how much tomato to put in…' Joe was starting to bounce slightly on the chair. 'Some even go wacky on whether to put three layers in, or even four,' Sam drawled, waving his hands 'jazz style'. At this, Joe could take no more.

'He put fucking cottage cheese in it! Who in their right fucking mind puts cottage cheese in lasagne! WHO?!'

'Me,' said Sam flatly. Joe's head now seemed to be on a swivel trying to find someone as angry as him. He failed.

'I don't think I've ever had a proper lasagne,' said Crowley. Joe stared at him straight in the face. Crowley could not tell if he had inadvertently insulted him until a smile began to creep across Joe's face and then he shouted.

'Ma! Make lasagne instead!' He waited for a response. 'MA!'

'I heard you shout Joe, but I must have gone deaf when it came to your manners,' a voice shouted from another room. Joe shifted a little in the chair.

'Please.' Another pause. The 'mother' pause that all children know.

'Okay, Joe,' she shouted. He began to smile again, and Crowley suspected it was more from relief and not being reprimanded again from his mother.

'Wait 'til you taste her lasagne. It's gonna be better than the day you died.'

'Can we deal these cards?' Ed snarled, passing the cards to Jack. 'Or maybe you want to ask your mom for some breadsticks.'

Jack split the deck in two and started to riffle the cards repeatedly. 'The game is No Limit Texas Hold 'Em. You all know the rules and as usual the winner takes all.' Jack continued to shuffle. Crowley was surprised as to how quick they were launching into the game. Any card games he had been to before were normally preceded with a few Martinis. But judging by this crowd they were not the Martini type. Sam looked like he was a beer man and Joe looked like he enjoyed a bourbon. Crowley chuckled to himself as he assumed Ed probably drank urine straight from a lion.

'Crowley, I forgot to mention we each put a grand in.' Crowley nodded silently and pulled his newly appeared £1000 out of his pocket.

'Dollars!' snapped Ed. With his hand still on his money Crowley looked at Ed.

'And yet the pound is worth more.' Everyone stayed silent around the table until Jack piped up.

'Well Ed, for this game let's play in sterling, seeing as Crowley is our guest. It's not like we can spend it anyway.' Ed slowly moved his gaze to Jack. The atmosphere became a little uncomfortable and before Crowley could intervene, Ed slid his dollars across the table and without emptying his hand pushed back a neater pile of pounds. Joe and Sam followed suit and eventually Jack changed his with a small victorious smile across his face.

'Now,' started Jack, 'more for Crowley's benefit, this is a game of not only skill but of trust. There is no point in us playing if we manipulate our cards in any way. The game and the winner must be true.' While all the men nodded in agreement, Crowley could feel Ed staring at him. He reminded him of a bully he had once encountered at boarding school, Mark Fellowes. He was the only bully who made sure he was caught which was why he was called

Masochistic Mark and the only person who enjoyed corporal punishment.

The night began to stretch out and Crowley wasn't sure exactly how long they had been playing. A few empty bottles were now littered around the room and the ashtrays began to show evidence of a long night. He surveyed the piles of notes that sat neatly in front of each man, except for Ed who preferred to gather his notes into an unorganised pile.

'So, Crowley,' started Sam, 'what do you think of your gig of being a spiritual guide?' Crowley talked of Sean and how he was a friend of Grace, a woman he had helped to allow him to cross over. He told them how much he liked Sean and how he felt he had another family back on Earth. A small laugh left Ed's mouth and Crowley looked at him. He was going to challenge him but then decided he wasn't worth it. The man was clearly unhappy and probably felt like that before he had met him, Crowley decided. But how anyone could be miserable when they were in Heaven was a whole new experience for him.

Joe was on his last gasps with only around £50 left. It wasn't unusual for Joe to be the first one under pressure. He was ever the optimist, expecting every inside straight or flush draw he would chase to come in. They rarely did. The dealer button had been rotating around the table all night and now rested in front of Sam. Sam had many times wished he could riffle the pack as expertly as Jack or Ed, neither of whom would look out of place dealing in a Las Vegas casino, but he knew from many failed attempts that it usually ended in disaster with cards spraying around the room like confetti or the pack bending slightly upwards on one side. Tonight, was not the night for him to practise the skill again. Ed was left of Sam and so duly posted the small blind of five pounds and instantly mocked Crowley for always being slow to post his blinds. Crowley didn't flinch or say a word as he lifted a ten-pound note and placed it over the line in front of him. Jack on the other hand was grinding his teeth whilst Crowley did this; he knew Crowley wasn't being slow, and this was typical Ed, who was now full of liquor. Jack could tell that Ed was not only fuzzy from copious amounts of whisky but also far too engrossed in his own game. Jack felt he was losing Ed and the whole point of the night. This was probably his last chance with not only Crowley, but his master as well.

'All in,' declared Joe confidently, who was sitting next to Crowley and was first to act in this hand. Joe took a large swig of whisky, put his hands behind his head and rocked back on the chair.

'Call,' said Jack as he placed his money over the line.

'Call,' repeated Sam.

'Go on then,' said Ed as he topped up his original £10 blind with two more twenty-pound notes. Crowley cupped his hands over the top of the cards and ever so slightly lifted the corner revealing the bottom card, which was the king of spades. He then dropped the corner and slid the card from the top to the bottom and repeated the process of lifting the corner to reveal his second card, the six of clubs. Crowley dropped the corner of the cards, so they rested flush with the surface of the table again and switched his attention from the cards to his neatly stacked notes. He knew his hand was a poor one, but he also knew that Joe, who was all in, could equally have a poor hand, and with nobody else raising and £200 of their money in the pot to play for, he felt it was time for a bluff.

'Four-hundred pubs,' he said softly.

Joe dropped the front legs of his chair back to the floor and placed his elbows on the table and rested his head on his hands as a signal of his re-engagement into the game.

He had no more moves to make but sensed things were about to get interesting. Jack and Sam duly folded, Ed however wasn't so obliging. He stared at Crowley and Crowley kept his gaze.

'I think this limey is full of shit,' Ed snarled, 'I'll see ya.' Crowley didn't move a muscle as Sam burnt the top card and dealt the flop calling out each card as it was revealed. 'Seven of Hearts. Ace of Diamonds. Seven of Clubs.'

Without hesitation, Crowley declared £500 which was easily more than half of what he had left. Ed slumped in his chair and Crowley knew his bluff had been successful.

'You were right the first time, Ed, I am full of shit,' Crowley said as he flipped his cards over and reached for the side pot containing £350.

'King six! King fucking six.' Ed banged the table in rage while Joe chuckled to himself knowing he was now out.

The night continued and while Crowley was enjoying playing cards he wasn't sure this was his type of company. He had never met them before and felt it would have been easier if he had maybe got to know their personalities a little better first. Ed was still rattled by the previous events and continued to play aggressively until it reached a point where Jack and Sam were almost out and Crowley was leading the way with £2,390. The dealer button was in front of Jack and after looking at his cards, Crowley silently dropped a neat £100 bundle over the line. Jack saw this as a sign of strength; Crowley was indeed a good poker player.

'All in,' smiled Jack, looking in Crowley's direction.

'I might as well,' said Sam, sliding his money into the middle. Ed shouted 'raise' as he dropped £500 over the line. Crowley wasn't expecting this move, but no one was more surprised than Jack. Sam and Joe gave him a sideward glance and could tell he was seething inside. The whole plan was crashing around them with a wrecking ball called

Ed's Ego. Crowley was trying to decide if this was a genuinely good hand from Ed or was this his act of revenge for earlier; either way Crowley decided he had to see the flop and called as he pushed the required amount into the middle.

'King of Hearts. Queen of Spades. Queen of Hearts.'

Ed couldn't believe it! Thoughts of how to get all of Crowley's money started to swirl around his head drowning out the whole objective of the night. He was trying to control his excitement as he double-checked that the pair of Queens he had seen moments earlier were in fact laying in front of him. He deliberated, then bet £500. Crowley kept his hand placed over his Ace and his King.

'All in,' Crowley said confidently, convinced his Kings and Queens with an Ace kicker were ahead. The thought of Ed having two Queens never crossed his mind. Jack, Sam and Joe looked on nervously. The grin that had appeared across Ed's face did not instil them with any confidence that he was sticking to the plan as Ed pushed his pile of cash over the line. He quickly flipped his cards to reveal the pair of Queens, making an impressive four of a kind.

'Fuck,' whispered Jack, shaking his head as the Queens hit the table.

'I only have two pair,' said Crowley turning his cards over to reveal his Ace of Hearts and the King of Diamonds.

'A pair of fours,' said Sam turning his cards.

'Eight, nine of Clubs,' followed Jack. Ed was already reaching into the middle of the table when Jack slammed his hand down in protest.

'It's not over yet, there's two more cards to come,' Jack snapped. Ed sat back, his grin growing ever wider; he knew there were two more cards to come but the chances of

Crowley to win the hand were as slim as Big Foot advertising Pretty Polly tights.

'King, King will give Crowley a better four of a kind,' said Sam.

'Or Jack, Ten of Hearts,' slurred Joe from the corner. They all mentally agreed, Jack, Ten of Hearts would give Crowley an unbeatable Royal Flush. The room fell silent; the tension, much like the smoke, could be cut with a knife as Jack picked up the deck and slowly burnt the top card.

'Ten of Hearts,' he said with a glimmer of hope in his voice.

'Told ya,' shot Joe. The room remained deadly silent. Jack hadn't put the cards down and continued dealing to the river in one motion, but it felt like an eternity. Jack knew how there was much more than five-grand on the line, much more than Ed's stupid ego, the whole of the plan was on the line. This was his last chance to win Crowley's trust. He closed his eyes as he fingered the last card and slowly opened his eyes to see what he had turned.

'Jack of Hearts,' Jack sighed. Ed sat stunned for a moment. His mind whirring if Jack had 'intervened' while Joe slapped Crowley on the back for a great game.

'Glad to see someone whip this man's ass,' smirked Sam. Crowley awkwardly smiled as he collected his money. He noted the clenched jaw from Ed. The man was clearly not used to losing.

'Well, I think we will call that an end to the proceedings, don't you?' Jack asked rhetorically. 'Will you be staying for more lasagne, Crowley?'

'Er…no,' Crowley stood awkwardly. 'If you don't mind I'll be getting back to the lovely lady wife.'

'Stay and have one more with us, don't you think boys?' asked Jack. Crowley was hoping they would say they didn't mind him leaving but Joe was soon to his feet and pressing on his shoulders to get Crowley to sit back down. As he did, he watched the reaction from people, mainly Ed.

The table was soon cleared and with fresh drinks and clean ashtrays they turned their attention back to Crowley. They talked at length about Heaven and how it differed from what they all imagined.

'Put it this way, I didn't think I'd have to work!' moaned Joe.

'It's hardly work is it. It's not like we are down mines, swinging canaries. Or dodging bullets fighting for our country, is it?' protested Crowley.

'We're still being told what to do,' growled Ed.

'But in the scheme of things,' Crowley argued, 'it's not hard or life threatening. Plus, I find comfort in knowing that we make a difference back on Earth. The whole idea of us and them feeling so separate that we were not sure that a Heaven even existed.'

'And how do you feel interacting with the living?' asked Jack. Crowley was not sure where this line of questioning was going. He had not mixed with that many people in Heaven, but he thought he was sure in surmising that all in Heaven were happy.

'I'm not sure what it is you are asking me,' replied Crowley trying to play it cautious.

'Well,' started Jack, 'we once had a conversation in Benito's about how the two worlds overlap, shall we say?' Crowley could recall the conversation and he wasn't sure it was one he wanted to return to. He started to think of Jennifer and Sean and realised he wanted to leave and be with one of them. 'And as I recall you were quite perspicuous in your views.'

'I was, indeed.'

'Do you think Sean feels the same?'

'I don't understand the question.'

'I mean, do you think Sean would like to reveal you in any way?'

'Like I explained Jack, Sean does tell people of my existence.'

'Ah yes, but some may feel excluded that they have never been able to see someone who has passed while some simply think he is a crackpot. Whichever way you look at it he must be on the receiving end of an awful lot of negativity. Would he not be relieved to be able to show people that you do actually exist?'

'What would be the point of being a guide when I would be able to talk to anyone then?'

'There'd be no need at all,' growled Ed.

'Like I said to Jack, us walking around on Earth for all to see would have catastrophic consequences.' Crowley's voice was transparent with concern.

'Don't you think you are being melodramatic? Also, do you think you are best qualified to speak on behalf of the human race?' asked Jack. Crowley stood, he was ready to leave. He had had a similar conversation with Jack about this before and he was sure he had made his feelings clear on the matter then. He did not want to repeat the conversation with an audience and especially with a belly full of whisky.

'I think my view would be echoed by most people. If that makes me a sheep running with the masses, then so be it. It's my belief and one that I am sure is right. For us to be wandering around on Earth and influencing matters in front of people takes away any shred of faith they had.'

'But surely it offers them faith. Knowing that there is a Heaven, knowing that there is more to life than they experience while they are alive. The comfort in knowing that they will see their loved ones one day. Knowing that we can intervene with matters on Earth to keep them safe, happy and like in Sean's case rich.' Crowley's skin began to prickle, and he could tell from Jack's face that this comment had been made on purpose to touch a nerve.

'Sean did not ask for this gift,' whispered Crowley, 'it was thrust upon him.'

'And yet, he uses it to make money. Why should that privilege only be given to a few,' asked Ed.

'Because by only giving to a few keeps the element of doubt! And with doubt comes faith and hope.'

'Not everyone on Earth believes in Heaven, Crowley,' spat Jack.

'Oh, I'm sorry. You confuse my thoughts with the limitations of your own!'

'What did you say?' hissed Jack.

'You pin all your ideals on the matter of us and them. People believe in a multitude of things when it comes to them dying. Including being collected by little green men to simply being put in a box and that being the end of it. You destroy everyone's beliefs no matter what they are! Now, if you will excuse me gentlemen, I will take my leave. I'm sorry the night has not gone how any of us planned and I apologise for my part in that.'

'Just before you go Crowley, am I correct in assuming that it's Sean's last night tomorrow at the Royal Hall?' Jack's steely eyes were fixed on Crowley. He immediately felt threatened and paternal toward Sean. He did not have a good feeling about this at all.

'You stay away from him, Jack. I mean it.' Crowley stood fast, his jaw locked, and a vein began to protrude on his temple.

'Goodbye, Crowley and well done on an excellent game,' smiled Jack. Crowley gave the room a deliberate once over and all eyes were on him. Then within a moment he was gone. A big sigh was let out around the table.

'He's a tough nut to crack,' said Sam. Jack's head was whirring with the events that had just taken place; Crowley was clearly steadfast with his beliefs. His mind wandered to his master and how he would tell him, and Jack could feel dread creep across his body. He needed a Plan B.

'We clearly are going to have to take him out of the equation. The end goal is still the same.'

'Do you mean, go straight to the kid?' asked Joe.

'We have no choice. We could be waiting forever to get Crowley on side and the master's patience has ran out. He has waited over thirty years for this and no matter what happens, this is the time. I'll see the master later and tell him that we are still forging ahead with the show, only some of the original cast will not be performing as planned. And Ed?' Jack raised an expectant eyebrow and smiled, 'freshen up a little, tomorrow you are going to be on television.'

CHAPTER 10

Crowley persistently knocked on the door until it opened. He was full of whisky and panic and felt this was the best place to come. The door opened and Nazriel stood before him in his usual calm and collected composure.

'I need to speak to you,' Crowley gasped pushing back Nazriel. Crowley began to pace around the very tight space, so it looked more like a warm up to an Irish jig on the spot. Nazriel closed the door, turned and stood watching his unexpected guest.

'Would you like a drink?'

'No, no,' said Crowley wringing his hands.

'Would you like to sit,' he asked calmly.

'No, yes, maybe I should, yes.' He plonked himself down on the sofa, but the handwringing continued. Nazriel slowly took his usual place beside his friend and waited for him to start. Crowley took a deep breath and began with the conversation that he and Jack had had in Benito's some time ago and then continued further with the revelations of the evening. Nazriel sat in silence and occasionally nodded to illustrate to Crowley he was still listening and understood.

'What am I to do, Nazriel?' Nazriel stood and walked over to his desk while Crowley sat on the couch with his legs shaking on the balls of his feet. He slowly cursed himself for making friends with Jack, especially knowing that something was always a bit off with him.

'Were the other men good card players?' asked his friend. Crowley stared at Nazriel. He began to feel that he had sought advice from the wrong person. Nazriel clearly had no idea or understanding what was being suggested. Nazriel sat down behind his desk and looked at Crowley squarely in the face. 'Well?'

'I think that's a stupid question!' Crowley got to his feet and started for the door.

'Answer the question,' Nazriel insisted.

'I think they were all very competent players. Have you not listened to a word I have just said? This is not about a card game.'

'Then I have been listening.'

Crowley stayed on the spot.

'I suspect,' said Nazriel, 'that the whole night was staged. You are the closest influence to the boy and for you to echo their sentiments and prepare him is only to their advantage.'

'But why him?'

'Why not him? He has half the world watching him at the moment and has a positive following. For him to channel and show the world what there is beyond, will only be seen as a good thing in their eyes.' The panic began to rise in Crowley again. How were they planning to do this? What would happen to Sean? What would happen to him? Would Heaven still exist as it was?

'Maybe, you should speak to Rucelle,' offered Nazriel.

Crowley began to laugh under his breath.

'Rucelle? And if I'm wrong, what will happen to Sean? His whole career will come crashing around him and his reputation will never recover. Rucelle will reassign me just like that!' He clicked his fingers with an air of permanency.

'And if you're right?' Crowley stood and placed the untouched tea back on the tray and turned.

'And if I'm right, then God help us all,' he whispered. Crowley walked over to the door and simply nodded at Nazriel before he disappeared.

* * *

'Sean!'

The banging on the door continued. Sean sat quietly at his dressing table mirror, willing Sue to go away for a bit longer. She knew he was in there so there was no point in pretending otherwise. He simply wanted to be left alone and had done all day. But his phone hadn't stopped with well-wishers for his final night at the Royal Hall. Sue had also been bombarding him with further offers being made for him to do a tour across the USA which she felt could be combined with a European tour as well. The whole thing sounded gruelling and added to his feeling of being overwhelmed.

'Give me five minutes, woman! I'm in the knack, for God's sake,' he lied.

His make-up was done, and he slowly tidied up his brushes into little pouches while he thought of the last year or so. In fact, he went right back to the accident when it had all changed. At times, he was grateful and at other times he was not. He could not really pinpoint as to why he was still unsatisfied. All he knew was that there were still days of darkness within him. He had begun to think that he was a sad soul that would never be happy with his lot. When he worked in the office for Bill at Moore Haulage he dreamed of being rich and famous just like everyone else. And now that he was, he was only too aware that he was still the same person and he still felt unsatisfied. The only difference now was he didn't know why or have an excuse. He had been given a gift that brought a lot of comfort to people and that in itself was the only part of his life that he truly loved. To see the recognition on people's faces when they knew what his cryptic messages meant. The relief of some faces when he brought closure for them and the sheer joy when people were just simply contacted and told that they were loved. But once out of the spotlight, the darkness was not only visual, it was a physical thing he could feel. He, at times, wondered if he was suffering from depression. He knew there was something deep inside him and at times he found it unsettling, but he didn't know what it was. Maybe, this was a lingering affect from the plane crash that he never had sought help for. But then at times he could feel happy, especially with his family and friends. He would be laughing with everyone but would feel like there was someone there, who wasn't laughing, who was ruining the moment. No one was there of course, it just felt like darkness standing in the corner of the room, judging him and reminding him that things were not all well.

His thoughts were disturbed by the clink of a glass and as he spun in the chair he could see Crowley, sat on his sofa with a bottle of wine in one hand and pouring it into a glass with the other.

'Crowley! You made me jump!' Crowley did not move or even look up. He continued to pour his glass to the very top, move to his lips and drank the glass in three or four greedy gulps. Sean watched him silently as he poured himself another glass, this one not as full and place the bottle on the floor.

'What's up mate?' Sean was never bothered by Crowley drinking. But he had not seen him drink like this before. As Crowley looked at him, Sean could feel the darkness envelop him more. Was it Crowley that made him feel like this? After all, he had only known Crowley since the accident. Did he give off some 'other world' vibe that he could feel negatively?

Crowley stared at Sean. He could see concern in his face and immediately felt guilty. He wasn't sure what to do or even say to the boy so in true Crowley fashion he turned to drink instead. The effects of the whisky were still within him and the wine was now adding that extra punch.

'Sean, Sean, Sean,' he said heavily, 'my dear, Sean,' he smiled. Sean began to panic about the imminent show. Would Crowley be fit enough for it?

'Hey, maybe you should knock off the plonk 'eh? At least, until after the show. I don't want to be telling ninety-year-olds that they should expect baby twins in the next nine months, do I?' He waited for Crowley to laugh but he didn't. He just continued to stare at him. Sean slowly stood and walked over to his friend, took the glass from his hand and walked back to the dressing table to put it down.

'You been arguing with the Mrs?'

'If only.'

'What is it then? Don't tell me you can't do tonight.' The question brought Crowley back to life as he realised that apart from the thousands in the Hall tonight and the fact that it was being televised, it was simply that Sean was relying on him, solely on him.

'I'm fine, dear boy. And yes, sorry I lied, Jennifer and I did have little spat earlier. You know what women are like and believe me they don't get any better up there,' he threw Sean a fake smile that Sean didn't buy. 'Tonight, is going to be huge for both of us.' He walked over to Sean and rubbed his shoulders with another fake smile. 'We shall play tonight like we have always done. Truthfully, honestly and with compassion. Have I ever let you down?'

'Yeah, that night when we opened in that little theatre called the Fern Gardens and you started off the show by arriving on stage shouting that you had been in bigger women!' Crowley burst out laughing, remembering the night. 'Put me right off, you did!' Sean started to smile as well until they were interrupted by the familiar knocking on the door from Sue.

'I know he's in there with you, so let me in,' she bellowed through the door. Crowley shrugged his shoulders as if to say the game was up while Sean walked over to let her in. When he opened the door, he was surprised to see Ambrose and Michael waiting with her as well. She marched straight in and clocked Crowley finishing off the glass of wine that Sean had put on the dressing table moments before.

'It's Bedlam out there and you two are in here having a bloody cheese and wine party. Was it you telling him not to open the bloody door to me?' She waved her finger in his face with her own not too far behind her finger.

'Tell this woman that instead of banging on doors like a new prison inmate she should spend her time investing in a decent bra and finding an alternative snack to the mountain of crab sticks she must be consuming each day to give her breath like Billingsgate.' He waved his hand in front of his face and turned away from her.

'Don't you wave your hand in front of me, like I've got bad breath or something,' she snorted. She flashed her gaze around the room making a mental list. 'Right,

Ambrose, check that Sean's suit is spotless and then get this place tidied up. Michael, I have no idea why you are here seeing as you are the bloody driver but as you are here can you go and fetch some bottled water from the stage manager or his assistant or someone. Sean, let me see your make-up.' Sean gave a quick flash of his face. She always wanted to check his face even though her make-up bag consisted of a lipstick that had lost its top about ten years ago and a mascara that was so dry she had to spit on the bristles before she applied. Only she was convinced that the glisten on her eyelashes was courtesy of Max Factor.

A tall man with greying hair popped his head around the door and spied Sean. Al was from the television company that was recording tonight's show which was scheduled to be shown next week with the DVD on sale before Christmas.

'Hey, Al.' Sean shook the extended hand.

'Okay Sean, we're all set up. Now remember, just as we went through this afternoon. Don't look at any of the cameras. If you see any of the cameramen running around, try not to look at them either. It'll just be someone shouting at them to move somewhere to get a better shot when we start interacting with the audience. Pretend we are not there and it'll come over completely natural which makes for better viewing.'

'In other words, I do my thing and you do yours,' concluded Sean.

'Exactly.' Al looked around the room nervously and started to back out. 'Okay, well I'll leave you to it, so you can...erm...you know...conjure Crowley up or whatever it is you do.' Al quickly skipped out of the room closely followed by Crowley who stopped at the door and shouted after him.

'Conjure him up! Do you think he's going to pull me

out of a bloody hat? I'll get him to pull me out of your bloody arse if you carry on talking to him like he's a bloody magician. He's a psychic medium, you cretin!' Crowley roared.

'Is he shouting at Al?' Sue turned to Sean, 'Tell him he can't be shouting at him!' Sue bellowed. Crowley turned at the door, looked at Sue and then at Sean.

'What part of this doesn't she get? HE CAN'T HEAR ME, YOU PENDULOUS BOSOMED WITCH!'

'What's he saying to me, Sean?'

'He said you all have to get out, all of you. He said don't shout me until it's time to go on.' Sue sneered at Crowley as she walked out of the room ushering the others to follow. Once they were alone, Crowley picked up Sean's jacket and helped him slip into it. He then silently nodded at Sean's shoes and without hesitation Sean picked up a cloth and gave the toes a quick and vigorous rub. He then patted his hair, which didn't move of course as it was full of lacquer and checked his teeth for foreign bodies. Crowley was near the door, taking a last large swig straight from the bottle of wine he had brought earlier. Sean watched his reflection in the mirror.

'Are you sure you're okay, Crowley? We can make them wait you know,' Sean offered as he turned and faced his friend. Crowley snorted, walked over to Sean and placed his hands on the young man's shoulders.

'And have a riot on our hands with scampi-breath Sue leading the way with a flaming torch? I'm fine, just had a little too much to drink.'

The knock came from the door to say that they were ready and with one last look Sean gave Crowley a huge hug. Suddenly Sean became aware of the audience noise which amplified a hundred-fold as soon as he opened the door. A man with a headset and iPad was waiting to walk with him down the corridor toward the stage. Crowley, as usual marched silently by his side as he listened to the crowd becoming more excited as Sean's introduction had started.

'Ladies and gentlemen, Mr Sean Allister!' Sean and Crowley stood in the dark ready to walk on.

'Abracafuckingdabra,' whispered Sean to Crowley as he walked on to the stage complete with a huge smile.

The evening started with Sean breaking everyone into the show gently. He made the odd joke about the cameras being there from a previous show and he had insisted they stayed there simply to make him look good. But as much as he joked he noticed that Crowley was prowling the stage like a predatory cat.

'What's up?' Sean whispered.

The look of panic on Crowley's face was not lost on the medium and Sean felt like he had dipped his toe into some icy water and wished he hadn't done so. He turned back to the audience and began to make some small talk and slowly build up to the moment when Crowley would normally begin to say who was there for Sean to pick. But Crowley's face told him something was wrong. Why wasn't he speaking? Did he have stage fright? Not now surely, not tonight. Should Sean have insisted he delayed the show to allow him to sober up a little? Sean, still talking, began to stare at Crowley with a look that was clearly saying 'pull yourself together'.

'No one is here!' Crowley mouthed back.

CHAPTER 11

Rucelle was shouting at a room full of panicked people as he stood behind his desk. Nazriel and Bathisma were also behind him as they too looked on the rabble of angels and spiritual guides working themselves up into a frenzy in the large white room.

'ENOUGH!'

The whole room became quiet as they stared at Rucelle, waiting for him to speak. They watched as he gathered his thoughts and took a deep breath. 'There is no point you all remaining here. Once we feel it is safe to open the portals, we will let you all know. But until then we have no choice but to lock all our channels down.'

'Does Death know about this?' came a voice buried within the sea of faces. 'I'm supposed to be intervening with a family who are about to get into an unsafe lift. His essence won't be able to keep up if the Protectors are not there to take some of the pressure off.' There were murmurs of agreement around the room from people with similar predicaments.

'Even Death cannot get through,' said Rucelle

reluctantly. Nazriel lowered his head realising the consequences of closing all the portals. He felt he had no choice but to tell Rucelle Crowley's story. There was no hesitation from Rucelle or even doubt. He had simply called for action straight away which had sent Heaven into a panic. This was an unprecedented situation, and all felt the place that they would get answers was here, in Rucelle's office.

'I take it that all angels and souls who are already on Earth are also stuck there?' said a small woman at the front.

'I'm afraid so.' The crowd began to talk again amongst themselves with no sign of moving. Rucelle felt helpless as he looked at the growing crowd and wondered if he had done the right thing. More questions were being thrown at him and he wasn't sure if he could answer them without actually answering them. But these people were not stupid, and he knew that he would have to come clean sooner rather than later.

A man in a red suit with a face to match came running into the room at the back and began to squeeze through the claustrophobic mass. Rucelle, Bathisma and Nazriel all spotted him at the same time and stepped forward slightly and even though the throng had moved to let him through they continued to speculate to their nearest as to what was going on.

'They've all gone, sir.' The man explained breathlessly. Rucelle slowly turned to Bathisma and Nazriel who were patiently waiting on the message.

'We're too late!' he whispered.

CHAPTER 12

Sean took a few steps toward his small table and picked up his water bottle again. 'What do you mean, there's no one here?' Sean whispered back. Crowley shrugged his shoulders and looked beyond Sean at the huge crowd who were still unaware of what was, or was not, unfolding.

Sean continued to drink his water, swallowing the liquid and the dread that fought to rise up against it. He could feel the sweat prickling through his suit and the stage lights felt like they were burning him on the spot. He could feel the room swimming beneath his feet and as he glanced sideways he could see the small red light of the TV camera firmly fixed on him like the eye of a Dalek. He wanted to run but his feet wouldn't let him. He willed himself to turn and consider the darkness that was filled with the hope from thousands. As he turned he could see Sue, Ambrose and Michael standing in the wings looking concerned. He then looked to the other side at Crowley who had moved to stand beside him.

'You have to wing it dear boy,' he croaked. Sean stepped forward and took a deep breath. How on Earth could he wing this? But then who was to know, if he came out with general things that could apply to anyone then at least he could give them a show, albeit an abysmal one. But he knew that's how a lot of other charlatans did it. If he knew anything by now it was how to entertain at the very least.

'So, shall we start then?' and he threw his arms out wide and his smile mimicked the same. The applause was loud, and Sean tried to leech from it some confidence while his thoughts ran through some past readings that he could tweak but as his mind formulated a plan he noticed that the clapping became erratic while some people began to gasp. At the front of the audience he could see some faces of people who were looking high above the stage and noticed the cameraman lowering his equipment as he did the same. He became aware of Crowley walking in front of him and staring upwards as he walked to the left of the stage. As Sean's gaze looked high to his left he could see what everyone else was looking at.

The small lights swirled gently high above the stage and were lowering very slowly. To call them lights, was not accurate, it seemed a swarm of fireflies had found themselves in the theatre and with each blink of an eye they multiplied. Sean was sure that even without the 'oooing' and 'aaahing' from the audience that the growing glow was not making a sound. The only sound that Sean could properly make sense of was Crowley's footsteps as he walked towards the descending scattered form. Sean stood transfixed, now unaware that he was supposed to be hosting a show and as he made a move to walk toward Crowley he stopped when Crowley raised his hand for him to halt. As the glowing particles floated nearer to the stage they began to converge into larger forms. At least a dozen were now taking the shape of a human form and like tuning an old black and white TV, they all came into view. The whole theatre was deathly quiet as three women and nine men looked out onto a stunned audience. Sean was still stood, rooted with disbelief and muted with fear.

The first to become stepped forward and ignored Crowley and slowly surveyed the room. Dressed as usual in his black trousers and turtleneck sweater he began to smile and raised his head toward the back of the theatre to ensure all would hear.

'Ladies and gentlemen. My friends and I are happy to finally speak to you all,' he spoke deliberately slowly. 'We have waited a long time for this day to come. So long.' He looked over at Crowley, smiled and turned back to the audience. 'Forgive our dramatic entrance. I do believe more of our friends will be appearing in establishments less grand than this.' He smiled again, and his eyes scanned over the darkness beyond. 'So aren't we the lucky ones.'

'Don't do this! Please!' begged Crowley. Jack turned around and gave him a disdainful look.

'My friend here, Sean's spiritual guide, is not happy at all. He's at a disadvantage you see as you still cannot see him,' he mocked.

'Who the bloody hell are you?' asked Sean. The men and women still standing still on the stage turned their gaze to Sean.

'My dear boy, we are the angels of fate,' replied Jack. 'We have been sent from Heaven.'

'No one sent you! You put this rabble together yourself,' Crowley hissed.

'And Ed has changed his shirt especially for this occasion,' teased Jack.

Sean's attention turned to the front row of the audience as he heard someone ask who the hell the new guy was talking to, to his very scared wife next to him. She stood, grabbed her handbag and made a bolt for the exit. Within moments, hundreds of people were on their feet including cameramen trying to make their way to an exit door. Jack's smile fell from his face and soon his arms were raised and moving in the direction of all the theatre doors.

'WE CAN'T GET OUT!' a woman screamed. The Hall erupted and became choked with panic as people pushed and struggled into the aisles to find a way out. Jack watched for a moment and clearly found the whole scene amusing while Sue, Ambrose and Michael ran onto the stage toward Sean.

They first felt it in their feet. A rumbling that could have been mistaken for the running crowd. But even the angels, except for Jack, began to look around as the shaking became louder to the point they could feel it in their bodies. The theatre began to feel like it was in the middle of thunderstorm and soon thousands of people were starting to crouch on the floor, expecting the roof to cave in from what sounded like an earthquake. Then suddenly it stopped and for a moment there was silence.

'Don't make me do that again,' Jack threatened. 'Now all, please return to your seats. The doors will open once the show is over, isn't that right Sean?' Jack said turning his attention to the original host. However, his smile fell as soon as he saw who was stood in front of Sean.

'Michael,' he whispered under his breath. Crowley caught the recognition. In that moment of studying Jack and then Michael, he realised.

'Get Sean off this stage, NOW!' bellowed Crowley to Michael. Michael stood rooted to the spot. 'I know you can hear me, damn you!' Michael grabbed Sean by the arm and Ambrose took the other side while they ran to the exit through the curtain and started running toward the dressing room. As Crowley watched them disappear, he turned his attention back to Jack who was distracted watching everyone silently sit back down. He had to stop him, all he knew was that he had to shut him up, somehow. But as he stepped from the shadows of the side stage, Joe and Sam appeared before him. They each in turn grabbed him and pulled him back into the shadows. Crowley tried to disappear and return to Heaven to get away, but he couldn't. For the first time since his death, he felt human.

'I need to get back on that stage,' he pleaded.

'Ain't gonna happen,' smirked Joe. Crowley threw Sam an imploring look who just shook his head in agreement with his friend and continued to pin Crowley against the wall.

'How could you do this?' The men remained silent.

'How many more came down? HOW MANY?' he screamed and managed to wriggle free enough to try and throw a punch at Sam. The two men pounced on him and as Crowley landed on the floor, Joe was soon on top of him.

'Too many for you to do anything about,' Joe spat. Sam stepped forward and picked up Joe and Crowley while pushing Crowley back down a corridor that was clearly a dead end.

'Don't make this ugly,' said Sam, still in the bored tone that he had when he was playing cards. Crowley brushed himself down while trying to get his breath back. He could hear Jack talking on stage but had no idea what was being said. His mind quickly went to Sean.

'Look, it's quite clear that we can't get out so can I at least go to Sean?' Joe and Sam looked at each other unsure how to answer him.

'Look, you are supposed to be getting humankind on side with this so why not start with one that could have a great deal of influence for you?' As the men thought,

Crowley tried his best to look as unthreatening as he possibly could and after the men gave him a once-over, they both agreed that it would be fine. Crowley turned and walked slowly towards the last door at the end of the corridor. As he opened the door, there they were, all sat in stunned stillness. Sean was the first to rise to his feet.

'Angels of fate?' he croaked. All eyes were on Crowley but instead of answering Sean he turned his attention to Michael.

'How long have you been able to see me? Hear me? And how on Earth does he,' Crowley pointed in the direction of the stage within the building, 'know you?' Ambrose looked at Michael and closed his eyes. Crowley saw the look. 'And you can see me too, I take it?'

CHAPTER 13

As Bathisma ushered the last few out of the office, Rucelle sat down and Nazriel felt the weight of the world was being supported by that one small chair. Lence, the man in the red suit, had since left giving a full report to Rucelle.

'How many got through?' asked Nazriel. Rucelle let out a long sigh.

'We average a presence of around five million on any given day. Sharply raised during wars and the obvious slight surge at Christmas. But Resourcing and Diversion Divisions have estimated that we currently have around 11 million unaccounted for in Heaven.'

'So, that means there are six million more angels and souls now on Earth than usual,' said Bathisma.

'And all that without a calculator,' sniped Rucelle.

'I should have said something sooner,' raised Nazriel.

'YES!'

The room became silent as all the men collected their thoughts. Rucelle quietly contemplated the rest of the report in which angels were scattered all over the world including Jack and his merry gang. While Rucelle knew that Jack may take centre stage on Earth he knew too well that Jack was not directing the show.

'Well, we can't keep the portals locked down for much longer. The Transitional Division should have had 100,000 new souls to process by now.' Rucelle sat further back in his chair and allowed a plan to formulate in his mind. 'Bathisma, fetch Anthony for me from Chartering and get Magda in here. Nazriel, I need you to be on hand to help me…let's say refurbish a room.' Both men nodded and Bathisma was soon gone. Nazriel stepped forward to Rucelle.

'I am so very sorry for my part in this.' Rucelle sighed and looked at his friend.

'We should have been more prepared.' Nazriel walked around to the front of his desk and waited for further instruction. 'Do you remember the Carcerem?' asked Rucelle. Nazriel nodded slowly inwardly shuddering at the thought of it. 'I never thought this day would come, but I need your help in creating a new Carcerem.' Again, Nazriel nodded. As abhorrent as the idea was, Nazriel trusted Rucelle. 'If Bathisma is back with the others before I'm back, tell them to wait. I have to see Mr Reeshon about our plan for a new Carcerem.' Without waiting for Nazriel to answer, Rucelle then disappeared.

It wasn't long before Bathisma returned with a man and woman who looked worried. Nazriel walked toward the man who relaxed a little once he set eyes on the Native American. He was dressed in a long-sleeved white top and white trousers, the same as the red-haired woman at his side.

'Anthony, Magda.' Nazriel smiled and embraced them both. 'Rucelle will be here in a moment. He is with Mr Reeshon.' Anthony and Magda looked at each other and raised an eyebrow.

'That bad eh?' said Anthony as he brushed his fingers through his long, thick greying hair. They all sat, except for Bathisma, who took his usual place behind Rucelle's desk while he waited for him. The others sat in whispers about the events that had taken place and the parts they presumed they would be taking in rectifying it.

Soon Rucelle appeared in the room, looking slightly flustered. He tried to mask it with a smile for his new company and instructed Bathisma to make some refreshments. With Nazriel, Anthony and Magda on one side of the desk, Rucelle sat down on the other to address his small army.

'I have called you both here as I am sure you aware of...' he coughed a little nervously, '...of the events that have taken place today.'

'We heard there has been a complete shutdown of portals. My division is completely in the dark as to what to do,' raised Magda.

'So, I take it you have not heard as to the reason why?' asked Rucelle. Anthony and Magda looked at each other and shook their heads. 'It seems we have a fair number of angels and souls who have descended to Earth to, how can I put this, make themselves known.' Anthony looked at Rucelle, slightly confused. They had had angels in the past who wanted to show themselves, make themselves known up to a point. But that was usually when the angel wanted to stay on Earth. It was also very rare.

'How many are we talking about, Rucelle?' asked Magda.

'Approximately, six million, two thirds of them being angels. Not including the five million who were simply doing their job.' Anthony stood slowly and leaned forward towards Rucelle with his hands flat on the table.

'Are you telling me, that we have millions of angels on

Earth showing themselves to people?'

'Not just to people, Anthony, to the world!' Anthony's bearded mouth opened but no sound came out. He slowly backed away and sat himself back down in his chair. 'It seems they want the recognition for all the work they do. They are not satisfied with it being interpreted as anything else but them. So, they are now on Earth spreading the word and no doubt illustrating the great power that we hold.' Anthony sat in silence while Magda began asking more and more questions about numbers and where they all were. Nazriel quietly listened to Rucelle answering Magda's questions but all the while could feel the anger rising in Anthony. He gently placed his hand on his but as soon as Nazriel touched him, Anthony shot to his feet again.

'How did we not see this coming?' Rucelle glanced at Nazriel. 'I mean, this has taken some organising. This didn't get decided one day and then it happened the next. Six million? This is a full-on rebellion!'

'We think this plan has been thirty years in the making,' Rucelle slipped.

'Thirty years? Are you serious? You had thirty years to prepare and we are only just hearing about this now!' Rucelle was starting to become flustered and unsure what to say next. Nazriel stood and walked over to the right of Rucelle's desk. He waved his arm and in an instant a landscape appeared. It was as if someone had opened the curtains and threw open a window. The view was of the yellow grasslands of Earth. The grasslands where people would dance and sing for the spirit of Nazriel. They all stopped talking and looked at the swaying tips of the grass, the blueness of the sky and inhaled the aroma of Mother Nature.

'When I was called, I would see that my people were at

the mercy of the land. They prayed for the rain for the rivers and crops. They prayed for their people to be as fertile as the land and yes, they prayed for peace. But nature can be cruel sometimes if you don't respect it and she knows when you have become complacent. She knows if man is too greedy for its resources she will turn on him no matter how much they prepare.' He turned to make sure his audience were still listening to him and once satisfied he was still holding their attention he turned back to the grasslands. 'Heaven is much like Earth. There is an order to nature and to interfere with her plan is much the same here as it was down there. The disease of man wiped out most of the Native American tribes. The diseases that the white man brought could not be cured with their medicines. For all their preparation, they were not prepared for man. Just as now, how were we to prepare for a threat that we only knew lurked in the shadows. Man is not prepared for us, we must act quickly before the world cocoons itself into a chrysalis.' He looked over his shoulder at Rucelle, 'Some men will not embrace being a caterpillar for long when they are told they can be a butterfly with wings.' Nazriel waved his arm and the view became white again.

Magda and Anthony sat for a moment. It was clear that these angels knew something, and had done for some time, but it was also clear they didn't know what it was or what was to come. The pressing issue was not what they should have done, but what they needed to do now.

'Nazriel is right. There will be some that do not fear death anymore now that they know, or think they know, what the alternative is,' said Magda.

'We need to move quickly,' said Rucelle. 'Anthony, as you are the best in Chartering I need you to pinpoint exactly where all these souls and angels are.' Rucelle passed a list to Anthony with a shortlist of names including Jack, Sam, Joe, Ed and Crowley. 'Once we know where they are, I need you Magda, to transition them back into a Carcerem.'

'Do we have one?' she gasped.

'Nazriel and I will create one while you try and find them, Anthony. I have spoken to Mr Reeshon and he has agreed that this must be the first part of our plan.'

'The first part?' asked Nazriel.

'I fear the road that winds before us will be long and unchartered in some respects. Well, certainly for us anyway,' Rucelle admitted.

'What if I can't find them?' asked Anthony. 'It's not that easy.'

'Well, if the Head of Chartering and the bloody patron saint of all things lost cannot find them then we are all doomed!'

Rucelle instructed Bathisma to spread the message that events were under control and to tell the Heads of all Divisions that Mr Reeshon was aware and approving plans as they spoke. He disappeared without delay and left Rucelle and the others in the office. Their attentions were turned to who had organised this. Magda and Anthony were in agreement that while Jack was always impressionable and a loose cannon he did not have the intelligence to orchestrate anything on this scale. They continued to speculate as to what type of person could do this and the lack of conclusion still left them frustrated.

'As soon as we have them all back I am sure we will have a clearer picture. Let's not forget we have Crowley down there too, in the thick of it,' Nazriel said.

Magda recalled her first meeting with Crowley soon after his death and remembered him as an ordinary man with ordinary habits. He liked to drink, flirt and at times he was immature. His transition to Heaven had been average and the path to becoming a spiritual guide was not extraordinary.

'This Crowley,' she began, 'as I recall he has a great capacity for whisky.'

'As I recall, he has a greater capacity to love!' snapped Nazriel. Rucelle watched the scene before him. This was the first time he had ever seen Nazriel lose his temper. While Magda had always been known for her dismissive attitude to some, it was well placed in the Transitional Division. A calculated brain was needed to keep the souls coming through, and worthy ones at that. While she didn't judge their ascension, she judged their soul. It's purity, it's journey and above all else, it's capacity. Her judgment placed you in a division in Heaven and only Rucelle had the power to override that decision. It didn't happen very often but in Crowley's case he had.

'Is that why you appointed him to be a Guide?' she drawled.

'Circumstances on his first assignment left us no choice but to transfer him. He was always appointed to Sean Allister, so the move meant…' he paused looking for the right words, '…less paperwork, shall we say?'

'And this Sean Allister? What's so special about him?' she probed.

Rucelle gave a small giggle. 'Special? You make it sound as if he was less worthy than anyone else we could have appointed this, in your words, "whisky swiller" to.'

'I did not say that, and I did not mean that Sean was unworthy!' Rucelle held Magda's gaze and hoped she would drop this line of questioning. It was completely distracting from the task in hand. 'I simply wondered why Crowley was appointed to someone he already knew. Was Sean not the best friend of Grace Hammond, the person he picked for his transitional task?'

'Really? I had no idea,' Rucelle replied dismissively. 'I'm not the one who put him in the Protectors' Division.'

Magda took the accusation personally. 'But I'm not the one who assigned Sean Allister to him.'

'Then that is something we need to look into. But right now, what we should be doing is sorting out how on earth do we get these angels back into Heaven and creating the Carcerem?' Rucelle shouted. Anthony shot up from the chair. He was feeling frustrated.

'One thing I know for sure is I need to find some peace and I'm not going to get it in here,' snapped Anthony. 'I'll be in my study, and I should like to be left undisturbed until I can figure out what to do. Do you think I could get that?' he asked rhetorically. 'Good!' He went to disappear until Magda announced that she would go with him. She didn't say goodbye, she simply looked at Rucelle, then turned to follow Anthony into the corridor beyond.

'There's more to this than he's saying,' she said, marching with Anthony at her side.

Rucelle breathed a sigh of relief as the door closed behind them. He mulled over the conversation and cursed himself for letting her get to him. He had known Magda for years but until this point he realised that he didn't really understand her. He didn't know what she liked to do when she wasn't working and then concluded that she probably worked all the time.

Anthony was relatively new, only being in Heaven for eight hundred years or so. He had brought order to the Chartering Division in finding all manner of things lost. It was rare that this was an object of some sorts as the people on Earth believed. His main aim was to find all the lost souls and bring them to the attention of the Protectors'

Division. But never before now had he been asked to find a particular soul.

Rucelle's attention was drawn back to Nazriel who sat quietly drinking some tea. His friend had been just that, a friend. A calming influence on all who came in contact with him and he was glad that he had taken Crowley under his wing when he asked him to. As he looked at him he noted that Nazriel had not looked up in some time. His face had an unusual look and Rucelle realised it was the look of worry.

'What is it, my friend? Do you think they know we know more?' asked Rucelle. Nazriel continued to drink his tea in silence while he collected his thoughts. He then looked up at Bathisma who walked over and took the empty cup away. No words were spoken but all the while Rucelle watched as Nazriel placed his hands on his lap.

'The Carcerem? It has been a long time since we had such a negative entity with our realms. I fear that it may bring unbalance.'

'The Carcerem,' Rucelle began gently, 'is not a negative entity. It is there for our protection which is surely a positive thing. The Carcerem is to contain the negative entities which by my reckoning have been here for some time already. The 'unbalance' as you say is already manifesting itself as we speak. Our actions are not to make the matter worse. The decision has not been taken lightly, but we simply do not have a choice. My only concern is do I have enough to give in its creation? My spat with Magda earlier makes me question otherwise.' Nazriel finally looked up and smiled at his friend. Rucelle held great power in Heaven and yet still doubted his own ability. He doubted his reactions and decisions that he had made and even though he had never made the wrong decision he still could not recognise his own ability. He chuckled lightly to himself.

'What?' asked Rucelle smiling.

'I just hope I can keep up with you.' They both began to give a little chuckle and the melody of it filled them with energy. They could both feel it rising within each other. If they were going to do this, then they had to do it now.

'Yes?' asked Rucelle, rising to his feet. Nazriel followed suit and smiled at his friend.

'Yes!'

They both slowly walked to the far side of the office and looked at the plain blank white wall in front of them which had earlier shown the grasslands on Earth. The two men walked side by side both in unison with their stride until they reached the wall. With Nazriel on the left and Rucelle on the right, Nazriel placed his left palm flat on the wall as Rucelle placed his right. Without looking at each other their remaining hands sought each other and as the angels touched a white brightness enveloped the room devouring them from view.

CHAPTER 14

'Could someone please tell me what's going on?' whispered Sean. He slowly looked around the room at all his friends. He felt that he'd walked in on a night out with mates when all the juicy gossip had already been spoken and he was finding it hard to catch up because everyone now was bored or pissed. Something huge had just happened and he felt that not only was he the last to know about it but also, he was at the centre of it all and he didn't know why. He watched as Michael and Ambrose sat down on the settee with an air of resignation, all the while Crowley refusing to take his eyes off them. The room was quiet and all that could be heard was a distant voice of Jack on the stage and Sue's heavy breathing. The room felt very small to Sean all of a sudden and a rush to escape came over him, but he knew that it was worse for him outside of the corridor. If he had any chance of getting any sense out of what just happened it would be in here. He slowly turned again and looked at Michael and Ambrose.

'Please?' he pleaded.

'We need you to sit down, Sean,' said Ambrose. Sean fumbled behind him looking for his dressing table chair all the while still staring at the two men sat on the couch. Crowley stepped forward and slid the chair under him, Sean didn't seem to notice. Crowley then walked to the corner of the room and found a similar stool and placed in front of the door and sat himself down. Including Sue, they had made a small circle.

'My real name is Ambriel,' started Ambrose.

'Am…Am…Ambriel?' stuttered Sean.

'Yes, Ambriel. I was sent here to help protect you.' Ambriel spoke very slowly and softly, never taking his eyes off Sean.

'Protect me? Sent here? What do you mean sent here? I found you in a hotel. I offered you a job.' Ambriel smiled.

'We were meant to meet, Sean,' Crowley shifted slightly on the stool.

'Do you work for the Protectors' Division?' he asked.

'I do.'

'Protectors' Division. Who the hell are they?' said Sean.

'The Protectors,' Ambriel started, 'are a force that help humankind. Crowley also works for the Division. We are here to do good things. Amongst a multitude of other things, we intervene to keep people on the path of their destiny. Crowley is here as your Guide, you are one of the lucky ones that can see us and hear us and there is a reason for that. My purpose is for you and has always been to tell you the truth and to be here when your calling came to be.' Sean continued to look at Ambriel, completely stunned. He slowly turned his gaze to Crowley.

'Can you please tell me what the fuck he is on about?' Crowley looked at Sean and then turned his gaze back to the two men.

'So, what's your name then?' Sean whispered to Michael.

'Michael.'

'But you're not a driver, are you?'

'No.' Sean stood up and instantly started to hyperventilate. He frantically rubbed his head to make the whirring stop. He looked at all the people in the room and felt he didn't recognise or trust anybody. His body was sweating with panic and he felt he couldn't breathe. He marched over to Crowley who was sat in front of the door.

'Get the fuck out of my way!' Crowley slowly stood up and gently took Sean's face in his hands and tightened his grip either side.

'You do not want to go out there, believe me. You need to hear this! I need to hear this! And no matter what is said or done I will not leave you. Do you understand me Sean?' Crowley could feel Sean's first tears seeping into the palms of his hands as they ran down his friend's cheeks. 'Do you understand?' he said more softly. Crowley could feel the gentle nod of Sean's head and slowly released his grip. He then pulled a handkerchief from his pocket and passed to Sean who took gratefully. Crowley sat back down, and Sean turned back and returned to his stool where he sat again in front of Ambriel and Michael.

'So, who are you then?' Sean sniffed looking at Michael.

'I too have been sent here to protect you and fight for you if necessary.'

Crowley felt a prickle all over his body as realisation set in. Some of it was starting to make sense. With wide-eyed wonder, he asked, 'So, you are THE Michael…Head of War Division?' asked Crowley.

'Yes, and if that man continues with his revelations and the millions of other angels that we feel have followed him, then there will be war.'

Angel's Rebellion

Crowley gasped. 'Millions? I thought this was just Jack and his "Stand By Me" gang.'

'Ambriel and I both felt it. There was a huge surge of angelic force on Earth just before Jack became on stage.'

'Felt it?' squeaked Sue.

'Yes.' He looked around at the confused faces and felt he wanted to explain. 'If you imagine you are in a huge empty hall, like this one say, and you had your back to all the chairs. If the room filled up suddenly you would feel it without having to turn around. You would just know there were people there and from the energy you would be able to tell if it was two or two hundred.' Sue nodded. 'That's how it felt to Ambriel and I.'

'So, all of these millions of angels that have come down, have they come for me?'

'No. Only Ambriel and I are here for you. And Crowley of course.'

'And you're all angels?' asked Sue.

'No. Only Ambriel and I are angels. Crowley is a soul, he is a Guide.'

Sue laughed at Crowley as she thought of his diminished role, but he completely ignored her. He was still trying to digest that THE Michael had been driving Sean around for months and had been able to see and hear him. He was also struggling to digest that Ambrose was Ambriel, a well-respected angel known for bringing and delivering truth. His influence had clearly been to make sure that Sean and Crowley had delivered their readings well and with love. Crowley wondered if Ambriel had not been there would Crowley have said different things to Sean in his readings.

'So, let me get this straight then, the surge that you felt were a load of angels. And angels are here all the time doing stuff that we don't know about?' asked Sean.

'The surge was angels and souls descending to Earth.

Only guides can talk and be seen among the living souls. Angels have never been seen or heard on Earth for over two thousand years until today,' explained Ambriel.

'You mean until a few months back when you two came?' corrected Sean.

'Yes.'

'So why did you two come first? I'm not getting this,' he quickly swivelled in his chair to look at Sue. 'Are you getting this?!' Sue wasn't sure how to answer. If she said yes, she would be lying and if she said no she feared they would start again and she didn't want to hear it again. She was struggling to process what she had heard already. She gave a shrugging, nod/shake of the head which was delivered in the way she intended as Sean was still none the wiser.

'Sean, listen to me.' Michael shuffled forward on the couch and sought for Sean's hands that were on his knees and gently took them in his own.

'You are part of a bigger plan. A plan that has been in the making for some time. A plan that we had no control over. But in that plan, we do have the power to protect you and keep you safe. All will become clear, I promise! But right now, we need to shut that man up out there and all the other angels that are destroying the one thing that lives in all of us and all of the living souls on Earth.'

'What's that?' uttered Sean.

'Faith.'

* * *

Jack's spirit was invisibly soaring on the stage with the sheer acknowledgement from the thousands of people in the Hall. It was better than he imagined. At times, the thought of today had filled him with dread but at this moment the power within him was intoxicating. Jack knew his master would be pleased. All of the planning that had gone into this day had finally come to this. The plan was always that Sean would be at his side to deliver the message but they had not foreseen that Crowley would have such a hold and influence on the boy. His master had explained that Sean would indeed be on their side as it was his destiny and while the timing was a little off, the message was still the same.

'We have walked amongst you for thousands of years,' he boomed, 'thousands!' He slowly strode across the front of the stage like a preacher warming up, trying to captivate his audience. 'People like Sean are simply conduits, channelling our message to you, the living. Telling you what we want you to hear, or not telling you, sometimes. Why is it up to people like Sean to decipher what you should or shouldn't be told? Why is it only them that can tell you what they hear? Who says that people like Sean are special? Who is it that decides only the few can have this ability to see and hear us? Why should you all suffer, simply because someone said you were not worthy of receiving the same gift as him? Because that's why you are here. That's what drove you to buy a ticket and see "The Great and Magnificent Sean". That's what your life has been filled with up until this point. Your suffering. We feel your suffering in Heaven. We feel your pain. And yet there are still higher powers in Heaven that tell us that we can only help the few.'

He stopped to face the side stage and could see Crowley, Michael, Sean, Sue and Ambriel walking towards him. They stopped in the shadows. They were there to listen. Maybe, they had realised that what he was doing was for the greater good. He then turned his head into the spotlight. Maybe, he could get Sean to listen.

'Think of a time when you have truly suffered.' He

began to walk again, allowing the now captive audience to digest his statement. 'The anguish, the tearing at every fibre of your body and soul, the helplessness and the loneliness. That's the worst bit, isn't it? That feeling of being utterly alone and unloved. That feeling that you cannot go on anymore, but you know you have to! Why? Hundreds of reasons that you have told yourself. It could be your children or parents or your job or simply that you are too afraid to end it all. All valid reasons I guess, I am not here to judge. But why did you have to face it alone? Because the higher powers in Heaven say you must face it alone! The higher powers say that they can't help EVERYBODY! The higher powers are IGNORING you! The higher powers are saying that you are not WORTHY of their help!'

'I'm not sure I can listen to any more of this,' whispered Ambriel.

'Look at them all,' said Crowley, craning his head toward the audience, 'they're listening to him.'

'But there are a few of us who can see your anguish, can feel your pain. Some of you have been lucky. Some of you have been touched by us. Those times when you think you have done something that has changed the course of your life. THAT'S NOT FATE! THAT'S US!' The huge hall stayed deathly quiet. Crowley turned to Sean and even in the semi-darkness could see the tears still rolling down his face.

'My dear boy.'

'If someone had to gate-crash my show why did it have to be someone that looked like the Milk Tray man?' sniffed Sean.

'Crowley, can you leave? I mean properly leave?' asked Michael. Crowley recalled his previous fight with Joe and Sam and then proceeded to try again without success.

'No. I've tried a couple of times.'

'They must have shut down all the portals to stop more angels coming through. It means we can't get through either. We're stuck here,' whispered Ambriel.

'Your life is not by chance,' shouted Jack to the darkness. 'Your life is already set. Your choices are superfluous as you will always end up where you are supposed to be. But that doesn't mean that it has to be hard. That doesn't mean that we can't help you. Ladies and gentlemen, this message is being delivered across the globe. The message that we are here. The message that we have always been here. The message that we now want to walk amongst you. We want to take away your pain. We want you to be happy. We want to take away your suffering. We want to be your friend and be there when you need us. The only difference now is that you will be able to see us and most of all WE WILL be recognised.'

'And there it is,' said Crowley, 'the true talk of rebellion. Little men that know no other way of being acknowledged than by throwing a tantrum. All this talk is so someone will take notice and pat them on the back and...'

Michael began to stagger and sway on the spot and started to fall back. Simultaneously, Sean and Ambriel saw and caught him by slipping their hands under Michael's armpits to take his weight. They gently lowered him to the floor while Crowley lowered himself as well. Confused and concerned they all looked at Michael who was now screwing up his eyes as if in pain.

'What is it?' asked Crowley.

'I can hear millions of prayers,' he was struggling to speak, 'all at once,' he said breathlessly. Crowley became more concerned as he watched Michael visibly deteriorate in front of him. Sean laid Michael's head on his lap and gently caressed his hair.

'And you?' Crowley asked Ambriel quietly.

'No. Only Michael can hear prayers that ask for protection from the Devil.' Crowley looked over his shoulder back to the stage where Jack was still addressing the audience.

'So, I guess not everyone is swallowing this Angel Aid crap.' Michael opened his eyes and started to take deep breaths. His colour started to return to his face and Sean could feel his body steeling underneath him. He started to get to his feet and Sean and Ambriel loosened their grip.

'You ok?' asked Sean rising up with him.

'Yeah. When you hear a lot of prayers all at once like that, it's called a flare. We don't get them very often but when we do, they can knock you for six, shall we say,' Michael smiled to pacify Sean.

'But one good thing, though,' turned Michael to Ambriel. 'If prayers are getting in, then prayers are getting out.' Ambriel smiled as he realised what Michael meant.

'Anthony!'

CHAPTER 15

Rucelle and Nazriel had finally finished creating the Carcerem. A task they did not enjoy as it not only took a great deal of energy to form, but it had been thousands of years since one had ever been in Heaven. The task would have been quicker with the aid of Michael as he had created the last one and they were not entirely confident that the confinement prayers would be strong enough. They consoled themselves with the fact that if they could get the rebels through and incarcerated then Michael would follow and ensure the Carcerem was strong enough to hold them until such time it was decided of their fate. Just as Nazriel was about to excuse himself to retire to his own office, Anthony arrived.

'Anthony?' said Rucelle. Anthony stepped forward and could feel the energy of the Carcerem. It made him feel sad, depressed and above all else hopeless. He instinctively took a step back in fear that the negativity would draw him to a place he would never return from.

'You feel it, too?' asked Nazriel.

'I don't think I have ever felt anything like it,' Anthony whispered.

'Or want to again?' stated Rucelle, who began to walk back to his desk. 'It still needs a bit of tweaking, but it should be enough to hold until Michael can get back.' Anthony turned and smiled to Rucelle. A gentle and knowing smile. Rucelle caught it and felt some hope. 'Please tell me you roughly know where they could be?'

'I know exactly where they are,' beamed Anthony. Nazriel stepped forward. He knew Anthony would come through in the end. His speed in the matter had surprised him though.

'Michael sent a prayer!' Rucelle stood again from behind his desk, his mind whirring with the simplicity of it all.

'I only shut the portals for travel. Not for prayer.'

'Indeed. He is with Ambriel. Sean is still with him. It seems Jack fancied himself as an entertainer and became on one of the largest stages in Britain. He's not sure about the other angels and where they are as he can't move from the building he is in. But he did say that the angels are all over the world spreading the message of our existence.'

'He's used Sean's show to showcase himself and his followers. I can't say I'm surprised. I take it his merry men are with him also?' asked Rucelle. Anthony nodded.

'Okay, well we can tell who was supposed to be on Earth and those that followed Jack. We just need to make sure we get all the right angels and souls into the Carccrem.'

'An angel's heart is pure and should be free of want. Those essences that have craved a human trait will be tainted,' said Nazriel. Rucelle thought for a moment of the prayers that he and Nazriel had placed on the Carcerem.

'The Carcerem will only hold a tainted angel or a corrupted soul. So, if we open the portals and clean the Earth of *all* angels and only the corrupted souls, then only the six million we need will be incarcerated?' Rucelle knew this to be true but still wanted some reassurance. Moving this amount of angels and souls was a huge task and holding six million of them was just as challenging.

'I believe so,' agreed Nazriel, 'but what about Crowley?'

'Crowley is a pure soul and will not be affected or feel the pull,' said Anthony.

'I doubt he would want to leave Sean, anyway,' said Nazriel confidently.

Rucelle sat back down in his chair, leant forward and with his elbows on the table, clasped his hands in front of his mouth. The co-ordination of this whole plan was feeling overwhelming. The pressures from above to clear this mess up was increasing and as the bigger picture came into focus he started to doubt his ability. He knew this day would come but had no idea it would unfold like this and would be on such a large scale. The timing of it all had to be perfect and it was the first time, in a long time, that Rucelle felt vulnerable. The first time in his life that he felt he needed help and had to rely on others to achieve it. He took a deep breath while under the scrutiny of Nazriel and Anthony.

'Okay, I need Bathisma back to open the portals while you stay here Anthony. I need you to ensure you have a fix on Jack and Michael. Michael will no doubt arrive here with Ambriel. Once, we are sure that the cleanse is underway I need you to come with me Nazriel. There is someone we need to see.'

Nazriel nodded silently and closed his eyes as if in prayer. As soon as he opened them, Bathisma had become in the room awaiting his instructions in his usual stance of hands clasped in front of him. Rucelle stood and slowly walked around to the front of his desk and joined Anthony and Nazriel and looked at Bathisma to follow suit.

Instinctively, they formed a circle and slowly looked at each other one by one. They all recognised that they were the best and the only hope to pull this off correctly. Each of them in turn having their part to play and without one they knew the plan would fail. Rucelle had his lowered as if in prayer while the other three awaited his instruction.

'The energy will be felt across the whole plain. As soon as you open the portal,' he looked at Bathisma, 'and you have locked on their ascent,' he looked at Anthony, 'then we must leave without delay,' his gaze finished on Nazriel.

'Are we ready, gentlemen?' Rucelle asked softly. He didn't wait for a reply, he simply took Bathisma's hand to his right and Anthony's to his left. Nazriel took their remaining hands as they now formed a united circle. They all bent their heads in silence.

Bathisma was the first. His head flew back and his whole body bright. The energy created was re-opening the portals. Anthony soon followed, his light just as bright as Bathisma's trying to lock on the rebels. Rucelle almost instantly was soon lost in his light as he created 'the pull' for the angels to return. Then Nazriel was the last to be consumed by the white as he amplified their combined energies.

* * *

Jennifer was in her kitchen, tearing off bits of tissue as she worried for her love. She knew Crowley would be ok but wondered if he would return. No one in Heaven could give her any answers as to where he was or if he was ok. But even though she fretted, she knew that if Crowley could get back to her then he would.

She stared at the pots and pans lining the shelves on the wall opposite her. The kitchen was the same as De

Mondford Hall the day she had last seen it when she was alive. While her and her husband had special places in their heart, such as Cullanamore beach in Ireland where Crowley had proposed it was always De Mondford Hall where they were their happiest. All the details were the same including some of its shabbiness and its funky smells. The only difference compared to the real De Mondford Hall was this one was warmer, and it didn't leak.

As she rose from the battered pine table that dominated the kitchen she walked over to the black iron kettle to make herself a pot of tea. Some Earthly habits had not changed. After filling with water, she placed the kettle on the range and went to retrieve the tea leaves from the old rusty caddy. But as she reached for the tin she felt her body drain in an overwhelming sense of tiredness. A tiredness she had not felt since she had been in Heaven. It felt very human and debilitating. As soon as she felt it the moment was gone, and her hand took a firm grip on the caddy. Something was happening. She wasn't sure what and she wasn't sure if it was good or bad, but she could be sure that it was related to the recent rebellion.

'Crowley, come back to me,' she prayed.

* * *

Back in Rucelle's office, the four figures could not be seen. The dazzling glow had consumed all its surroundings. Then through the light Nazriel could be seen first and he stared straight in front of him until he could see Rucelle. As soon as their gaze was locked, they disappeared.

They were soon stood in a highly manicured garden that seemed to stretch as far as the eye could see. Perfect grass was underfoot that stretched until broken by sculptured bushes and shrubs. Flowering trees peppered the perimeter and a heady smell of magnolia hung in the air. While there was no sun in the sky, the view was bright and warm. The sound of water could be heard and although they could not see them it suggested there were fountains in the beautiful grounds.

They both stood and slowly drank in the very agreeable scene. They made no move to find him, they knew he would come looking for them. They both looked at each other and raised their eyebrows expectantly when they heard the footsteps approaching from inside the house. Huge open doors carried the sound to where Nazriel and Rucelle stood. As they cast their gaze in the direction of the open doors, he stepped onto the shiny, grey stone patio.

'Rucelle. Nazriel. It's been a long time since we were in each other's company,' he sneered.

'Christian,' hissed Rucelle, 'I would say it's a pleasure to see you again but that would be a bare-faced lie.' Christian licked his lips. His hands were still in the pockets of his white pants that matched the collarless white shirt. Rucelle noted that he was periodically clenching his jaw. The whole smooth act was not convincing either of the angels. 'How on Earth did you ever think you would get away with it?'

'Who is to say I haven't?' Christian snapped. For a moment Rucelle could feel panic inside him. Had they overlooked a small detail? Did Christian have someone else as his puppet apart from Jack? Had they left Anthony and Bathisma too soon? If they hadn't left, Christian could disappear, he wasn't to be underestimated.

'You know what is written,' said Christian. His eyes, almost black, were burrowing for answers in Rucelle. Rucelle gave no reaction.

'Then that explains your confidence,' Rucelle said flatly.

'Even you Rucelle cannot change what is written!'

'But we all have the power to change the *course* of the inevitable. Even the humans that you pathetically wish to control.' Christian started to slowly walk towards Rucelle, his jaw still clenched, and the hands stuffed in his pockets were now visibly fisted. As Christian pressed his face nearer to his rival, Rucelle spoke. 'Did you not feel the surge, Christian? All your rebels, or should I say rats, are now following Jack the Pied Piper to the Carcerem as we speak.' Rucelle finished with a menacing smile. He could see the realisation sweep across Christian's face. He could not only see it he could feel it.

'The Carcerem?' Christian was slowly backing away from Rucelle. He knew why they were here. It wasn't just to gloat, it was to arrest him.

'Don't even think about becoming somewhere else. The whole time we have been here, my good friend,' he pointed to Nazriel, 'has been reciting the Instacian Prayer.'

Christian had noticed Nazriel but had not noticed that his lips were indiscernibly moving as he discreetly prayed. If he couldn't become, then he could run. Another angel would need to touch him for him to become in the Carcerem. He continued to back away and he wasn't sure where he could run to.

'You have to touch me first,' Christian said in a panic.

'I don't have to. He will,' Rucelle nodded and his gaze shifted to just behind Christian. As Christian spun on the spot his face was inches away from his old aide, Bathisma. And before he had a chance to open his mouth, Bathisma firmly placed his hand on Christian's shoulder. The instant white light was gone as quick as it came leaving Rucelle and Nazriel standing in the garden alone. They both looked at each other. The feeling of relief was beginning to envelop them and as soon as they felt it they both dismissed it.

'We are not out of the woods, yet.' And they both disappeared.

Rucelle and Nazriel were soon back in the office. Anthony was still there and Bathisma was standing in his usual spot, behind the chair of the desk, in his usual manner. Magda was also waiting.

'Well?' asked Rucelle as soon as he became. He looked at Bathisma who simply nodded.

'Please don't nod at me like you are pumping oil! What's the status so far?' he snapped. Bathisma looked a little taken aback. He had never been on the receiving end of Rucelle's temper. Oh, he had witnessed it many a time and had taken some pleasure in the spectacle of it all.

'Sorry, sir. Christian is contained.'

'And the rest?' Rucelle shouted, his gaze sweeping toward Anthony and Magda.

'They are still transitioning. Moving eleven million angels and souls is not like rearranging your CD collection!' said Magda.

'A what?' Anthony looked intrigued.

'A CD is something from the twentieth century. It played music. Apparently, they didn't last long. It was replaced with something called an Empty Three player, I think,' she tried to sound convincing and as she was the only one in the room who had the most contact with fresh Earth souls they were all convinced.

'An Empty Three. How fascinating,' sighed Anthony.

'I'm sure Magda would love to enlighten you on the merits of the pedal bin or why the human race is enthralled by a thing called memory foam, but in case it slipped your notice…' he sarcastically smiled and pointed toward the Carcerem, 'but we are moving…well, I would say a fair amount of angels and souls, wouldn't you? I mean, okay it's not exactly on the scale of when the Black Plague hit, so we can't reminisce about the good old days but it's still a pretty busy day.' His smile was becoming wider to the point where he looked slightly maniacal. 'So, can we please get on?' he asked rhetorically, 'if it's not too much trouble?'

Anthony and Magda gave each other a sideways glance and then lowered their gaze in an apologetic manner. Rucelle continued to stare at their slightly bowed heads until he was satisfied he had made his point.

'When will we know that we have everyone in there?' Rucelle asked Magda.

'The Carcerem will know and we will feel it. But there is one thing I need to point out,' her voice was concerned and as Rucelle turned to face her she stepped forward. Her voice was low and raspy. 'The earthly death toll is starting to increase. The transitional plane is flooding with human souls.' Rucelle looked at her for a moment, his face blank. He was trying to compute how their action had created such a side effect. The realisation of what they had done was starting to become clear.

'We've removed the angels from the Protectors' Division,' he said in a whisper. He looked at his feet as he started to walk back to his chair behind his desk and as he sat he continued, 'That means all babies currently being born haven't received their mapping from the Birth Division either,' he leant back into his chair. 'The Birth Division will soon catch up but there are people dying and it's not their time!'

Anthony walked over to Rucelle's desk. 'But surely, what has been mapped will override any premature deaths. After all, what is mapped cannot be changed.' Magda stepped forward and joined Anthony and addressed them both.

'Indeed, when a life is set with a certain time of death, that cannot be undone. But the mapping also states all the points as to when the Protectors will intervene and guide. You take that away and the mapping…well…the mapping is now simply what was planned.'

'So, all these people are now dead before their time and the rate will increase with every passing hour,' Rucelle said deflatingly.

'Not quite,' said Magda. Rucelle and Anthony looked at her.

'They are in limbo, a suspended state of transition,' whispered Nazriel from the corner of the room.

'Exactly,' confirmed Magda. 'These souls are not alive or dead. Their circumstances on Earth have allowed their soul to transcend but their mapping prevents them from dying and entering Heaven or even the transitional plane.' Magda took a seat opposite Rucelle and could see him visibly shrinking before her. She felt responsible to give him some hope.

'The good news is, these souls have no idea what they have been through. When we are sure we have the Carcerem sealed, my division will make sure all the souls are back in their respective bodies. But we do need to be quick and I mean within an hour, so we can return the souls back to their original bodies,' she finished.

'And if they can't return to their original bodies?' asked Rucelle. He switched his gaze from Magda to Nazriel.

'Welcome to the world of reincarnation,' Nazriel shrugged.

'Recycling?!' snorted Rucelle and stared back at Magda.

'Well, if you can think of anything better, then tell me and I'll do it. But I'm not sure what choice we have if someone has been on the receiving end of a bomb and his body now looks like mince!' she retorted. Rucelle sighed and inwardly admitted that he had no choice. As much as he hated reincarnation he knew in this situation there was no alternative. Part of Heaven's job was to bring peace and serenity to all souls. A human body that held two was an inward battle that the human brain could not cope with very well. A lot of humans had ended up in mental institutions as they could hear voices, completely unaware that their body now housed another soul. Others, more in tune, were very aware of a previous life and had learned to supress the personality of the other in some way. Only ascending into Heaven would bring these souls peace as they once again became independent of one another.

Rucelle sat back and mulled over the options once again. There was very little choice and it seemed whichever way he looked it just created more problems. He leant forward in the chair and with his elbows on his desk and clasped his hands together in front of his mouth.

'It seems whatever we do there are consequences,' he sighed. 'Okay, as soon as the Carcerem is contained we need to open the usual portals and get all the innocent angels back to their jobs. Magda, I need you to liaise with the Birth Division and give them a list of all the souls currently in limbo. They will go nuts with all the new mapping they need to do for the bodiless souls. If they cause you any problems tell them to come and see me and you might want to mention I have the Carcerem in my office; that will probably shut them up. Anthony, you go with her to speed up locating the bodies of those that can be re-souled. Nazriel,' he swung his chair to his right where Nazriel was still standing, 'I need you to tell me when the Carcerem is full and more importantly when Michael and Ambriel are back.' He swung his chair further to his right to Bathisma who was stood behind him. 'And Bathisma, you better send Death a fruit basket or something. He's gonna be pissed off.'

CHAPTER 16

Sue sat on the couch and periodically flicked through the news channels on the dusty television the boys had wheeled out from the corner of the room. It clearly hadn't been used for years as a burning smell of dust began to permeate the room and obliterate all remnants of Sean's Creed aftershave and fake tan.

Soon there was breaking news, and all the other channels began to follow suit with the same report. The angels were disappearing, some of them mid speech. Footage, sent in by phone wielding observers showed angels trying to run from something that couldn't be seen. Some showed they had no idea that they were about to involuntarily leave. Michael and Ambriel were making their way back to the stage.

'Do you think Anthony heard us?' asked Ambriel.

Michael smiled and continued to walk. 'I like to think an archangel's prayer is a pretty powerful one. Especially, when it's amplified by this cool leather jacket,' he smirked, tugging at the collar. Up ahead they could see the silhouettes of Crowley and Sean still standing in the wings.

The boom of Jack's voice could still be heard. Crowley turned to see them approaching and raised an expectant eyebrow.

'It's done. He should be able to find us and pass the message that Sean is safe.' Sean spun around.

'Pass the message to who? Who needs to know I am safe?'

Crowley too looked at Michael and wanted an answer, but Michael's face did not change and had no intention of giving an answer.

'Jesus Christ, I need a drink,' whispered Crowley. Sean looked at his guide for a moment, sighed and then with an air of reluctance rooted into the inside breast pocket of his jacket and pulled out a hip flask. Crowley's eyes lit up as he looked at the shiny silver canister like a child in a sweet shop. Sean silently passed the flask over and looked back at Jack on the stage.

'You might want to save a sip of that for yourself,' said Michael to Sean who turned to him. 'The news is showing videos from people all over the world of angels being pulled back. I'm presuming the portals are reopening and any minute now,' he nodded toward Jack, 'this bunch of pirates will be going.'

'Seriously?' An air of excitement started to quell the dread that had enveloped them for what seemed like days but was in fact, only hours. Sean's mind was thinking of the here and now and then jumping ahead to six months' time and wondering what people would be making of all this then. He realised that he still had a part to play, albeit a small one. His actions now would not only shape his career moving forward but could also influence the attitudes and beliefs of some.

Crowley was still gripping the flask in his hand ready to take another gulp of the brandy within when Sean quickly snatched out his hand. They all watched as Sean took a huge mouthful and then as quick as it was gone the canister was thrust back into Crowley's hand.

'Sean?' Crowley reluctantly asked. Sean buttoned up his blazer and started to tug at the hem of it to pull the wrinkles out.

'Sean, don't go out there!' Ambriel second-guessed Sean's actions.

Michael gently took Sean's arm as he continued to pull the cuffs of the shirt down over his wrists. 'Don't!' Michael pleaded. Sean looked at Michael directly in the face with steely determination and put a hand on each of Michael's shoulders.

'I have...' he looked over Michael's shoulder at Ambriel, 'archangel?' Ambriel shook his head. 'Regular angel?' Sean pushed. Ambriel gave a slightly smiling nod with a lack of enthusiasm at being described as a *'regular angel'*.

'So, I have an archangel, a regular angel, a spiritual guide and a woman that looks like she was weaned on spare ribs looking out for me. I'm fine, I can do this.' He fixed his gaze into Michael's piercing blue eyes and felt the archangel's shoulders slightly relax under his clutch. He took a deep breath, looked toward the stage, stretched his face into a wide and welcoming smile and stepped from the wings onto the open stage. Jack looked to his right and could see Sean striding toward him with his arms outstretched.

'Ladies and gentlemen, how about that? Jack, is it?' Sean smiled at Jack waiting for him to answer and as he was about to draw breath, Sean interjected. 'Everyone, give Jack a big hand.' Sean began with the clapping and soon a few in the audience began to follow suit. He continued to clap and smile at the darkness waiting for the whole hall to join in. He periodically clapped in Jack's direction who stood dumbfounded and noted that Joe and Sam were looking at Ed for some indication as to whether they should join in the clapping.

'Thank you, thank you!' Sean, still smiling, stopped clapping and started to wave at people to cease their own. Eventually the hall returned to being quiet, but the atmosphere had changed. It felt more... Sean's.

'Soooo...' started Sean, he tried to peer at some faces in the front rows, 'the big reveal, eh?' He gave a little snigger and looked back at Jack whose dumbfounded face reminded him of Charlie's when someone once walked into his butcher's and asked if he did vegetarian sausages. The only difference was Jack was not wielding a meat cleaver. 'My friend here, Jack,' he spat, 'and his 'er...' he looked over to the back of the stage where Joe, Ed and Sam stood, '...what shall we call you lot then? Followers, cronies, hangers-on...I know, how about leeches?'

A loud "HA" could be heard from the wings and Sean knew instantly it was delivered by Crowley. Jack went to speak, and Sean quickly placed a firm hand on his chest which shoved him slightly. Sean turned his back to the audience and covered his lapel mic.

'These people came to see me! You've had your turn, now you just smile and let the people get their money's worth, okay?' Before Jack had time to respond Sean spun on his heel and smiled back at the audience. 'It's true what Jack says. Well... some of it,' he snorted. 'Yes, there are angels and guides and God knows what else walking amongst us.' He began to stride the stage as he normally did in one of his shows. He had once taken his mum to a Billy Connolly concert and noticed that Billy moved around that stage a lot. It gave the impression he was trying to be part of the room and not just simply talking to it.

'But you are an intelligent lot, right? You knew this, otherwise why would you be here?' He smiled and spied a bearded man sat next to his young girlfriend who was hanging on to every word Sean had to say. 'Except maybe this guy,' he pointed, 'you didn't come here because you believed. You are clearly here to earn some Brownie points with your girlfriend, aren't you?' Sean looked at the crowd and gave a huge smile and the laughter from the front row began to ripple throughout the hall. 'Don't blame you either, kid. She ain't letting you have any 'yee ha' on your looks alone, is she?' The room was up. The laughing levels increased, and it filled Sean with strength.

'Anyway, just so you all know. Jack's message has been delivered by millions like him all over the world this evening. It's all over the telly. So please don't think that you have been singled out and you are all going to be abducted and come back with a glowing finger, dragging your arse like E.T. No, nothing like that. These people are simply giving you some hope and reinforce the message that psychics like me have been trying to tell you for years, that there is something on the other side,' he said softly. He turned and shot Jack a penetrating look. 'However, don't for one-minute think that you have no control over your life or your destiny. It just simply isn't true. No one made you who you are, no one made you make all the good and bad decisions you made in your life,' he looked back to the front row, 'and no one told you that shirt and trouser combo was a good choice, did they sir?' Sean laughed. 'Nooo, you thought that get up was an excellent choice all on your own!' The crowd began to laugh again. 'One thing I learned tonight though,' he turned and looked at Jack, 'is that they have incredible egos in Heaven. I get the feeling that Heaven might be a bit like an Oscars' after-show party.' Jack could take no more and stepped forward, his face was set.

'ENOUGH!' he bellowed. Sean spun around, Jack's face was thunderous. But Sean could feel the redness of anger rising in him and once it was charging every nerve in his body, there was no stopping it.

'Quite!' responded Sean. 'That's exactly what we all thought when you wittered on about us all "being alone",' he mimicked Jack with a moaning tone, 'and "we're here to help you". This is life mate, not Tesco!' Sean turned back and smiled to the audience. 'Angels appearing, I admit…well…it's a big day for all of us but it's no different to when they found out that Jesus rose again after being crucified, or when they learned the Earth was round and we were not the only planet in the universe or when we read that Charles was sleeping with Camilla when he was still with Lady Di. Huge news, undoubtedly, and we have all been privileged to have witnessed this monumental moment in human history. But you'll be leaving here tonight and still have to stand at the same bus stop to get home and still moan in the morning that there isn't enough milk for your Coco Pops. And why? Because life still goes on!' Sean walked toward the wing on his right and could see his angels, Crowley and Sue watching him and listening to every word. He gave them a wink and turned back, looking toward Jack.

'Now I thought I should stand here, as you will be leaving us soon Jack.' Jack shot Sean a panicked glare. 'Yes Jack, I can feel the energy in the room starting to shift and I feel…' Sean pressed a finger on his forehead for dramatic effect, 'yes, I feel that while you may have told them plenty and not all of it true…' Sean could see Joe beginning to disperse into a million specks of light, closely followed by

Ed then Sam and the rest of the angels they arrived with. The timing of this could not have been better than if Sean was in control himself, '...that you forgot to tell this beautiful audience the power of their own energy.' Sean faced the audience and in the glare of the spotlight raised his arms and closed his eyes. 'Ladies and gentlemen, join most of us in this room who, with our energy, are banishing this negative force back to where it came.'

'What the hell is he doing?' whispered Ambriel in the dark.

Crowley, who had not taken his proud eyes off Sean for a moment, even when polishing off the brandy said, 'He's putting on a show! And a marvellous one at that!' He laughed. Sean, keeping his arms outstretched, raised his head as if looking to the Heavens.

'Channel your energy!' Sean instructed. Without looking back into the darkness Sean could hear the gasps as all the angels including Ed, Joe and Sam began to disperse and float toward the ceiling. The millions of lights from them never quite reaching the edges of the Hall before they disappeared. Jack, in a panic, stayed rooted to the spot, only moving his head to peer into the wings to spy Crowley. He could see his silhouette and the fleck of the white glint in his eye. He went to stride toward him and became aware the pressure on the soles of his feet had disappeared. He could feel the pull and with all his might could not resist or reject it.

'This isn't over yet, Crowley!' Jack shouted. Crowley stepped forward slightly, so the stage light could illuminate his face.

'You're damn right, this isn't over with,' Crowley hissed. He watched as Jack began to disperse more and as he did he raised the hip flask, smiled in Jack's direction and took a large celebratory gulp. The action was not lost on Jack before he finally disappeared. Crowley's smug feeling was interrupted by a tap on his shoulder; it was Ambriel.

'Michael and I can feel the pull. We will be leaving soon. If Sean is still on the stage when we have gone, tell him we will either be back or at least get a message to him through you.' Crowley, still concerned and confused looked at Ambriel's face searching for answers.

'What the hell has all this got to do with Sean?' he looked over Ambriel's shoulder to where Michael was standing. 'I don't understand, so what the hell am I supposed to tell him?'

'The truth. Always, the truth.' Ambriel smiled.

Crowley snorted. 'The truth? From two angels who disguised themselves as an assistant and a chauffeur. From two angels who could always see me as Sean's guide and never once gave any inclination that they could...' Crowley looked down and could see Ambriel's feet starting to shine and splinter.

'Crowley!' shouted Michael, 'we will tell you everything that we know, but right now it seems we have somewhere else to be. In the meantime, look after Sean and keep Sue away from the bloody media.' Michael gave a soft laugh, but Crowley was in no mood to join in the humour.

'So, thank you all for joining me tonight and what a special audience you have been to share this wonderful historic moment with. Good night!' Crowley turned his head to the stage and could see Sean bowing to the audience to thunderous applause. He turned his head back to speak to Michael and Ambriel, but they were gone.

Crowley, disappointed, was left with too many questions and he knew that Sean would be adding some of his own, to which he knew no answers. The Hall began to fill with the noise of energetic chatter and a keenness to leave the building. Who could blame these people? They had no idea what they had been through, never mind how to make sense or comprehend it. Sean came bounding over.

'Any drink left in that flask?' Sean asked breathlessly. Crowley reluctantly shook his head. Sean marched off in the direction of the dressing room muttering, "stupid question", under his breath. He stormed into the room to find Sue, sat transfixed in front of the TV. As she jumped to her feet, Crowley entered the room.

'Is there any booze in here?' Sean snapped. Sue began to fidget with her fingers and while still stood to the spot, gave the room a quick glance.

'I don't think so, ducky,' she whispered. Sean looked at the TV and could see the news channel talking about similar events as to what they had just experienced. Sean turned to Sue, suspiciously.

'How long have you been in here?'

'Erm…not sure…,' Sue replied nervously.

'Are you telling me that while I was giving the performance of my life due to a bunch of ghosts coming down and gate-crashing my show, you have been in here watching the telly?' His face was moving closer to Sue's, who began to twist and pull her fingers more.

'Sorry, Sean. I was watching to see if anyone had videoed you. I can't believe the stuff they have been showing and yet no one has sent anything to ITV or BBC or any of them about you.'

'That's all you are interested in, isn't it? Media, hype, publicity, the bloody image machine. All the time I have been on the stage trying to make sense of whatever the hell just happened, you still sat here and watched the telly. Even the revelation of angels being on the staff can still not tear you away from the thought of how much exposure we had and is there any money to be made from it!' A shocked Sue raised her eyes, but Sean wasn't taken in. 'Don't give me the look of indignation. I'm the only one who can act around here and tell the truth as well.' He moved his face closer to Sue's. 'Now do us a favour, go and find me and Crowley a couple of nice bottles of something.'

'Yes, Sean.' Sue was relieved to be able to leave the room. She quickly scooped up her handbag from the couch on her right and smiled weakly at Sean.

'Don't take too long, Sue. I know how you love to listen to the audience spilling out, but this is one night when I am truly not interested.' His back was turned and she caught Crowley's eye who gave her a look that told her she should go.

Sean, with his back to Crowley, stood at the dressing table and was slowly closing lids on various make-up palettes. Crowley watched him for a moment and wasn't sure what emotion Sean was feeling right now. He didn't want to be the idiot that asked how he was or what he was feeling either as he wasn't sure how he felt about it all, never mind Sean.

'Don't be too hard on Sue, you know what she is like. She probably...'

'Where's Michael and Ambriel?' Sean interrupted without turning. Crowley stopped, and he too started to fidget. All he was going to do was to add to Sean's frustration. The level, however, was dependant on him, he supposed, or how long Sue was going to be. He had no answers or booze. A situation that Crowley could not cope with at the best of times.

'Sean, they were pulled as well as Jack and all the others. They left just before you had finished. They hoped that they would still be there to say goodbye to you before...

well … before they erm…Christ…' Crowley wasn't sure what to say.

Without turning, Sean very calmly and slowly continued to tidy the dressing table. 'Why would they be pulled? They had done nothing wrong. Or had they?' He let out a small sarcastic laugh.

'No, no, no, Sean. They had no choice. The angels have been pulled all over the world.' He tried to be reassuring.

'Then why didn't you go?' He turned and with a sneer said, 'oh, but you're no angel are you? You're just some "guide". I mean, your level of importance is clearly low for them, so they just left you here. Why didn't they want you back, Crowley? Was it you that told Jack where I was, because you obviously knew him, didn't you? I saw you, I saw your face.' Crowley felt stunned at what Sean was saying to him. He could feel himself prickling all over and wondered if he was being pulled. He looked at his feet and could see that they were still there and as the prickling rose it started to feel familiar. He remembered the last time he felt like this was in an art gallery in New York with Grace. That was the last time he was truly angry. 'They didn't get pulled,' continued Sean, 'they just simply left you. And now you are stuck here. I didn't know you could get barred from Heaven. Will you…'

'ENOUGH!'

Sean immediately closed his mouth. He wanted to say more but he knew that he had done what he wanted to do and that was blame Crowley for this whole mess. He stood staring at him.

'Sit down,' Crowley asked. But Sean stood firm. He continued to stare at Crowley. 'Sean Allister, I am here with you, I am dead, and I am nearly SOBER!' Crowley stepped forward to Sean until he was inches away from him. 'And

I am not going to have this conversation with someone acting like a petulant teenager. Now you do as I ask and sit down.' Sean continued to stare. 'NOW!'

As Crowley bellowed, Sean gave his head a little shake as if he had just come out of a trance and did as he was bid. He walked over to the couch and sat down. He shuffled himself into the back of it and pressed his knees together as he placed his hands on each of them. Crowley could see that his anger had clearly rattled Sean and by the looks of things Sean was not sure how to act. Crowley's anger began to drain as quickly as it has rose and he looked at Sean. Sean continued to look at his knees as he resisted the urge to fidget and Crowley studied him trying to judge what was going through Sean's mind, but he struggled. He wasn't sure if Sean was angry, upset, sorry or even ashamed at being told off.

As Crowley continued to look at him, he noted that Sean had not made eye contact with him since he had shouted. That was it! He wasn't used to being shouted at. This boy, man even, had not had a male disciplinarian when he was younger. Sean was in territory that he had never experienced before and clearly didn't know how to react. Before Crowley could speak, Sue entered the room. She was waving two bottles, one in each hand and was panting like a hot dog. Crowley entertained the idea that she had ran but judging Sue's frame the only thing Sue would run for was an ice cream van.

'Remy Martin or Martell?' she asked breathlessly from the door. She took one look at Sean and made up her mind she had no intention of stepping into the room. She wanted to get back to the hotel and have a large drink herself. Crowley stepped forward and swiped each bottle from her.

'There is no such thing as 'or',' he said flatly and walked

back to the dressing table to put the bottles down. Sue looked at Sean who was still staring at his knees.

'Sean, he can't take the two of them. I just told the man on the bar back there that I would come back with the money and one of the bottles,' she moaned. Crowley began to peer in a couple of dirty cups that were on the dressing table and silently decided that they would do. He began to unscrew the top off the brandy.

'Tell her she needs to get a taxi, Sean.' Crowley didn't look up. He began to pour a large amount of the brown liquid into each of cups.

'Michael's gone. You need to get a cab, Sue.'

'What about Al? What about the TV cameras and the cameramen?' asked Sue. Sean raised his eyes and could see a cup being handed to him.

'That's what I pay you for, isn't it? Sort it Sue, and make sure they do not bother me,' he said coldly. Still not looking in Sue's direction he took the cup but could see out of the corner of his eye that she had stormed off. Crowley slowly walked to the door, shut it and then took a seat in the chair on the opposite side of the room to Sean. With the bottle still in one hand, Crowley drained his cup in one satisfying gulp. He then refilled his glass and placed the bottle on the coffee table that sat between them. Sean took a gentle sip at first. He wasn't sure he would like it. He wasn't even sure he wanted a drink now. He felt like he wanted to jump in a cab and go somewhere, anywhere, but here. He slowly raised his eyes to try and observe Crowley and was taken aback when he could see that his piercing blue eyes were staring straight at him.

'Shall we start again?' Crowley asked with an expectant gaze. He didn't wait for an answer. 'But first Sean, don't you ever speak to me like that again! Or anyone else for that matter! Now, if you've finished having your tantrum,

I'll tell you exactly what I know.'

Crowley began to tell Sean about how he met Jack and then later how he met Joe, Sam and Ed at a poker game. He told him of Nazriel and how they had been concerned with what Jack was planning. He continued with revealing his own fears and how Jack had asked him to join them, but he had refused.

Sean finished his drink and shuffled forward on his seat until he could reach the bottle sitting on the table. As he poured himself a larger one than the measure that Crowley had just given him, he thought about what his guide had told him. The questions spinning around his head were so big that some of them he couldn't put into words. He wasn't sure where to begin as he couldn't tell when all this had started.

'All of this still doesn't explain what all this has to do with me? It doesn't tell me why Michael and Ambrose…I mean Ambriel were here to protect me. Why do I need protecting?'

'Everyone here on Earth has a Protector,' Crowley said trying to reassure Sean.

'But not everyone has angels protecting them that they can see, do they? Even Michael said that. He said angels have not been seen on Earth for two thousand years until me. I mean, what happened two thousand years ago?' Sean took a large gulp of his drink then as his eyes grew wide he spat, 'JESUS!' Sean stood up, his whole body stiff.

'Jesus, am I Jesus?!'

'I feel it necessary to also spit my drink just to illustrate the absurdity of your conclusion,' drawled Crowley, 'but as I am not one to waste a perfectly acceptable brandy or my time on such a ridiculous assumption, I feel a categoric 'no' should suffice.'

'How the bleeding hell do you know? You can't be

sure?!' Sean was shouting as he looked down on a very relaxed Crowley.

'Seeing as you still don't understand who Michael is, you cannot turn water into wine – which is such a crying shame, and you wouldn't be seen dead in sandals I think it's fair to say you are not the new Messiah.'

'What do you mean, I don't understand who Michael is?' Sean began to sit back down.

Crowley smiled, 'What do you know about the archangel Michael?' Sean sat for a moment and tried to recall what little knowledge he had about the angel.

'I know that John Travolta played him in a film and it was one of his worst films ever,' he paused for a moment, 'until he made Face Off with Nicholas Cage.' Crowley looked at Sean, slightly confused.

'Michael or John Travolta?' asked Crowley.

'John Travolta, of course,' Sean scoffed rolling his eyes. Crowley took his turn to shuffle toward the bottle for a refill. He felt this was going to be a long conversation.

'Can we leave John Travolta out of this?' He gave Sean a withering look before continuing. 'Michael is the head of the War Division. It was Michael who incarcerated Lucifer when he thought it was a good idea to…you know… stir things up a bit.' Crowley settled back into the couch and watched Sean digesting this information. 'Sean, I have to say for someone who is privy to the workings of Heaven and Earth, I thought you would have googled a few details if you felt your knowledge was a little limited when it came to these things.' Sean threw back the contents of his drink down his throat and banged his cup on the table.

'Seriously? You are going to have a go at me about not knowing about stuff that I didn't know I was supposed to know? How the hell am I supposed to know that my driver is not a driver and that instead he is the Muhammed Ali of

Heaven? Oh My God.' Sean lowered his head and shook it from side to side.

'What?' asked Crowley concerned.

'Is it wrong that I thought Michael was hot? I mean the leather jacket and…oh God…that's just so wrong, isn't it?' Crowley started to laugh.

'Sean, even Michael thought he was hot, so I really wouldn't worry about it. I think narcissism trumps fanaticism.' They continued to drink in silence and the thoughts in their heads became fuzzier.

'This is big, isn't it?' said Sean. Crowley didn't answer and the silence spoke volumes. Did Rucelle know? Of course, he knew. Only Rucelle could orchestrate the return of all the angels. What happened to Jack and the others? Was he, himself, part of the plan? Did he start something off when he showed himself on the plane? And what about humanity? How had this changed things? What damage had been done? Could it be undone? Should it be undone? Crowley let out a big sigh.

'Yes Sean, this is big.' Sean sat up slowly, put his cup down and looked straight at Crowley.

'Then as soon as you are allowed to fly or whatever it is you do to go back to Heaven, then do it. And do us a favour.' Sean braced himself, 'Never come back!'

CHAPTER 17

Michael and Ambriel were soon stood in Rucelle's office. It felt as if they had simply blinked and that action alone had transported them from the Royal Hall to the familiar Heavenly office.

'Welcome back,' said Rucelle who was perched on the end of his desk. The two angels looked around to gauge their environment and the company. Nazriel, Magda and Bathisma were also in the room and a beaming Anthony stood to their right. Michael returned his smile with a sense of gratitude.

'So, you heard me then?' As Michael went to return his gaze back to Rucelle he began to feel strange. It was a fear of something and he wasn't sure why he could feel fear. There was no one in this room to be feared or was there? As he studied each of their faces he realised the fear was penetrating him from outside and not within. He slowly raised his left arm and as he did so, he could feel the concentration of negativity pulsating towards his fingertips. He dropped his arm immediately and gasped.

'You've built a Carcerem?' Michael whispered. Rucelle

stood and slowly walked to Michael's side who had not moved since he became. Instead of looking at the angel, Rucelle looked in the direction where the Carcerem was.

'We had no choice, Michael.' Michael let out a sigh. The tiny sound could not hide the deafening disappointment within it.

'We need you to protect it, us, and seal it properly. Nazriel and I did the best we could. But as you can feel it, our first attempt is a little unstable, shall we say?' Michael turned to look at Magda.

'All the angels have now transitioned,' she began, 'and all of the rebels are now in there.' Michael's eyes began to search for the invisible Carcerem. In his mind's eye, he could see it. It was there but where it began and where it ended no one knew. Not even those who had created could tell. The Carcerem was a force, not a thing.

'How many?' asked Michael.

'Nearly six million,' Rucelle replied flatly. Michael looked at Rucelle and then Nazriel. He knew they wouldn't be joking but something made him want to see their faces just to confirm.

'Well, Jack has been a busy boy, hasn't he? We had no idea the numbers of angels and souls that descended were on that scale. Even in the short time that they were there they may have caused so much damage. Not all the witnesses had someone like Sean to try and make some accepting sense of it.' Magda looked at Anthony and raised her eyebrows. The last sentence was not lost on Anthony either.

'Well, to tell you the truth Michael, this was not down to Jack. But I am sure that Jack would be very flattered if he knew that you thought he had choregraphed all of this.' Rucelle gave a sarcastic smile.

'Then who?' asked Ambriel. Rucelle slowly walked back

to his desk and gently lowered himself into his chair. He took his usual pose of placing his elbows on the table and placing his fingers in front of his lips.

'You remember Christian, don't you Michael?' Rucelle studied Michael's face and watched as the realisation flooded the angel's face. Michael could indeed recall Christian. And all this was now starting to make a bit more sense. He inwardly chastised himself for ever thinking that this was led by Jack. Christian, indeed, was very clever.

'Is he in there?' asked Michael. Rucelle nodded. Michael slowly turned to face the direction in which the Carcerem was in. He took a tentative step forward and instinctively all the others in the room took a few steps away from it.

'Do you need any help?' asked Rucelle. Michael began to raise his arms.

'No, I got this.' His head was thrown back with the sheer force of white energy that burst from within Michael. All the other angels in the room were enveloped by it and patiently waited within its vacuity. How long they waited was not measured and made no difference when the task was completed. Michael, still in the same spot, was lowering his arms while Rucelle stood up and walked over to Michael. Immediately, they could all sense the difference in the room. The positive energy was back and they all felt something that they had not felt in a while. They felt hope.

'Well done, Michael. I take it that we too are now protected?'

'If you mean, can you go in there, then yes,' confirmed Michael. He caught Rucelle glancing at Nazriel. 'So, are you going to tell me any more about what this is all about? I mean what about the Guides that are still down there, like Crowley? He has a wife here, you know.' Rucelle placed an arm around the archangel's shoulder.

'It might be an idea if you explained to Jennifer just

exactly what has been going on.'

'But I don't know what is going on! Well, not fully anyway.' protested Michael.

'Then simply tell her what you do know and what you are comfortable with telling her.' Before Michael could say anything, Rucelle dropped his arm and turned his attention to Magda. 'Now the Carcerem has been sealed, you can make a start on returning the portals back to complete normality. The Birth Division need to catch up with mapping and we need to get the Protectors back as they were. I'll also need a report on the reincarnation situation and make sure you send a copy of that to Death. Anthony, could you spare anyone from Chartering? I need someone down there to compile an incident report. We need to start thinking about damage limitation and about future measures.' Rucelle felt that he was able to think more clearly now and wondered if it had anything to do with the Carcerem being sealed.

'No one is going to want to go down there with the portals opening and closing like the mouth of a Koi carp!' argued Anthony. Rucelle thought for a moment.

'Send Jude,' he instructed.

'Seriously! Jude? He's a pain in the ass!' Anthony was astounded.

'Then you won't mind him leaving your division for a short while. He loves to report, the recent incidents will not faze him, and he can kill two birds with one stone by sorting out a few desperate cases while he is down there.' Rucelle smiled triumphantly and ignored Anthony's tutting.

'Magda, I am sure you could use Bathisma's help. Ambriel, why don't you go with Michael and see Mrs Crowley? Now, if you don't mind I also have some work to do so run along and we will re-convene later for a status report.' With reluctance, except for Bathisma of course, they each disappeared from Rucelle's office and soon only he was left and his trusted aide, Nazriel. Nazriel noted how Rucelle's shoulders slumped slightly as soon as everyone had left and walked around to the front of the desk. Rucelle raised his eyes and looked at the kind face of his loyal friend.

'You do not need to take all of this worry on yourself, Rucelle,' Nazriel started softly. 'We are all here to share the burden.' But Rucelle felt the burden was his. He felt that all this was his fault. Well, not all of it, but he felt that they should have been better prepared. After all, they knew it was coming. Nazriel could sense the torment that Rucelle was inflicting upon himself. They all could have done so much more, and the truth be told, Nazriel felt that things were not over yet.

'Will you come in with me?' asked Rucelle. Nazriel smiled and stepped away from the desk. He raised his arm toward the Carcerem and indicated that he would follow. Rucelle stood and slowly walked toward the Carcerem and once Nazriel was by his side they took a step forward together.

Within the step they had entered a room of white. Only this room had no walls or floor or a ceiling. Their feet moved forward as if walking on solid ground but there was no ground to see. The Carcerem was void of anything tangible and completely vague of what it contained. Its atmosphere was unmoving as if in a state of unconsciousness. To describe it as a room gave the impression of limits. Yet, the Carcerem had no limits. Its emptiness was interminable.

Nazriel nodded to Rucelle and they instinctively moved forward. Far ahead, they could see a figure. He looked quite still in a sitting position and as they advanced, the image became clearer. They could tell he was not sitting on anything that had a form and the position he was in was not of his own making. They stopped as soon as he smiled. Apart from talking, it was all he was capable of doing.

'Love what you've done with the place,' Christian chuckled as his eyes looked around the vacuum. 'Very…you.'

'I'm glad you like it. I would have hung some pictures on the walls but…well, there are none,' Rucelle finished sarcastically.

'And Nazriel, always a pleasure. Tell me have you two come to entertain me? After all, it seems you are now the new double act. I hope you are here to perform a magic show as from what I have seen so far, illusions are your speciality.'

'Oh, Christian, I would never be so bold as to even attempt to follow with a performance after Jack's spectacular theatrics. I hear he would have been a hit if he possessed any charm. Still, I'm sure your little protégé will have plenty of time to polish up his act in his new home. It's just such a shame that none of us will ever see it.'

'Your arrogance and naivety fill me with such joy, Rucelle.'

'Even in here, you still show no remorse.'

'You always assume incarceration will create remorse. But the essential ingredient for remorse is regret, which I do not have. While I am in here I really only have two options of feeling left to me. Regret or hope. And I choose hope.'

'Well, if you are hoping for a playmate or a magazine subscription I think you will find that you and hope will soon part ways.'

'Why are you here, Rucelle? What is it you want?'

'I want to know how you ever thought you could get

away with this? How on Earth did you not envisage that you would end up here? You were here during the creation of the last Carcerem. And yet, you followed the same path of ones before and never entertained the idea that it would lead to this.' The silence fell between them and Rucelle studied Christian's face. His eyes were downcast and without the addition of body language Rucelle was struggling to gauge Christian's reaction or even his thoughts. He gave a sideways glance at Nazriel who had not taken his eyes off Christian since they had entered the Carcerem.

'Nazriel, I think we are simply wasting our time here. Let's go.' Rucelle and Nazriel began to make their way when Christian interrupted.

'Well, you are certainly wasting Nazriel's, aren't you? I mean, why did you bring him?' Nazriel and Rucelle stopped, looked at each other and then looked at him. It was clear to both that Christian had something further to add. 'I mean, no offence Nazriel,' Christian gave a disconcerting smile, 'but it's not like you were here when they made the last Carcerem is it?' He smiled wider and looked directly at Rucelle then back to Nazriel. 'I only say this as you seem to be a wise man, a lot wiser than your friend here. You see, if you were here for the last one I am sure that you would remind your friend that he has not...' Christian turned his gaze to Rucelle and his eyes began to darken, '...abided by the laws of Heaven.' Rucelle could feel his anger rising. Was Christian suggesting that placing him in the Carcerem was unjust? Rucelle squatted down in front of Christian and as he got closer to his prisoner's face, his anger became more amplified.

'Nazriel might not have been here, but you were.' Rucelle's voice was almost a whisper. 'And any angel that walks the Earth for their own purposes IS breaking the laws of Heaven.' Rucelle threw Christian a last look and turned to catch up to Nazriel. They were soon leaving the Carcerem when they heard Christian shout.

'I think you'll find the law states that any angel who will not serve humanity is breaking the law.' Rucelle and Nazriel stopped and gave each other a sideways glance but did not turn. After a short moment, they continued to leave. 'Check it out, Nazriel,' a distant Christian could still be heard, 'when you next read a book and you are drinking tea from your dirty little mud cup.'

If Christian said any more after that, Rucelle and Nazriel did not hear him. They were now stood in the office. Both men were silent and Rucelle made his way to his usual position of being seated behind his desk. The worry on his face was clear and Nazriel felt there were no words, he simply stepped back and disappeared.

* * *

Michael and Ambriel lifted the huge brass knocker of De Mondford Hall and gave it a firm rap. They didn't wait long for the large door to open and reveal Jennifer and a small boy clinging to her legs. She held onto the door and half of her Laura Ashley clad body was hidden behind it as she peered around.

'I'm sorry to interrupt you, but are you Jennifer?' asked Michael. Jennifer looked confused and she quickly looked at the two men from feet to head. The dark-haired Michael in a black suit, shirt and tie seemed very different to his blond-haired friend who was dressed the same, only white.

'Yes.'

'We know your husband, Crowley.' In an instant, Jennifer knew who they were. She instantly felt relieved and hoped they had some news for her.

'Michael?' She turned and looked at Ambriel, 'Ambrose?'

Ambriel smiled, 'Yes, but it's Ambriel. We can explain if you wouldn't mind letting us in.' Her face brightened, and she opened the door wider, so they could step into the vast entrance hall.

'Come in, come in,' she said excitedly. She noted her voice was a little shrill and wasn't sure if she was excited because they were bringing good news, or if she was nervous because they may be bringing bad. After shutting the door, she stooped down to her son, Max. He was clutching a Spiderman figure in his fist and looked on suspiciously at his mum's new guests. 'Max,' she said, 'run upstairs and play. I won't be long. Mummy needs to talk to her friends for a bit. Then I'll be up, and we can make a den. How does that sound?' she tried to be encouraging.

'Okay, Mummy.' Then without another word, he ran upstairs and disappeared down a hallway. She shut the door and with a welcoming smile asked them to follow her into the kitchen.

'I've just made some tea. Please, come and join me.' She didn't wait for an answer. She quickened her step and walked in the direction of a large wooden door tucked into the corner of the huge hall. Ambriel and Michael took their time in following her as they craned their necks admiring the history oozing from surface. The large blue carpeted staircase dominated the room which split halfway to lead left or right to a particular wing of the larger house. The portraits of ancestors adorned the colourless walls and looked down on the angels as they glided through. A stain-glassed window at the top of the staircase flooded the hall with a welcoming glow that transformed the vast space into almost cosy.

As they entered the kitchen, Jennifer was popping the

lid on the tea pot. She looked up and smiled and the angels made their way to the large, battered, pine table. They both gave a little smile and gently scraped their chairs out across the polished stone floor. In silence, she made the tea and Michael noted that her hand gave a slight shake. The anxiety was clear on her face and Michael could tell she had been worrying about her husband for quite some time. He reached out for her hand.

'He's okay. He's safe,' he said softly. They both watched her with genuine concern as she sank into the chair that was behind her. The relief on her face made her instantly lose ten years and Michael noticed suddenly how much younger she looked than Crowley.

Michael, with help from Ambriel, relayed the story of Jack's arrival at Sean's show and how the portals were all closed and that they still were to human souls. They also revealed that they were angels and had been sent to Sean to protect him and Crowley and Sean had only just found out.

'Sorry, you're angels?' Jennifer was confused.

'Well, technically I'm an archangel. Ambriel is an angel.'

'Why were you sent to protect Sean? And why have you changed your name?' she looked at Ambriel.

'Rucelle didn't tell us everything so we only know what we have told you. All I can say is Sean Allister is a very special human being. It seems that Rucelle has been watching him for some time, but we were only sent for after the plane crash. As for my name change…well…' Ambriel struggled to answer and began to smile.

'He just fancied giving himself a whole new identity when we were sent to protect him,' Michael teased.

'So says the man who wore hair gel and a leather jacket,' Ambriel laughed but Jennifer didn't join in. She didn't care that these two men purged their need to play dress up, she still had questions.

'After the plane crash, Crowley was given a new role as a Guide after speaking to Sean on a training mission. The Protector didn't show up and my husband felt he had no choice but to show himself and Rucelle went mad. Is that why you two were sent then? Because Sean didn't have a Protector? And I'm sorry, but why in the hell does Sean Allister need protecting like this?' The men cast their gaze at their cups; they were not sure how much they could tell and judging from the silence from each other they both took this to mean that they had reached their limit in revelations. 'Did you know that my husband already knew Sean before he was appointed to him?' The men looked up at her. 'When Crowley first died he helped Sean's best friend, Grace. Sean doesn't know that; don't you think that's odd?'

'Why is that odd?' asked Michael.

'Of all the people in the world that Crowley could have been appointed to, he was sent to him. I didn't think you could do that for fear of humans putting two and two together. I mean Sean is now an international star, surely when he is on stage he says who he is talking to?' Ambriel thought for a moment and recalled a conversation that he had witnessed between Crowley and Sean. He told Jennifer that Sean wanted to give Crowley a name so his audience could relate more to him as opposed to "just listening to voices". But Crowley had argued that it would turn them into a double act and even though Crowley's presence was extraordinary, the gift belonged to Sean. They soon settled on simply being referred to as his guide so then at least people knew that it was only one person and he was male.

'So, I don't think Sean has ever revealed Crowley's

name not even to his friends. The only people who knew his name were us, the people who worked for him,' said Ambriel. Jennifer took a sip of her tea.

'So, when will my husband be able to come back?'

'It shouldn't be too long,' Michael tried to reassure Jennifer.

'And remember, he is still with Sean,' said Ambriel.

'I just hope he is okay, well…both of them, really.'

The three of them finished the pot of tea and speculated as to the effect that the angels and their recent act would have had on Earth. After Jennifer had heard the story of how Sean had handled it, she adopted a new level of admiration for him. She only hoped that others would dismiss it as a hoax or accept the new knowledge and simply continue with their lives. Both were a big ask.

After an invite of staying for supper, which was gratefully accepted and a tour of De Mondford Hall, the two angels made themselves comfortable as Jennifer's guests. They not only felt it was comforting to her, but they also knew that Crowley would be grateful that they had looked out for his wife. There was nothing for them to do anyway, until they received word that Rucelle was ready to see them.

* * *

Nazriel became in his study, standing by his desk. He had just left Rucelle and he was certain that Rucelle was harbouring the same thoughts and doubts that he was. Christian's words were still echoing in his head, "any angel who will not serve humanity".

The laws of the Carcerem were created long ago and the need to study it had never presented itself to Nazriel, until now. The Carcerem had only ever been created for one purpose, which it had since served. There were many people in Heaven who had since forgotten that there ever was one. A negative dimension within Heaven is not something angel or soul is comfortable with. However, until such times as the occupant or occupants were judged, the Carcerem was the only place that could hold and control an angel or soul.

Nazriel walked over to his shelves which were silently groaning under the weight of all the knowledge held within the books. But Nazriel knew what he wanted would not be found in his usual offerings. He stood perfectly still in front of the bookcase, closed his eyes and focused all his energy and desires on one thing. When it was clear in his mind he imagined his study as it was when he arrived, the only difference being that the shelves were all empty. It was a strange sight to see as they had always been furnished with a variety of books placed in no particular order and in no particular fashion. With his mind's eye, he placed the object he desired on the empty shelf and once satisfied it was in place, he opened his eyes.

The scroll looked lonely on the shelf but even in its isolation and blandness it was still imposing. Nazriel took a deep breath and reached for the rolled-up paper and carefully carried it to the couch opposite and sat down. He cautiously unfurled the paper as if touching it would disturb its contents. It was not a long document, it didn't need to be and as Nazriel read it the purpose of the Carcerem became clear. With a sigh, he gently placed the paper on the couch. Reading the scroll had only raised more questions.

* * *

After holding an assembly to various Division Heads,

Rucelle's weariness was now evident in all of his actions. The enormity of all that had come to be weighed heavily on him and for a fleeting moment he wished he was someone else. He had known that this day would happen but the way it would happen was a guess made by a few, including him and the thing that frustrated Rucelle the most was that he didn't know how it was supposed to end, he was too busy mopping up the after effects to focus on what they were aiming for. His mind was always centred, and his decisiveness had always been the motivation for others around him. This was the first time he didn't know what to do and what he did, he doubted.

He had become on a warm sandy beach and sat cross-legged with his eyes closed enjoying the sounds of the waves that fizzed in front of him. This was his place. This was his place he liked to come to when he needed to think. He sat for some time trying to focus his mind and when he finally began to relax a little he could hear his name being called. Someone was in his office. Rucelle stood and turned and could see Jude in the distance waiting for him. Jude was in his office and gave a little wave to Rucelle to confirm it was him calling. As Rucelle walked along the sand, the beach began to disappear, and the familiar floor of his office returned underfoot. Once he was at his desk, Rucelle gave a large arced wave of his arm and the beach disappeared from view and the office became complete.

'Jude,' Rucelle said as he sat in his chair. The tall black man, dressed in a casual white shirt and trousers to match, gave Rucelle a welcoming smile. His teeth were slightly crooked, but the delivery was as warm as his honey brown eyes.

'Hey, Rucelle. I got that report for you. You wanna get the others or you fine me doing this now?' Jude asked eagerly.

'The others have been called. They should be here in a moment,' Rucelle said slowly.

'You ok? Looking kinda peaky there.' Jude's smile slipped a little out of concern for Rucelle.

'You'd look peaky after what we have been through,' said the voice behind Jude. It was Anthony. There was no smile exchanged between them. Magda soon followed with Bathisma and lastly, Nazriel. Only Rucelle saw the change in Nazriel.

They all took a seat except for Jude who walked around to Rucelle's side of the desk. As he stood over him, he placed a report in front of Rucelle but turned the pages for him as he spoke. He summarised the report in his own unique casual delivery like it was no problem being asked to give the status on the human reaction to recent events.

'Okay guys, the word on the Earth street is more than half think it was a hoax,' he shrugged his shoulders with a smile to everyone and an air of *"that's fortunate"*, 'but the rest are a real mixed bunch. Some of them will fall into a transformation category at some point in the future, which can vary greatly from person to person.'

'A transformation category?' asked Nazriel. Jude turned and smiled to explain.

'Yeah, you know, those people who in future say "so" or "nothing changed", when in time they realise that what they think they know or don't know had no effect on the rest of their lives.' Nazriel nodded, remembering how fickle a human belief could be.

'But it's how influential the rest could be, that's the danger,' he said sombrely. Rucelle looked up at his colleague. 'Let's not be naïve about this crew. There could be a lot of influential people in here who can make these numbers grow substantially. There's a lot of evidence being thrown around through media coverage which is making some people listen. For these people, and those they can influence, there's no going back. They know we are here and they know we exist.'

'But do they?' argued Anthony. 'How do they know that this might not have been an elaborate show by some religious sect to try and make people be good and kind?' Anthony looked around the room for support, but all eyes stayed on Jude.

'Because I don't know of some "religious sect" that can disperse their essence on live TV. Do you?' Jude raised his eyebrows. His problems with Anthony went back as far as he could remember. While people initially prayed to Anthony for certain things they would eventually pray to Jude for him to answer. Anthony resented this and tried to make the point that Jude was only as good as a mop. Jude would wind Anthony up by saying at least he could deliver. Anthony didn't like Jude's casual style and Jude found Anthony too formal and hot-headed.

'Magda?' asked Rucelle.

'All the Protectors are back with their original souls except for those that do not have a body to be housed in. However, most of these souls have been appointed to a human that we feel has the level of mental strength to house another soul.'

'Until they start jumping off bridges,' muttered Jude. Magda shot him a withering look.

'We can only hope we have done our best with the only option we had. But no doubt you will be running in here with a report in the future, outlining how we all cocked up,' spat Magda.

'How you guys play chess down there and change people's lives ain't nothing to do with me. I just tell it how it is.' Jude put his knuckles on Rucelle's white desk and leaned forward on them to edge closer to his audience. 'But don't be thinking that six million angels can appear on Earth and not bother someone.'

'Are we talking hysteria here?' asked Rucelle. Jude stood up and tried to smile.

'There's a reaction, a big one. But truthfully?' Jude shrugged his shoulders and gave a little chuckle, 'I think I saw a bigger reaction when Elvis died.' Anthony shook his head in disbelief at the comparison. Rucelle looked around the room. He wasn't sure if Jude had given a good report or a bad one. Rucelle asked Jude to take a seat and thought for a moment.

'What about mapping?'

'The Birth Division have all caught up,' confirmed Anthony.

'Death?'

'I saw him earlier. He was not a happy angel knowing that he had sent souls to Heaven only to find out that a lot of them were sitting in limbo. But once I told him that he looked like he had lost weight he seemed happy enough,' said Magda.

'So, Death is sorted,' said Rucelle. 'Birth Division have caught up and limbo is now empty. So, all we need to do is open the portals, so the Guides can move around. As far as humankind goes all we can do is wait and see how this manifests. We may need to send some Guides to Earth that can be seen. Once they have integrated and pass for humans they can then spread a well-constructed message that gives doubt to recent events. What we say needs to be carefully thought out but now we have some time on our side we can be confident in our projection of impact.'

Nazriel stood up and looked a little reluctant to speak. He looked at his colleagues who seemed puzzled by his interruption. Nazriel pulled a rolled-up scroll from his sleeve and passed it to Rucelle.

'What's this?' he asked taking the scroll.

'It's the original document that was drawn up when the first Carcerem was created.' Rucelle began to unfurl the paper. They all sat in silence while Rucelle looked at it. The look on his face was hard to read. They could all tell that whatever it said was not good, but how bad, they could not be sure. Rucelle read the document and re-read it again to be sure that he was correct in his understanding. They waited for an age for Rucelle to speak and Magda could bear it no longer.

'Rucelle?' Rucelle looked up and stared at Nazriel for a moment. Nazriel did not flicker and only waited for Rucelle to speak.

'In short, the Carcerem cannot be used to house angels or souls indefinitely. It can only exist as a transitional dimension until judgement. However, the judgement that the Carcerem was built for was for those *"who will not serve humanity"*.' Magda began to look around at the others. She did not understand but for some reason could feel panic rising. She looked back at Rucelle and then at Nazriel with an imploring look.

'It can be argued that the angel rebellion *was* to serve humanity,' said Nazriel. They all sat digesting this information. Did that mean that Christian and all the others had to be released? Could all the angels go back?

'So,' started Rucelle, 'if the Carcerem can only be used for transition then we have to have a judgment made.' Nazriel nodded. 'We cannot just keep them all in there.'

'So, you're saying that we can't just keep these bandits in there because of a piece of grammar?' Jude asked incredulously. 'Because that piece of paper argues whether they served or didn't serve? Well, what about us? What about what we say? I mean, isn't our judgement good enough? Isn't the fact that they have had a profound effect on the belief system down there enough to say that they weren't serving humanity, that they were helping themselves?!'

'I hate to say it,' started Anthony, 'but I agree with Jude. Let's just make a judgement and send them where they need to go.'

'And where is that?!' shouted Rucelle. 'Because the last time we had anything like this we created a place like no other. And I'm not so sure that what Christian has done is anything like Lucifer's antics. But I'm not the one to judge and neither are you!'

'You need to speak to Mr Reeshon,' suggested Nazriel in a composed voice trying to calm the situation. Rucelle let out a huge sigh. Just when he thought things were starting to settle, then this. He agreed that he needed to speak to Mr Reeshon. His judgement was absolute, and no one could argue once concluded. They just needed this to be sorted quickly so they could try and bring some normality back to the people on Earth.

'You all wait here, this shouldn't take long.' Then Rucelle left. They all sat in silence for a while contemplating the latest revelations. Each in turn tried to imagine what the effect would be if Christian was allowed to go free. Had he and his followers actually broken any law? The veiled existence of angels surely was not maintained on an assumption? And could the intentions of the Carcerem be changed? Could it not hold an angel or soul forever? Even though six million were now housed in the Carcerem each of them felt they were alone. They never saw another spirit or interacted with anything other than the white light. And while some thought Hell the ultimate torture, there were some who thought existing forever in the void and limitless abyss of the Carcerem was far worse. And when Lucifer fell, was he evil? Or did Hell make him evil? Would sending Christian and his followers to a place of judgement make them regret? Did Lucifer regret? Would Mr Reeshon be prepared to make a judgement like this? Could he and should he be influenced? The lives and souls of many were to be considered, each of them with different needs, goals and reasons. None of them looked at each other. Each of them sat staring into space waiting for the judgement to be delivered by Rucelle.

After what seemed like an age, Rucelle finally became back in his office. All, except Magda, jumped to their feet. It was completely an involuntary action by them all. Rucelle looked at them one by one and then gestured for them to sit. Once they had, Rucelle took a large breath and began.

'The course of action that Mr Reeshon has suggested seems to be the only option available, if indeed it is an option.' He sounded defeated already. The option clearly was not what they were hoping for, to keep the Carcerem as it stood. 'As the law of initial incarceration is to isolate those who will not serve humanity, it seems that Christian has indeed, found a loop hole. While we know that to make humans aware of our existence during their life is forbidden,' he paused, the disappointment was unmistakable, 'it seems there is no law to uphold this.'

'What?!' whispered Jude.

'Yes,' Rucelle stuttered, 'we have nothing to enforce.'

'So, we have to let them go?' asked Nazriel.

'We can't do that!!' Anthony began to panic.

'Wait! Wait!' Rucelle gestured for them to calm down. 'Mr Reeshon and I feel that while Christian's actions might not have broken any written law he has certainly broken a code that we all live by. This is the only thing we can take advantage from.'

'So, he can stay in the slammer?' asked a hopeful Jude.

'For now.' There was a collective sigh of relief and for a moment they began to smile. Rucelle felt it necessary to push on. 'However, the Carcerem is still only a transitional dimension,' added Rucelle.

'Then we can kick Christian's ass and all his other mutineers to Hell or some other godforsaken place,' Jude suggested, still smiling. They all nodded in agreement but also noted that Rucelle didn't.

'He has to be judged. We have to listen to his case and reasons in the Curia. A case has to be brought forward before Mr Reeshon and only then will he decide if what Christian has done was against serving humanity.'

'Can't Mr Reeshon write down a law that says you can't just start popping up like zits on a 15-year-old and get away with it? We all thought that this was the law anyway, so what difference does it make?' said Jude.

'The difference is there was no written law that states what he did was wrong, and you cannot judge anyone on a law that some will say doesn't technically exist.' Rucelle could not hide his frustration.

'So, let's put a case together and get this done. Between all of us we can get this sorry excuse for an angel out of our hair for good. Right?' Jude looked around looking for support. Even Anthony looked encouraged and looked at Rucelle for a reassuring smile, but it didn't come. Rucelle began to pace his office from one end to the other. All the while, he looked at his feet and if there was a stone to kick to distract him he would have been grateful for it. Anthony looked at Jude who began to look more confused. What was the problem? Rucelle stopped and looked at them all and knew what he was about to say would banish any idea of pushing a hearing with Mr Reeshon in the Curia.

'Christian's debatable sin is against mankind. And only

someone who has been part of mankind can argue for them in the Curia.' They all sat for a moment trying to understand what Rucelle had just said.

'So, are you saying that as angels we cannot argue for humanity? Only a human soul can do this?' asked Magda. Rucelle nodded. Nazriel stepped forward. While he knew his suggestion might not be popular, he felt there was no other choice.

'Crowley?' asked Nazriel.

'I asked. Mr Reeshon said no.'

'But I'm sure with our guidance…'

'And plenty of coffee,' mumbled Magda out of the side of her mouth. Nazriel shot her a disappointing look.

'I'm sure with our guidance,' he continued, 'he could rise to the challenge.'

'For once, Nazriel, I do actually agree with you. For all his faults, Crowley has demonstrated a natural want to bring harmony and love to people's lives. But Mr Reeshon has made it quite clear,' he paused, knowing he was about to crush all hope from his faithful servants, 'that only a person who has sacrificed their own life for the sake of all humanity, can speak for all of humanity.'

They all sat stunned. It was hopeless. It was over.

CHAPTER 18

Crowley sat for a moment and stared at Sean. He mulled over the fact that if indeed, he never came back as Sean had asked, what would the consequences be? Well, Sean's career would be over for a start. Did Sean think of that? Would Sean even be bothered? He suspected in the long-term Sean may come to regret that decision. Maybe financially, certainly emotionally. While Sue craved the thousands in the halls, Sean was happy with the one that he could help.

How did he, himself, feel about never seeing Sean again? It was not something he had ever contemplated or envisaged. He had always thought their journey would continue until the day Sean would be in Heaven as well. Maybe, as Sean got older and the performances stopped, the reasons for visiting Sean would change but he had never considered the fact that he would never see Sean in his retirement years. He had always expected Sean to be a huge part of his existence.

Crowley wondered if Sean had the strength to deal with all the aftermath of the last few hours. At a time like this, he suspected that the world would turn to psychics, mediums and anyone else who felt they could offer answers, whether fake or genuine. But someone of Sean's reputation would certainly be hounded. And not just by those in the media but by Joe Public himself. People would want to hear what he had to say even when they were not sure what they believed in. And now that they felt they had some proof it was not unrealistic to think he may be persecuted.

He watched Sean open the second bottle, completely unaware he was being studied.

'And what, may I ask, do you plan to do with the rest of your life?' asked Crowley.

'I'll go back to Bill's. He'll have me back in a flash. Or I might go to New York. I've got friends there,' Sean sniffed. Crowley thought of Grace and wondered if he should tell Sean of their past. Within a moment he dismissed it. It served no purpose and would make no difference.

'Oh yes, I'm sure you could go back to pushing invoices in a haulage firm and pretend none of this ever happened. You honestly think that you can go back to your old life after the career you have just had?'

'Why not, it worked for Curly Watts,' Sean said sarcastically. He looked at Crowley waiting for him to acknowledge the fact then realised he had no idea who he was talking about.

'You know, the fella from Coronation Street, married Racquel,' Crowley still looked blank. 'Ended up in Freshco's?' he pushed.

'Racquel?' asked Crowley.

'The barmaid from the Rovers Return. The pub in the show. Ken Barlow gave her French lessons.' Crowley was still baffled. 'Jesus, Crowley, did you watch anything that wasn't on the History channel?'

Crowley didn't think it would help his argument to add that he had spent a number of years homeless before his death and television was not something he felt he needed in Heaven. However, he didn't want Sean thinking he was quite as stiff as he believed.

'I'll have you know my taste in television was rather eclectic. I was very fond of Hart to Hart as I recall, neither historical or highbrow!'

'You only watched that because you like redheads so don't kid me...you like a bit of action,' Sean retorted.

Crowley could not argue. The reason for him tuning in week after week was indeed to leer at Stefanie Powers.

'Well, never mind about my taste in television programming. I do not believe for one minute that you will go back to Bill's or to America and be able to lead the life you once had.' Sean drank the contents of his cup before pouring himself another one. He leaned over and topped up Crowley's too. He knew Crowley was making a valid point and trying to go back to any normal life after recent events would be hard. But it wasn't impossible, was it? Maybe, going back to Bill's would be a bit of a stretch but he had a fair amount of money in the bank and that gave him options.

'I could travel for a while, lose myself for a bit and figure out what I want to do next and while I'm travelling all of "this" will have died down. People will forget about tonight and who I was.' Crowley sat wide-eyed for a moment. As much as he loved Sean, he was still dumbfounded by his naivety sometimes. He could feel a slight shake in his hand and knew it was about to become worse, so he put his cup on the table.

'Sean, I truly despair with your ignorance and sheer

inability to comprehend situations that could and should have an effect on your being! I cannot believe that you have no idea or understanding of what happened here tonight!' Crowley stood up, if only to alleviate his raging energy. 'All across the world are hundreds of thousands of people that need answers. They may not be the right ones,' he stopped and glared at Sean who could not bring himself to look at Crowley, 'but any answer may pacify them than none. And who else will they listen to? I'm not saying that you are the one to put the world straight, but you certainly are someone who can help a few. And you want to go off travelling? For thousands of years, man has wondered if celestial beings truly existed. They've now been told, inaccurately I might add, that the whole point of living is to be used as a pawn for an angel's amusement! And you?! You don't, for one tiny second feel that someone who has been protected for months by an angel and an archangel, has a duty to understand? To ask why? For someone whom I have admired for their ability to empathise and understand the human soul, you shock me to the core to not think, in some way, you are not part of this!'

A shocked Sean raised his eyes to see Crowley on the point of hyper ventilating. He had seen Crowley angry, on a frequent basis, when Sue was around but never like this. As he looked into Crowley's eyes he immediately felt shame but as he allowed the shame to wash over him the fear in him rose again. It wasn't ignorance that made him want to run, it was sheer terror. Just as he was about to ask Crowley to sit down, the door opened and there stood the Hall's General Manager.

'I'm sorry Mr Allister, but we need to lock up now. I think you are the only one left in the building as everyone wanted to go home early, so I am going to have to ask you to leave. You can collect your things tomorrow if you wish.' The man walked into the room and Sean knew he wasn't going to leave without him. As he put his cup on the table, Crowley gave Sean one last look, buttoned up his jacket, smoothed himself down and marched out of the room. Sean's eyes followed him, and the manager looked in the direction of the door to see what Sean was looking at. There was nothing there and the manager began to feel a little uncomfortable.

'Will your driver be outside, Mr Allister?' The man tried to be bright in his attempt to chivvy him along.

Sean slowly stood and walked over to the hanging rail opposite. He pulled his coat from the hanger that Ambriel had hung it on earlier and gave a gentle smile. He turned back to the manager and said softly, 'I think I'll walk tonight, mate.' Before Sean reached the door, the manager felt compelled to speak.

'Do you think what happened tonight…well…you know…was real?' Sean looked at him and could see his eyes were full of questions, but this would be the question, that not only him, but probably everyone needed to know first.

'I dunno, mate,' whispered Sean.

'Well, if people like you don't know, then who does?' he questioned. Without a goodbye, Sean turned on his heel, hung his head and slowly walked in the direction of the exit. And as he reached the main doors that led to the busy main road, he didn't notice Crowley disappearing.

Crowley became at home. He found himself stood with his back to the fireplace which was emitting a small amount of heat from a pile of dying embers. He concluded that Jennifer was in the house somewhere but just hadn't been in this room for a while. He knew exactly where she would be.

She was sat, facing the door, at the large pine table stroking the sides of a steaming mug and even though he only caught it for a second, he knew her mood was melancholic. He could tell that she had been worrying for some time. The sound of the door made her jump with a start and for a moment she sat staring at the familiar face trying to process if he was really there. The twinkle in the true blue of his eyes gave her the jolt that pushed her to her feet and made her run into his outstretched arms. She buried her head into his chest and wrapped her arms around him. She could feel his kiss on top of her head and as he rested his chin there she heard him emit the longest sigh. Only for the necessity of an explanation, they would have stayed like that for the rest of the day. Jennifer pulled her head away from his chest and craned to look at him without loosening her grip around his waist. He looked down at her and gently smiled.

'Tea or something stronger?' she chuckled.

'Tea's fine.' He was still feeling the effects of the brandy that he had shared with Sean.

She poured the tea in silence as he sat. After his first soothing mouthful, he proceeded to tell her everything that had happened while he had been with Sean and she listened intently trying to make sense of events, past and present. He continued up to the point of leaving the venue and feeling a surge within him. It was then he knew that he could leave and return to Heaven and there was nowhere else he wanted to be than with her.

Jennifer told him of how all the Directors of Division had been sent into a tailspin with the events and how all the souls could physically feel the moving of the angels en masse.

'Michael and Ambriel?'

She looked at Crowley with a look of amused confusion. 'Well, they came to see me not long after they got back.'

'Ah yes, Starsky and Hutch! I really cannot make head nor tail of that. Do you know that they could see me and hear me the whole time? Well, of course they could, they are angels but how I did not notice is incredible.'

'You wouldn't notice your pants were around your ankles if you had a bottle of red in your belly or your hand!' she teased. He shrugged and smiled with an air of defeat at her accurate prediction.

'They kept talking of a plan,' said Crowley.

'I know, they were hinting at that here.' They sat mulling over the facts again. Crowley could see Jennifer's mind whirring.

'What do you know about Sean? I mean his family or his friends or his life? What is it about him?'

'Sean is the epitome of extraordinariness and ordinariness all in one person if that makes sense.' Jennifer looked for more. 'When you see him on stage and how he connects with people he is a spectacle to watch. He has the ability to make you want to protect him and yet, you are not sure why. When you are in his company, there's something that makes you feel comforted, I cannot explain it. But, on the other side, he is the most ordinary man you could ever meet. He grew up with his mum, his dad left when he was a baby, and then she married when Sean was in his late teens. He moved away from home as his sexuality was the talk of the very small town he grew up in. He went to work in an office, the same one where Grace worked, and that's it.'

'He has no strange habits or beliefs or anything?' she probed.

'Well, apart from his psychic abilities, he smokes twenty

a day, likes a wine and his wee is probably orange due to fake tan ingestion,' he smirked. Jennifer shook her head then raised her mug to drink her tea.

'There's something else, there has to be!' Jennifer stood and walked over to the kettle to refill, her mind still racing. 'I wonder if they knew that Jack was going to that place at some point and this isn't about Sean, that this is about Jack. I mean, he just came up to you in a bar, didn't he? What if this is about him? What if Michael and Ambriel just used Sean to make sure they were in the right place at the right time?'

'Plausible, I guess.' Crowley frowned as he tried to recall the last few months and would that conclusion fit.

'But Ambriel said that Sean "was a very special human being". Isn't Ambriel the poster boy for truth and communication?' asked Jennifer.

'So, he cannot be lying about Sean then. But, that could also mean that he was special, as they knew that Jack would appear at one of Sean's shows. You should have seen Jack up there Jen, he paraded around that stage like he was bloody Gordon Gekko from Wall Street. For a moment, I lost all hope until Sean went back on stage.' Crowley mused for a moment. 'He has such a presence, one could feel quite envious.' He looked at Jennifer who sat back at the table. 'But then I remind myself of his inability to create a five-letter word in Scrabble and quickly feel grateful for my extensive vocabulary,' he laughed. She gave a little giggle and squeezed her husband's hand.

'We're not very good at this investigating malarkey, are we?' she shrugged.

Crowley's voice became low with the reluctance to leave. 'I have to go and see Rucelle. Maybe he will have some answers.'

'What? Now?!'

'I'll be back, don't worry. They need answers as much as I do. Plus, Sean has said he doesn't want to see me again and I'm not sure how that works. The longer I leave it, the more damage I may be inflicting without realising it.' Jennifer's heart sank; she had just got him back. Crowley could see the disappointment washing over her face, but he had to go. He stood, and as she did the same, he caught her by her shoulders and pulled her back to his chest. 'I'll be back soon, Miss Marple.' He bent his head and gave her a kiss, stepped back and then disappeared.

Crowley was stood in front of Rucelle's office door. Before he knocked, he wondered what he should say. Where should he start? He hoped Michael and Ambriel had told him most of it and he only had to speak of the moments when he and Sean were alone. He began to feel like an intruder, and somehow, he had been caught in all of the crossfire. He knew that it was a silly idea to think that Rucelle would ever give him information. He was here to simply report on what had happened and to receive instruction on what was to happen next. Hopefully, it would be over fairly quickly. He was just about to raise his hand to knock when the door opened, and a smiling black man greeted him.

'Here he is,' said Jude. Crowley could see beyond the man's shoulder into Rucelle's office. He could see Rucelle, FBI agent Bathisma, Magda, Nazriel and a couple of other angels who he did not recognise including the warm, friendly angel who had opened the door. Jude patted Crowley on the back and indicated for him to step into the office. Crowley smiled and tentatively walked forward and when he reached the black angel's side he stopped when he noticed the angel's hand being offered.

'I'm Jude. I hear the desperate,' he said softly and winked at Crowley. The angel had obviously heard his thoughts when he was outside the door. He took Jude's hand, gave it a grateful shake and only stopped when a tall, good looking man with greying hair moved forward, also offering his hand.

'I'm Anthony,' he smiled. Crowley shook Anthony's hand and switched his gaze from him to Jude.

'I'm very pleased to meet you both.' He then slowly looked at all the angels in the room and finally rested his gaze upon Rucelle. Crowley could see a change in the angel. Rucelle always had an air of superiority and a presence of authority about him. This Rucelle looked very different; this Rucelle looked tired and vulnerable and in a strange way, hopeful. Nazriel stepped forward, his face was warm and welcoming and Crowley was grateful for his advance.

'Nazriel,' Crowley whispered as the angel stepped forward and hugged his friend. Crowley felt the friendly pat on his back before he was released from the warm embrace. As Nazriel stepped away slightly he turned and indicated to an empty chair to the side of Rucelle's desk. It was in front of where Nazriel was originally standing and Crowley was sure that it was not there when he first walked in. Picking up on Nazriel's hint, he walked over to the chair and once satisfied that it was okay, he hesitantly sat down.

'I feel we have some explaining to do,' offered Rucelle.

CHAPTER 19

He stood in the street, not sure what direction to take. He briefly considered heading back to the hotel, but he was sure that Sue would give him no peace. Without a purpose for standing on the spot he began to feel exposed, so turned to his right and began to walk down the busy street. There were a few people heading to where they needed to be, and the traffic was still steady, but Sean could tell it was not as congested as normal for this time of night. Usually, walking through this part of town at this time of night could only be achieved with patience and a sense of rhythm. Being out of step with your immediate population as you walked along the pavements could result in someone breathing heavily down your neck or feeling you were being piggy-backed by the person in front of you. It was quiet, nothing like the conga line that was normally shuffling through.

Sean turned the collar up on his blazer and tried to hunch down in it as much as he could. His fists were stuffed tightly into his trouser pockets and he walked poker stiff straight to his unknown destination. It wasn't a particularly cold night, but Sean was freezing. The effects of the brandy were clouding his head even though he didn't feel drunk. After walking for half an hour, he cast his gaze up to get his bearings. The street was quiet and yet familiar. There was not a soul to be seen but Sean could see in the distance a building that stirred a recent memory. He headed toward it and once he reached it, he could tell the old church of St Bart's was closed. His disappointment was tinged with a sense of desperation. He didn't know London that well and had no idea where to head next.

His thoughts were interrupted by a peal of laughter and as Sean turned, he saw the pub over the road. Two men were leaving and heading back in the direction from where Sean had come from. They didn't notice him and why should they, he thought. Sean directed his attention back to the pub and the shafts of orange light from its Georgian leaded windows bathed the dark pavement. He hesitated in succumbing to the inviting glow as he already had had enough to drink but as he looked to his left and right and saw only bleakness he found himself walking toward the large wooden door of the Rising Sun pub.

As he walked through the door his nostrils filled with the smells of ale, aged wood and a hint of bleach. The floor was wooden and as solid as the panelling that dominated the walls, bar and partitioning of various areas of the public house. The deep yellowing ochre walls and ceiling gave it a sense that it was confident in inviting you in and helping you to relax. There were not many people in the pub and only a few had given him a brief curious glance as he walked toward the bar. A young woman offered her services and she shouted her goodbyes to a regular as she placed the diet cola in front of Sean. He smiled in appreciation, silently paid her, walked to the far end of the room and slightly out of sight from others he took a seat on one of the two low stools at a small round table.

He sat for a moment collecting his thoughts but mainly thought of Crowley. Where had he gone? He wondered if had been allowed back in Heaven or if he was walking the streets. Was he waiting in the hotel for him? He had regretted some of the things he had said already. He thought of Ambriel and had there been any sign of who he truly was. He thought of Michael and could feel his cheeks prickle with a blush as he recalled some of his daydreaming that involved the archangel. He gently closed his eyes as he hoped that Michael did not have the ability to read his mind during these last few months.

He pulled out his mobile phone to distract himself, but it was to see if anyone was wondering where he was. His home screen was littered with notifications from various news sources about the developments of the angels appearing and then disappearing. He raised his eyes to see if the few people that were in the pub were talking of the events. A couple in a far corner looked like they had no idea what was happening outside of their obvious love bubble and a small group of men that he had passed when he walked in, were too far away for him to hear. He turned his attention back to his phone and as he started to read some of the news items he noticed a man was heading in his direction. Sean carried on looking at his phone trying not to catch anyone's eye when suddenly the man took a seat on the remaining low stool in front of Sean. Sean hesitantly raised his eyes, still gripping the phone. The face was kind, smiling and familiar.

'Hello, Sean,' he said. Sean nervously smiled to one side of his face. He remembered him.

'Hello, Father O'Carroll,' he smiled. The priest beamed at being recognised.

'I'll have that pint you promised me, if you don't mind?'

Sean was taken aback and recalled the last conversation they had had in the chapel. Sean had indeed agreed to buy him a pint on their next meeting. He wanted to protest but wasn't sure if it would sit well with his conscience with the company being a priest and especially after today's events.

Sean obediently walked to the bar, requested the Guinness, walked back and placed it in front of the Irish man. The man smiled at the contents then raised his pint expectantly. Sean picked up his cola and they silently tapped their glasses together. They each took a sip and as Sean lowered his glass back to the table, his gaze followed it. The priest however, continued to observe Sean and noted his sense of awkwardness.

'So, how've you been sleeping?' Sean looked up slightly confused.

'You know, the dreams and that?' the priest asked. Sean remembered confiding in him about his strange dream in the chapel only a few days before.

'There are much stranger things happening in the day than at the night now,' Sean muttered.

'I take it you heard about all these people claiming to be angels,' the priest scoffed. Sean snapped his stare back to his drinking companion.

'Claiming? So, you don't believe it then?' he said defensively. Father O'Carroll calmly picked up his glass and took a slow and deliberate drink of the black contents. He lowered the glass and gently licked the creamy evidence still left on his lips as he leant forward to rest his forearms on the table. He was stroking the side of the glass completely aware that Sean was waiting for his response.

'I seen as much as anybody. People popping up and then disappearing in various places going on about how we are all here dancing a jig with only angels hearing the music. But I'm not so sure,' he shrugged. Sean stayed silent and raised an eyebrow at his naivety. 'Oh, I believe that what happened tonight is one of the strangest things that I and many others have witnessed, but I'm not so sure I believe that my whole life has been for their entertainment,' he raised his hand casually toward Heaven.

'But how much more evidence do you need? You saw them! There's hundreds of videos of them being uploaded every minute,' Sean waved his phone.

'I know.'

'So, do you think they just came down here, fed us a load of lies and now they are back in Heaven having a laugh as they watch us?' Sean folded his arms ready for a debate.

'I doubt it's like a scene from Jason and the Argonauts,' the priest chuckled. 'But I'm pretty damn sure that God didn't create all of this simply for theatrical purposes. If he did, then why give us a sense of achievement, a sense of wanting, a sense of simply being different from anyone else? If we were put here simply to amuse a higher being, then of all the people that have walked this Earth, why hasn't one person become aware of it? Why hasn't one person had a sense of it? Why hasn't just one person even had a notion of it?'

'Well, maybe no one has been close enough to God to know what all this means!'

'Including Jesus?' Sean sat, slightly stunned into silence. He could not argue his point further. He wasn't sure now what the point was he was trying to make. He dropped his arms and shoved his phone into his blazer pocket and picked up his cola to finish.

'Look, I just came in here for a bit of peace and quiet. Not to debate about God, Jesus and angels and stuff.' Sean took a sip of the cola then put the half-filled glass back on the table. He got to his feet and was about to say goodbye when he was interrupted.

'Well, you can't go yet,' Father O'Carroll smiled. Sean looked down on him quizzically. 'The first pint was for the chat in the church, but you still owe me a pint from your promise.' The man lifted his glass, opened his mouth and throat wide and poured the rest of his pint within. With a satisfying smack of the lips he pushed the empty glass toward Sean. 'I'll have another in there, thanks.'

Sean stood for a moment. Was this man taking the piss? He had only come in for a soft drink and was now watering the local priest. He wanted to protest at the promise was for one pint not two, but again the guilt or even sheer kindness came to the fore and moved his feet back to the bar with the expectant empty glass. By the time he walked back, Sean had decided not to join the eager recipient in watching him consume it. Father O'Carroll noted Sean's impending departure.

'Please, Sean, sit down. We are simply having a healthy debate and an enjoyable one I might add, compared to some once they have spied the old dog collar here,' he pointed to this throat. 'Please,' he waved his hand toward Sean's empty chair. Sean walked back around the small table, realising he didn't want to go back to the hotel and resisted the urge to say that he was not buying him any more Guinness, especially at London prices. The silence fell between them for a little while and for a moment Sean forgot that he had someone in his company. His mind was still racing through not only this evening but various points of his whole life. He started to come around to the priest's idea that they were not there for the entertainment of others, as Sean had concluded that apart from the last year, his life had been pretty unremarkable.

'Do you have family, Sean?' the priest asked.

'I do, though not many. My mum and stepdad live in a little place called Clune and I've got an aunty and some cousins but that's about it. I class my friends as family to be honest with you. Not that there's many of them but the ones I have are dear to me.

'You say, your stepdad. Where's real dad?' Sean sniffed and swallowed as he continued.

'The "lovely" Chris left my mum when I was tiny and ran off to Scotland the last she heard. Never sent a penny or a card. She once told me that she was relieved with each Christmas and birthday he didn't appear. I think she admitted it because she felt guilty and wanted me to forgive her for feeling like that.'

'And did you?'

'If you knew my mum and saw the way she loved me, and fought for me, and the sacrifices she made for me, then you would know that I never felt she needed forgiving.'

'Forgiveness isn't always about the act of absolution. It can simply be found in pure acceptance of something that you or others have no power to change.' He took a sip from his pint. 'Did you ever look for him?'

'I thought about it and then realised that what I wanted didn't exist. The dad in my dreams was not the man that walked out on my mum. The one that left us was a selfish bastard, so why would I want to find that and welcome it into my life? I have met and discarded enough bastards to fill that church over the road. So, just because I am biologically related to one doesn't give me enough of a reason to break Mum's heart.'

'Hear, hear!' Sean was surprised by his friend's reaction. He thought he would get a further definition on the word forgiveness at the very least.

'But you are right though,' continued Sean, 'something is only worthwhile if you have the power to change it. If you don't, then why waste your energy on it. You just have to accept it, live with it if you have to, and then move on.'

'But, if the angels, or whatever they are, are to be believed then did we ever have the power to change anything in the first place?' asked Father O'Carroll.

'Christ knows. I find it hard to believe that some of the crazy decisions I have made were actually made by an angel who was as stupid as me!'

'And there lies my argument! If we are here for no other purpose, then why do we have a sense of regret?' They both sat for a moment, consumed with thoughts of past regrets and silently both concluded that deep in their hearts the decision was firmly down to their own sense of judgement.

Sean was aware there was only a mouthful of cola left in his glass and knew that he should make a move. Periodically, he could hear the faint buzzing from his vibrating phone and knew that he needed to check in with someone soon. He picked up his glass, drained the contents and smiled at his friend.

'I'm gonna have to go,' he said slightly reluctantly. 'No one knows where I am, and they will start to worry. Listen, sorry if I seemed a bit short earlier,' said Sean.

'Ah Jeez, stop your worrying. I enjoyed it. I'll no doubt see you again?'

'I doubt it. I was only here to do a bit of 'erm…temp work. It's finished now, so I'll be heading back home tomorrow.' Father O'Carroll took a firm grip of Sean's hand and clasped his other around it.

'I think we can both agree that the events of the last few hours have taught us that we are part of bigger plan and our part in that is yet to be revealed. The only difference from today than yesterday is we know where the answers are and what difference we alone made.' The man's handshake felt strange and Sean felt a little uneasy with the parting words and the priest's final look. Sean simply smiled, pulled his grip away and walked toward the exiting door.

'I hope that Guinness was all right, love,' shouted the barmaid. 'The pipes on the barrel were playing up before and I wasn't sure it was pouring properly.'

'Oh, it wasn't for me it was for my friend. He looked like he enjoyed it anyway,' he shrugged.

The barmaid looked over at Sean's empty table and looked confused as Sean waved in its direction and walked out.

CHAPTER 20

'How are things back on Earth?' asked Rucelle.

Crowley could see that Rucelle was trying to look calm, but his eyes told a different story. They reminded him of a homeless man he once knew when he lived on the streets. The man, named Wally, never seemed to sleep. He would curl himself up in his favourite doorway of an old bank and even though he looked comfortable his eyes would be darting with every sound and move of the night. Crowley had put it down to his nerves at being so vulnerable. Either that, or it was the copious amounts of Listerine he consumed.

'I left before I could evaluate the aftermath of it all,' admitted Crowley.

'You left?' Rucelle raised an eyebrow.

'I was asked to, by Sean.'

'So, you just left?' Crowley started to feel a little guilty about leaving, but then as he processed his thoughts he came to the same conclusion.

'What was I supposed to do? The boy asked me to leave. It's not like I could go back to my apartment in the city and pop the telly on with News at Ten and a microwaveable meal. Where am I supposed to go? I felt that I could leave and did. I have a wife and a son, and I knew that they would be worried.' Crowley looked around the room and felt he was being judged. 'Forgive me, but I was not aware I was sent to be Sean's babysitter. In fact, I am starting to question what was the point of me being there at all?'

Rucelle moved forward in his chair. 'I beg your pardon?'

'I know there is more to this than meets the eye! Why did you send me to someone who I already had a loose connection with? Was me being sent to Grace the start of all of this?' Crowley knew he sounded accusatory.

Magda slowly crossed her legs. 'You chose Grace, Crowley. You were not *sent* to her,' her tone was flat and cold. His mind cast back to his first encounter with Magda not long after he had died. She had asked him to pick someone that he could have a positive effect on by performing an unknown task. He had picked Grace, a stranger, at random because she was the last person who had spoken to him when he was alive. Grace happened to be Sean's best friend.

'But did I choose Grace? Or was this part of all the puppetry that Jack wants us to believe? And by choosing Grace was I ultimately choosing Sean? But why Sean, I ask? I mean what does someone like me have in common with a man who thinks a good day is downing a bottle of vodka, dancing to Madonna and having a pizza delivered in under twenty minutes?' he snapped. Nazriel caught everyone's attention as he walked towards Crowley. He stood in front of his seated friend and crossed his hands behind his back.

'If that is how you see Sean, then we, and I include Sean when I say we, have no further requirement of you. Once this is all over we can reassign you to another division where your reasons for being are far clearer.'

Crowley looked up at the deep brown eyes. He could not see any warm emotion behind them and immediately felt alone. No one in this room was on his side. He might as well get transferred to another Division and put all this involvement behind him. He took a deep breath and stood up and after a brief moment of looking at Nazriel, he turned his attention to the door and made his way toward it.

The room was silent, no one said a word. He reached for the smooth glass door knob and just as he was about to turn it he felt overwhelmed. He couldn't tell if it was past guilt or future regret. Or was it simply Sean? He thought of Grace and how she had given him a reason to carry on, even though they didn't know what they were trying to achieve. Was this so different? Why did the goal always have to be in sight to give one a sense of direction? Surely the path of life was all about the journey of constantly solving, discovering and ultimately learning. He knew that they knew more, certainly Rucelle knew more than he was willing to reveal. Maybe, he should at least allow them the courtesy of divulging a heavily edited tale. With his hand still wrapped around the door knob he turned to face Nazriel who was stood in front of Rucelle's desk.

'For some reason, I can't leave. When a gut as large as mine is telling me to stay, it's kind of hard to ignore,' he smiled meekly.

'You see, my friend, you have always had a choice. Always!' Nazriel emphasised. The point was not lost on Crowley. He knew he could leave if he wanted to and no one would persuade him to stay. The fact that he chose to stay gave him hope that Jack's devastating revelations were not entirely grounded. Nazriel smiled and walked back to his original spot against the wall and while everyone silently watched Crowley return to his seat.

'And just for the record, that is not how I see Sean.' Rucelle turned slightly in his chair to Bathisma.

'Bathisma, could you please fetch Crowley a whisky?' Bathisma spun around and a faint clink of cut crystal could be heard.

'What would you like in your whisky? Ice?' Bathisma asked over his shoulder.

'Don't be absurd,' as Crowley recoiled in horror.

'Then what would you like in your whisky?'

'More whisky,' joked Crowley. No one laughed but he did catch Nazriel pressing his lips together and his eyes were dancing. Bathisma placed the large whisky on Rucelle's desk, who then gently pushed it across for Crowley to reach. He stared at the glass and as he stretched to claim it he said, 'I have only ever been given a whisky twice in my life without having to ask for it. The first, was when I was told my father was dead and the second, was the day I lost De Mondford Hall,' he took a large sip. 'Tea is usually served with the deliverance of bad news in Britain,' he looked around the room. 'I think I managed a whole pot on the day when I heard John Wayne had died.'

'Would you prefer tea?' asked Bathisma.

'No, I prefer whisky,' he laughed. But no one laughed at the joke. They were clearly waiting for him to stop talking. He composed himself and cupped the whisky in his two hands and rested the glass on his lap. He looked at Rucelle expectantly and waited for him to start.

'I will not lie to you Crowley, but I will admit that I cannot disclose all that I know. And trust me when I say that there are people in this room who are in the dark with some details as much as you. I will omit some detail simply for you and Sean's protection. Now, I know your general characterisation of Sean hides the fact that you truly care for the boy; that is not lost on any of us. So please believe me when I say that anything we ask of you or Sean is only for good. You may not see or believe it at the time, but I really need you to trust me. We cannot resolve any of this diabolic situation that the human world and our world finds itself in if I am to be questioned and interrogated at every turn.' Rucelle leaned forward on his forearms that were resting on his desk. He lowered his head to lock Crowley's gaze. 'Do I make myself clear?'

Even though Crowley felt he had the right to know everything when it came to Sean he felt he had no choice but to accept the terms offered. While Rucelle was understood to be cold and unemotional, Crowley knew he was a man of his word and that was enough for Crowley at this point. And as he nodded in agreement he could visibly see Rucelle relax a little as he reclined back into his chair.

'We have always known this day would come. Well, when I say 'always' I mean for the last thirty years when this was planned. We performed some cautionary tasks at the time when we discovered there was a plan or rebellion of some sort, but we did not have the power to change the event itself.'

'If you knew this was going to happen then why not banish the people who were planning it?' asked Crowley.

'You have been aware for long enough to know that there are things we cannot change once they are written. We can influence, manipulate and in some cases, persuade a change of path but the eventual point will always come to be.' Crowley remained silent. 'I will admit that you were sent to Sean on purpose,' Crowley drew breath to interrupt but Rucelle continued. 'We scoured the Earth for a long time to find a suitable person to guide Sean and I do not mind confessing that I had begun to lose hope. Some of us…' Rucelle cast a glance toward Magda, 'are still yet to be convinced that you are that person, and that I made the right choice. But trust me when I say, that I wholeheartedly believe that I was right in choosing you.'

'I take it Bob Geldof and Bono were on the list?' teased Crowley. Again, no one laughed.

'What you will learn and what we ask of you will not be easy to comprehend but you must trust me and even if there is any doubt of my actions you surely must know that Nazriel would not allow anything that he felt was not necessary.' Crowley looked over at Nazriel who gave a respectful bow of his head.

'How did you hear of this plan?' asked Crowley.

'Bathisma?' asked Rucelle. Bathisma stepped forward, still clasping his hands in front of him.

'Christian was once my friend,' his voice seemed to echo shame. He stepped back to his original spot and looked at the floor. Crowley looked around the room to see if anyone else was intrigued by this cryptic clue. All the faces remained the same and he concluded he was the only one who didn't know who Christian was.

'This feels like a sub-standard celestial version of Jeopardy. Okay, I'll play. I'll take "who the hell is Christian" for fifty points.'

'Christian is the brains behind all of this,' Rucelle started.

'I thought it was Jack!'

Rucelle gave a gentle, sarcastic laugh. 'Jack is a mere soldier in all of this, doing his master's bidding. I'll admit he did a fine job multiplying his numbers with angels and souls but no, Christian was the one who led the rebellion. He was the one who initially rallied any like-minded individuals in his quest for angels to be part of the living plane. When Bathisma learned of his future plans, he came to me and alerted me. We tried to find actual evidence of this plan, but Christian had not only disappeared but had been clever in covering his tracks. Due to his loyalty, I then offered Bathisma a position in my office and once Christian returned, he felt he could not trust Bathisma anymore. But by then we knew enough to know we could only wait for the day and deal with whatever we could at the time. This is now the time.' Crowley took another large drink from his glass and kept his gaze firmly on Rucelle. 'Christian and all the angels and souls that followed him are now in the Carcerem,' Rucelle added. Crowley was confused again

'I'll take "what's a Carcerem" for another fifty points?' No one laughed at the joke and he now wasn't sure if it was because of his inappropriate humour or that angels didn't know what a game show was. Rucelle continued.

'It's a bit like a holding prison, but not like any prison you can imagine. Visualise a place where you are surrounded by people who cannot see you, a place where there is no end or beginning, a place where there is nothing you can see, a complete vacuum of nothing.'

'Sounds like the day I got lost in Milton Keynes.' Bathisma moved forward with a fresh glass of whisky for Crowley and removed his empty one.

'Is it a good idea to keep plying him with alcohol?' quipped Magda. Her lips were set in a thin line and Crowley could not believe he once thought this woman attractive.

'My dear, I have yet to be in a situation where whisky was not a good idea. And if you are worried that I might become inebriated then that ship has already sailed as I arrived here with a bottle of brandy already making itself quite at home within the confines of my stomach.

However, I will stop drinking if it makes *you* feel more comfortable as I am told the most incredible story of my life!' Magda shifted in her chair and gave a little tug at the hem of her jacket to regain her composure. She looked away from Crowley and gave an exaggerated glare of attention toward Rucelle. Crowley pursed his lips and he too looked at Rucelle.

'As I said, the Carcerem is a holding prison. It is only used while judgement is made.'

'But you said you have all the evidence you need. You know it was him, so why not send Christian and his cult to wherever you send people when they cross the line?'

'It is not that simple,' began Nazriel. 'The reason for the Carcerem is to hold an angel or angels that have not served humanity. To serve humanity is the reason why we are here, all of us. It is the point of our being. Some people will say that what Christian did was for his own gain. Some may say that what he did was for the benefit of us all and that angels should interact with the living and be applauded for their influence. But some, including us and for the majority of the angels and souls on our plane, believe that human kind was created for a higher purpose. The purpose is not something we know, but it is something we individually believe. There is no right or wrong answer. But what we do all agree on, is that the choices of humanity shape this plane and without its existence and widespread belief of 'whatever' in the human soul, we would not be who *we* are! Christian has overlooked the fact that hope, within the human soul, is what gives *us* purpose. Do you understand?' Crowley lowered his head and gazed into the amber contents of his glass and thought of a necklace that his mother once wore.

'Mama wore a necklace,' he began, 'it was a silver heart. Well, half of one. The other half of the heart was worn by my aunt, her twin sister. She used to say that the necklace only became whole when my aunt would visit, and they would giggle as they pressed it together. But looking back, it was all about them. They only felt whole when they were together and each of them held the belief and hope that in those long periods of absence that they would always wear a silly little trinket. They believed in each other to keep wearing it, as it was the thing that identified them as a twin. If one had stopped wearing it, then without a doubt, it would have had a devastating effect on the other. They were each buried still wearing them. So, yes in a strange way, I understand that one cannot exist without the other and crushing the belief and hope in one is damaging to all.' He allowed the story to settle and took another breath. 'So, am I right to believe that Christian will be released to cause havoc again?'

'Not quite,' began Rucelle, 'Christian will have to be judged.'

'Like in a court?'

'The Curia.' Crowley looked puzzled and Rucelle continued. 'The Curia is in all sense and purpose, a court of judgement.'

'And who makes the judgement?'

'A highly respected being that has cast judgement since creation.'

'God?!'

'No. It is not God!' Rucelle looked at Nazriel. 'Have you not taught him about God?'

'A rebellion got in the way,' said Nazriel calmly.

'Well, for now,' Rucelle turned back to Crowley, 'just accept that there is not a man called God who is about to intervene with this.'

'Well, let's hope he is busy cleaning up Christian's mess or at the very least giving Bournemouth a makeover.'

Rucelle rolled his eyes and studied Crowley. Was he really understanding what had taken thirty years to unfurl? Was he placing too much hope on this soul? Should they have just left Sean in Michael's and Ambriel's protection? Nazriel had argued that it had to be a human soul to connect to Sean. A period of trust had to be formed and ultimately a bond. Nazriel had pointed out that while an archangel had abilities far more reaching than a human soul, an archangel would never truly understand the complexities of raw emotion. Only another human soul would be able to not only understand but could in some ways actually feel another person's pain. This was why Crowley had been their choice. And while Rucelle knew he was judging Crowley he also reminded himself that his humour was part of a unique blend of qualities that made him their best choice.

'Bournemouth isn't that bad surely?' There was a faint hint of surprise from everyone in the room at Rucelle attempting humour.

'They have more sloped kerb stones to accommodate the wheelchairs than any other place on Earth. You're up and down, up and down. Taking a short stroll from one end of a street to the other can make you feel positively sea sick,' joked Crowley. Rucelle laughed a little, not knowing if that was an appropriate response seeing as he had never been to Bournemouth.

'Joking aside, we must all be clear on our next steps and how to bring this to the Curia. We cannot afford to lose on this, for all our sakes,' Rucelle said sombrely.

'But you haven't told him the best bit yet,' sneered Magda.

CHAPTER 21

Sean was running around the streets. He was out of breath and didn't know what direction was best. He was coughing as the masonry dust swirled in his lungs and tears and snot streamed from his face. Whichever way he went the exploding churches, mosques and synagogues continued to block his path. The banging became louder and he could hear someone shouting his name. He desperately tried to run toward the voice and it was becoming louder. He felt in the dense dusty fog he was nearly upon whoever was shouting when an almighty bang woke him up.

The door opened slightly and from beneath the covers he could see Maggie poking her head through the gap and turn in his direction. She stepped into the room, already armed with a cup of tea and after placing it on the bedside table she walked to the window and snatched open the curtains.

'For fuck's sake, Mum!' Sean sat up and squinted at the piercing light of day.

'I'll give you for fuck's sake! You've been in this room for nearly a week now and today is the day when I say ENOUGH!'

'What?' Sean moaned.

'You heard! Now get that tea drank, get out of that bed and get your arse in the shower. This bloody room stinks and it's coming from you!'

'Charming! What the hell happened to "good morning"?'

'I said that six days ago, the day you came back from London, and the day after that, and the day after that. Now get your backside out of that bed and I want you downstairs in thirty minutes and if you're not I'll be back up here to wash and dress you like a child,' she stomped toward the door and disappeared.

'Don't forget to unleash your flying monkeys!' he shouted. 'Witch!' he whispered under his breath.

He sat up properly in his bed, patted the quilt around his body and reached for the tea. He began to sip from the cup and could hear Maggie talking to Charlie downstairs, no doubt telling him that she had read the riot act to him. He suspected last night when he had turned off his bedside lamp that Maggie would probably lose her patience today. He had only been downstairs to return his dirty dinner dishes or to fetch another bottle of water. When they were both out he would root through the food cupboards looking for comfort food. There was none, which told Sean that his mum currently had Charlie on one of his diets. Sean, knowing Charlie's lack of willpower, was confident that there would be a small pile of confectionary sitting in the glovebox in the old Range Rover.

He toyed with the idea of heading back to Lanson today, but it was only fleetingly. The fallout from a couple of weeks ago was still huge news and although Sue called

Maggie to ask after his health he suspected she only wanted him so she could alert the media and get him back in the spotlight. His mum and Charlie had been great in protecting him since he left London. At the hotel, he felt vulnerable and exposed when various people began to call asking him for his opinion on the recent events. The number grew each day and once he realised that Michael, Ambriel or even Crowley were not coming back he felt very alone and he knew the only place he would feel better was home. He slowly climbed out of the bed and walked toward his window and with a click and a push he gave it a wide-open swing.

'Sounds like he is up,' said Maggie from the downstairs hall where she had been craning her neck trying to hear some movement. 'I think he was having one of his nightmares again.' Charlie, who was sat at the breakfast bar, closed his newspaper and folded it before putting it down. 'He was shouting before I came in.' Maggie continued, 'I could hear him from halfway up the stairs. Has he spoken to you about these dreams?'

'No, love.' She saw the empty plate in front of Charlie and whipped it away before submerging it into a bowl of bubbly hot water. Her hands became still in the water as she clutched the plate and looked out of the window into the garden.

'Charlie?' she asked, a little dreamily. He spun lightly on his bar stool to face her and she looked over her shoulder at him. 'Do you think what they were saying was true? I mean, have we been walking around and an angel tells us where to go, or what to wear or even when to wash this plate?' Charlie slipped off his stool and walked over to his wife. He stood behind her and slipped his arms around her waist and rested his chin on her shoulder.

'Does it matter?' he asked. 'I mean, what difference

does it make if an angel makes me do things. If it is true, then I would like to shake my angel's hand because that means an angel brought me you and Sean and made us find our home. What's so bad about that?'

'But I don't know what to believe anymore? Does this mean that there is no Heaven? We just all turn into angels and come back to Earth to help people? I always understood it that once you were gone, you were gone, and you went to a better place.'

'Well, you were always far more spiritual than I ever was. I still struggle to understand what Sean does.'

'Do you think there's a God?' she whispered.

'I've no idea, love. I'm still figuring out how to find Radio 4 in the car.' Charlie smiled, kissed her cheek, let go of her waist and walked over to the breakfast bar where he picked up his newspaper and headed for the lounge. Within a few seconds she could hear the low voices coming from the radio as it did every Sunday morning in Charlie's routine.

Maggie continued with the dishes and put them away and once satisfied the kitchen was clean she pulled the wet washing from the washing machine and padded out to the garden. She felt a sense of satisfaction when the wind tried to pull the billowing pegged sheets and she could see Sean watching her from the kitchen window. She smiled and toddled back to the kitchen with the empty laundry basket.

'Want another cup of tea, Mum?' asked Sean, filling the kettle.

'Oh, yes please, son. Charlie will probably want one as well.' She walked to the utility room and popped the basket back and as she returned to the kitchen she gave her hair a push from her face. 'Windy out there today. Those sheets are probably dry by now and no doubt Dorothy is on her way. I must find my broom.' She pretended she was looking to the sky for a falling house and then smiled at Sean, 'You cheeky sod!'

Sean smirked as he popped a tea bag into each of the three cups. He made the tea and after delivering one of the cups and a kiss of good morning to Charlie he headed back to the kitchen where his mum was sat on one of the sofas at the far end of the kitchen.

'Bring your tea here, son. I want to talk to you.' He collected his cup from the worktop and silently debated whether to sit next to her on one couch or to sit opposite on the other. He concluded that she had not really seen him in days and knowing Maggie she would want to squeeze, hug, pat or cuddle periodically throughout the conversation. She looked pleased when he settled in next to her and she watched him as he sat back making himself comfortable. Maggie stayed perched on the edge with her hands clasped on her lap like the Queen. Sean knew it was going to be one of 'those' chats which meant it was going to be deep, probably emotional and no doubt be peppered with mild interrogation.

'So, come on Mum, spit it out.'

'Let's start with the dreams shall we,' she said softly. Sean could feel his skin prickle beneath his cheeks. He knew he could explain the dream, but he also knew that he would struggle to explain why he was scared. Probably because he didn't know himself. He debated with the idea of not telling her, but he knew that his mum wasn't stupid, and she would be able to see through any casual dismissal. He also knew she was tenacious and if she didn't get an answer today then she would simply ask him again tomorrow.

He took a deep breath and began to tell her that he had been having the same dream for a few weeks. He told her of the churches and that he was alone in the dream and that he was always running. When she asked him what from, he confessed he didn't know and he wasn't sure if he was running from something or to something or trying to find something. All he knew was that whatever it was, it certainly had something to do with him. He told her that he would sometimes wake up sweating from the dream, like he had actually been running.

'Do you think it's a message? Maybe from 'up there'?' she nodded Heavenward.

'I thought that, but now I'm not so sure. Anyway, I am sure it will pass. It probably would have stopped ages ago if it wasn't for every news item or TV show banging on about angels and stuff,' he sniffed.

'What do you expect, Sean? The world has been turned topsy-turvy these last couple of weeks. The churches are fit to burst with people looking for more answers and I heard on the news that the suicide rate has shot up with people thinking they will turn into angels and thinking they can go around and tell people what to do.'

'Well, that's just stupid,' he mumbled.

'Is it?! Who knows what is real anymore? I mean you're supposed to have a sixth sense, is there an angel sat with us now?'

'How the hell would I know? I had a spiritual guide, that's all!'

'That's all, he says. Well, if it's no big deal why has the phone never stopped ringing with people from TV shows wanting you to come and explain what is happening? People think that you might be able to explain. You have a gift and you are one of the few people in this game who has a decent reputation.'

Sean remained quiet. He wondered how much he should really tell her. At what point is it that you say something to your own mother and she thinks you might be crazy? He had deliberated repeatedly about what he should say, and if he did, how much he should say. He knew why he was indecisive. It was because here, in this house, he went back to being plain old Sean Allister. It was here that he could truly be himself and he wouldn't be judged. The only other place he felt like that was with Crowley. He pushed Crowley to the back of his mind, unable to deal with the thought and the hurt he had inflicted on his friend.

As if Maggie could read his thoughts she said, 'Tell me about your spiritual guide?' Crowley came galloping back. He could see him walking out of the dressing room, heavy with disappointment. He wanted to say, 'not now' to his mum, but if it wasn't said now, then he would have to later on.

'I haven't seen him since that night,' Sean picked some invisible lint from his jean-covered knee cap. 'I told him I didn't want to see him anymore.'

'But doesn't your whole gift rely on...what's his name?'

'Crowley,' he replied flatly.

'Crowley? I thought it would be more...well, you know, cosmic, spiritual.'

'Well, his real name is Moondance Unicorn, but he likes to be called Crowley.' Maggie smiled at his joke.

'And yes, I do need him to perform mediumship. But I told him I didn't want to do it anymore.'

'So, what do you want to do?'

'Maybe go back to Bill's, or go travelling.' He could hear now just how ridiculous that was.

'I love you Sean, but sometimes you can't half be a silly prick!'

'I know,' he unconsciously pouted. 'Look Mum, that's only half the story and if I tell you the rest I think you are either gonna freak or call the doctor or both.' Maggie put her cup on the table in front of them and slowly reached for her son's hand and gave a little squeeze.

'Sean, there is nothing you can say that will make me think you are crazy. You have been surprising me since the day you were born.' She cocked her head to one side to try and read Sean's face. 'Have you heard of a caul?' Sean looked at her confused. 'A caul is a thin piece of membrane that covers a baby's face when it is born. Some people call it a veil. It's supposed to symbolise a special destiny for that baby.'

'I never knew that.'

'So, when I heard about your ability, shall we say, I was not surprised. But, I will admit I was a little disappointed.' Sean looked hurt. 'Not in you! Never in you! I just always had a feeling that it would be something unique. Don't ask me why. But I am sure all parents feel like that about their children. I just never spoke to enough mums I suppose to find out if what I was feeling was normal.' Sean now felt he could tell her. All his indecisiveness ebbed away, and he was sure she would listen and help him try and make sense of it all.

'Well, I think what I am about to tell you might help you make sense of some of those feelings. But before I tell you, can we ask Charlie to come in? Your reaction to this will be huge and I don't want to feel weird around Charlie not knowing how he reacted when you tell him.

'I won't tell him if you don't want me to!'

'Mum, this is too big to keep secret from him. Plus, he deserves to know.' She gave a nervous nod of her head, stood up and with a quickened step, walked through the kitchen toward the lounge. He could hear her speak and then the radio being turned off and soon Maggie was back, accompanied by Charlie. Maggie took her seat again and Charlie sat opposite with a concerned look.

Sean took a deep breath, wiped his sweaty palms along his thighs and began. They never interrupted him as he told them of how he first met Crowley, Sue's ability to see him but not hear him and how his gift worked. His story continued of needing more staff and how he ended up employing Michael and Ambrose. He then revealed when he had his first dream and told Charlie of what they contained. His flow was constant until his story reached the last night on the stage of the Royal Halls. They could see Sean was starting to struggle and Charlie gave Maggie a concerned sideways glance.

'So, Michael… is…um…' he began to rub his face, a sign when Sean was distressed, 'he…um…oh Christ…'

'What?' pleaded Maggie. Sean looked at her square in the face.

'He's the…erm… okay, he's the archangel Michael.' Maggie's face remained the same. 'You know! Like THE archangel Michael!' Sean switched his gaze to Charlie who looked dumbfounded. 'And Ambrose, isn't called Ambrose, his real name is Ambriel and he's an angel as well. He apparently is the angel of communication or something.'

'Christ!' murmured Charlie. Sean carried on about them being there for his protection and that they had disappeared on the night and he had not seen them since.

'He said I was part of a bigger plan.'

'What plan?' asked Charlie.

'They disappeared before I got an explanation.'

'Why do you need protecting?' whispered Maggie. Sean shrugged his shoulders and stared at his knees while Maggie and Charlie continued to stare at him. Charlie felt numb and wasn't sure if he had heard it all correctly as the story in his head was too incredible. Then the silence was broken by a loud sob. Sean raised his hands and covered his face and began to shake as the sobs came faster. As quick as a flash, his mum slid nearer to him and pulled his head to her chest. Sean moved his hands into two fists underneath his chin while his mum clutched him closer.

'You don't think I'm mental, do you?'

'NO! God, no!' They both shouted in unison. Sean continued to cry into his mum's chest until he was reduced to sniffing hiccups.

'Do you think Crowley would come back? If you asked him I mean,' questioned Charlie.

'I'm not sure. I was pretty horrible to him and when all is said and done he is my friend, family even, and I miss him. I know that might sound strange, but he's as real to me as you are.'

'It doesn't sound strange at all,' said Maggie, 'and Charlie is right, you need to try and contact Crowley. Maybe, he can make some more sense of it all, especially the bit about you needing protection.' Of all the detail she had been told, it was the comment about protection that concerned her the most. Was her son in danger and if so, who from? Was it that man that had appeared on Sean's stage that night? She tried to tell herself not to worry until they had some answers if they could get some answers. But one thing was for sure, Sean was not leaving her house until she was satisfied he was safe. Her mind jumped to Sue back in Lanson.

'Sue has been on, every day. Do you think you should call her? Maybe, let her know if she still has a career?' Maggie could not hide her disdain.

'You really don't like her, do you Mum?'

'No, I do not! As far as I'm concerned, she took advantage of people before you, and is still doing it now only on a bigger scale. The woman calls here every day and only asks if you have you spoken to the media yet. She doesn't ask how you are or anything!' she snapped.

'Be fair, Mum, if it wasn't for her I would never have got the bookings I did.'

'Oh, please! You honestly think she spent hours ringing around venues to get you booked. The phone rang here enough times for me to know that they came looking for you. No, Sean, she had a very easy job and she made a very easy living and all of that is under threat now. She was in the right place at the right time and took full advantage of the situation.'

'But she saw what happened to me on the plane and she could see Crowley.'

'And that entitles her to ten percent?!'

It was starting to dawn with Sean that Sue had indeed changed, or had she? It was a bit of a private joke between him and Faye at how much she stretched the truth about what she could 'see' and it all seemed harmless fun. But looking back he could see that she was playing with people's lives and emotions and even though it was tiny she revelled in that sense of power. Sean had simply made it all a lot bigger and it fed her hungry ego. He wondered if she had thought about Michael, Ambriel or Crowley since the night in the halls. It didn't take him long to convince himself that she probably never gave them a second thought.

'You should get your mum to be your booking agent. You should hear her on the phone,' Charlie mimicked Maggie with a posh voice and raised his nose in the air for comedic effect. "Mr Allister is currently unavailable for comment. However, once his spiritual rehabilitation has concluded I will ask him to return your call to discuss an exclusive interview".' They all began to laugh, especially Maggie.

'I need to see what's been happening in the world,'

declared Sean. 'Do you mind if we go in the lounge to watch a bit of news?' Without a word, they silently walked to the lounge. Maggie and Charlie took their usual seats while Sean hunted for the remote control. He soon settled in next to his mum and flicked through the channels until he came across a group debate that involved the Archbishop of Lettenbury, Iqbal Shafi, a representative from the Muslim Council and Samuel Jacobs, the Chief Rabbi of the Commonwealth.

'Tell me gentlemen, have you experienced within your own faith, the violence that is being subjected upon the Vatican? And do you feel the need to go into hiding as Pope John has eventually had to do for his own safety?' asked Miriam Clooney, a well-respected political interviewer and journalist.

'We have all experienced some sort of threat since the revelations,' began Mr Shafi. 'However, I am not sure that I agree that the Pope should go into hiding.'

'Do you simply want Pope John to remain a target?' asked the Archbishop sarcastically.

'This is a time,' Mr Shafi responded, 'probably the only time where the people no longer feel their chosen religion.'

'I beg your pardon?!' interrupted the Archbishop.

'Please, do not misunderstand me. I feel, certainly from when I speak to people in my community, that the details of what we believe in each of our own faiths has been challenged and, in some respects, even crushed. But one thing that has remained in all is hope and faith. We now know there is something else.'

Miriam Clooney interjected, 'So what you are saying Mr Shafi is that where some believe in Christ and some in Allah and so on, that this is what has been challenged the most?'

'Indeed. We now know that there is a heavenly plane

and that we all will transition to this plane upon our death. It is the same for all.'

'But how do we know that these angels who revealed themselves to us are not just part of something very small on the next plane. How can we be sure they represented all faiths? How do we know for sure that there isn't more than one paradise?' asked Mr Jacobs.

'These are questions being asked by everyone and Pope John needs to be there for his people. This is the most challenging time for all religions, especially their leaders and for me I feel he should be present.' Miriam Clooney swung in her chair and faced the camera.

'Join us after the break when we will continue with our discussion and invite Hollywood star turned preacher Tim Ferryman to give his views since the revelation.' The title music began to jingle, and Sean picked up the remote control and clicked the television off.

'Is that what they call it? The Revelation?' asked Sean.

'Seems to be,' sighed Charlie.

'Is this what it's been like since then?'

'Pretty much.' Sean stood up and slowly walked to the lounge window. His mum and Charlie just watched him stare out for a couple of minutes. Then he turned and perched himself on the windowsill.

'So, all this revealing and telling people that they will be going to a heaven or somewhere after they die hasn't exactly brought comfort, has it? I mean, it seems to me that everyone is more confused than ever!'

'They don't know what to believe, son,' shrugged Maggie.

'So, what was the bloody point of it all? And the weird thing,' started Sean, 'is why haven't they been back since? Why just deliver the message and then hear no more? I mean why reveal their purpose and our purpose and not....

well…I dunno…I mean…not do anything more? Do you know what I mean?'

'You need to contact Crowley. If anyone has any answers, then surely he is your best bet.'

'And if he doesn't?'

'Then we join the masses in not knowing. But let's take advantage of your advantage, eh?' Maggie smiled.

'Okay, I'll do it later. But it takes a lot of energy to do it you know, and I'm gonna need a lot of sustenance to reach into the far lands of the dead.' Maggie turned her gaze slightly as she could see Charlie beginning to smirk.

'So,' began Maggie, 'what will you need to converse with those that have passed?' her sarcastic tone was not lost on Sean and he too began to smile.

'Can I have a bacon butty with a large fried egg on top and some hash browns, please? Oh, and if there is any black pudding that will no doubt make the difference between standard and high definition communications,' Sean joked.

'Any black pudding indeed?' Charlie sniffed and reached for his paper, opened it with a snap and raised it so they could no longer see his face. Maggie and Sean smiled at his pretence of being annoyed. 'You wouldn't think you were the stepson of a butcher.'

CHAPTER 22

Crowley was sat in his usual chair in Nazriel's study and waited for his tea to be passed over to him. He accepted the tea and waited for his friend to sit and join him. They both sat silently staring in front of them as they each caressed their cups and occasionally tried to drink some of the scalding brew within. It was Crowley who eventually broke the silence.

'You haven't told me everything, have you?'

'No,' Nazriel said flatly.

'I mean I kind of understand how the Curia works now, and the Carcerem. But I didn't understand the bit about someone representing humanity. Why can't you gentlemen do that?'

'Only a soul can represent humanity, not an angel. While an angel understands what a human soul is and its complexities, it cannot understand its spirit.' Crowley looked more confused.

'The spirit is the part of the soul that once belonged to the living. Angels have never "lived". So, fundamentally an angel cannot understand...desire.'

'Well, I think Christian missed that memo then,' Crowley sniffed.

'Christian is an angel, but a very different one. He has experienced things he should not have. He has been exposed to events that he should never have encountered. He "feels" things because of these experiences.'

'He feels desire?'

'Yes.'

'And that's bad?'

'For angels, yes.'

'And Michael?'

'He is an archangel. You can count on your fingers the archangels. They are…a bit like an advisory service, shall we say.'

'But archangels don't usually protect people, do they?'

'No, they don't.' Crowley's head was starting to spin. Why was Michael protecting Sean then? He wanted to ask but felt his understanding was splintering off and decided to try and keep his mind as tidy as possible. He felt if he could follow the line of the past, the present and the plans for the future then some of his questions may be answered along the way.

'So, back to the court thing then, have you brought me in here to tell me that it is up to me to convince the powers that be that what Christian did was bad and he needs to do a "bit of bird"?' Crowley attempted a cockney accent. Nazriel gave a curious look. 'Incarceration,' Crowley clarified.

'Not quite.' Nazriel leaned forward and set his cup on the small table in front of him. 'What I am about to tell you is only known by a few. It is something that, believe me, if we had any other option we would take it. But through all what I am about to say and ultimately ask of you, you must remember that we have NO other choice. This is the only way. You cannot argue the point, you can only agree to do it or to not. There is no in-between. Do you understand?' Nazriel finished firmly.

Crowley looked deep into his friend's eyes that seemed to have darkened within moments. He knew whatever he was about to be told was not only of great importance but that his subsequent decision would be greater. He too leaned forward, placed his teacup upon the table and then settled back into the chair to await Nazriel to begin.

'I understand,' said Crowley.

CHAPTER 23

Sean could hear Maggie and Charlie close their bedroom door on the far side of the landing and after hearing the flush of a distant toilet, he knew they had settled into bed. He wanted to wait a while before he called for Crowley. He wanted to make sure they were asleep as he wasn't entirely comfortable talking to Crowley and thinking they might be able to hear the one-sided conversation.

    Sean was already in bed and only the low glow from his bedside lamp cast any light at all in his dark bedroom. A lot of his room on his far right-hand side could not be seen as the lamp's rays could not penetrate that far. He sat for a long time staring into the dark. He wondered if he really wanted to do this and put off speaking to Crowley until tomorrow. There was no guarantee that he would respond anyway. He waited and closed his eyes for a moment to soothe the sleepy sting and when he opened them he could see Crowley emerging from the blackness from the far side of his bedroom. Crowley walked towards Sean and gently sat on the bed. Sean could feel the bed depress and the quilt tighten around his legs and once he was sat, Crowley offered a gentle smile.

'Hello, Sean,' he whispered.

'Hello, Crowley,' Sean whispered back. 'I'm so sorry,' recalling how things were left in the Royal Halls.

'We need to talk,' Crowley emitted a long sigh, 'about a great deal, I'm afraid.'

'I know what I said was awful and I know I probably hurt you. But I didn't mean it. Well, I mean...I did at the time, but it was just because of everything that happened that night and I thought by telling you to go away would mean that things would go back to the way they were and I would feel normal again which I know is stupid but it's just....'

'It's fine, Sean. Please let's just forget about it,' consoled Crowley as he shrugged. Sean was about to push his point further, but something told him that Crowley did indeed want to forget about that night because he had something else to say, something more important. Sean cocked his head to one side to study Crowley's face more and he sat forward in the bed to scrutinise further.

'Are you sober?'

'I am. Horrible isn't it? How do people go through life with this unforgiving clarity?' He gave an unconvincing chuckle. Sean felt a slight panic rise within him. For Crowley to be sober it could only mean that what he was about to say had to be said right or Heaven had run out of booze. Sean plumped for the former as the latter already existed and it was called Hell.

'Let's start talking about your dreams, shall we?' Sean silently nodded. He knew they meant something and he was finally being offered an explanation. 'Have you not drawn any similarities between your dreams and the current state of human faith?' asked Crowley. Sean thought for a long time. He recalled every dream he had had. Some of the detail was different in each one, but essentially, they were all the same. Sean running, buildings falling and the sense of being alone. Crowley patiently waited for Sean to come to some of his own conclusions and watched Sean's face turn from scowling recollection to a scared conclusion.

'Have these been premonition dreams?'

'Do you think they have?' asked Crowley.

'I think they are foretelling the downfall of religions and stuff. All the buildings in my dreams are places of worship and they're falling down. And that's exactly what is happening in the world right now. No one knows what to believe any more and the very foundations of their beliefs have been shaken.' Crowley smiled. 'Am I right?' Crowley nodded. 'But why am I on my own? There's never anyone else. Do you think there may be others having this same dream?' Sean felt his answer straight away from sheer instinct. 'No, it's just me isn't it?'

'So that makes you special.'

'What's so special about me though?' Crowley let out a huge sigh and looked at his feet. The task before him was huge and he had agreed to endeavour to complete it once Nazriel had asked him. He too had understood that there was simply no other option.

'Jack, the Milk Tray man, was not the leader of the rebellion as I thought. He was doing the bidding of an angel called Christian. Christian, at this point in time, is locked up in the Carcerem, a jail for want of a better word.' He was talking slowly to ensure Sean's understanding.

'So, what's the problem then? Because there is a problem, isn't there? I can tell by your face,' Sean pushed.

'The Carcerem cannot be used as a permanent hold for the angels. Its very existence in Heaven has a negative effect on all. It cannot remain on that plane indefinitely. And so, we must decide what to do with its inhabitants.'

'Can't you send them all to Hell? Hell does exist doesn't it?'

'Oh yes, there is a Hell. But we cannot just send people there willy-nilly. Do we, as a human race, just condemn people?'

'Well no, we have a court and a jury and men in curly wigs to decide all that,'

'Exactly, and Heaven is no different. They call the court the Curia.'

'The Curia,' Sean whispered back to himself. 'But what does that have to do with my dreams and being on my own?'

'The set-up of a Curia is not unlike a court here on Earth. There is no jury, but there is a judge and there is a defendant and a prosecutor.'

'So, who has Christian got as his lawyer? Johnnie Cochran?' said Sean in a mocking tone.

'That is one of the differences, the defendant and the prosecutor do not have legal representatives, they each must defend or argue and convince the judge, and it is the judge alone who then decides their fate. The good thing about the Curia is that no one can lie once they are within its confines, so we can take all at face value and not feel the need to suspect any answers given. However, that doesn't mean that people may omit or edit their answers to suit. So clever questioning is paramount in cases such as these. Not that there has ever been a case such as this before,' Crowley sighed.

'And the bad thing?' probed Sean.

'The bad thing is there is no appeal. Once the judge has made his decision it is final. So, there is only one crack of the whip so to speak.'

'Shit,' whispered Sean. He sat for a moment trying to absorb what Crowley had said. He realised it explained why there had been no contact from angels since that night.

Sean eventually peeled back the quilt to reveal a pair of hairy legs that were thankfully housed higher up in a pair of pyjama shorts. The legs swung to the side of the bed and walked towards the curtained window. Sean swiped the curtains open, fumbled to open the window and threw it as wide as it would allow. He then reached into the drawer of his desk under the same window and pulled out a packet of cigarettes.

'She'll smell it tomorrow, but I'll worry about it then.' He popped one into his mouth and with one flick of his lighter his cheeks were soon drawing in as he took a large pull on his cigarette.

'Your mum disapproves of smoking in the house?'

'Mum disapproves of smoking, full stop. Did you ever smoke, Crowley?'

'Only in my younger days. My sister Sarah and I would often enjoy clandestine meetings in the ballroom for our nightly puff.'

'The ballroom?' Sean mocked.

'Well, it was the least used room in the house.'

'Oh, of course, said Sean rolling his eyes, 'Heaven forbid you smoked in the library or the billiard room.' Crowley wanted to defend his story but dismissed it as soon as the feeling arose. Sean Allister and Hugh Crowley had very different upbringings, it didn't need to be argued about, especially tonight.

Crowley remained on the bed and watched Sean half hanging out of the window as he tried to direct the smoke into beyond. Sean smoked his cigarette in silence and began to form a list of questions in his head. Once he had finished, he flicked the butt as far as he could in the hope it would land in Charlie's bushes. He eventually slid off the sill and tiptoed back into the bed, leaving the window wide open.

'I have to do something, don't I? I have to help the prosecution, don't I?' Crowley silently nodded. Sean went to speak and then Crowley stopped him.

'Before you ask anything else, I need you to understand something further,' said Crowley. Sean closed his mouth and waited for the next instalment. 'The prosecution is there to defend mankind. Their job is to ensure that humanity is restored, and the equilibrium and purpose of Heaven and Earth is brought to balance.'

'You mean to try and make things like the way they were before?'

'I don't think that is possible now. But this case will mean the difference between repair or ruin.' They continued to talk into the night about the aftermath since the revelations and how all religions were feeling some sort of positive and negative effect. Sean and Crowley talked of that night in the Royal Hall when they last saw each other and why they both behaved the way they did. Sean also admitted how he had missed Crowley and occasionally referred to times in the future when they may put the show back on the road. Sean noticed that Crowley offered no reaction to this and felt this was not the time to interrogate that point any further, well not tonight anyway.

They had talked all night, especially about his mum and Charlie and their support. They continued until they talked themselves back to the now and how the Curia case would be presented.

'So, will one of the angels be arguing on behalf of humanity?' Sean hoped it would be Michael. He felt Michael understood what had happened more than most, seeing as he had witnessed the rebels in full force.

'An angel cannot represent mankind. It has been made very clear that only a soul can do this. A soul is from someone who once lived.'

'So, it has to be someone who once was a human and then they died, yeah? Well, that only leaves you then. You can't just have any soul doing this. It has to be someone who understands what's going on down here. Plus, you know loads of big words and I can get the laptop and watch some old Judge Judy episodes and get some tips on how to keep arguments on track and how to insult people without swearing. You can ask Ambriel to be your little runner like Judy has. So, when they come in and say, "I've got a letter here that says humanity owes me two-thousand years back-pay in acknowledgement and gratefulness and I still haven't received a cent", you get Ambriel to run over and get the letter. Judge Judy makes some great faces when she reads the letters, we can practice that...' Sean was desperately trying to find some humour in the dark conversation, if only to help him cope.

'I can't,' whispered Crowley.

'Oh,' Sean abruptly stopped. He felt all the wind being sucked out of his sails. He noticed that Crowley looked disappointed. 'Is it because you like too much sauce?' Sean tried to sound sympathetic.

'No, it is not!' He shot Sean a withering look. Sean sat back into the pillows and began to pick at his nails. 'The reason I cannot represent humanity is for the simple reason I am already dead. The rules of the Carcerem, laid out in ancient scrolls, state that it can only be used to house those that *"will not serve humanity"*. To determine if this is the case then judgment within the Curia will decide. But the Curia further states that only a person who has sacrificed their own life for the sake of all humanity, can speak for all of humanity.' Crowley turned to stare at Sean who stared back for what seemed like an age. Crowley could see Sean's lips moving slightly in a repeated pattern and eventually a sound accompanied the moving.

'Sacrifice?' Crowley nodded. Sean calmly climbed out of his bed again and made his way back to his desk and retrieved his cigarettes. He didn't bother leaning toward the window once he had lit one. He stood with his back to his friend and stared into the dark night. The only thing that could be heard was the faint crackle of the burning tobacco when Sean took a drag.

'Sacrifice their own life? It's me, isn't it? Only someone who can prove their worth is deemed worthy enough to represent the whole of the bleeding planet Earth. And I mean the thing is, there are plenty of people out there willing to top themselves and to have their names on top billing in Heaven but…erm…,' Sean's voice was starting to crack. The huge lump that was forming in his throat felt like it was going to choke him. 'Do us a favour? Can you go down to Charlie's drinks cabinet in the kitchen and get me something…anything?'

'Of course,' Crowley stood and made his way to the bedroom door. Without turning Sean added, 'Nice and quiet, eh?' Crowley lowered his head and barely making a noise, shut the door behind him leaving Sean alone in his bedroom.

Most of his body felt numb. He couldn't even feel the ground beneath his feet. But he could feel the satisfying smoke fill his lungs and the dizzying swirl in his brain. He looked toward the sky and wondered how far you had to go before you reached Heaven. He wondered if they could see him now or were they all just waiting patiently for Crowley's return and deliver Sean's decision. After all, he didn't have to do what they were asking. He didn't have to involve himself any further. They could just find someone else and hope that their second choice was a good enough choice. Just because he had been their first, didn't necessarily mean he would be good at it. What did he know about prosecuting and defending? He wasn't sure if he understood which was which! Even though he had a gift of mediumship, it didn't make him all that special, surely. There were plenty of others that had the same gift as him that could probably be more eloquent. But did they know how it all worked up there? After all, he did have some inside information which gave him the advantage. But did he know that much? Couldn't someone else be brought up to speed? Would there be any consequences for him if he failed? Would he be punished also?

His thoughts were interrupted by a small click and he turned around to see Crowley creeping back through the door. One of his pockets was bulging and he was clutching a bottle of Grey Goose in his hand. He resumed his place on the bed and relieved his swollen pocket of a glass. Sean took his place back in the bed and waited for Crowley to pour him a drink.

'You not joining me?'

'Not tonight.' He passed Sean the glass and then proceeded to screw the top back on.

'Why me?'

'Would you believe me if I said it was your destiny?'

'Yes, I would,' croaked Sean. 'But surely I still have a choice. I mean, what if I say no? It can't be that much of a done deal; otherwise why would they ask you to 'ask' me if it's already predestined?' Crowley did not answer. He wanted to say very little now. The decision that Sean had to make, had to come from him. The consequences of Sean's decision, had to sit well within his conscience.

There was no point in trying to convince Sean to do anything if he later regretted it.

'Sean, I know what they, and I for that matter, is asking is a huge thing. I cannot tell you what to do, but do know this, that whatever you decide I will stand by and defend your decision to anyone who challenges it. I will remain your servant, my love for you will not change. But unfortunately, I cannot help you decide one way or another, and for that I am truly sorry.' Sean sniffed as he fought back the tears that began to well up in his eyes.

'Not your fault, is it,' Sean mumbled. Crowley slowly rose to his feet and Sean looked up earnestly at his friend.

'I must go now. But I will return before sunrise, I promise.' Crowley walked over to the far end of the room and disappeared before the darkness could envelop him. Sean sat in the bed and began to stare at his drink. He still had a million questions and he felt the only person who could give him the answers had now just left. Who else could he talk to? It wasn't as if he could knock his mum out of bed and tell her that he might have to sacrifice himself to keep some lunatic angel in his place. He lifted his glass and took a large gulp and closed his eyes to try and stop his head from swimming. Maybe, if he could just ask Crowley when he came back, what he would do if he was in his situation.

When he opened his eyes, he was shocked to see someone standing over his bed. He dropped the glass and shot off the bed toward the bedroom door and as he was about to shout he recognised the face.

'Father O'Carroll?!' he squeaked. The front of Sean's body was pressed against the door ready to bolt. How the hell was the priest in his bedroom? Had he come through the open window? Not unless he was Spiderman, Sean told himself.

'Sorry, Sean,' he drawled in his thick Irish accent, 'didn't mean to make you nearly blow your load there.' The priest spied a chair near the desk under the window and pulled it over to the side of the bed. 'Will you not get back into bed, Sean. I know you think you're God's gift, but your legs are brutal, man.'

Sean loosened his grip on the door handle and slowly stepped away from the door, keeping his gaze firmly on Father O'Carroll. He gradually made his way back to the bed and little by little covered his legs with the quilt.

'Am I dreaming?' whispered Sean.

'Do you think ya are?' he smiled. Sean shook his head slowly. He studied the priest more as he sat beside his bed. His posture was the same as Charlie's when he came to visit him after the crash. 'Well, probably best to trust your gut there,' joked the priest.

'How did you get in here? Where did you come from?' Sean began to pat his quilt at his knee, 'and why the hell is my quilt wet?' he squealed in disgust.

'Jesus! You're firing the questions out like a feckin' Tommy gun!' The priest placed his hands on each thigh. 'Your blanket's wet there because you threw your drink over it.'

'Oh, yes,' whispered Sean. He was gently rubbing the wetness and became aware he was scared to look at the priest. Father O'Carroll still seated on the stool began to shift around as if taking in a better view of the room. His eyes were darting everywhere and the longer he looked the more satisfied his face became.

'Not a bad room you have here. Yes, very nice,' he nodded toward Sean's bedside lamp. 'You could do with another 40 watts in that bulb though. I feel like I should be listening to your confession,' he chuckled. Sean did not smile. 'So, have you spoke to Crowley then?' probed the priest. Sean snapped out of his nervous demeanour and looked at his visitor straight in the eye.

'How the hell do you know about Crowley?'

'Oh, come on Sean, don't be an eejit! Did you think Dr bleeding Spock transported me into your room?'

'I dunno! You might have come in through the window!' The priest turned and looked at the first-floor window and the desk that sat under it.

'You're right there, Sean. I managed to haul all sixteen stone of me up your plastic gutters, shoehorn meself through that tiny gap in the window and not only not break any of that crap on your desk but also manage not to break a sweat either,' he said sarcastically, 'all in silence!'

Sean continued to stare at him. His clothes were the same as they were when he met him in the chapel at St Bartholomew's. His manner was the same and Sean could detect a faint smell of Guinness pervading the air. He studied his body language and concluded the priest seemed very relaxed. *If I was dreaming,* thought Sean, *could I not tell myself that I was dreaming? How do I know any of this is real?* For a moment, Sean tried to concentrate on the sounds coming from the window. He was listening for falling buildings. But all he could hear was the swish of the dense foliage of the leylandii trees at the bottom of the garden.

'Are you like Crowley?' Sean asked flatly.

'Yes and no,' he sat up slightly to deliver the rest. 'Ah sure, I'm dead. Have been for a while now.' Sean raised his eyebrows. 'Don't worry, doesn't hurt a bit,' Father O'Carroll chortled. 'Well, the thing is you see Sean, I can't get into the big house until I do the big man a favour,' he pointed upwards with his thumb and a large grin.

'So, are you just walking the Earth until the 'big man' says yes?' asked Sean.

'Not exactly. I can come and go as I please, but I'm

kind of in the waiting room for now. We all go there first, well, not all of us, but most of us anyway.'

Sean managed to smile, frown, shake his head and shrug his shoulders all at the same time. He had no idea what the priest was on about or if it was important enough to understand seeing as he wasn't sure if he was awake or not. Father O'Carroll smiled.

'Are ya keeping up, Sean?' Sean bobbed his head slightly.

'So, what's the favour you have to do?'

'We'll come to that in a minute,' and he waved his hand dismissively. 'So, Crowley has told you all about the carry on. One minute we were all sitting there having a drink and the next we get word that all hell had broken loose on Earth,' he squinted into the distance, 'and I was in Heaven. Jesus Christ, Hell, Earth, Heaven, I think my brain's gone fizzy.' He shook his head for comedic effect and continued. 'Anyway, there was a wee bit of panic and then I felt the tap on me shoulder there and this big fella, Bathisma, said I had to go with him and the next thing you know I'm in this beautiful white room. I know, very predictable.'

Sean raised his knees under the quilt and felt slightly more protected. He wasn't sure from what, but it felt better all the same. 'And there in front of me was Magda,' the priest stopped to enjoy the memory, 'ah, Sean, she was like a young Maureen O'Hara with all that red hair. But when she spoke she was no Maureen O'Hara, let me tell you. There was no nonsense out of that one!'

'So, who is Magda?'

'She's an angel. And that's not a term of endearment, I mean she really is an angel. And she said…well she told me…' he trailed off. Sean sat forward expectantly. 'Well, she just said I was to come and have a chat with yer,' he nodded in affirmation.

'A chat?' snapped Sean. 'A chat?! You're telling me that some redhead pulled you and told you to come and have a chat with me at half past three in the morning?! Behave!' Sean flung his legs out of the bed for the third time and stomped to the only other place he had been to in his bedroom this evening. He found his cigarettes on the desk, lit one up, then stood at the foot of the bed with one hand on his hip staring at the priest. 'So, you're not here to talk about the Curia or the jail or bleeding ancient scrolls that say someone has to kark it to save all of mankind?'

'Crowley was thorough, wasn't he?' mumbled Father O'Carroll.

'And he was sober. It was weird!' he snatched a drag of his cigarette. The priest sat quiet for a moment and continued to look up at Sean who started to feel uncomfortable under his scrutiny. He turned towards the open window where he carried on smoking and fidgeting. He flicked the butt in his usual fashion and walked back to the bed but instead of getting in he knelt on top of it and faced his visitor.

'So, let's chat then.' Sean sounded irritated but was clearly determined to find out why the priest was here. Father O'Carroll remained silent, a trick he had learned from years in the confessional box. He realised that people would be more conversational when the only alternative was uncomfortable silence. He could see Sean was silently winding himself up.

'Have you always been dead? I mean, with me? Were you dead in the church and the pub?' A memory came flooding back to Sean. 'You were dead in the pub! That's why that barmaid asked if I liked the pint that you drank. And that's why you made me buy your ale because she couldn't see you! So, were you dead in the church then?' his tone was interrogating.

'I was.'

'So, why've you been haunting me? What's all that about?'

The priest took a deep breath. 'I'm not haunting you,' the priest said in an exasperated tone. 'I'm here because of your dreams, of course. You told me about your dreams.'

'Did you make me dream?'

'No,' he chuckled.

'Then it's true, then?' Sean slumped slightly on the bed and began to realise that everything was connected. 'They are a message for me,' he lowered his head in mild defeat. The priest leaned forward and sought Sean's hand in his lap. He gently pulled it toward him and cupped it with his other hand.

'Sean, this "thing" or whatever you want to call it, I won't deny is monumental. The impact that it has had on all the mysteries that we liked being mysterious has been damaging beyond words. That simple belief in something beyond our time here has been shaken to its core. And I'll not lie to you, Upstairs are in a bit of a tizz. They're kind of making this up as they go along, I think, otherwise they would have asked someone a bit more qualified than me to get involved. But this is an unprecedented event. I mean whoever heard of an angel having an ego, I ask yer?'

'But you said you didn't believe they were angels that night.'

'No, what I actually said was that I didn't agree with what the angels were saying. Oh, they definitely came down that night and left the whole world in devastation and Heaven in confusion.'

'There's people killing themselves over this,' whispered Sean. 'They think they will have eternal life and still be able to be around their loved ones.'

'I know.'

'Crowley told me about the Curia. He told me how it works and who does what,' said Sean softly. The priest, still cupping Sean's hand, tilted his head to one side and could see tears forming in the soft brown eyes. 'If I don't do it, then who will?'

'Does it matter?'

'Well, yeah. I mean you can't just have anyone doing this, can you? They have to be carefully selected on merit and heart and hope and stuff. They have to be special, don't they?'

'That's why you are top of the list,' he said gently. Sean's tears began to roll slowly down his cheeks and he made no attempt to wipe them. The priest wasn't sure if Sean was aware they were there.

'I can't think,' Sean admitted. 'I dunno what I'm supposed to do. I'm not sure I'm strong enough to do this, or if I am the best person,' he sniffed. The priest sat still for a moment with his head tilted so he could see the young man's face. Over the years of catching glances of parishioners in the dim confessional boxes he had never seen one so full of anguish as this. He knew he shouldn't have thought it, but it wouldn't go away. The thought popped into his head and now he couldn't shake it off. After silently deliberating to himself he convinced himself that the powers that be would understand that what he was to do next was with the best intentions. Father O'Carroll sat up slightly and took a deep breath.

'Sean, I want you to do me a favour.' Sean raised his increasingly red eyes and looked at his visitor. 'I need you to trust me and do exactly what I say. Do you trust me,

Sean?' The priest looked at Sean imploringly and Sean knew that not only did he trust this man but, in some way, he felt he was being looked after. Sean nodded silently. 'Then close your eyes,' he said softly. He watched Sean take one last look at him and then without a word Sean closed his damp lashed eyes. 'I want you to remember when we first met, Sean. I want you to try and feel the seat beneath you. I want you to try and remember the smell of the old place, but most of all I want you to remember me being there. I want you to see me there, Sean. I want you to hear my voice and the things we talked about.'

Sean began to recollect their first meeting. He could see the back of Father O'Carroll before he sat back into his wooden chair. He could hear the slight rustle of his snug jacket as the priest made himself comfortable. He remembered the hardness of the seat and the blue kneeling cushion on the floor. He could see all the empty wooden chairs in the chapel except for the ones that Sean and his new-found friend were sat in. He could see the grey stone walls and the feeling of its age began to envelop him.

'Now, I want you to breathe in and try to smell those burning candles.' Sean took a long, slow and deliberate sniff. The delicate ashy aroma filled his nostrils and he could see their soft dancing glow to his left. 'Can you smell them, Sean?' he whispered. Sean dipped his head slightly. 'Now open your eyes,' he sighed.

Sean slowly drank in his surroundings as the priest let go of his hand. It was there, all of it, just as he remembered. He then stopped, in a dreamlike state, as his eyes rested on the painting of the Madonna and her baby, hanging on the chapel wall of St Bartholomew the Great.

CHAPTER 24

When Sean realised where he was, he did not feel the need to question why he was there, or if indeed he was there. His mind was still double-dutching from feeling conscious to unconscious. It had been a strange night, a strange few weeks, months even, and Sean now felt he was at a state to accept and not to look for a definitive answer. He wasn't even sure what the question should be.

He gazed upon the painting on the wall of the Madonna with her child and began to wonder what she was thinking, where and who she went to when she was troubled. Did she have a place to go to that brought clarity to her mind? He then remembered what the priest had said when they first met.

'It's true,' started Sean, 'she does help you think.' The priest took a deep breath or was it a sigh of relief.

'And what is it you are thinking about, Sean?' Sean thought of his first encounter with Crowley. He thought of him in his flat and how they had drunk tea which seemed absurd, now he knew Crowley. He thought of their first few shows and how an article in the local paper had raised his profile nationally. He thought of how lucky he was to have such an excellent reputation in the charlatan riddled industry of mediumship. He thought of the joy he had brought to countless people and the tears that had flowed with the words he had offered. He thought of how his mum and Charlie had been incredible in their support and kept him 'normal'. His thoughts of Sue were a marbling of gratitude and disappointment. He thought of Ambriel and his calming way. Maybe, he should be here to help him think. He thought of Michael and wondered if he could see him now. Were they all looking down on him? Could they see him in this church staring at the painting? Could they feel him pushing the most important question that needed to be answered not only out of his mind but out of his very pores? Could they feel his fleeting but crippling panic as soon as he gave the question a momentary deliberation?

'I'm thinking I don't want to think about what I need to think about.'

'What is it your frightened of?'

'Dying!' Father O'Carroll gave a small amused snort. 'You think this is funny, do you?' snapped Sean.

'Ah, no. It's just…well…I'm dead and I'm no worse for wear for it.' Sean gave him the once over. He wasn't sure he entirely agreed seeing as the priest and Crowley had not had a change of clothes since he had met them. Should that be something he needed to contemplate? Was that part of the dying process to tell someone what you wanted to wear for all eternity? 'Sean, death doesn't just bring pain it also brings relief and not just for the one that passes. Those who are left behind experience both emotions as well.'

Sean thought of various people in his past who had experienced loved ones dying, especially those who were ill. The varying illnesses experienced by them made no difference to the result. But the thing they all had in common was their relief at the eventual death. Whilst all being sad, of course, they were content once they were dead. It was not only about the person being free of pain, it wasn't just about the constant care that some of them demanded, it was sometimes because the living were able to have normality back. It might have felt different from before but being given normality was sometimes the greatest gift to those left behind. Could he be the person that offered this normality back? Was humanity sat by the unknown bedside of an unknown person, waiting for normality?

But what if he didn't die? What if someone else did this? What if that person was the wrong choice? How would they choose that person? What if they failed? Could we live in a world where angels walked amongst us, telling us how to make decisions and what thoughts to have and who to speak to and what to say? Could we live in a world where all humans became nothing but grateful puppets? The thought made him shudder. What would happen to places of worship? Would we need them anymore? Could the human soul take on an identity that it had never experienced? Did it have the resilience and the ability to adapt to a whole new world of now and beyond? And what if the second choice succeeded? Would he ever know who it was? Would the world ever know who it was? Could Sean live with himself knowing that someone else had been able to achieve the thing he was asked to do and then bottled it? How would he be received in Heaven when he eventually did die? Would he go to Heaven, even? What if this decision affected his eternity?

He thought again of his mum and Charlie. If he asked them what he should do he wondered how they would answer. In a flash, the scene was before him. Mum in a panic and telling him that he couldn't do it. Charlie calmly drinking the whole scene in and then telling Sean that it was up to him. Then his mum shouting at Charlie for not dissuading him from this terrible fate. Then Charlie calmly telling his mum that the decision was bigger than them and it was up to Sean and his conscience to decide. Then his mum crying and then eventually saying Charlie was right. No one could help him decide. It was his decision, and his alone.

'No one can help me with this, can they?'

'I'm here to help you,' consoled the priest.

'Yeah, but you can't make the decision for me.'

'No, Sean.' Sean went back to the Madonna. He knew for sure that whatever decisions she had to make she never had one like this.

'Maybe, if I knew who is next on the list…maybe, that would help me?'

'Sean, maybe you should stop focusing on who is second and think about who is first. Maybe, think about yourself in the third person. If you knew someone exactly like you and everything about them since the day they were born would you want them to do this?'

Sean remembered the story Maggie had told him of the caul over his face when he first came into the world and its spiritual significance. He thought of himself being a generous man and apart from a couple of vices and appalling taste in men he was a good and sensible. Would whoever was second on the list have a CV that matched his? And even if they did, did they have the tenacity, the understanding and above all else the passion to make this right? He doubted it.

'There's not gonna be many like me is there, Father?'

'No. There's only one Sean Allister,' the priest smiled.

'Have you ever looked up the meaning of your name, by the way?'

'What? Sean?'

'No, Allister.' Sean shook his head.

'It means the defender of mankind,' he said softly. Sean slowly moved his gaze away from the priest and stared wide-eyed at the Madonna.

'It's predestined for me,' he sighed.

'I'm sure you would have still been at the top of the list even if you had a surname like McGreedy or Clutterbucks or something.'

'Clutterbucks?' Sean giggled.

'Sure! I had a man in my parish called Tony Clutterbucks. Permanently in confession about wanting to inflict harm on those around him. I used to think that if he changed his name they would stop taking the mick and he wouldn't permanently feel in a state of wanting to kick ten bells out of people's arses,' he finished. Sean smiled and carried on looking at the painting and silently Father O'Carroll did the same. They sat in the quiet, both quite still. Now and again they could hear a faint flicker and a purr from a candle flame. But the noise of traffic that usually could be heard, was not present. The murmur of a city beyond the church walls had been hushed to a still, eerie silence. As Sean thought of his mum and Charlie, he eventually spoke up.

'I want to go home, if we can?'

'Sure, we can.' As Sean turned to look at the priest and await his next instruction he could see him back on the stool beside his bed that he was now kneeling on again. His surroundings seemed noisier and the whispering trees beyond the open window reminded Sean why.

Sean slowly uncurled his legs from beneath him, swung them to the opposite side of Father O'Carroll and headed for his desk. He opened the drawer and the priest mistakenly presumed that he was reaching for his cigarettes. Sean pulled out a card that was still in its cellophane wrapper. The picture on the stark white front of the card was a simple silver outline of angel's wings. He had bought the card to give to his friend Grace when she lost her dear old friend, Kate Mortimer, last year. But he realised he had forgotten it as he stood at the graveside. After that, there never seemed to be a right moment to give her the card as he had said everything to her that he had wanted to write.

The pen had eagerly rolled to the front of the drawer when he opened it and Sean was grateful for its readiness. He then peeled the cellophane off and discarded it into the bin beside the desk. He missed, but he didn't notice. Father O'Carroll sat in silence as he watched Sean write. He noted that Sean showed no emotion while he was writing. He could have been writing a note to the milkman for all his face gave away, but the priest knew for certain that the eventual recipient of the card would not be as restrained with their feelings as the author. Sean slid the card into the envelope, scribbled on the front and then placed it back on the desk. He then walked back to the bed and instead of kneeling back onto it, he sat on the edge facing the priest.

He was about to speak when he noticed Crowley emerging from the darkness at the far side of his bedroom again. Sean felt relieved that his friend had returned. Crowley, with a hint of a smile sat on the bed next to Sean. He gave a small courteous nod to Father O'Carroll who in turn gave a friendly acknowledgement with a smile.

'I'm glad you're here,' said Sean.

'I'm glad you wanted me,' shrugged Crowley.

'I did, and I didn't even realise it until I saw you.' Father

O'Carroll, who too was glad of Crowley's presence, also felt a tinge of jealously. He had become fond of Sean in the few interactions he had had with him and had always envisaged that when the time came he would be alone with Sean. But he soon recognised that Crowley was an important part of not only the plan but to Sean and he soon felt appreciative and blessed that he was part of it too.

'I want to do this.'

'Are you sure?' asked Crowley. Sean lifted his knees up and swung his legs behind Crowley's back to lay back down on the bed. He stared at the ceiling for a moment to collect his thoughts.

'I can't stay in a world that's in such a state knowing that I could have made a difference, I couldn't live with myself. So, by not doing this, I'd be condemning myself anyway, if that makes sense. I know I might royally fuck all of this up, but I have to try, don't I? And I know you guys are saying that I have a choice, but really…I have no choice. It has to be me.'

'Spoken from the soul of a truly brave man,' proclaimed the priest. Crowley nodded in agreement and could feel his heart swelling with pride for his courageous friend. Sean turned his head to gauge Crowley's reaction when he was distracted by someone else coming into the room.

'What the…?' stuttered a dumbfounded Sean. From the darkness appeared a tall black man. He didn't just appear, he rushed into the room as if he was on fire. He seemed excited, nervous and relieved all at the same time. Sean noticed that neither Father O'Carroll nor Crowley didn't flinch at his arrival. The man, who wore sunglasses, gave a flirty smile and headed to the bed. His long, silk coat was made from brightly coloured patches that had been sewn with gold thread and as he moved the glint in the garment danced in the gaudiness. His shirt beneath was black and buttoned to his Adam's apple and his baggy Aladdin style silk trousers were just as dark as they sat at his slim waist. His afro hair was shaved at the sides, but the top had been preened to a perfect wedge which had been intentionally cut to slant slightly to one side.

'Hello boys,' his voice had a slight feminine squeal about it. Sean went to sit up, not because of manners but more that he was completely aghast by the sight before him. 'Oh, don't sit up dear, on my account.' His accent was American and his voice was breathy. With a mixture of amusement and fascination Sean watched as the new arrival waved his hand as if invisibly patting Sean back down on the bed. The man moved in between Crowley and the priest and went to sit on what seemed like fresh air. But by the time he smoothed his coat satisfactorily around his rear, a small stool appeared exactly like the one that was under the priest. Sean, still wide-eyed and staring at his new visitor, began to shuffle up the bed slightly until he was in a sitting position.

'Well, isn't this cosy,' the man giggled as he crossed his legs and clamped his intertwining hands around his higher knee.

'I feel like I'm in a scene from Back to the Future!' said Sean.

'A back to the what?' The man quickly looked at the priest, then Crowley, then back to Sean for a clue.

'I think,' Crowley began, 'that Sean is alluding to your attire.'

'It didn't sound like a compliment,' he sniffed.

'Did you miss the nineties and noughties and now? It's like you got dressed after watching a Duran Duran video.'

'I'll have you know that this was designed by a very talented man from the fashion house L'eau de la Créativité!'

'More like L'eaud of old shit!' Father O'Carroll unsuccessfully tried to supress a laugh and the black man looked hurt.

'Ah, he's only codding ya, so take that puss off your face and tell him who ye are,' and he gave the new visitor a nudge on his shoulder. The man quickly composed himself, smiled brightly and held out his hand. Crowley and Father O'Carroll stared at the outstretched hand.

'My name is Keziah, and you must be Sean,' he squealed. Sean sat up some more to take his new guest in. The man was very feminine and had an air of immaturity about him and even though his fashion sense would be perfect for a gay rendition of the film The Lost Boys, Sean liked him. He took the outstretched hand but didn't notice Crowley or Father O'Carroll raising their eyebrows then quickly looking at the floor.

'So, what brings you to this impromptu party?' asked Sean.

'I'm an angel!' Keziah said in a delighted tone.

'Oh,' drawled Sean, slightly unimpressed.

'I'm here to take you,' he beamed.

'Take me where?'

'To Heaven of course, I'm the Angel of Death,' Keziah laughed. Sean sat bolt upright on the bed and continued to stare at Keziah.

'Fuckin' hell! That escalated quickly!' snapped Sean. He quickly gave Keziah another obvious once-over. 'Why're you dressed like that though?' Sean gave him a confused look.

'This again!' Keziah shook his head in exasperation. 'I REFUSE to wear some horrid black gown that does nothing for my figure. And a hood?! Please! This...' he patted his slanting afro, 'takes more manicuring than any of your country's English Gardens. Why, why, why do people only want to see me head to foot in black, carrying a scythe and moaning like mating bull. My job is bad enough without me being depressed because of bad clothes and a bad attitude.' He shook his head with the abhorrence at the suggestion.

'Don't you like your job?' quizzed Sean.

'I'm the Angel of Death, dear. People are rarely pleased to see me.' He squinted his mouth to one side and leaned a little toward Sean, 'Especially old white people from Alabama.' He then drew an invisible circle in front of his face to illustrate the problem. 'And I'm sooooo busy! I don't get holidays even though I've been promised for thousands of years. Not one day! Every day there's someone waiting for me to give them that final push. And let's face it, death is sooooo depressing! I asked for a transfer to maybe spiritual guide,' he briefly smiled at the thought, 'but I'm not allowed because I'm an angel and that position is for souls only. Not exactly in keeping with our Inclusion Policy, but I don't make the rules. Then I asked if I could be in the Birth Division.' Keziah smiled dreamily at the ceiling and added in a breathy tone, 'But they felt my artistic side might get in the way and I would be tempted to 'zhush' a little bit too much with soul mapping.' His face changed to a disappointed look and dropped his gaze back to Sean. 'So, they now just have me on file until a suitable position comes up that I may be interested in.' He tried to finish with a hopeful tone, but he was fooling no one and Sean felt very sorry for him for a moment but then slowly he could feel a laugh rising in him. It eventually became evident as it burst on his face as a huge smile.

'Are you telling me that you are a reluctant Angel of Death?' he laughed.

'Reluctant and ragged! It's hard to keep up.' Sean quickly had a thought.

'Are people waiting to die at this very moment and you are waiting for me?' Sean began to feel under pressure.

'Oh no dear, it doesn't work like that. Death is everywhere,' he saw Sean's confused look. 'I'm everywhere. I'm not like a soul that can only be in one place. I'm like a feeling, a thought, a reaction. I'm something that is all around,' he finished dramatically with a wave in the air.

'So, you can be in two places at once?' pushed Sean flatly.

'The limitations of the human soul,' he said disappointingly, 'but I suppose so, yes.' Sean stared straight ahead and thought of all the people who were now being greeted by Keziah. All over the world people were popping their clogs and being escorted to the Pearly Gates by an MC Hammer lookalike. Crowley turned to see Sean's face and wondered if everything had moved too fast. Should he have warned him of Keziah and the whole process of death? Should he have given Sean more time by sewing a little doubt in his mind?

'So, are we ready to go boys?' smiled Keziah. Sean jumped off the bed and headed to the desk to find his cigarettes. He had his back to them all as he put the small flame to the tip and pulled hard on the other end to entice the flame to work harder.

'I just need a smoke and a think first. I have to be sure I am doing the right thing,' and he closed his eyes to contemplate his ending.

'It might be a little late for that, dear,' Keziah squeaked. Sean spun around and noticed that another person was sitting on the bed behind Crowley. Crowley and Father O'Carroll stared at Sean, not looking at the additional guest. Sean frowned and squinted at the slightly obscured man propped up against the pillows and as he moved to see him more Crowley and Father O'Carroll could see the shock begin to ravage Sean.

The man on the bed was Sean.

CHAPTER 25

Sean's funeral was so well attended they spilled out into the large gardens in front of St Michaels and All Angels Church. Maggie had insisted, to a lot of silent confusion of the mourners, that the service be carried out in a church thirty miles away from Clune. His death had been a shock to not only those in Clune and Lanson, where he lived, but nationally and internationally. His reputation in mediumship had escalated his celebrity status very quickly and, until the Day of Revelations as it was now being called, his career was about to embrace another level of stardom. But many of the mourners knew Sean before he was famous. Old school friends sat amongst his previous co-workers, as they sat amongst TV presenters, radio DJ's, soap stars and pop stars. All of them having one thing in common: their love and respect for Sean, who had been taken from them suddenly and prematurely.

At the front of the church sat Maggie and Charlie. Charlie's brother had also come with his wife and children and they sat stony-faced looking at the large picture propped on an easel to the side of Sean's coffin. Behind them, were Sean's closest friends including Faye and Sue. To Sue's right sat Grace who had flown from New York with her fiancé, Todd, and Grace's parents Dai and Penny had also joined them on the same bench.

Maggie's face was motionless and expressionless. She almost looked doll like, as if someone had painted her face onto a blank mannequin. Oh, she had cried, she had screamed like an animal when she discovered his lifeless body on his bed. Her whole being felt as if it was shredding as she tried to shake him back to life. Charlie had used all his strength to eventually prise her off his body so he could make sure that Sean was indeed dead. And though he too wanted to scream, he couldn't, as it would have tipped Maggie into a state he wasn't sure she would ever recover from. A voice inside him shouted at him to be strong, to keep it together, to help his wife.

When the body had been taken away from his room, Maggie had gone to bed and had planned never to leave it for the rest of her life. She wanted to stay in the bed until she could see Sean again. She felt that her reason, her point, her life had gone. Charlie had roused her a few hours later, and as she began to protest he insisted she sat up to read a card that he had found on Sean's desk addressed to "My Beautiful Mother".

The card had sat on her bedside table for two whole days. She couldn't bring herself to open it. She knew it would be the last time she would 'hear' Sean. And while it stayed there unopened she felt that she had a piece of him to look forward to. But then as the funeral arrangements began, she wondered if the card held any wishes for his end and the panic began to rise thinking she would get it wrong.

She read the card as she sat on his bed, smelling one of his denim shirts. It was one of the few items in his wardrobe that hadn't been laundered. He didn't like his denim being washed too often. He liked to be smart, but he always said that denim should look a little shabby, a little creased, a little lived in. Only Charlie had seen the contents of the card and it would remain like that forever. There were no wishes in the card. The card was full of reasons. The card was full of responsibility. But most of all the card was full of love.

She had admitted to Charlie, as they lay in bed in the dark, that she understood and they both cried as they clutched each other about how proud they were of their son. And even though the pain was unimaginable for them both, he had done the right thing. They were only disappointed they were not with him at the end.

In Maggie's mind, as she looked at her beautiful son's picture before her, she knew she was unique. She knew she was probably the only mother ever to say she was glad her son was dead. She knew that the world was about to change, and the world had her son to thank. But they would never know. But it didn't matter, she knew. She would miss him, but she was not sad. She and Charlie would see him again and then they would be a family once more. No one saw the corner of her mouth twitch slightly with a tic of a smile.

The rest of the funeral became a blur for Maggie and Charlie. They had insisted that the funeral reception be at their house and after the crematorium a handful of people, mainly family, joined them in Clune. They graciously accepted people's sympathies and promised to consider calling people whenever "they needed to talk" and the last of the mourners were packed off by seven pm. Maggie was in the bath by eight.

Charlie had stayed downstairs and by the time his rosy-cheeked wife descended the stairs there was not a trace of the day left and the house became eerily normal again.

They made their hot chocolate together, put a few chocolate digestives on a small plate and toddled to the lounge and instead of Charlie sitting in his usual armchair, he sat on the couch beside his wife. She reached for the remote control and as the television slowly came to life she sat back into the warmth of Charlie's awaiting hug.

'And now we wait,' she whispered.

CHAPTER 26

Crowley, Father O'Carroll, Keziah and Sean stood in front of the door that Crowley had recently knocked. Sean had no idea where he was. He remembered seeing his body on the bed and then an overwhelming feeling of joy, happiness, peace and light. He wasn't sure how much time had passed, and he knew he had spoken recently to his three companions, but he couldn't remember what was said. He was sure that he was safe and in a strange way he felt peaceful. The door opened, and a beaming face looked at Sean.

'So, are you Peter or Paul then?' joked Sean.

'I am Nazriel, and I am most honoured to finally meet you, Sean.' Nazriel stepped forward and embraced Sean without warning. While being embraced, Sean cast a sideways glance at Crowley who looked positively chuffed with the whole scene. 'Come in, come in,' insisted Nazriel gently guiding Sean through the door. As they walked into Nazriel's study Sean noticed another man waiting for them at the far end and then saw Nazriel slightly taken aback.

'Bathisma?' enquired Nazriel.

'I'm here for Jesse O'Carroll,' he delivered in a flat tone. They all turned to look at the priest.

'Your name is Jesse?' smirked Crowley. The priest blushed.

'Ah, me da was into the Wild West,' he stuttered. 'It could have been worse, me brother was called Geronimo.'

'Geronimo O'Carroll? That would fetch a hefty score in scrabble,' Crowley joked.

'We called him Gerry after he ran out of people to punch who laughed at him.' He turned to Sean, 'Well, I guess this is it, now.' He stretched his arms wide and stepped forward to embrace him. Sean too stepped forward and accepted his love.

'Guess the big fella is happy with you, then?' said Sean referring to Father O'Carroll's reason for meeting Sean in the first place. The priest smiled and as he placed a hand on each of Sean's shoulders he gave him a final look.

'I hope to see you again, Sean.'

'And when I do, there'll be a Guinness waiting for you.' The priest pulled away, shook Crowley's hand and then walked toward Bathisma. They both disappeared before he reached him.

'And that is my cue to go,' Keziah announced. 'Busy, busy, busy,' he began to walk out of the door.

'Wait!' started Sean. He wasn't sure how to word the question without it sounding strange but then he was now in a world of strange, so he supposed it didn't matter. 'How did I die?'

'Well, I gave you an undiscovered heart condition that you have had since birth and people think you simply died in your sleep,' he said in a victorious manner. Sean thought of his mum and Charlie and felt it was a good reason for them to tell people what had happened to him, even though he was confident they knew the truth. Without another word Keziah was gone.

'Well, I guess I won't be seeing him again,' muttered Sean.

'Not unless you plan on dying twice!' Crowley smirked and then without being asked took a seat in his usual place.

'Please?' Nazriel pointed to the couch for Sean to sit and as Sean sat down, Nazriel began to busy himself with tea.

'No offence, Nazriel but you couldn't rustle up something a bit stronger, could you?' Nazriel turned to look at Crowley and while he did not approve of how much he drank he had to admit to himself that the man deserved a drink of his choice after what he had achieved.

'Whisky?' enquired Nazriel.

'Now there's a sport,' grinned Crowley, 'and vodka for my recently deceased charge here.' Sean looked around Nazriel's study and was surprised at how normal it all felt. Even though he had chatted at length with Crowley as to what Heaven was really like, he was still surprised to see it was as his friend had described.

They were soon all seated and sipping their drinks, except for Crowley who even though guzzled his with the thirst of a lost Arab, the contents did not diminish as he rested his glass in between his bouts of gulping.

'So, what happens now?' asked Sean. Nazriel placed his cup on the small table in front of him and sat up slowly.

'That is up to you,' he smiled.

* * *

Rucelle sat alone in his office with only his thoughts for company. Bathisma was now dealing with all the new entrants that fell under his department and all the other angels and archangels were waiting on Rucelle's further instructions. He thought of thirty years ago and the decisions they had made. He thought if they could have avoided Sean's death. But then he thought of the shift in Heaven and the damage on Earth and then would always come back to the same conclusion that the recent and past events were mostly out of their control and their reactions and actions were their only choices.

He had prepared for Sean's arrival. He had prepared for the Curia. He just needed to prepare Sean for the Curia, as once they were in there, it was all down to him. He had a short time to teach him the ways of the Curia and a shorter time to coach him on questions he should ask and answers he should give. He might not be able to speak but that did not mean he couldn't make his voice heard, even if that meant it was through Sean.

Rucelle felt nervous at meeting Sean and he struggled to understand why. It was Nazriel who offered the suggestion of Sean being the first person that Rucelle actually needed, and he was probably right. In the Curia, Rucelle would have to trust that Sean would remember his teachings and as most people had not been in the Curia before, they could only prepare so much and this only added to Rucelle's anxiety. Nazriel had also made the point that Rucelle must gain Sean's respect. Trust and loyalty would not be enough for this new soul. For Sean to understand the enormity of what lay in front of him, Rucelle had to recognise that Sean was a unique person with unique qualities.

He began to walk around his office, trying to order his mind when the expectant knock pealed from the door. He took a deep breath, walked to the front of his desk and beckoned for them to come in. The door opened, and the three men took a moment to peer in before silently entering the room. Sean who was sandwiched between Nazriel and Crowley, could not look away from the pale blue eyes that were quickly studying him. They silently sized each other up and could not conclude their initial thoughts just yet.

Rucelle stepped forward and offered not only a handshake but also a smile and as Sean shook his hand he noticed Sean looking to his right. There was nothing there that could be seen but Sean looked uncomfortable.

'Sean?'

'It's great to finally meet you,' Sean's voice was barely a whisper.

'Please, take a seat,' he looked at Crowley and then at Nazriel. 'Crowley, I am sure your lovely wife is waiting for you. Nazriel, thank you for delivering Mr Allister.' Rucelle's word was final. It was not up for debate and Crowley and Nazriel knew not to question their expulsion. Crowley gave Sean a last look of encouragement and then disappeared with Nazriel. Sean, feeling a bit awkward, took his seat and waited for Rucelle to begin. However, he felt he was still being watched to his right and wondered if there was someone there. Rucelle caught him again casting his cautionary gaze.

'Are you okay, Sean?'

'I'm still getting to grips with…well…all of this,' and he waved his hand to demonstrate. 'Can I ask, though? Is there someone there? Watching us?' Rucelle frowned slightly and then looked to Sean's right. *Could it be?* he thought.

'I assure you, Sean, there is no one watching you.' Sean was not convinced. Rucelle walked around to the back of his desk and took his seat. He sat forward and placed his clasped hands on top and offered a smile. 'I take it you are up to speed with everything?'

'Not everything.' Sean not only suspected there was more to say but had hoped that Rucelle would fill in some of the gaps. 'I mean, they've told me about the Curia. But I am not sure what it is I am supposed to do or say.'

'That is my job. By the time we have finished Sean, I am confident you will not only be our best chance at defending mankind but will also restore balance to our world and the world you have just left.'

'Glad someone is hopeful,' sniffed Sean. Rucelle took his tone to be lack of confidence and felt the only way to restore it was to jump straight in with his teachings.

After settling in with some refreshments, they made themselves comfortable and Rucelle slowly began with the history of the Curia, how it came to be and how it had only been used once before. Sean nodded throughout and only asked a few questions. He was grateful that Rucelle was explaining things in a way he could understand, which surprised him. Rucelle went on to explain why there was no jury, in the traditional sense, and that the judgement could only be made by Mr Reeshon.

'And why is Mr Reeshon the be all and end all of all of this?' Rucelle cast his gaze downwards and smiled.

'Mr Reeshon understands sin. He understands temptation. He understands the importance of mankind and he also understands banishment,' Rucelle finished.

'What? So, has this fella been to Hell?' gasped Sean. Rucelle gave a little chuckle to himself.

'No, Sean. Mr Reeshon has been to Earth.'

'Oh!' Sean was still confused. If the qualities to be a judge was temptation, sin and banishment then he felt he himself was more than qualified after a few drinks on a Friday night.

'So, is Mr Reeshon a soul?'

'Mr Reeshon is not a soul nor an angel nor archangel.'

'So, what is he then?'

'He is Adam,' Rucelle said flatly. Adam Reeshon, thought Sean. It didn't ring a bell. Should he know him? Was there some connection to him and this Adam? 'Adam was banished from Eden because he sinned,' said Rucelle. Sean felt a jolt through his body.

'What? The Adam? Like the "Adam and Eve", Adam? That Adam?' Sean stared in disbelief.

'The name Reeshon or Rishon means the first.'

'Oh, my fucking giddy aunt,' sighed Sean.

Rucelle continued until Sean agreed that Mr Reeshon was indeed, a unique person and in a case like this, his knowledge and empathy should stand them in good stead. However, even though it was not a given, they still had to give a solid reasoned argument as to why Christian should be banished. Rucelle resumed his thread and moved on to the writings of the Carcerem and how it could not be a permanent state within Heaven. Whilst not telling Sean where it was, he did say that it was in the vicinity and was being constantly monitored. He also explained the environment of the Carcerem which Sean winced at and wondered of all the things that angels did for humans back on Earth why they couldn't create a place like that for all the bad people. What felt like an age, they continued to talk, and Sean became more relaxed in Rucelle's company. He felt he had a greater understanding of what to expect in the Curia but not what to say. Sean asked for Rucelle's advice.

'I feel I should give you a list of questions, a script so to speak.' Sean frowned at this.

'A script? Something you want me to learn word for word?'

'I suppose so, yes,' smiled Rucelle.

'Sorry mate, but I thought you were going to give me

some pointers. I didn't realise that you wanted me to vomit something out verbatim.' Sean began to sound frustrated.

'Please don't get me wrong, Sean. I do not doubt your abilities. It's just that we can't take any chances with this, and I…I mean we have to be sure that this is done correctly.' Sean sat stunned. His stare into Rucelle's blue eyes was only relieved with his occasional and purposeful slow blink. 'I'm sorry, Sean. I get the impression you think I'm offending you,' Rucelle's tone had changed. He sounded slightly irritated.

'I am offended, quite frankly!' he snapped. Rucelle looked a little taken aback by his bluntness. 'Can I just condense this,' began Sean, 'into a few simple sentences? Are you telling me that I left my family, my friends, my whole bleeding life which I am sure still had a few years left, to come here and be an 'extra'? You could have gotten anybody to 'follow a script'. But hang on, no you couldn't! Because some bloody ancient text says that a human soul has to sacrifice themselves to even enter the arena in the first place.' Sean was now becoming increasingly angry.

'Sean, there is no need to get excited about this! You too have an input.' Rucelle tried to reassure but this just wound up Sean even more.

'You don't get it do you? I'm not going to make a difference. You are!!'

'Please do not raise your voice at me, Sean!' Sean stood up and blindly looked around.

'How the fuck do I get out of here?' He gave a slightly panicked laugh, 'I don't even know where the hell I'm supposed to go!' And then instinctively he called Crowley and Nazriel at the top of his voice.

In an instant, they were both standing in Rucelle's office looking very confused and slightly ill at ease with the shocked look that was evident on their superior's face.

Sean spun and looked at them both.

'Can you get me out of here? Now! Steven Spielberg here is a fucking joke!' The shock soon appeared on Crowley's and Nazriel's face and then quickly changed to concern. Crowley looked over at Rucelle who was now on his feet but still stood behind his desk, clearly agitated. *What on Earth has happened,* thought Crowley. He wanted to talk to Sean but knew he would be too emotional to get any sense out of him. The air tasted of disappointment and Crowley could see that Sean was clearly upset.

'Nazriel, could you please take Sean back to your study and I shall be with you shortly. I want to speak to Rucelle.' Nazriel silently obeyed his friend, took Sean by the arm and they disappeared leaving Crowley locked in Rucelle's gaze.

'Well?' asked Crowley who was aware that he was still half drunk and needed to sober up quickly.

'The boy became excited, that's all. He just needs to calm down and realise that I am talking sense.'

'And what sense would this be, Rucelle? I've known Sean a long time and yes, I know he can be hysterical and dramatic, but I have only ever witnessed it at times when it was justified.' Crowley was trying his best to remain calm.

'I simply told the boy that I would help him with his questioning.'

'He called you Steven Spielberg. It sounds like you might have been directing him what to do.'

'I mentioned the word 'script' and that seemed to trigger him.' Rucelle was trying to play the whole scene down and gave an unconvincing shrug of his shoulders.

'You want him to follow a script?'

'Yes, but only in the sense that we have all the important facts covered. I did say to him that he could have an input in this, but he didn't seem to like that suggestion at all. I'm sorry Crowley, but I feel you are standing there in judgement of my actions and I will not tolerate it, from you or the boy! We cannot take any chances with this! Do you want to see Christian and Jack and all of them wandering around Earth practically breaking their own arms as they try to pat themselves on their backs? I am not prepared to take the risk and if that means that I have to tolerate a bit of sulking from the boy to achieve this then so be it!' Rucelle was practically hissing through his gritted teeth, but Crowley could only feel more anger rising in him.

'The boy?! His name is Sean!' snapped Crowley. Rucelle stayed silent. 'At all, of what I am sure was a well-constructed and probably clinical delivery of the facts, can I just ask *at all*? I mean, forgive me if my presumption is not founded,' Crowley walked toward Rucelle's desk, 'but did you thank Sean at all for what he has done?' Rucelle's face did not flicker and Crowley was now confident in his belief. 'Did you empathise with his unique situation that I, and quite frankly you also, have never experienced? Did you refer to the fact at all that he gave his own life for not only those on Earth, but for the sake of Heaven too?' He continued, almost prowling, toward Rucelle. 'Did you acknowledge at all that what he did was one of the most selfless acts that any of us have witnessed?'

Rucelle's face began to soften whether it was realisation or the fact that he didn't know how to react to someone talking him in this way, Crowley wasn't sure and didn't care either. 'I take it from your penetrating silence that you didn't. I take it then, that you brought "the boy" in here and tried to make him feel valuable by simply saying that any suggestions he wished to make to your "script" would no doubt be considered. But at the end of the day, this was your production and I am sure you made it plain that you ultimately wanted control over everything and that he should be grateful!'

'I'm trying to help,' Rucelle's voice sounded cracked and Crowley was not mistaken to hear that it was also laced with fear.

'You are no better than the people we are trying to condemn,' spat Crowley. Rucelle's eyes grew wide in shock and disbelief at the accusation. 'You simply want to use Sean as a puppet. You want to play him like a pawn in this universal game of chess.'

'That's not true,' Rucelle stuttered.

'Oh, but it is! You are completely ignorant to the fact that it is not Sean who needs you, it is you who needs Sean. We all need Sean! This has been his destiny since the day he was born, if not before and whether any of us like it or not, including Sean, this is HIS cross to bear.'

Rucelle lowered his head and his gaze and stared at the edge of his desk. Looking at Crowley was making him feel uncomfortable and listening to him was even worse. Had he made a mistake? Crowley could see defeat slowly eating away at Rucelle and allowed it to nibble at him. Rucelle needed to realise the damage he was causing, the irreversible result if they followed his actions and ultimately where the blame would lie if they failed. If there was to be failure at the end it needed to be simply that, pure failure, without the spiciness of blame added to the mix.

Crowley pulled up a chair and sat in front of Rucelle's desk. He took a large breath and hoped he could recover something from the mess they all had had a part in creating.

'You know,' Crowley started, 'it wouldn't hurt for you to talk to Michael and Ambriel. Maybe ask them about Sean and how he can change when he's in front of an audience.'

'The Curia is not the London Palladium,' Rucelle muttered still looking downward.

'Oh, I'm sure Sean is well aware of that. But when he

knows he is being watched, when he knows that people are listening to him, a very different Sean emerges and it's very hard not to...' he paused looking for the right words, '...it's very hard not to be consumed by him.' Rucelle looked up, his eyes almost childlike, his face hopeful. 'Most of us, if not all,' continued Crowley, 'are afraid of Christian and all who follow him.'

'But not Sean?' asked Rucelle.

'I'm sure he is. But see the thing with Sean is, once he is out there, you do not see those fears. It's like he's invincible. But the most marvellous thing about him is...well...it's like he can see into your soul. He can see your deepest want and make it happen with a few words. And it's not just about the living feeling comforted or relieved, he makes it believable. I've seen him make the hardest sceptic believe. Not that there are many of them left in the world now. But to a see a grown man change from cynical to shocked has always been down to Sean. It's not what I have said, it is the way he has delivered it to make it believable and those added extras that we describe as consolation and liberation are not lost in what he says but are arrived at subconsciously, they are not paramount in Sean's message.' Rucelle's raised an eyebrow. He looked expectant. 'Michael and Ambriel will tell you the same as I,' said Crowley who stood up and watched Rucelle mirror his actions, only Rucelle continued to walk and headed toward Crowley. 'Tell Sean what he needs to know and let him deliver it in his way,' Crowley said softly. 'I'll speak to Sean and ask him to come and see you once he has calmed down.' Crowley headed towards the door and as he reached the handle he heard a croaky Rucelle say thank you.

'Don't make a mess of this again. Only a few humans believe in second chances and hardly any will go for a third.' Rucelle gave Crowley a weak smile and watched him open the door and close it behind him. As soon as Crowley disappeared outside Rucelle's office he became in Nazriel's study. Sean was sat on the couch and looked startled when Crowley arrived.

'It's like the Starship Enterprise around here,' said Sean, and Crowley began to laugh.

'Just get the hang of it while sober. I once did it after a heavy session with Richard Burton. Believe me, becoming when you haven't gotten the hang of it, on Chivas Regal and a bottle of Cinzano, for old time sake, is not an experience I wish to repeat or my dear wife to clean up after again.'

'Ew,' Sean pulled a face in disgust. Nazriel stepped forward and indicated for Crowley to sit down.

'Rucelle?' asked Nazriel.

'Ah Rucelle,' began Crowley, 'the only control freak I know who can't control himself.' Nazriel smirked. 'I tell you, if that man ever walked the Earth he would work in something like IT. Those people who like to think they control the nerve centre of big organisations and yet would probably foul themselves in a small thing like a power cut, while the rest of the world would be grateful to find a half-lit birthday candle, a match and simply continue with life.'

'He's a freak, I'll give you that,' said Sean sulkily.

'Come now, I admit Rucelle can be…a little trying shall we say. But he carries us all and it has never felt so weightier for him as it does right now.'

'Did he tell you what he wanted me to do?'

'He did, and I think he realises now what a silly thing it was to ask you. I am sure when you go back…'

'I'm not going back!' Sean interrupted.

'I am sure *when* you go back,' Crowley ignored his outburst, 'he will listen to you and you will find him more amiable.' Sean began to sulk, and Crowley caught Nazriel raising his eyebrows. 'Sean, listen to me. Rucelle is not known for his tact, don't take this personally. Please give him one more chance.' Sean gave Crowley a slightly disappointed look. 'If not for you, then for me…please,' Crowley asked.

'I'm not doing what he said!'

'He knows that, and he knows what he asked was a silly idea.'

'If I do this, then it has to be my way.'

'He knows,' sighed Crowley.

CHAPTER 27

'How long have I been here?' asked Sean. He put down his pen and looked over at Rucelle who glanced upwards from reading his scroll. Rucelle pinched the bridge of his nose and squinted.

'A while, I suppose. Would you like some refreshment?' offered Rucelle.

'No, I mean, here,' Sean gave a general glance around him, 'in Heaven...or dead?' Rucelle spun his chair gently to the white table behind him and with a wave appeared a pot of tea, a small jug of milk and two china teacups complete with saucers. He stood, then took a few steps to stand in front of the table to begin to make the tea and paused for a second to turn to Sean and smile.

'It was Crowley who taught me the art of patience through making a cup of tea, believe it or not?' grinned Rucelle. 'I can make a cup of tea appear anytime I want but Crowley made me feel the satisfaction of making it for myself. He taught me that being patient always brings a more satisfying result.' Rucelle finished pouring from the pot and added a dash of milk to each cup and marvelled at the confined but billowing cloud. Rucelle returned to his desk and passed a cup to Sean.

'But surely in Heaven you could magic up a cup that's even better than what you could make?'

'Never! And I've tried. But as Crowley correctly pointed out, it does not have the added ingredients of patience and determination.'

Sean began to laugh. 'Were you and Crowley pissed when this profound conversation took place? Patience and determination! It's tea!!' Rucelle gave a nervous cough and blushed a little as he sat down.

'Well, back to your original question about how long, well that all depends. We have no concept of time up here as you have gathered by now. But if you still feel the need to quantify it then, at most, a couple of months.'

'Really? That long? Or is it? I can't tell anymore. It's so weird not being able to feel time and I'm starting to feel like I don't understand it anymore either.' Sean daydreamingly took a sip of his tea. 'Anyway, how is Christian and his rabble of rats getting on?' Rucelle noticed that an unaware Sean gesticulated to his left.

'I try not to think of them too much,' Rucelle lied and then without a word they turned back to their desks, began to read again and almost simultaneously picked up their pens to make notes. Now and again, Sean would cast a glance over to his left. He wondered if he looked a certain way would he be able to catch a glance of something. He never did.

A while later, Rucelle began to re-curl the scrolls that were now scattered across his desk and started to pile them, pyramid fashion as he went along.

'I think we can call it a day now,' sighed Rucelle. Sean silently began to tidy up his area, closing books and tapping a large amount of paper into a neat pile. 'How are you finding life with the Crowley's?' asked Rucelle.

'Jen is lovely, too good for him. She makes a mean shepherd's pie as well. I think Crowley is getting narked because she keeps giving me first choice for the meals,' Sean laughed.

'I have no doubt that Crowley is enjoying your company immensely,' said Rucelle. Sean watched Rucelle as he moved all their reading material onto the table behind his desk. He had warmed to Rucelle after Crowley's dressing down as Rucelle was clearly trying to make an effort in listening and understanding the points that Sean would raise during their lessons. He knew that Crowley would visit Rucelle from time to time and no doubt talked about how things were progressing. Sean never asked, he didn't feel the need to. However, he once asked Jennifer as to why Crowley had so any meetings with Rucelle and Jennifer, although in the dark as much as Sean, felt they were to keep Rucelle on track more than anything. Sean trusted Jennifer and her explanation was good enough for him.

Sean began to wonder about the Rucelle outside of the office. Was there a Rucelle outside of the office?

'Rucelle, can I ask you,' started Sean, 'when I leave, where do you go?'

'Go?' asked Rucelle, slightly confused. 'I stay here.' Sean stared in disbelief and thought Rucelle might have misunderstood.

'No, I mean, where do you go to after here? When you have finished work?' Rucelle felt more confused than before.

'But I never finish work, Sean. And to me it is not work, this is my...' Rucelle looked around his office and struggled to find the word. What was the word? Was there a human word for what he did? Sean could see him searching for something and knew.

'Reason,' said Sean simply. Rucelle looked relieved at the answer offered and he smiled in agreement. But even with the fact that Rucelle's purpose had been qualified, Sean still felt that there could be more. 'What do you enjoy doing though?' Rucelle sat at his desk and he looked at Sean. No one had ever asked him what he did. Was it because everyone knew he didn't leave? Or was it because no one wanted to ask him? Was it fear of him or were they simply not interested? He caught Sean still looking at him, waiting for an answer and then it dawned on Rucelle that he didn't have one.

'I don't know,' whispered Rucelle. Sean's mouth was slightly agape.

'All work and no play make Jack a dull boy, Rucelle, and we are deep in dishwater territory here.' Sean thought for a moment and had an amusing idea. Right, you are always giving me homework so instead this time I'm gonna give you some.' Rucelle raised his eyes and Sean could see a little excitement in the glint. 'I want you to either read a book and I mean proper read it. Not sticking your hand on it and absorbing it or whatever it is you do. I also want you to listen to some music. Not heavenly stuff, earth stuff and not in your head either. You have to listen to it from outside.'

'I don't know any Earth music,' confessed Rucelle.

'Yeah, but you can request anything you want up here, just like that,' Sean snapped his fingers. 'And no ads!' Rucelle frowned slightly when Sean laughed. 'Don't worry,' Sean dismissed his misfired joke. 'Get yourself a list of successful songs on Earth and take it from there. When I come back you can tell me all about it like we are on a late-night-arts show or something.'

'I don't know where to start though,' Rucelle started to look slightly panicked.

'Get the list and start with the A's.' Sean stood and could see Rucelle was about to protest but Sean was enjoying giving him this project too much and didn't want to offer an opportunity for Rucelle to object. Sean's "see ya, Squire" was still hanging in the air for a moment after he disappeared from the office.

Rucelle sat for a moment and wondered if Sean was being serious. Did he really want him to physically read a book? And music? What was the point? He knew souls could not exist without song, but he was an angel, he was very different. But something deep within him did not want to disappoint Sean and he felt that on this occasion he should be a little flexible, if only to keep Sean happy and still be receptive to his teachings.

Rucelle thought for a moment, waved his hand over his desk and two books appeared, one larger than the other. He lifted the larger one and inspected its cover, then flicked to a page that he knew would give him assistance.

'A-Ha, ABBA, ABC...' he muttered to himself as he traced his finger down the list. He put the book back on his desk and picked up the smaller one. As he looked at the cover he was intrigued to think that the human race was interested in a book about ties and from the title they were only grey ones. He turned the book over and read the synopsis on the back and concluded that it was not about fifty shades of a grey tie, but a love story. He should have known that the best-selling book on Earth at the moment was a romantic piece and he would tell Sean, once he had read it, just how predictable and schmaltzy he knew it would be.

He picked up the books and placed them on the table behind him with the scrolls and decided he should speak to Nazriel. He soon called to the angel, and as he turned in his seat to receive him Nazriel was before him. He smiled and without a word took the seat that Sean had recently vacated.

'I felt I should give you an update on how things are going.'

'I did wonder,' said Nazriel.

'We are more or less ready. I think that Sean would have been happy to have done this a long time ago.'

'They do say that you can overprepare.'

'I know. I just want to make sure that Sean understands everything.'

'Have you told him everything?' asked Nazriel.

'No.' Rucelle leant back in his chair.

'If Sean feels he is ready and Mr Reeshon is ready then I do not see any point in delaying this further. Things on Earth are now stabilising a little, but there are a growing number of groups that are now embellishing on what they know or what they think they know. With each differing detail a splinter group is formed, and they meet to discuss their beliefs and convictions.'

'It sounds like they have replaced a number of religions with…well another number of beliefs with their inconsistent, contradictory and varying degrees of truth and illusion,' sighed Rucelle.

'The human race craves social and emotional stability and while the modern pre-existing structure of religion has by and large been eliminated, they still feel the need to organise themselves. These groups can still be defined as before with polytheism or monotheism as some still believe the angels were sent by one.'

'Well, they were in a sense,' shrugged Rucelle.

'Christian is not a God. But if their new-found faith brings steadiness, security and a sense of belonging then I have no doubt that the human race will emerge with new found faiths as did the followers of Vedism, Ashurism and Tengruiism.'

'I forget the faiths of time gone by,' mused Rucelle. 'I also struggle to understand this "need" the soul has. Why can they not be satisfied with their existence in isolation? Why do they look for more, whether it's angels or ghosts or aliens? And when they are presented with something different, what happens then? They either fall into a collective chaos, which brings war and destruction, or if one poor soul experiences something, then they are ridiculed.' Rucelle shook his head in exasperation. 'I will never understand the human soul!'

'Do you want to?' asked Nazriel. Rucelle was silent for a moment as he mulled the question over. He lowered his head as he answered Nazriel.

'Sometimes I do. Only lately have I found this.'

'You are growing close to Sean, it is understandable. This is the most time you have ever spent with a soul. It is bound to make an impression on you. But Rucelle, I must ask you...'

Rucelle interrupted, 'I know what you are going to say, and the answer is no. I cannot tell him. We may get away with this and he will be none the wiser and it will save a lot of unnecessary hurt.' Rucelle was now on his feet.

'But if we asked Crowley, I'm sure he would be able to explain...'

'The answer is NO!' Rucelle spat. Nazriel lowered his head. He knew it was a long shot. He would have been more surprised if Rucelle had agreed. Nazriel slowly rose to his feet, keeping his gaze to the floor but completely aware that Rucelle was waiting to lock his gaze.

'You know best, Rucelle,' Nazriel whispered and walked to the door to leave. Rucelle was still standing at his desk watching his friend. Then still looking at the door, Nazriel spoke.

'An animal's strength is not measured by his mind or his body. It is measured by his spirit. I do hope you have taught Sean well enough to give him the strength to face what is a battle that only he can fight.' Nazriel looked over his shoulder to look at Rucelle, 'And still have the strength to fight for mankind.' Nazriel kept his gaze for a moment then without another word he disappeared. Rucelle sank back into his chair and whispered to himself.

'What have I done?'

CHAPTER 28

Sean could hardly breathe. His cheeks were hurting and occasionally he had to apologise to Jennifer for knocking into her as he rolled around the couch in laughter at a very drunk Crowley who was sat at his piano singing new lyrics to famous tunes.

'Shifty eyes…' went the chords to Dr Hook's Sexy Eyes, '…and he'll send you to hell, will old Rucelle, with his shifty eyes.' Crowley finished his song with great gusto and took a bow at the end. He then drained his glass of Macallan and jumped to his feet.

'How do you cope with him, Jennifer,' asked Sean sniffing and trying to compose himself. With that, Crowley stuck his backside out, pushed his chest forward and began to strut toward them both on the couch.

'Cos, she wants my body and she thinks I'm sexy, come on Jenny let me knooooww!' Crowley lowered his head toward Jennifer for a kiss.

'Well, Mr Stewart,' she turned with a smile to Sean, 'and your one and only fan, I shall bid you both good night.'

Crowley was still stooping with his bum in the air, his face still close to his wife's.

'It was Rod, wasn't it?' Crowley turned his head slightly to look at Sean. 'She was more of a Mick Jagger fan. Isn't that right, darling?' he turned to face her.

'Well, I won't be getting any satisfaction, tonight will I?' she smiled sarcastically.

'TMI!!' shouted a drunk Sean, waving his hand at them both. Jennifer rose to her feet and Crowley straightened his posture as she did.

'My dear, Sean,' began Crowley, 'I do believe you have now been upgraded from guest…to family.' Jennifer bent down and kissed a smiling Sean goodnight and then kissed her swaying husband before she left the room. Crowley was staring at the door still long after she left.

'I love her, Sean.'

'I know,' Sean sighed.

'Too good for me.'

'I know.'

Crowley walked to the couch and plonked himself down on the seat Jennifer had just left. 'I particularly love her warm bottom,' Crowley buried his own further into the couch with a satisfying grin. He then sat back and allowed the couch to envelop him further and he began to stare at the fire. Sean stood and walked to the drinks tray, filled his glass with vodka and made his way back to the couch. He silently sat, leaned back and rested his head on Crowley's shoulder as he too began staring at the fire. With each crackle from the burning logs within the flames, it ignited thoughts and questions of what was to become. Sean thought of the Curia, Rucelle, Maggie and Charlie. Crowley's thoughts were of Sean and if his optimistic spirit would not only prevail but would ultimately triumph. He and Jennifer had tried to ensure that his worries were left in Rucelle's office. They wanted him to be able to switch off, if only for a short while. While they recognised that Sean was an extrovert, he had many layers and deep within those layers were his grief over his mum, Charlie, his friends and his wanting of his old life with its natural balance of expectancy and unpredictability.

They sat for an age until the fire was almost out. Their drinks had been drained long before, and only for them noticing the room becoming darker as the glow from the fire began to die, they snapped out of their trances. Crowley jumped to his feet, swiped the glass from Sean's hand then walked over to the drinks' cabinet.

'I'm not ready to retire yet. Let's have some company eh?'

Sean's eyes lit up! 'Please, please, please say Judy Garland!'

Crowley raised his eyebrows. 'What! After last time and have Jennifer back down telling her where she will shove that trolley and it won't be going clang clang clang any more. No, I don't think so. I think we'll just have some boys round. What do you think?' Crowley looked over Sean's shoulder toward the couch and as Sean turned around his face flushed. On the couch wearing a huge grin was Ambriel and sat next to him was a less enthusiastic Michael.

'Michael, Ambriel,' Sean said.

'Surprise!' Crowley tried to sound enthusiastic. Ambriel stood up and began to walk toward Sean who instinctively began to do the same. They soon embraced and within it Sean realised just how much he had missed his friend. Michael, dressed in angel attire of black tunic and black trousers, stood and waited for Ambriel to release Sean and once he did he stepped forward with his arms wide. Feeling a little awkward, Sean stepped forward and hugged his friend, aware of his burning cheeks. Crowley was soon shaking their hands and patting them on their backs.

'Well Sean, all we need now is Eammon Andrews to bring out your old maths teacher,' as he began to belt out the theme tune to This is Your Life. Once he had realised his audience was unappreciative, he attended to everyone's drinks and then sat himself down. Michael and Crowley sat opposite Sean and Ambriel, who were still beaming at Sean.

'So, how are you settling in?' asked Ambriel. Sean took a deep breath and tried to pretend the last two minutes of them both appearing was perfectly normal, even though deep inside he was wondering why they had not seen him since that night in the Royal Halls on Earth.

'I'm settling in fine. Crowley and Jennifer are looking after me a treat and Rucelle has gone all Mr Miyagi on me getting me ready for the Curia. He reckons it'll be soon. I just want it over and done with to be honest with you. Anyway, what about you boys? What have you been up to?'

'You mean, why haven't we seen you?' asked Michael. The room fell silent and the atmosphere changed dramatically.

'Yes.'

'Rucelle asked us to stay away,' confessed Ambriel.

'Why?' asked Sean.

'He felt...we...well...he felt...I...would erm...you know...' Michael trailed off.

'No! What?' Sean hoped it wasn't what he thought it was. Michael began to squirm, feeling a little tongue-tied.

'Distract you,' Michael mumbled.

'Shit,' Sean was barely audible. Crowley, in a flash, could sense what had happened and more importantly what hadn't happened and decided to plough in.

'Sean, is it fair to say you had a crush on Michael?' Crowley began light-heartedly. 'I mean who wouldn't? Even though I am a male with red blood that only rushes for the ladies, I can understand why an archangel who dressed from head to toe in body-hugging black, with a leather jacket, a dazzling smile, perfect jet-black hair and a bum like a peach would not be worth a second glance.' Crowley looked at the fire and in an instant the flames were high, and Crowley could see the reddening face of Sean. 'But is it also fair to say that since you have found out he is not a sexy chauffeur...'

'Not helping,' interrupted Sean.

'Okay, since you found out he is the archangel that kicked the Devil's arse, would you say that your feelings toward him have changed?' Crowley tried to sound leading.

'What is this? A shit version of Oprah?'

'Well?'

'Don't embarrass him, Crowley,' Michael waved his hand without looking at Sean. Sean realised in that moment that Michael was just as embarrassed as he was and the only way for it to go away was to talk about it.

'Okay Michael, yes I had the hots for you. But when you look like a cross between John Travolta and George Clooney, from his days in ER I should add, then what do you expect?'

'To be fair Michael, you could have worn anything,' said Ambriel trying to sound supportive.

'Yeah, why didn't you dress like Ambriel in his...' Sean looked at Ambriel who began to look hurt, 'in his clothes that make him look very handsome and...erm...modest, yes modest.' Ambriel started to smile, even though it was a little forced. Michael looked at Crowley for support.

'He's right you know,' Crowley began, 'you could have worn anything. You were only a flick and a click away from

West Side Story.' Crowley then stepped his foot to the side, gave an exaggerated click and burst into 'Tra la la la la Amereeeca!' Sean stared at Crowley in disbelief.

'Look, let's just get this over and done with. Yes, I liked you. Do I now? I don't think so. The angel get-up reminds me of the staff from a tanning salon in Lanson, sorry. And to be honest, I have more important things going on in my head right now. While I don't agree with Rucelle warning you away, I understand. It was a crush, nothing more and I am sure if Ambriel was in the same gear then my attraction would have been towards him.' Sean looked at Ambriel who looked rather pleased with himself. 'Now, can we please change the subject before Crowley moves onto My Fair Lady!'

They all silently stared at each other and then began to look around the room for a distraction. It was Michael who started first. A small snigger but they all heard it. Then Ambriel started, his shoulders giving a little shake. It was infectious! They were all soon laughing and above it all was Crowley's booming chortle.

They spent the next few hours catching up on what had happened since the angels had left Earth. Sean talked about meeting Rucelle and the preparations that had taken place for the Curia. Michael explained that the Carcerem had only been used once before for Lucifer and how they had hoped they would never feel the need for it again. It was Sean who brought up Christian.

'So, does anyone know what he is like? Rucelle keeps preparing me for the technical side of things and how it all works and what not, but whenever I ask him about Christian or Jack he never seems to answer me properly.'

'Well, Jack you've already met,' Ambriel pointed out.

'Yes, but you would hardly say I got the measure of him. I only watched him for about an hour.'

'Wasn't that enough?' asked Crowley.

'I could tell he was a smarmy git. And the others? Well, they wouldn't have looked out of place on a children's TV show. But it's not just Jack that is speaking for the defence is it? Christian is the main one. So, have any of you met him?'

'Sorry, no,' they all muttered in near unison.

'See what I mean? How the hell can I go for the Achilles heel when I don't even know what shoes he's gonna be wearing?' Sean cupped his face in his hands.

'Who is the scariest person you ever met?' asked Crowley. Sean looked up confused.

'You what?'

'Seriously, who was the scariest person you ever met? There must be someone in your past who you knew and that it didn't matter what you said they would always know what you thought or what you were going to say and always had a better answer than you.' Sean mulled for a moment as he stared into the still roaring fire. His eyes lit up as soon as he homed in on someone.

'I know, it was my science teacher. His name was Mr Gibbons and he knew I was crap at science, all those cells and stuff. He picked on me mercilessly and I think he actually got a kick out it. He was a right bastard!'

'It's always a teacher! Mine was the same. Mr Samuels was our Housemaster who once shouted at me to make my bed while I was in the shower. I told him I would attend to it once I had finished, but he wouldn't take no for an answer. He dragged me from the shower block into the dorm and watched me while I made the bed stark naked. He then told me in no uncertain terms that in future if he was to call me, regardless of what task I was undertaking, I was to run immediately and do his bidding.'

'Did he ever shout you again?' asked Sean.

'Indeed, he did, and I did as I was told.'

'Were you naked again this time?'

'Only from the waist down. As I recall I was suffering from a nasty intestinal infection which resulted in me defecating myself on the wooden floor with each and every step. I promptly collapsed as I attempted the last envelope corner due to a temperature of one hundred and one and awoke in sick bay with my buddies telling me that the Headmaster was not happy with Mr Samuels and instructed him to clean the faecal matter away. Such a shame in a way as it was the beginning of term and the floors had only just been polished.' They all sat in stunned silence, Crowley completely unaware of the term "over sharing". 'So, what I am saying is my dear boy, is imagine for now that Christian is this Gibbons chap. If you can prepare imagining what he would say, then that may stand you in good stead.'

Sean, still trying to banish a half-naked Crowley from his mind, decided that this may be good advice for now. He could not imagine anyone worse than Mr Gibbons, well not until he heard about Mr Samuels anyway.

'Do you think in the meantime you could see if Nazriel knows him?'

'I will ask,' said Crowley.

Crowley and Sean continued to tell the angels stories of their childhood, who were fascinated by decisions made on pure emotion. They interrogated them both about the desire for sweets and what addictions felt like. They questioned as to why a human would do something if they knew it was wrong or dangerous.

'But you are not a bunch of robots up here, are you?' started Sean. 'I mean you know it's dangerous driving around London, but you still did it. And I've seen you eat on Earth. Are you telling me that you felt nothing when you did that?'

'In Heaven our pleasure sensors are very different to how they are on Earth. When we ate on Earth it was simply a charade. I could not feel it or smell it or even taste it as my body did not require it. But in Heaven it's very different. My being is designed for this plane not yours.'

'And yet Crowley and I can get pleasure from both?'

'Yes, because the human soul is required for the Earth plane and destined for this.' Sean looked confused.

'For an angel, eating on Earth is a bit like us eating at a Toby Carvery,' started Crowley. 'There's a degree of satisfaction, but you know you'd only do it again if you had to.'

'Ooooh,' drawled Sean, 'I get ya.' They continued to talk through the night of varying subjects including season ten of Grey's Anatomy, why women drive 4x4's in the city, why dogs are better than cats and whatever happened to Barry Manilow's face until Crowley interrupted.

'I have Nazriel calling me to his office. I am sorry gentlemen, but I feel I may have to call time on these proceedings.' Crowley stood and began to clear some glasses away. The angels stood and waited for Sean to rise so they could embrace him.

'We probably won't see you now until the Curia,' said Ambriel to Sean as he gave him a quick hug. 'Lots of luck.'

Michael stepped forward. 'You'll be fine. We have always had faith in you.'

'Will you both be there?'

'We will,' said Michael. Sean opened his arms and hugged Michael and waved to Ambriel to join him for another group hug.

'I'll see you gentlemen in the Curia,' Crowley nodded to the angels, 'and I'll see you later,' he said to Sean then disappeared.

Crowley soon found himself outside his friend's office. He gave the door a gentle knock and was soon greeted in by his Native American mentor.

'You rang,' drawled Crowley as he watched Nazriel walk to his desk. 'I have to warn you, the boys and I have had a few liqueur chocolates this evening. Very potent they were and surprisingly moreish,' he joked.

'I have simply asked you here to find out how Sean is, but I take it he is doing well and enjoying a fine selection of your robust confectionary.' Nazriel raised an eyebrow. Crowley sat down in his familiar spot and looked at his friend.

'He's scared Nazriel, and who can blame him? He has no idea who he is dealing with to prepare properly and he refuses to talk about what he plans to do. Well, he refuses to talk with me. I hope he talks to Rucelle and they have formulated some plan. But practically speaking I don't know if I am helping.'

'Your job is to look after Sean and his emotional wellbeing. You must leave the rest to Rucelle and me.'

'Rucelle and me? That suggests you know a lot more than you care to tell.' Nazriel shifted in his chair unsure of what to say next. 'Oh, it's okay Nazriel. I know you know more than you are letting on. But tell me this, have you met this Christian?'

'I have.'

'And what is he like? Sean was asking, and we could offer no answers for him and I promised him I would ask you.'

Nazriel's face did not change, 'You must tell Sean to focus on the goal and the obstructions in achieving it.'

'I call Christian an obstruction.'

Nazriel sniggered to himself, 'I agree. But a sound argument is hard to contend. It should not matter who is presenting it. Tell Sean to focus on his convictions and not to worry.' Crowley felt there was more. He wondered if he should push it. Were they leading Sean into a den of lions? Did they actually know what Christian was like? Was he simply the bad guy to them? Could he trust Nazriel? He felt ashamed for even thinking it. But why would they not tell them more of Christian or the arguments they would present? Crowley kept returning to the same unsatisfactory conclusion. This was not Earth, and this was not a court case with barristers in wigs and men built like sheds who worked for HM Prisons scattered throughout the court.

'I know your ultimate goal here is to bring peace on Earth but my ultimate goal is to make sure Sean is okay.'

Nazriel stood and walked to Crowley and sat beside him on the couch. 'As is mine,' he whispered, 'and believe it or not, as is Rucelle's.'

'I'm not so sure about that,' sniffed Crowley. Nazriel smiled to himself knowing that one day his friend would see that there had been a great change in the higher angel lately. What confused Nazriel was whether it was Sean, Crowley or both that had initiated this enrichment within him.

'Rucelle is talking of events taking place soon. He feels there is no more preparation to be done and the rest can only be conducted by pure reaction to events. It also has to be said, that the presence of the Carcerem cannot be held in abeyance for much longer.'

'So, should I tell Sean or leave that to Rucelle?'

'What do you think? You know him best.' Crowley cast his mind back to the numerous performances that he and Sean had conducted together. The delayed openings due to Sean's nerves being calmed in a dressing room with the aid of a vodka, a pep talk from Ambriel, and then a berating from Crowley. It always followed the same suit. How was Crowley supposed to calm him down? His usual speeches of people loving him and paying good money just to see him and how wonderful he was, wasn't going to work here.

'Well, unless you can think of something better, but if you tell him that he is to go to the Curia in a few days' time they'll be able to hear him wailing back in Lanson. Don't give him a build-up or a chance to think about why the hell he is doing this. Leave it until the last minute.'

'If you're sure.' Nazriel watched Crowley nod. It was slow, but his eyes showed determination and Nazriel trusted him. 'I will tell Rucelle. He will set the wheels in motion so to speak.' Crowley stood up to leave and return home.

'You will look after him won't you, Nazriel? And Rucelle? This boy is very special to me.'

'Crowley, you will soon realise just how special Sean is to all of us.'

CHAPTER 29

Jennifer was drying the last of the dishes in the kitchen when her husband walked in. She didn't speak to him. Lately, he had become more withdrawn and quiet and it seemed he was only gaining company from his own thoughts. He had tried to act cheerful when he caught himself being reserved or if he became aware of Jennifer's concerns, but the effort was too great sometimes. Jennifer knew that he was waiting for the call from either Rucelle or Nazriel. And now he had come to tell her it was both of them.

'It's time isn't it?' she asked with her back to him.

'It is,' and even though his voice was soft, she could hear the crack within. She spun around on the spot and forced a large smile onto her face.

'Well, I guess I had better put my party frock on.'

Crowley too forced a smile, walked to the kitchen door, opened it slightly and called Sean's name out. When he turned around his wife was already changed into a tailored black dress, a long string of pearls, matching earrings and her hair was swept up into a French chignon.

'I figured once we were in there, I could lose the pearls,' she shrugged.

'You look splendid, darling.' They could hear Sean approaching across the floor from the hall outside. He soon bounded in and stopped in surprise when he saw Jennifer.

'Blimey, Jen! You look like you're ready for Breakfast at Tiffany's.' Jennifer blushed and looked awkward. Sean took this to mean she felt embarrassed by the compliment which endeared her more to him. Crowley spun to face Sean and gave him a huge smile. He placed his hands on each of Sean's shoulders.

'We are off to a party!' Crowley lied.

'You are?' Sean looked pleased.

'No, you are. I mean, we are. All of us!'

'Oh,' Sean was now confused. 'Who's?'

'Yours!' Crowley beamed, but he felt his insides being torn. 'It's a good luck party. A chance to let your hair down. It'll be fun.' Crowley looked at Sean who was wearing a grey t-shirt and matching lounge pants. 'Rucelle, Magda and a few others will be there, so you may want to smarten up a little.'

'Really? A party for me?' An excited Sean looked off into the distance over Crowley's shoulder. 'How about this?' Crowley stood back to see Sean wearing a suit. The colour was French navy, but the white shirt underneath buttoned to the collar made the colour more vibrant.

'Tie?' asked Jennifer.

'Sean doesn't wear ties, do you Sean? It distracts from his feet,' Crowley explained. Crowley looked at Sean's black shiny lace up shoes. The sides of the sole had been hammered with silver stars. 'Jimmy Choo?' asked Crowley.

'You're learning,' Sean beamed proudly.

Crowley walked toward his wife. She did not fail to

notice that he wrung his hands as he approached her. He offered the crook of his arm into which she slipped her own.

'Shall we go?' he said. Jennifer and Crowley walked towards Sean and Jennifer offered her other arm and just as Sean took it, they all disappeared.

They became in a room that was almost black. Only for three shards of light that created three sharp columns ahead of them, there was nothing else. Sean could not tell if he was in a room with no further light or if he was part of the darkness. He plumped for the idea that it was supposed to be dark and they would all shout 'SURPRISE' Earthly style. But the atmosphere within the room felt strange. It felt oppressive, confining and slightly threatening. Sean was not sure he was going to like his party after all. He could still feel Jennifer in the crook of his arm and the slight tug as she began to walk toward the shafts of light. As they got nearer, Sean could make out a figure moving forward. He flashed through the middle shaft and almost immediately a fourth, but larger beam of light descended in front of the original three. In the beam stood Rucelle.

'Fuck me, I thought it was my party,' whispered Sean to Jennifer. She said nothing, and they continued to walk towards Rucelle. He was dressed in his usual white suit and Sean felt slightly disappointed that he had made no effort to change for this special occasion. Sean could feel his eyes squinting slightly as the light began to creep upon them and they eventually stepped in front of Rucelle. Rucelle tried to offer a small smile which made Sean feel nervous. Something wasn't right.

'All a bit atmospheric isn't it? Sean joked.

'You can leave now,' Rucelle instructed the Crowley's.

'I'm not leaving him just yet,' insisted Crowley. Jennifer

unhooked Sean's arm, gave him a silent kiss on the cheek, offered a meek smile and then walked to where Rucelle had earlier appeared. Sean watched her leave. He then tried to study Rucelle's face which offered no answers. He turned and looked at Crowley, who did not look happy.

'What's going on?' asked Sean.

'It's time, Sean,' Rucelle glanced around his immediate surroundings. 'You are in the Curia.'

Sean could feel his being burning. He felt as if all his nerves were being electrocuted in one big wave. The feeling was overwhelming. He didn't know what to do or say. He kept looking at Crowley and waited for him to say it was all a joke and soon the music would be blaring with a tune from Kool and the Gang. Crowley, feeling ashamed he had betrayed his friend, looked down. Sean looked back at Rucelle. Why do it like this? Why not tell him? He wasn't even prepared. Or was he? Well, if he was prepared, then why not simply tell him? Why all this secrecy? It's not like he didn't know this day was coming. What difference did it make to tell him a few days before?

Crowley knew he would be able to handle it. Then Sean remembered all the times when poor Crowley had practically forced him onto the stage because of his nerves. The times when he had acted like a petulant teenager refusing to perform. The times when Sue had to remind him he could be sued if he did not take to the stage. Sean lowered his head and sighed. They didn't have time for his histrionics. They didn't have the patience for his drama and this was not the place to make it all about him. He understood, and in some way agreed, that this was probably the best way. He looked over at Crowley who was still staring at the floor and then looked at Rucelle who was still bathing in the sharp shaft of light.

'You two organise a good luck do? You couldn't

organise a trail of traffic behind a hearse!' Sean smirked. Rucelle relaxed a little.

'I'm sorry Sean, but we were advised this was the best way,' whispered Rucelle. Sean looked over his shoulder back at Crowley.

'Advisor now are we? I thought it was too good to be true, you keeping quiet about a party.' Crowley looked up slightly and could see Sean was smiling at him. 'You did the right thing. None of these needed to see the Sean from the Winter Gardens, did they?' Crowley looked over to Rucelle.

'We locked him up in a broom cupboard until he calmed himself down,' Crowley admitted. Rucelle gave an amused nod.

'Well, as you know Crowley, you cannot stay. So, if there is something you want to say before you leave then now would be the time. Mr Reeshon will be here any moment,' Rucelle pushed. Crowley stepped forward and Sean could see him better as he was now half-bathed in the light. He reached out and took the young man's hands, then took a deep breath.

'I want to see the Sean that I saw in the Royal Halls. I want to see the Sean that makes everyone listen. I want to see the Sean that I miss. And instead of thinking about all the people you help that are in the audience that have come to be loved and remembered, I want you to think of your mum. She is the one that loves and remembers you the most. She was immensely proud of you, Sean, and if you make her proud then that's all that will matter, to all of us.' Sean could feel the lump rising in his throat.

'Okay, Crowley,' he croaked. Before he could say another word, Sean threw his arms around Crowley's waist and pressed his chin against his shoulder. Crowley closed his eyes, pulled him even closer and gave him a long gentle squeeze. He eventually pushed Sean from his body by his shoulders, gave him one last look and with a slight nod to Rucelle he walked into the darkness to join Jennifer.

'Is there anything you want to say to me, Rucelle?'

'Mr Reeshon will come in a moment. He will be seated there,' Rucelle pointed to the middle shaft of light. 'You will be here,' pointing to his left, 'and the others will be there,' pointing to his right. 'You can ask whatever you feel is necessary but make sure it has purpose. We will all be watching over there and you will be able to see us once Mr Reeshon arrives, then you know what to do. We have been through all of this. You can call anyone you see fit to support you, but it must have a purpose.' Sean continued to look to Rucelle, his face expressionless.

'But is there anything *you* want to say to me, Rucelle?' Sean's voice was almost imploring. Rucelle's shoulders sagged a little as he turned his gaze to the floor to collect his thoughts. He then looked up at Sean.

'The one thing that unites souls and angels is hope. It is one of the rare things we have in common. Everyone up there is hoping that you do well. They are hoping that the balance between Heaven and Earth is restored. They are hoping that mankind will channel new paths for their future and their beliefs. But the one thing that I have without question is faith. I know you can do this, and it's not just because I have taught you, it's because of your unique soul. And you are unique Sean, please believe this. There is no one in Heaven, or on Earth, like you, and I am sorry for ever doubting you when we first met. But I have no doubts now, they have all been replaced with my utmost faith in you, my dear Sean.' Then Rucelle stepped forward and gave Sean a gentle kiss on his forehead. It was the sweetest kiss Sean had ever known.

'Ready?' Rucelle whispered. Sean took a deep breath.

'Ready.'

With a dramatic swoop, Rucelle turned and almost immediately the back of the room became bathed in light. Hundreds of people were seated, ascending as far as the eye could see. The lower rows were filled with familiar faces including Michael, Ambriel, Magda, Jude and Anthony who were seated together. The Crowleys sat to their right with Crowley behind where Sean should stand. Nazriel was to their left and an empty seat awaited Rucelle. At least they were all near him.

Sean then became distracted. A tall black man dressed in similar clothes to Rucelle's, only black, made his way to the now softened shaft of light. The light now revealed a high glass table to which the gentleman could sit. Sean watched him as he climbed the few steps to reach his place and noticed that the table could not be made of glass as his lower body could not be seen as he sat down.

'I am Mr Reeshon, could you please approach the bank?' His voice was deep and velvety, and Sean thought of drinking chocolate.

'The what?' asked Sean.

'The bank,' Mr Reeshon could see that repeating it was still not helping. 'This table. Me!'

'Ooooh,' and Sean quickly scooted over to Mr Reeshon and gave a nervous giggle. 'You look nothing like your pictures,' Sean joked recalling a children's bible from his infant school where Adam looked more like Justin Timberlake.

'And you don't look like your picture in your current passport,' Mr Reeshon raised an amused eyebrow and Sean felt a little surprised at the witty retort.

'Rucelle has explained everything to you and you are comfortable to begin?' asked the judge.

'I am, sir.'

'Then who do you call?'

Just like that, thought Sean, no introductions or an opening speech as to why they were all there. Up until two minutes ago he had been worried if he could remember all the moves to The Locomotion and now he was in the middle of the Curia. He looked down at his feet and studied his Jimmy Choo shoes and then concluded that this brand brought him nothing but constant and ill-timed surprise. But then with a closed-eye breath, he remembered all his teachings with Rucelle and he knew he was ready. He raised his head and stepped forward to be heard.

'I call Jack Remington, please sir.' Mr Reeshon stared at Sean and Sean stared back. Should he have not asked for Jack?

'Well, call him then?' pushed the judge.

'What? Just shout out his name, you mean?' asked Sean.

'Unless, you prefer to use a whistle?' Mr Reeshon asked sarcastically. Sean looked over at Crowley who gave a wide eyed sharp nod. Sean lowered his head; he could feel his nerves getting the better of him. *You can do this*, he told himself. *I want to see the Sean that I saw in the Royal Halls*, he could hear Crowley's echoing voice swimming in his mind. Sean took a deep breath and focused his mind. She soon came to him. She was carrying a cup of tea and he was lying on the couch waiting for her to sit back down next to him, so they could carry on watching something on the TV. 'Thanks Mum,' he heard himself say when she passed the tea.

'I call Jack Remington,' shouted Sean and as he raised his head he caught a glimpse of Crowley who sat like a proud dad.

From Sean's far left, he could see the familiar figure making his way towards the glass table. Jack's steely eyes locked onto Sean and without looking where he was going he perfectly navigated his way to his seat and sat down with an air of pretension. Before Sean walked over, he gave a fleeting glance to the angels and souls that were watching him. In a way, it felt no different to the many venues he had performed in while he was touring. He became aware of his walk and slowly made his way towards Jack.

'Mr Remington. How does it feel to be back in the land of the living?' Sean caught Jack's confused look, 'or the dead, whichever you prefer?' Jack stayed silent. 'But it's fair to say you did prefer the land of the living, did you not?'

'In some respects, yes.'

'Tell me Jack, you don't mind if I call you Jack, do you?' Sean didn't wait for a response. 'Tell me, when did you come up with the idea of angels being recognised for their deeds?'

Jack mulled for a moment, 'I didn't come up with the idea.'

'Oh, so was it one of your friends. Let me see, who were they? Sam? Joe? Or was it Ed?'

'It was none of them,' Jack sounded bored.

'No, I didn't think so. Ed doesn't look like he could formulate a lather on his scalp never mind a plan within it.' Sean could hear a few chuckles around the room which gave him a little tingle. 'So, am I correct in presuming that everything was masterminded by Christian?' Jack shifted a little in his chair.

'Well, yes. But we did help.'

'Oh, I know, I saw your help, in the Royal Halls as I remember. But…well…you didn't really have any say in the matter, did you?'

Rucelle leaned over to Crowley. 'Where is he going with this?' he whispered.

'As Sean always says, you have to find the Achilles heel

and Jack's is his rather over-inflated ego,' he whispered back.

'I'm sure my master will agree that my input was invaluable.' Jack was showing a little frustration. Sean gave an exaggerated laugh.

'Your input, as you call it, could have been performed by a trained monkey. As I recall, the spotlight was soon shifted once I arrived back on stage. Your audience was hardly captivated.'

'You know as well as I do, the only reason my performance was cut short was due to us all being pulled back!' Jack was starting to lose his temper.

'Your performance?' Sean scoffed. 'Seems to me, you were saved by the bell.' Jack shot to his feet, glaring at Sean, his mouth in a tight thin line.

'Sit down, Mr Remington,' Mr Reeshon said calmly. Jack stood firm and continued to stare at Sean. Mr Reeshon moved his gaze to Jack and slowly repeated himself. 'Sit down, Mr Remington.' Jack did as he was told and slowly returned to his chair, keeping his gaze fixed on a smiling Sean.

'So, none of this was your idea?'

'No.'

'You were simply following orders from Christian.'

'Yes.'

'And there was only Christian? There was no one else? He was your only master?'

'We all followed Christian.'

'Then I have no more questions.' Jack looked a little shocked and so did Mr Reeshon. Sean walked over to Mr Reeshon but spoke in a voice for all to hear.

'A man cannot make a change on his own. He needs his followers to help. On Earth we had Hitler, Stalin and Pol Pot to name a few. These men could not have achieved what they did without their followers and believers. We should not lose sight of the fact that all the angels that followed Christian are not without blame and if we condemn one we must condemn them all. For even the small part that Jack played in multiplying Christian's numbers, he did it of his own free will. A sheep can sometimes be just as dangerous as the shepherd.' Mr Reeshon nodded and turned to Jack.

'You are dismissed Mr Remington. You are to return to the Carcerem until conclusion.' Sean gave Jack a last glance and then slowly walked back to his glass table where Rucelle looked eager to speak to him.

'I thought we said we would find out when it was all planned and how Jack rallied the angels to support,' Rucelle whispered.

'What's the point? We know he had millions of angels, and we know it was planned before today. It makes no difference.'

'So what difference have you made there?' he spat.

Sean smiled, 'I'll tell you the difference, Squire. Jack has admitted that it was all Christian's idea, so we know we are not overlooking some other clever dick. We could condemn Christian not realising that there is someone else in the background ready to take over when all the dust settles. We now know that this was all contained with them and they are all contained in the Carcerem. We don't want any nasty surprises in here or in the future, do we? Also, we need to make sure that all the angels involved are condemned as well and not just those that listened to Christian. They are all dangerous in my books and they all deserve to be punished. I didn't die just to see Christian go down and then me walk into Benito's to see all his mates crying over him!' Rucelle stared at Sean unsure what to say. He then began to smile, and he turned his gaze to Crowley.

'Told you,' Crowley said proudly. Rucelle beamed back at Sean and for the first time Sean noted that he looked a little excited which filled Sean with confidence. Jennifer was smiling and nodding in approval. However, Sean noticed that the smile from Nazriel looked a little forced. He quickly brushed it away and walked over to Mr Reeshon.

'Shall I call again now, sir?'

'Yes please,' Mr Reeshon instructed. Sean was nervous, this was the main event. He would finally meet him, and he knew he was ready for a fight.

'I call Christian,' he boomed with confidence, if only for show. Sean walked back towards his glass table near Crowley and Rucelle. He wanted to wait until Christian was settled before approaching him. He wanted him to wait for him. He wanted to look like he was in control.

Sean could see him approaching. He could see he was dressed in white, similar if not the same as Rucelle's outfit. The man looked like he was carrying a little weight around his middle which affected his gait as he walked. He could see, as he approached, that his hair was grey and was brushed back from his face. His face was slightly tanned, and Sean could see the dark brown eyes staring back at him. The eyes were familiar and with each approaching step Sean could feel the dread and disbelief coursing through his body. He had seen those eyes before. He had seen them in a photograph, an old photograph of a much younger man but the eyes were the same.

'Oh my God,' Sean's voice was strained, and he groped for his chair. Crowley looked at Christian who was sitting down, his eyes fixed on Sean who was now a deathly white. He stood quickly, took a few steps and then dropped to his knees beside Sean.

'Sean, what is it? What's wrong?'

Sean stared at Christian and a tear rolled down his face.
'Sean?' Crowley repeated.
'It's my dad. It's Chris.'

CHAPTER 30

'I must call for a recess!' shouted Crowley to Mr Reeshon.

'A what?' asked a confused Mr Reeshon.

'A suspension of proceedings, a temporary termination, an adjournment,' Crowley looked at Rucelle.

'A break, sir,' Rucelle said calmly.

'We've only just started!' The audience began to rumble, and Crowley looked around in a mild panic.

'I beg you sir, please!' urged Crowley. Mr Reeshon could see that Sean was in no fit state to continue and looked at Rucelle disappointingly.

'Very well.'

Crowley looked at Rucelle and then back at Sean. 'Your office! Now!' Crowley then grabbed Sean and within a moment they were back in Rucelle's pristine white office. They were soon joined by Nazriel, Michael, Ambriel, Magda, Jude and Anthony. A dumbfounded Sean took a seat and kept his gaze on the floor. After watching Sean sit down, Crowley flew at Rucelle.

'YOU KNEW!!'

'SIT DOWN!' Rucelle shouted.

'You knew! You promised me! You said you had his best interests. How in hell's name is this man his father?!'

'SIT DOWN!' Crowley looked around the room; they all stood looking slightly ashamed.

'You all knew! You let him stand there and you watched him fall to pieces and you knew! This boy has given up EVERYTHING!! Everything! And not one of you could tell him.' He rounded back to Rucelle. 'All your bloody meetings and teachings and lessons and promises and not one word. Not even to me to prepare him.'

'We didn't think he would recognise him! He was a baby for God's sake!' spat Rucelle. 'Now I will not ask you again, SIT DOWN!'

Michael and Ambriel squatted in front of Sean. 'We didn't know. We swear,' said Michael. He tried to put his hand on Sean's knee and without thinking about it Sean brushed his hand away.

'You wouldn't have said even if you did,' hissed Sean. They all stared at Sean who slowly raised his head and then stood up. He silently walked to Rucelle who was stood behind his desk. 'Mum kept a photo of him. She had it hidden, for years. She didn't even know I knew it was there. She was pregnant with me in it. Don't ask me who took the photo, 'cos I couldn't bloody tell her that I found it! I couldn't tell her that I would spend hours looking at his face and wondering if he was thinking about me. I couldn't ask her why the man in the photograph fucked off and left us. I couldn't ask her a bloody thing. So, all I knew was what he looked like.' Sean was now standing tall in front of Rucelle's desk.

'I hoped you would never need to know. I'm sorry Sean. Maybe I should have listened to Nazriel...'

'You knew?' spat Crowley to Nazriel. 'Oh, this just gets better!' Crowley was shaking his head.

'Does *he* know?' asked Sean to Rucelle. Rucelle looked at Nazriel who nodded to him.

'Yes,' Rucelle whispered.

'How long has he known?'

Rucelle took a deep breath. 'Christian has always known. He is part of your destiny. He made it so.' Crowley spun on the spot back to Rucelle.

'What do you mean, he made it so?' The room was silent as they all waited for the penny to drop. 'Are you telling me that Christian IS an angel? How can he be an angel if he was on Earth? I thought after this revelation he must be a soul.' Crowley was as confused as Sean.

'Many years ago, Sean, we learned of a plan for angels to walk amongst the living souls. By the time we knew of the plan, Christian had disappeared. Then by the time we found him he was with your mother and she was pregnant. A human soul being pregnant with the offspring of an angel was unprecedented, we were in the dark. All we knew was that Christian had always made you part of his plan. Upon your death you were to be at his side.'

The whole room began to talk, and Sean's mind was swimming and he felt like he was about to faint. The room kept spinning and spinning. He was supposed to help Christian. This was his destiny. He could hear his mum saying he was special and she knew he was destined for greater things. Was this it? Was he supposed to change mankind in support of his father's plan? Did his mum have any inclination that he was different? How do you not know that you are with an angel? How do you not know that you are half angel? Had there been a moment in his life when he thought he was different? He couldn't hear the answers to any of his questions. Was that because there were no answers or was it because all he could hear were other people's voices? How could they not tell him and allow this humiliation? He trusted Rucelle and it had taken him a while to do so. He should have trusted his first instincts. Did this make any difference as far as Christian was concerned and the judgment? It shouldn't, but he felt it did. The only thing he could do was see that judgement was made and see what happened after that. Did he want anything to happen after that? Did he want to know his father? Charlie popped into his head. Charlie may have come late in his life, but he was there for the most important bits and without Charlie he wasn't sure how those bits would have panned out. His mum had learned to live without him and she must have loved him at some point. So, would it be so hard for him to live without a man he didn't even know? Did he want to know the man that tried to change the balance of Heaven and Earth? They were shouting all around him. The room was becoming louder and louder and he could hardly hear himself think.

'SHUT UP!' Sean screamed. Rucelle went to open his mouth and Sean shot him a look. 'Don't you dare say another fucking word!' He turned and looked at them all in the room. 'I can't trust any of you! You've all lied to me one way or another. I'm not even sure I am on the right side anymore.' Then he disappeared.

'Where's he gone?' Magda gasped.

CHAPTER 31

Sean found himself in a garden. A beautiful, manicured garden that stretched as far as the eye could see. He could hear water running and correctly presumed that a water feature was sprinkling somewhere. He turned on the spot and could see a house, or was it a house? No doubt, a home magazine would describe it as a palatial villa, Mediterranean in style.

Its walls were painted in a rich yellow, but there was a definite nod to England when it came to the outside of the property. The tall glass doors were open, and Sean could see flashes of gauzy voile dancing at the edges. Even though the doors were wide to the world, he knew no one was home, he knew where they were. He was confident he could step in to the property and there would be no one there to challenge him.

He walked towards the house and could see the back of a large empty chair at an antique desk. The desk was clearly placed so the occupant of the chair could swing around and admire the immediate view. *And why not?* thought Sean. As he stepped into the house he gazed at the room beyond.

The yellow walls continued in the interior and throughout the house from what he could see through the large arches on either side of the desk. The chandelier above the Persian rug confirmed to Sean that whoever decorated this house certainly had good taste. While the antiques might not be to his liking he could appreciate the beauty of some of the pieces, in particular the Fabergé clock that sat on a marble topped oak table.

He had only taken a couple of steps into the house and was still behind the chair. He looked at the empty leather topped desk, and only for a small brass stand that held a bottle of ink and a protruding pen was the suggestion it was a working desk. The tan leather chair looked casual next to the desk and was clearly chosen for comfort. Sean went to reach and touch the head of the chair, but as his hand came into his line of vision he instinctively pulled it away. He didn't want to go any further and he didn't want to touch anything. He could have if he wanted to, but he simply didn't want to, he had seen enough.

He took a few steps backwards and knew the edges of the door were beneath his feet and with a final step he was standing back on the patio in the garden. He looked to his left and could see a heavily cushioned garden sofa and a low table. He was happier outside, he felt he could breathe, so he headed towards the sofa, a perfect place to think.

He sat for a while, completely still and revelled in how calm he felt, but then he was only allowing his mind to deliberate the present. The garden, the house and what form the distant water feature was. He imagined beautifully carved ladies pouring water from simple jugs, their faces happy and serene. Sean did not want to find them, he was perfectly happy with his own image. He wondered if he should be more surprised as to how palatial the house and grounds were. What did he expect? He hadn't expected anything as he had not thought about him for years and when he did he always imagined him in Scotland and for some reason he always had dirty fingernails. Sean smiled to himself, he couldn't have been any further from the truth.

Why here? he thought. Was it because he was on his mind when he became? Did some unseen force send him here to help him understand? It was none of them and Sean knew why, it was simply in his heart, that need, that want, he had to see. It was then he allowed himself to think and slowly Sean allowed it all to flood him, the recent memories, the Curia, the angels, Crowley and him, Chris. He chastised himself for the way he reacted, but a part of him told him that he reacted the way anyone else would, but what part of him said that?

Were they all still in Rucelle's office? Could they continue without him? He knew not, and guilt began to creep through him, prickling him to return. *Just a few more moments,* he said to himself as he closed his eyes and tried to relax and listen to the distant water. But then he heard footsteps, light steps on the patio and as he opened his eyes, a relieved looking Crowley was gently smiling at him. Sean smiled back at him, he wasn't surprised to see him.

'Did you really count to a hundred before you came looking for me?' asked Sean. Crowley walked over to the couch and sat himself down beside his friend. 'I suppose Anthony helped you find me?'

'Actually, no. I simply put two and two together,' said Crowley. Sean smiled at his shallow reasoning, when in fact Crowley had found him because he understood him, probably more than he understood himself.

'Is it time to go?' asked Sean.

'No, Rucelle has spoken to Mr Reeshon and we will continue when WE are ready to continue. You've had quite a shock and I've told them…well…' Sean raised his eyebrows. 'Well…I've said some things which do not need repeating and it's not important anyway,' Crowley said dismissively. Sean could only imagine what he said and knew it would have been said from this man's huge heart and Sean could physically feel a surge in love for this wonderful soul.

'So, how do you feel?' asked Crowley.

'Dumb.' Sean shrugged, and Crowley shifted in his seat for more. 'How did I not know? How did I not see this coming? And the way I reacted! Why couldn't I have stayed calm? How could I not know that I was different?'

'But you did, Sean. Since I have known you, you have always felt unsatisfied. You thought then it was because of men or your job or money or a number of things. But this last year has proven that it wasn't any of those things and yet you still felt that there should have been more, didn't you?' He leaned towards Sean who simply nodded. 'You told me in the moments on the plane when you thought you were about to die you felt disappointment, you felt unfulfilled because you felt that there was more. Well, this is more! You were right! You're a special boy, I knew it, your mum knew it and everyone that came to see you or watched you on TV knew it. So, you shouldn't feel dumb, you should feel relieved.'

Crowley was right, all the signs had been there. That feeling of being different his whole life that he had labelled with homosexuality, loneliness, not having a father, not having a great job, having the gift of mediumship. But who could blame him for these labels? No one, and he shouldn't blame himself and for the first time, he felt relief.

'Is Rucelle striding around his office like an expectant father?' Sean joked.

'Surprisingly, Rucelle was more concerned about you

than anything else. He even chucked Magda out,' Crowley sniggered.

'I can't stand her, she's so judgemental.'

'That's her job.'

'No, her job is about keeping harmony within the Divisions by placing the right people in the right place. She needs to "feel" people more, not judge them on sight and if she can't help what she thinks she could try and help what comes out of her mouth. She reminds me of Sue in a way,' Sean looked up and thought of his manager. 'I wonder what she's doing now?'

'The last I heard she was offered a TV deal to investigate strange happenings since the Day of Revelations. A pilot show aired which found Sue in County Wicklow talking to a farmer who claimed to have trapped an angel in his milking machine. Reviews were mixed including whether the farmer should be the star of the show, was this a cure for lactose intolerance and did his milk give the consumer celestial powers, and if so could he offer skimmed.' Sean shook his head and gave a small titter at the thought and was glad that Sue had continued in the entertainment world.

Crowley looked at the garden and admired its beauty. The house he was not interested in, bricks and mortar never impressed him, it was always gardens that Crowley felt at home in. He stretched his legs out and leant back into the sofa.

'Let's have a little siesta, eh? Then we'll head back and let Rucelle know whether it's a boy or a girl.' Crowley closed his eyes and craned his head to the higher heavens. Sean watched him and slowly followed suit and the two of them lay there, one satisfied that he had been found, and the other satisfied that he had found him, and just for a moment they allowed nothing else to consume them.

They lay for a while and Sean could hear the questions in his head. But in the calmness of the garden he told himself that it was not up to him to answer them, it was up to those who knew. But did he want to know? Of course, he did. How could he continue in the Curia and not know? How could he give it his best and answer the questions of mankind if he had unanswered questions in himself? Would Rucelle tell him what he needed to know? Did he trust him? He concluded that he did, but that wasn't to say he still found Rucelle secretive, controlling and maybe a little naive. After a while, his thoughts were interrupted by a snoring Crowley and it was then Sean felt that they should go, if only to stop the incessant noise. He gave Crowley a shake and let him come to terms with his surroundings for a moment.

'We better get back. It's been hours, I think,' Sean said softly. Crowley sat up and tried to rub some energy into his face.

'I was having a lovely dream. I was being massaged by Ursula Andress and she was promising me a Pernod like I've never tasted before and a Melton Mowbray pork pie. Bizarre!' he chuckled. He then slapped his knees, stood up and watched Sean do the same. 'Ready?' Crowley asked.

'Let's walk for a bit, just before we go back,' suggested Sean. Crowley, thinking it was a splendid idea, pointed to the openness of the garden and allowed Sean to take the lead. They were soon in a slow stride together walking through the gardens with the house behind them and they began to talk of embarrassing moments in their lives.

'What's the dumbest thing you ever did then?' asked Sean. Crowley thought for a moment.

'A barmaid in Stoke on Trent.'

CHAPTER 32

Rucelle was sat in his office, waiting patiently. They had all been and gone, some several times. Anthony, Jude, Michael and even Ambriel came, if only to pass on news to Jennifer. They had all assumed that as Crowley had not returned he must have found Sean. But as Rucelle began to wind himself up with not knowing what to do next, it was Jennifer who told him that Crowley would look after Sean and he should trust her husband to do the right thing. After all, was that not the reason why Crowley was appointed to Sean in the first place? Nazriel agreed with Jennifer and told Rucelle that patience would bring clarity and they needed that now more than ever. He thought maybe he should see Jennifer again. Would she be able to enlighten him on what to expect when they did return? Would Sean return to them? How sure was she that Crowley had the ability to convince Sean that he was on the right side?

In a blink of an eye, he found himself staring at the huge brass knocker hanging on the door of De Mondford Hall. Did he want to be here? Would she even let him in? He tugged at the collar at his neck and gave himself a little shake before he gave a firm rap on the door. It wasn't long before she was there, half hidden behind the huge oak door. She didn't seem surprised to see him and Rucelle was relieved that she greeted him with a warm smile.

'Tea?' and she cocked her head to indicate to him to come in.

They were soon in the kitchen and without speaking Rucelle sat at the pine table while he watched Jennifer make their drinks. He was grateful when she slid a large mug of steaming brew towards him as she sat down to her own.

'I don't know why I'm here,' Rucelle confessed.

'Of course, you do. You're worried about where they are and that's understandable.'

'And you're not?'

'No. No, I'm not,' she smiled. 'Crowley will bring Sean back when he is ready and not before, and that's what we all want isn't it?' Rucelle nodded. 'You can't do your bit until my husband has done his, so you just concentrate on that instead of wondering what's happening with the bits you can't control.' Jennifer took a sip of her tea and kept her gaze on Rucelle who was staring into his mug. 'You see, that's it, isn't it? You're not used to not having control, it's an alien feeling to you. Well, welcome to the community of hand wringers, nail biters and head rubbers,' chuckled Jennifer and Rucelle allowed himself a small smile. She was right, but she hadn't summed him up entirely, it wasn't just about the Curia or Christian or even Mr Reeshon.

'Do you think they'll forgive me?' whispered Rucelle.

'Why don't you ask them yourself?' said a smiling Jennifer as she stood up and began to walk beyond Rucelle. He turned to see Crowley and Sean standing at the kitchen door and watched as Jennifer and her husband embraced. Rucelle searched Sean's eyes that were staring straight at him for an indication of how he felt. When Crowley pulled away from his wife he noticed the silent exchange between Sean and Rucelle.

'Jennifer,' he boomed. 'Drinks! We gentleman have a lot to talk about, don't we?' Crowley marched forward and pulled out the empty chair next to Rucelle and indicated to Sean. 'You sit here, young man. Rucelle, you make yourself comfortable again.'

'Are we not going back to my office?'

'Indeed, we are not.' Crowley headed to the kitchen cupboards and began to rummage through a crammed cupboard full of glasses. 'This place helps me think and it's my home, and Sean's for that matter, and I feel we are at our best where we feel most comfortable and no offence Rucelle, but your office is as comfortable as pissing in a field at night when you can hear the hum of a nearby electric fence.' He placed three glasses on the table and looked over at his smiling wife.

'Whisky?' she giggled.

'Yes, and vodka and I have a hankering for a Pernod,' he caught Sean smiling, 'and whatever Rucelle wants.' He looked down at Rucelle. 'What do you want?' Crowley realised that he had never seen Rucelle have a drink before. Rucelle began to stutter and for some reason start to look around the kitchen for inspiration. Crowley turned to Sean. 'What's a good drink to start Rucelle on, do you think?' Sean wanted to laugh. The whole unexpected scene was amusing him, and Crowley looked determined to keep the mood upbeat and energetic.

'Cider?' suggested Sean.

'A first cider should be consumed at the back of something, like a bike shed or a supermarket. To say you had your first cider at De Mondford Hall could subject him to ridicule for the foreseeable future.'

'From who?' laughed Sean.

'From me!' said Crowley. 'Darling, get this man a Babycham and we'll see if we can get him upgraded to a Dom Perignon before this whole sorry tale is over.'

While Crowley cleared the mugs away from the table, Jennifer was soon back with three bottles on a tray instructing them if they required mixers they should get them themselves. She then walked over to a seated Sean and gave him a kiss on the cheek.

'Nice to have you home,' and after giving Sean a little squeeze, she left the kitchen. Crowley began unscrewing tops and started to pour the drinks.

'Have you seen A Few Good Men?' he asked Sean and Rucelle. The angel looked blank. 'Well, I'm Tom Cruise, so you'll follow my lead.'

'What does that mean?' asked a confused Rucelle.

'It means you're Demi Moore, so drink your Babycham,' said Sean as he pushed the glass in front of Rucelle. Sean locked his gaze and smiled and Rucelle could feel relief flood him and it wasn't lost on Sean. Sean could see in that moment that Rucelle was grateful, it was an emotion that neither Sean nor Crowley had witnessed before.

'So,' started Crowley, 'we've done it your way, Rucelle with your Top-Secret file approach and the hope that people don't know what their dad looks like and look where it got us. So, now we are going to do it my way and my way is quite simple. We are going to start at the beginning again about how Christian and Maggie…' Crowley looked over to a blushing Sean, 'well…you know…' he squirmed in his chair. 'You can spare the details of that and just take it from him buggering off and what happened next.'

Rucelle looked at his fizzy drink. It looked pleasant enough but was it a good idea for him to drink it. He knew Sean and Crowley were watching him and expected him to taste it before he answered any questions. He lifted the glass and swallowed the dancing liquid in his mouth. Crowley looked at Sean, who raised his eyebrows then shifted his gaze back to Rucelle. It was silently understood between them not to enquire as to what Rucelle thought of his drink and to continue as though nothing had happened.

Rucelle began to talk of Bathisma coming to him and revealing what Christian was planning. He admitted to Sean that they knew that Christian was planning a rebellion but even in Heaven they had to have proof and the only evidence they could find was a pregnant Maggie and that wasn't enough. After all, Maggie could not be called as a witness. In the end, they only knew enough to prepare, not to accuse. It was only on the Day of Revelations that they had proof of a rebellion and only now could they take action.

'But why?' asked Sean. 'I don't get it. Surely, he must have known that he was against the powers of Heaven and that was a battle he was bound to lose.'

'Don't forget, we haven't won anything yet,' reminded Crowley. 'And we are dealing with a man, or angel that firmly believes in his cause and that carries a lot of strength regardless of who you are up against.'

'I agree with Sean though,' began Rucelle. 'We need to understand why.'

CHAPTER 33

Sean, sitting at his glass table, looked down at his notes that he had made in his last meeting with Crowley and Rucelle. Over the last few days, they had tried to gain an advantage in trying to fathom out the mind of Christian. Some of his reasons were obvious but some were debatable, even amongst the three of them. Rucelle and Crowley had offered advice and suggestions on how to proceed next and once Sean had took his time in coming to terms with recent discoveries, Rucelle informed Mr Reeshon they were ready to continue.

Mr Reeshon was the first to arrive in the Curia and after taking his seat, he nodded at Sean to indicate he was ready to proceed. Sean slowly stood and after pulling on the hem of his blue navy suit he walked towards the bank.

'Let's get on with this pantomime, eh chief?' Mr Reeshon raised his eyes in slight amusement as Sean took a few steps back.

'I call Christian,' shouted Sean as he looked to his left. He peered into the beyond and from a far-off white he could see the familiar frame and gait of Christian. The man walked with confidence, with purpose and with a smile he took his seat, all the time watching his son.

Sean walked over to him and as he neared, he could see that he had only aged a little from the photograph. His hair was grey, but his face was the same apart from the smile. He recalled the memory of the photograph. Was he now seeing it with new eyes? Was the man in the photograph smiling because he felt smug or was he smiling because he was with his pregnant mum? Was there even a difference?

'So, Christian, you don't mind if I still call you Christian, do you?' The audience sniggered, unware of the jibe.

'So, you know,' Christian smiled.

'Irrelevant details as far as I'm concerned,' said Sean dismissively.

'You're half angel. I hardly call that irrelevant,' he sniffed. There was a gasp from the audience which shook Sean a little. He looked over at Rucelle and Crowley who both gave him an encouraging smile.

'I'm also half soul, but now is not the time to brag.' Sean tried to muster the "performing Sean". It was the only thing he could rely on. He told himself that each night he had walked onto the stage he had no idea what was ahead of him and this was to be no different. He had to think of this as a show, otherwise how would he cope? 'Can you confirm to me that you and only you formed the idea of angels walking amongst those living on Earth?'

'I can.'

'Can you please tell us why?'

'Why not?' Sean looked at Christian and waited for more, but he sat silent.

'Please could you explain,' he drawled his last word, 'why you felt this change was good?'

'Of course.' He took a breath which reminded Sean of

himself just as he was about to capture his audience. 'It is written that we were created to serve mankind. Our whole being is to provide, protect, attend and ultimately deliver the human soul. It has been that way for thousands upon thousands of years. And yet nowhere is it written that this must be veiled. Our existence through the ages of man has always remained, and so has the tarnish of scepticism. Our nebulous sightings have been ridiculed and driven the few to our plane.'

'So, are you saying people have killed themselves simply because they have seen an angel? So how is that a good thing?'

'No, we have not driven the soul out. The fellow human has done that with their contempt.'

'But there are now thousands of people killing themselves since the Day of Revelations.'

'Did they name it? How quaint,' he smiled to himself. 'But you forget, these deaths are not to escape cruelty. These deaths are to seek peace.'

'Peace!' Have you seen it on Earth? Oh no, I have forgotten, you've been holed up in the chokey, haven't you? Well, let me tell you this, there is no peace on Earth. There is only chaos.'

'There wouldn't have been chaos if I had been allowed to stay. The plan barely had a chance. It's quite laughable that it is being called The Day of Revelations when we were not given the opportunity to show what good could become of it.'

'Opportunity? You talk like you had a right. If this plan was so good, then why didn't you just come out and tell people? Why all the secrecy and the cloak and dagger? Surely a man of your intelligence could launch a decent marketing campaign,' Sean laughed sarcastically. 'I mean all the people you had on hand up here to help you. You should have just called Moses!'

'They would never have listened,' he gritted his teeth and looked toward Rucelle. Sean looked over to Rucelle whose eyes were unblinking, reminding him of a wide-eyed bush baby. Sean realised in that moment why Christian had not shared his plan.

'Oh, I get it. They may have listened, they may have even agreed. But they would never have had you as their leader, would they?' Sean turned back to Christian and knew he had touched a nerve. 'Rucelle has an ego that even Atlas couldn't carry, and you knew you were no match for it. The Angel Council might have sided with you, but they would never have let you replace Rucelle and you knew it! So, you thought you would take your chances and go it alone. Maybe find strength in numbers. Well here's a tip for you seeing as I've had the pleasure of Jack Remington, next time go for quality not quantity.'

'And that's exactly what I did,' Christian grinned. 'Why do you think I went to Earth in the first place? You are a Nephilim. You are unique. There is no one like you Sean. You are more powerful than you realise, or haven't they told you that?' He craned his head around Sean to look at Rucelle and all the other angels. 'Being half angel isn't like being watered down, my son. Being human and angel is a force that we all dream of.'

Sean stood for a moment and stared at his father's face trying to comprehend that even he was part of the plan. His mother may have thought she fell pregnant accidently, but it was clear that Christian had orchestrated the whole thing all along.

'Why her?' he whispered. Christian sat forward and rested his forearms on the table, his face softened, and he waited for Sean. He wanted to see Sean beg with his eyes and soon it was there. The needing, the wanting, the essence of a soul.

'She was beautiful. I'm sure she still is. I knew she would take care of you. I knew I wanted her to be the mother of my child.'

'Scotland?'

'I returned here.'

'Did you think of us?'

'Every day, Sean. Every day,' he replied.

'Then why didn't you try and contact us?'

'I barely managed it the once. So, I made sure that I would see you again and that one day we would be together. Your birth angel mapped that you would die in a plane crash and be at my side and then we could be together. Your mother had you in life and I would have you in death.'

Sean's mind was transported back to the jumbo jet. He could hear the metal ripping around him once more, he could smell fuel and he could see Crowley. He looked over at Crowley who was practically balancing on the edge of his seat. He gave Christian one last look. He never loved my mother and he sure as hell didn't love him. Lanson, Clune, Scotland, Heaven, it didn't matter where he was. The fact was he didn't love them and never did. Christian never thought about him at Christmas or hoped he was having a nice birthday, Christian had only ever wished for him to be dead! With a look of disgust that was not lost on Christian, Sean spun on his heel and strode toward his desk.

'Mr Reeshon, I have no more questions.'

'Christian, you are to return to the Carcerem until you are called again for further questioning or judgement.'

Sean did not look at his father leaving. His mind was shooting backwards and forwards trying to piece everything together. His whole life was starting to feel like a puzzle and for him to put the jigsaw together he knew he would have to start all over again and this time make sure he had all the pieces in the box.

Sean sat back at his glass desk and shuffled through his papers. He remembered making notes during his studies in Rucelle's office. One of the scrolls had offered details and the laws associated with mapping. He remembered that it had to be delivered in a concise, and some would say, clinical way. There was no emotion when a baby was mapped, and he smiled as he remembered Keziah's story of his unsuccessful applications to transfer to the Birth Division. Would his own mapping offer clues as to the outcome of this? Would his mapping reveal if mankind and angels were to live side by side? He scoured his notes and once he was satisfied in how to proceed he stood and walked over to the judge.

'Mr Reeshon, I would like to call the angel who mapped my life when I was born,' he asked in a hushed tone.

'Then you need to call Glesiah.'

'I call Glesiah,' Sean shouted. He looked over at Rucelle who lowered his head. Sean stood and waited by Mr Reeshon's desk for the angel. He expected a man so was surprised to see a beautiful blonde lady approach the glass table on the left. Her clothes, tunic and trousers of course were cream, pearly and iridescent. Her shiny blonde wavy hair sat perfectly around her shoulders and reminded Sean of the Timotei shampoo girl. Her skin was like porcelain and beneath her long lashes were the bluest of eyes. She smiled at Sean and as he walked towards her, he felt a warmth wash over him.

'Hello, Sean. I see you have grown into a fine young man.' Her voice had a feminine deepness to it and it glided over Sean like silk.

'Thank you, Glesiah. I take it you remember me?' Sean asked softly.

'I do.'

'You remember my mapping?'

'Yes, you were mapped to grow up with your mother, an only child. Spend your whole life in Lanson...'

'Yes, yes...what I am interested in is my death. What did you map for my death?'

'You were to die in a plane crash on a trip back from New York.'

'But that didn't happen.'

'But it should have. The mapping cannot be changed!'

'But it can,' said Mr Reeshon. Sean shot Mr Reeshon a look who continued to look at Glesiah to explain further.

'Another angel would have to be present for the speed needed to remove the mapping before it is imprinted on the baby's soul and there was no other angel there,' insisted Glesiah.

'But I was there,' said Sean. 'Half of me is angel and it's fair to say that you had never mapped a...nep...a... Neppypin!' The angel smiled.

'A Nephilim. No, you were the first and I didn't even know. But while you may have resisted the mapping, you couldn't change it. You were still a baby and applying mapping needs an understanding of the universe.'

'But could my angel bit that was resisting, allow some time for another mapping angel to swoop in?'

'I suppose, that is possible.'

'Thank you, Glesiah. You've been an angel,' Sean laughed at his slip. 'You know what I mean.' He walked to Mr Reeshon. 'I have no more questions for Glesiah.'

The judge instructed the angel to leave and awaited Sean's next instruction. Sean knew it was a long shot, but it was the only thing that made sense. He wasn't sure if anyone would come forward but surely someone must have existed. But at least if he was wrong then he could be sure that it was only him that had interfered with the mapping on his soul and in that case he had a lot of homework to do on half humans/half angels. He felt all he had to run on was his instinct and a little embarrassment could be endured if he was wrong with his first presumption.

'I call the second angel who mapped my life.'

Sean waited and looked beyond to where all the other witnesses had come forward. There was no movement and with each passing second his hope ebbed away. There must have been someone else. Or was it the fact he was half angel mean that he did not have a predestined path? He wasn't sure where to go next. Should he call Christian back? Maybe, Glesiah was wrong and he had changed his own mapping and ultimately his destiny. Who could tell him how much of Glesiah's mapping had stayed on his soul?

'I don't suppose there is a thing called a mapping MRI scan?' he muttered to himself.

Just as he was about to return to Mr Reeshon, he became aware of watching the back of a man walking toward the glass table. His long black, thick plait shone as he stepped into the shaft of light. He turned and smiled at his friend.

'Nazriel?' whispered Sean as he took slow steps towards the familiar angel and watched him slowly sit. When he reached the table, he was still not sure what to say. He had to forget that he was a friend. He had to treat him with suspicion if he was to get any answers at all.

'Nazriel, did you contribute to the mapping on my soul?' His voice was almost childlike.

'I did, it was after Glesiah. We were the only two.'

'Can I ask why you interfered with my destiny? Why did I not die when I was supposed to?'

'You are very clever to realise the part of you that is angel cannot be mapped. The destiny of an angel is pre-written, we are here to serve. I too, was in the delivery room but Glesiah was not aware I was there. I was hoping to reach you before she, but I was too late and as I arrived she was breathing into your soul. However, as she left she did not notice the essence emanating from you. I thought I could reverse the mapping, but some was already in your life force including your involvement with your father and his plans. So, by being able to manipulate your death by only a few short months we felt it may give us time to prepare you. The crash was already part of your timeline, so we had to use that point to change your destiny.' Sean expected something more profound. He thought Nazriel would tell him what his life was for, why he was there and all the things he had changed. But there was nothing. Only that when he was born and Glesiah had finished with him, he looked a bit misty.

'So, all you did was change the date of my death.' Nazriel looked down and Sean read disappointment.

'I suppose.'

'Was it worth the effort?' Sean sniffed.

'We are still yet to judge.' Sean looked at Nazriel and felt huge disappointment. Crowley was right to berate him. He should have said something.

'I have no more questions, Mr Reeshon.'

'Nazriel, you may return to your seat,' instructed the judge. Sean walked back to his desk trying not to catch anyone's eye. He could feel the whole argument crashing around him. The case had started to become about him, not the Day of Revelations. Sue had always chastised him for making everything about him and this was the best example by far. He wasn't sure how he could even get the case back on track. Should he just hold his hands up and tell Mr Reeshon to make a judgement. He eventually looked up and could see Ambriel and Michael talking. He thought of the journeys they had taken together, the analysis of performances over breakfasts, then he thought of Michael taking him to St Bart's church in London and how he had met Father O'Carroll and how Michael was sent to protect him. Why did he need protecting? Surely, you don't send an archangel from Heaven to protect someone if their destiny was to simply die a few months later. He needed protecting because he was special. His mum had told him that, she had said since the day he was born with the caul over his face that he had a special destiny. And why didn't he allow the mapping in his life force? He didn't believe it was just because he was a baby. There was more, and he knew deep down what it was. But was he ready to do this?

He walked over to the bank and requested a break, to Mr Reeshon's relief. Recent events and revelations had taken its toll on all of them and a period of digestion would be welcome. After the judge announced there was to be a suspension in proceedings, Sean could see the angels and souls disappearing as far as the eye could see and he made his way back to his glass table. He looked over at Rucelle and Crowley.

'I need some time to think. I'll be okay, honestly. But please don't try to follow me or find me,' said Sean. Rucelle and Crowley looked at Sean and then at each other in surprise. When they looked back, Sean had gone.

CHAPTER 34

Crowley and Rucelle were sitting in the snug of De Mondford Hall. They each buried themselves in the velvety red Captain's chairs that faced each other and silently watched Jennifer place a tray on the small low table between them. No one looked at each other. They only watched Jennifer's hands place two crystal balloons on the table followed by a square shaped decanter, its amber contents highlighting the monogram 'DMH' etched upon its smooth, flat face. Once she was finished, she turned, took the few steps down into the wider drawing room and left through the door at the far end.

Crowley took a quick glance at Rucelle who was sat staring, slightly catatonic at the recent arrivals on the table. He shifted forward in his chair, grabbed the decanter and with an effortless pull, the stopper was out and the contents were waterfalling into two glasses.

'This is a Remy Martin Louis XIII cognac. It's a step up from Babycham so you might want to take it a little easy. This drink is not only exceptional due to it being matured in specially crafted oak barrels, it is also good for shock.'

'I thought tea was good for shock?' quizzed Rucelle. Crowley, slightly impressed at Rucelle remembering, shuffled back into his chair.

'No, I said tea was served. I didn't say it helped. No one wants tea when they are in shock, but no one wants to argue either.' Rucelle, satisfied with the response reached for his glass. 'Sip it,' Crowley instructed.

They sat in silence for a while and throughout Crowley watched Rucelle. He wanted to say a multitude of things to the angel but resisted. He wanted to wait for Rucelle to open up, if indeed, he would. He wondered what he was thinking, which was strange as Rucelle was normally so vocal. Crowley noticed that Rucelle was mirroring his own intake of cognac and convinced himself that he was doing this absentmindedly. Eventually, the silence was broken.

'Do you think Sean is okay?' the angel whispered. Crowley felt the warmth ripple through his body and let out an involuntary sigh. 'I've made so many mistakes Crowley, and I fear that Sean is the one paying for them.'

'What is it you like about Sean?' Crowley asked casually.

Rucelle allowed a smile to creep upon his face. 'His tenacity, his hunger, his independence, his...' Rucelle searched for more and found he could not put into words what it was he felt about Sean. He only knew that he had never felt like this about anybody.

'Yes, he's all of those things,' Crowley could see Rucelle was struggling a little, 'but you know the thing I love about him? His self-doubt. I love the way he sees his flaws and makes them the best thing about himself. That constant doubt has made him stronger, made him speak in front of thousands of people, made him tell his parents of...well, all of this, made him sacrifice himself for everyone. He didn't do it for awards or for praise or recognition, he did it because even though he thought he wasn't good enough for the accolades he received, or a good enough son, or a good enough soul to help us all, he still did it. There are many people on Earth and in Heaven for that matter who have an unbending belief in themselves and when they achieve something they want the pat on the back, the medal, the trophy and ultimately the ego fed in huge bootlicking portions. But Sean has asked for nothing in return because he doesn't believe he deserves it and that is what makes me love him more.' Rucelle looked at his nearly empty glass and silently agreed with all he had just heard. He then drank the last in his glass, sat forward and reached for Crowley's glass to refill.

'This is nicer than Babycham,' he said as he picked up the decanter. 'I'm not sure what to do next.' He passed a full glass back to Crowley and shuffled back into his chair. 'I've been reading your human books and they are confusing and contradictory.' Crowley raised an eyebrow, 'Sean has been giving me homework,' he chuckled slightly. 'I have to read and listen to Earth music.' Crowley gave a bemused snort. 'Some of your books are firm in the belief that someone who says they want to be alone, don't actually want to be alone.'

'That sounds like a chick's book,' said Crowley dismissively.

'While others say they want to be alone and when they are offered company they can turn...well...quite vocal.'

'Again, a chick's book.'

'What should I do?'

'Read anything by Hemingway.'

'Seriously, Crowley!'

Crowley began to laugh. The thought of Rucelle sitting in his white office surrounded by scrolls while he tried to digest and understand the human soul was an amusing mental scene.

'Human books, of the fictional variety, are simply to entertain. They are not to be used as a guide in understanding the human soul. Think of the soul as an uncoloured drawing. If we each had the same drawing and were told to colour it in they would all be very different. Angel mapping goes so far in giving us the outlines, shall we say, but it's up to the soul to colour it in. People judge souls individually and I recommend you do the same.' Rucelle thought for a moment.

'I suspect then, that Sean does want to be left alone and he will come back in his own good time.'

'Fifty points to Rucelle, you can now go through to the next round,' joked Crowley. The joke was lost on the angel, but he laughed all the same. Crowley took a large gulp of his cognac and watched Rucelle retreat back to his thoughts. 'Just tell the truth Rucelle, however hard it may be.' Rucelle looked up to protest. 'I know you haven't lied, but you have misled with your omissions and that can be just as damaging. Your reasons for what you did I am sure were justified at the time you did them. But recent events have shown you that even a straight path may have some potholes along the way and we have to negotiate these to reach the end.'

'I understand. I just hope Sean understands why we did what we did and why we have tried to protect him from certain details.' Rucelle let out a big sigh. 'I didn't realise the human soul was so complex. Everything is so veiled, mysterious and confusing.'

They continued to talk for a long time about human culture and creativity and how it could be expressed on Earth through books, music, art, architecture and cinema. Rucelle constantly quizzed about how something could be evaluated better than something else and became frustrated with what he deemed as unsatisfying answers. They talked of music and Crowley was amused that Rucelle was working his way through the Guinness book of hit singles and albums.

'I'm only up to F,' admitted Rucelle. 'It's very time consuming. I have to listen to them out loud as well. Sean seems to think it sounds better.'

'I'm surprised he hasn't given you a deck and insisted you only listen to vinyl,' Crowley chortled. Rucelle gave a confused look which turned into surprise as Crowley jumped to his feet, pulled his chair out slightly and after dropping to his knees began to rummage behind his chair. As he stood up, a baffled Rucelle looked up at a beaming Crowley.

'I had the original to this,' started Crowley as he took a few steps down into the drawing room. He made a slight right and Rucelle could see him lift the lid on what looked like an empty wooden box. Crowley cajoled the black disc from its square home and after a brief inspection placed it in the box. 'I think it went with all the others when De Mondford Hall was auctioned off.' Rucelle could see the black disc starting to spin as Crowley lifted something long and placed it gently at the edge of it. 'Welcome to the world of vinyl.'

A slightly echoing voice began to fill the room and with a contented smile Crowley returned to his seat. He hadn't heard the song in a long time and he allowed himself to enjoy it. He watched Rucelle as he listened to the operatic tones and waited for his reaction when the turning point of hard rock pricked all of his senses. At this point he wanted to laugh, he wanted to applaud as he saw the slight head nod of each beat from the totally engrossed angel. The song eventually finished with the familiar fading note of a distant gong.

'Well?' asked an eager Crowley.

'I'm not sure to be honest. It sounded like a number of songs mashed together and I found the lyrics a little bleak at times and struggled with the relevance. I mean why was it necessary for Scaramouche to know if he could do the Fandango?' Rucelle wasn't sure he was saying the right thing, after all he was new at this game.

'Yes, yes, yes I agree the song does incorporate a selection of genres and the lyrics are at times...well...ludicrous. But did you enjoy it?!' he persisted. Rucelle thought for a moment and quickly concluded.

'Yes, I think I did,' he smiled.

'And don't think I didn't notice your head banging. Are you sure you are an angel and not a soul?' Crowley laughed.

'I don't think I have heard that song before.'

'You'll find it in the Q's.' Crowley hinted. 'And don't tell Sean that I made you jump a few letters.'

They drank more cognac and talked of everything but Sean. It seemed to be an unspoken rule as they continued through the day, evening, night, however long they had been there. They didn't even discuss recent events and what was to come. They were nearing the end of the decanter when they were distracted by the opening of the drawing-room door.

'Look who arrived in my kitchen,' Jennifer walked further into the room to reveal Bathisma from behind the door.

'They're ready,' he said flatly.

CHAPTER 35

The remaining angels and souls were all seated back in the Curia when they became. Without delay, Crowley, Jennifer, Bathisma and Rucelle sat in their vacant chairs. They each stole a glance at Sean who sat at his glass table referring to his notes. The recent arrivals were not even sure he had noticed them returning to their seats. He only looked up when he became aware of Mr Reeshon arriving and taking his seat at the bank. It was then Sean stood and walked over to Mr Reeshon.

'I wish to call Rucelle,' called Sean. Mr Reeshon raised his head in surprise. He wanted to advise Sean that to summon a head angel was not usual practice. But then again, this was not a usual judgement. He looked at Sean for a moment and in that moment, he realised that they had all under-estimated this soul or half soul. While he and Rucelle had pored over the details on how Sean should be instructed and what he should know and shouldn't know, they had all failed to see that at the centre of all of this was Sean. The nucleus of this whole judgement was not Christian, it was in fact, him.

Mr Reeshon turned his head toward Rucelle and gave an expectant look for him to attend. Rucelle looked surprised at Mr Reeshon's silent request but knew he had no choice. He stood, smoothed down his white tunic and slowly walked passed Sean to the glass desk beyond. As Rucelle made himself comfortable, Sean walked towards him. The silence in the Curia was eerie but familiar to Sean. It felt like those moments when he would call out from the stage if anyone in the audience knew who he was talking to. There was always a moment of silent anticipation as they all waited for the voice to cry out that it was someone they knew. This audience was no different. They were all waiting to hear if Rucelle was the person that they all thought they knew.

'Well, I didn't think it would come to this,' said Sean to Rucelle. Rucelle did not move or show any emotion. But unknown to Sean, Rucelle was scared, not of Sean, but of the unknown.

'Can you confirm to everyone that you knew of the plan before I was born?'

'I did know of an uprising, yes.'

'And isn't it true that when you did learn of it, it was too late and Christian was expecting a baby with my mother?'

'Yes, by the time we found him, your mother was due to give birth. Glesiah had already been appointed from the Birth Division.'

'So, was your plan to send another angel to map my soul before Glesiah but somehow Nazriel missed the bus?' Rucelle looked confused. 'Nazriel was late.'

'Yes.'

'So, was it you who sent Nazriel?'

'Yes, it was. We, the Angel Council, felt the only way we could change your destiny was to change the mapping of your soul. But, by the time Nazriel arrived, part of the mapping was already imprinted on your lifeline.'

'Did you consider that a Nep..Neppything could resist a mapping?'

'No. It was fortunate for us that you did. We underestimated you being half angel and how that would intervene in some way.'

'So, the plan, as far as you were concerned, was by changing my death date would show me the devastation on Earth before I ascended to Heaven. That way you could almost guarantee that I would automatically be on your side. Then all you had to do was teach me what to say, Christian would be banished, and everyone would think you were...a hero?'

'I wouldn't quite put it like that.' Rucelle sounded irritated. Sean glared at Rucelle.

'Well, what other way is there of looking at it?'

'Not every detail of your life is mapped, Sean! Nobody's is, otherwise you wouldn't be human! And for my part, that is the detail that I didn't understand, and I admit I underestimated it. I underestimated you and for that I am sorry! I wanted to tell you who you were as time went on. I thought you might even guess at some point. But then it...well...it became more and more difficult and I just couldn't risk it.'

'Risk what? Me taking Daddy Christian's side?' spat Sean.

'No!! Risk you being disappointed in me!'

Sean stood dumbfounded. His mind became cloudy. Had this angel developed feelings for him? Had this angel been looking out for him all along? Sean turned and looked at Crowley. His eyes were red and glistening and he was clutching Jennifer's hand.

'I sent Crowley to help me understand your human soul. At first, yes it was all rather clinical. I needed to know your limitations. I had watched you all your life and as far as I could see you showed no signs of being a Nephilim. In some ways that was good as maybe you wouldn't be the jewel that Christian thought you would be. But in some part, it was disappointing, as I thought the angel in you would rise and well…help make all this go away.'

'What the hell do you think I am doing here?! I'm not a warm up act you know! Me dying is trying to make this go away. Me sitting with you and Nazriel day after day is trying to make this go away! Me standing here and trying to unpick the last thirty years of my life in front of a gazillion souls and angels is trying to make it go away!'

'I'm sorry.' Rucelle lowered his head. 'Sean, everything changed when I met you. I have learned the consequences of disappointing people. I have learned the agony of not being truthful and I have learned I am not as apathetic as I thought I was. I will admit that thirty years ago I looked on you as no more than a puppet to help us when the time came. But now I look on you as my teacher, my mentor and my friend. I still wanted to protect you when you came to us, but the reasons why began to change.'

Sean slowly walked away from Rucelle trying to process everything he had just heard. Changing the date of his death was not just a small detail. To Heaven, it made all the difference. How would Sean be able to understand the consequences of Christian's actions without actually seeing the consequences for himself? He looked at Michael and Ambriel. They had been nothing but pawns in this plan and it was unfair of him to show disappointment in them when they had simply been doing their job. He looked at Nazriel; he too was the same. He had simply tried to put stronger brake pads on a freight train that they all knew was going to crash in their world one day. Sean walked back to Rucelle.

'So, my destiny? As far as Christian is concerned?'

'Your destiny states that you and Christian will stand and change mankind. This we now know as The Day of Revelations.' Sean nodded. There was nothing more he could ask. He felt exhausted.

'I have no more questions for Rucelle, Mr Reeshon.' Rucelle rose from his seat and walked back to his chair. He was a very different man to the one who had left it previously. Whether he was a better man was yet to be concluded and the conclusion was entirely up to Rucelle and him alone.

'Do you want to question anyone else?' asked Mr Reeshon, 'or do you draw the line at interrogating a head angel?' His humour was gone.

'I don't wish to question anyone else.'

'Good. I now need to review all I have heard in the Curia and question decisions made over the last thirty Earth years. I feel this may take some time,' he warned. He rose from his seat and as soon as Mr Reeshon had left the Curia the angels and souls began to disappear also.

Sean took a large breath and walked over to his glass table. Most of the Curia was now empty except for the cluster of supporters behind Sean's desk. Jennifer could see them all hesitating in what to do next, so she took the few steps down and joined Sean in tidying up his papers.

'I'm okay, Jen,' Sean whispered, 'I'm just gonna take all this and go somewhere on my own.' He didn't look at her.

'No, you will not!' Jennifer pushed her finger under his chin and raised it so he had to look at her. 'See that lot over there?' She pointed to them all as they looked slightly bewildered. 'That lot at one time or another have been at your side or watching you since the day you were born because of…this.' She waved her arms around to illustrate what 'this' meant. 'Don't turn your back on them because they were trying to protect you and love you, I won't have it. Now I'm not going to question where you've been recently but don't think for one minute you can just come and go as you please. You live in my house and you live by my rules and when I say you are coming home, that is exactly what you are going to do!' She turned to the others. 'I want you all back in the hall and we are staying together until Mr Reeshon calls us. Do you understand?' The small group began to nod, and Jennifer turned back to Sean and looked expectantly.

'Yes, Jennifer.'

The angels and souls looked a little relieved when Sean and Jennifer disappeared together.

'Feisty little thing your Mrs,' said Michael.

'Indeed. I don't think I've seen her that worked up since she found our one-eyed dog with Max's lollipop protruding from the hollow socket. Watching my wife cut it from its sticky fur while using language only heard on a naval ship or a delivery room, is an image that will resonate with me forever.' Nazriel clasped his hand over his mouth to muffle a laugh and hide the evidence. 'See you back at De Mondford Hall then,' Crowley said, before he disappeared. Soon they all began to follow suit and disappear until the Curia was empty.

Crowley found Jennifer and Sean in the kitchen. She was barking instructions at Sean to make some sandwiches and to make some of them vegetarian as she moved around the kitchen pulling things from drawers and cupboards.

'There's only us who bother with eating,' said Sean, trying not to sound argumentative. 'The angels aren't bothered.'

'They say that until they see a plate of mini bruschettas and then they're all walking around with cheeks like hamsters. Don't be fooled with this no desire stuff. That all goes out of the window if a black pudding is in sniffing distance.' Sean looked over at Crowley who simply shrugged his shoulders.

Sean turned and pulled some bread from the bread bin while Crowley fetched the butter and two knives. They stood side by side and began to butter their way through each slice. When Jennifer was satisfied they were busy she announced she was going to check the others were in the drawing room.

'You okay?' asked Sean as he continued to butter.

'I am. You?' Crowley responded casually.

'Yep.' Sean couldn't leave it at that as much as he wanted to. 'I went to Christian's house.'

'I thought you might.' They carried on in silence and when they had finished the bread Crowley began to move the fillings that Jennifer had ready on to the worktop for them to finish the sandwiches. Once they were all done and cut into small triangles, Sean found a large plate and they both arranged them until the plate was full and the worktop was empty.

'That's not going to be enough,' said Sean.

'Let's take these through, see if they are settled, and then we can come back and make some more. Only this time I want some pickle on them,' he moaned. Crowley picked up the plate and Sean followed him as they made their way to the drawing room.

When they entered, to their surprise everyone was there complete with a full plate of food in their hand. Crowley looked at the plate of sandwiches and then at Sean.

'What was the point of making these if she was just going to cheat and make it all appear?' pouted Sean. Jennifer swooped over and took the plate from her husband's hands.

'I hope you two have made friends,' she whispered.

Crowley stood rooted to the spot as he watched her place the plate amongst at least a dozen others on a table beneath the window. She looked a little annoyed when she walked back to see that neither he nor Sean had moved.

'Mingle then,' she muttered from the side of her mouth in their direction. The two men immediately walked further into the room. Anthony, Magda and Bathisma sat on one couch chatting amongst themselves while Jude, Nazriel and Michael sat opposite. Ambriel and Rucelle were stood over the record player, clearly discussing how the contraption worked. They all stopped for a split second to look at Sean and Crowley and even though it was quick, they all noticed that they did it. It was an uncomfortable feeling, so they quickly resumed their chatter if only to fill the brief silence.

Crowley made his way to Ambriel and Rucelle and after a brief discussion Crowley went to the snug and retrieved an LP. Sean watched as Crowley instructed Ambriel what to do and soon they could all hear the opening bars of Frank Sinatra's Witchcraft. He turned and looked at Sean.

'I have a soft spot for old Frank,' he smiled. Sean smiled back and soon Jennifer was at his side pushing a drink into his grateful hand. Sean could see that Crowley had no intention of returning to him or the kitchen and realised he had no choice but to join in.

The day wore on and the night wore on or was it the other way around. Who knew? Sean had now spoken to everyone at some point, except Rucelle. At first it wasn't intentional. He had sat with Jude and talked at great length of human inventions and how he would have liked to have invented the pill that cured cancer. He sat with Michael and discussed the coolest style icons of the 20th century and looked on in disgust when Michael said he thought it was the Fonz.

'That explains a lot,' offered Crowley.

He sat with Anthony and asked him what people prayed for most to him.

'It used to be house keys but these days it tends to be mobile phones,' he said disappointedly.

He sat with Magda and Nazriel who quizzed him about competitiveness and why there was a need.

'So, you know who is the best,' replied Sean.

'But why do you have to feel the best? Why do you have to display that you are better at something than someone else? Why do something that will make other people feel bad?' asked Magda. Sean gave lots of examples but struggled with reasons as to why the human race did this. Crowley soon waded in.

'My dear, Magda, if we didn't have a competitive streak then we would not have invented Sky Sports, the board game or Miss World! And everyone would be walking around in beige!' It still didn't help Nazriel or Magda understand, and they looked bemused at Sean who was laughing at his friend's explanation.

He talked with Ambriel in the snug about him adjusting to life in Heaven and soon the conversation turned to him talking of his mum and Charlie.

'I do hope they are getting on with their lives, especially Mum,' he smiled.

'I'm sure they are. It's been a while now since you left them. I think to them it's been about six months.'

'Six months? It was only the other day that Rucelle said two!'

'Would you be surprised to know that if we measure time here like you do on Earth then we have all been in this room for nearly two weeks?' Sean's mouth gaped open. It felt like six hours, ten at most or maybe a day. He couldn't be sure anymore.

'That means I've been avoiding Rucelle for a nearly a fortnight.' Ambriel nodded with a chuckle. 'Think it might be time I made a move?' Ambriel nodded again.

'You stay here, and I'll leave. I am sure when he sees you alone he will come over.' Ambriel didn't wait for Sean to agree, he simply stood and walked over to join Crowley and Michael who were discussing cars.

Ambriel was right. As Sean sat quietly in the snug he could see from the corner of his eye Rucelle look over and make his way towards him. As Rucelle stepped up to the snug he hesitated for a moment.

'Can I fetch you a drink, Sean?' Rucelle raised his own glass to illustrate that he wanted Sean to join him.

'I already have one thanks,' said Sean as he lifted his own. 'Do you want to sit?' Sean glanced at the empty chair. It was the same chair Rucelle had sat in when he was here with Crowley. He stepped into the snug area and gently sat in the chair. The silence fell between them and they each felt a little awkward.

'So, have you been doing your homework?' asked Sean, he offered a small smile and Rucelle looked relieved.

'I have, I'm up to F in music and feel I should widen my taste in literature. Crowley recommended Hemingway and Michael said when he was your driver and he was waiting for you he would read GQ. Crowley seemed surprised at that and told Michael he thought he was more of a Beano reader. Do you think I should add these titles to my list?'

'Most definitely!' snorted Sean. Rucelle waited a little for Sean to compose himself.

'Can we talk?' Rucelle asked. Sean simply nodded.

Crowley was stood with Jennifer as they looked into the snug. He stared and began to sip more frequently from his glass.

'Do you think I should go over?'

'Don't you dare,' whispered Jennifer. 'They need to sort this out, they need to sort their feelings out. A lot's been said, and a lot has not been said. Just leave them to it.' Crowley did as he was told and began to mingle again with his guests. He was pleased they all seemed relaxed and that there was a constant buzz of conversation. He smiled as he watched Ambriel take it upon himself to be the DJ and whenever another angel tried to use the record player he would insist they leave it to him and shoo them away. Jude was soon sitting by Crowley who began to thank him for inviting them into his home.

'I can't remember the last time I talked this much,' confessed Jude. 'I mean I thought I knew all about the human race but the things I have learned since being in here. I mean, did you know that women wear shoes that hurt them because they think it makes their feet look pretty? And that people spend money to try and win money?'

'Yes, that's called gambling.'

'I know, right! Why don't people just keep the money that they have and then they are guaranteed to still have the money?'

'Where's the fun in that?' asked Crowley.

'Who said anything about fun?' Jude was more confused than ever. He was about to question the concept more when he saw Sean and Rucelle stand in the snug. Sean made his way down the steps and Rucelle slowly followed him. As Rucelle slowed and stopped behind one of the couches, Sean continued and stood in front of the fire. He gave a little cough, and everyone realised that he wanted to speak to them all.

'I just want to say a few things,' he croaked. He gave another cough and cleared his throat. 'I just want to say thanks to Jennifer for making us all realise that we are in this together. I think we all know that without her rant in the Curia we would all be sat alone, winding ourselves up. Well, I know I would, so thanks Jen. I also want to say thanks to Michael and Ambriel. I never got a chance to say it until now about how lucky I was to have their protection and their friendship. I also want to thank Nazriel, my own Mr Miyagi, who has been with me since the day I was born, and no doubt made me a better person before and after I died. I want to thank the rest of you for your support even though I know I have got on your nerves and you never showed it.' A few in the room gave a little laugh. 'I want to thank Crowley who has been like an amazing big brother to me. I'm not going into it all now but without him I would not have had the courage to be the person who I dreamed of being. And apart from my mum and Charlie, he truly is the person I love most in the world.' Sean's voice broke at the end as he watched Crowley wipe his wet face. Sean looked at his feet and gave a huge sniff.

'And lastly, Rucelle.' Everyone turned slightly and looked at the angel. Rucelle stood awkwardly behind the couch and gripped the gold ornate moulding that edged the red velvet seat. 'I just want to say I understand, I agree, and you were right.' They all look confused but not Rucelle. He looked satisfied and they all witnessed a physical change before their eyes. It wasn't just relief, it was love and though no one understood entirely, they could all feel the change between these two men and it felt wonderful.

'Now all that's out of the way, can we play that thing called Twister?' asked Magda.

CHAPTER 36

'We call Christian for judgement,' shouted Mr Reeshon.

This was the moment they had all been waiting for and they had waited for what seemed like a very long time. In the beginning, they were all impatient and wanted to be called back to the Curia. But as time passed they all began to feel it, that feeling of dread coupled with wishes of it not coming at all. As they all stayed in De Mondford Hall they could pretend that all was well in the world. It all came to a halt a few hours ago with the call and with military precision they soon cleaned themselves up and reverted back to the characters they were before.

As Sean sat at the table waiting for his father to arrive, he looked at all his friends. Just looking at them filled him with the last few breaths of strength he needed. He noticed Nazriel looking to his right and Sean followed his line of sight and could see Christian walking in and making his way to his glass table at the far end of the Curia. Sean then stood, tugged at the hem of his blazer and took a deep breath.

'Now it's my turn not to disappoint,' and smiled at

Rucelle. Christian was seated at the glass table when Sean walked over. His posture was relaxed which angered Sean. He wanted to shout, *"sit up you fat bastard and show some respect"* but he could hear his mum saying, *"all you will do is amuse him"*. The last thing he wanted to do was make this man laugh. Sean stopped at Mr Reeshon's desk unsure of what was to come next.

'Christian,' Mr Reeshon started, 'this is your final opportunity to convince me that your actions were not only within the laws of Heaven but to the benefit of mankind. When you have concluded Mr Allister will have the same opportunity. Neither of you will be able to return to your concluding argument. Do you both understand?' They both nodded. 'Then please begin.'

Sean watched Christian rise from his chair and walk toward the centre of the Curia and as he did Sean returned to his seat. He knew as he walked back that Crowley and most certainly Rucelle were hoping that he was going to produce a stellar argument, but the truth of the matter was, he had no idea what he was going to say. All he kept thinking about was his mum.

'Angels and souls,' Christian began, 'some would say that this is an unfortunate day. Unfortunate in the fact that we are here to decide whether what I did was right or wrong. But others, including myself would say that this was a great day indeed. For this is the day when history is made. This is the day when we embrace the change that has been inevitable for thousands of years.'

'He's talking like it's in the bag,' Sean heard Crowley whisper to Jennifer.

'The law of Heaven and the role of an angel is simple. It is here to serve mankind. And have we not performed our duties in accordance? Our Protectors have saved millions of lives. The Birth Division have created human souls that still astound humanity. The War Division has helped evolution and Death keeps the scales of mankind precariously balanced. All of this has been imperceptibly choreographed to the human soul and why? Why must they be oblivious to these footlights of their existence? I know of not one reason. The balance of angel and soul has existed since the beginning of time and I can see no reason why this cannot be on Earth as it is in Heaven. My belief in this open co-existence was so strong I performed an act that was unprecedented. I created a Nephilim.' He gently pointed in Sean's direction. Sean could see the look of pride on Christian's face. But it was not a look of pride that he had a son, it was a look of pride at creating a Nephilim and Sean felt nothing but repugnance.

'Now, some might say that this was purely to add strength to my cause, and they would be right!' Christian paused and could see a number of shocked faces. 'To make such a fundamental change for our co-existence is because it was not I who needed the strength, it was all of us. A Nephilim would ensure our stability. We have served mankind without recognition or reward, but that is not what drives me and my many followers to do this. We do this to teach. Over the years of intervention, we still witness man at the centre of destruction, depression and devastation through indecisiveness, poor compromisation and delegating blame to unsatisfactory resolutions. When all the time the blame was entirely theirs, and what did they learn? Nothing! We stand by and intervene and influence where we can, but man still does not learn. But we can teach. We can teach man how to make a difference to not only his world but to those of his fellow men. We can teach that there is no such thing as good luck. Luck is a man-made veil to account for decisions that have been made by us. We can teach them what the word consequence truly means and why an action we undertake can have a far-reaching result. We can teach them that there is no such thing as fate. Fate is the mapping of their life line and as we all know, humans crave to know what the future holds for them and now we can tell them.'

'Sue won't be happy about that,' Ambriel whispered to Michael.

'But ultimately, as man knows of our existence they can now stop asking the question, *"is there a Heaven?"* Surely, that is reason enough to pursue with angels and souls living side by side. If man knows of a higher plane, then surely he will promise himself to be good which in turn is for the benefit of mankind! Good people do good things and if they are ever in doubt then we are there to counsel them in the right direction.'

Christian walked further back into the Curia to make sure all could see him. Sean had listened intently to him and had admired him throughout. He could not help comparing himself to him. His mum was shy and unassuming and would blush if she had to raise her voice at a busy train station. She had said over the years she had admired Sean's natural ability to talk to people and was constantly amazed when she had seen him perform. She would even sometimes drop the line, "I don't know where you get it from", and at the time he would always cast his mind to the hidden photograph of a man and a pregnant and happy woman.

'I make no apologies for my actions, and those of my followers. How can I be sorry for something I know is right for us and for those on Earth? I feel to repeat the Day of Revelations and allow its natural course is for the benefit of mankind and I respectfully ask Mr Adam Reeshon, Our First, to judge in my favour.'

Christian stood before Mr Reeshon and gave a small courteous smile.

'Thank you Christian. Please be seated as we now hear the conclusion from Mr Allister.'

The murmurings were rippling throughout the Curia. Sean kept his eyes on Christian and wasn't sure to still admire him as he winked before he walked back to the far glass table. It was in that wink that Sean found his tongue. It was that wink that gave Sean his passion. He looked at Crowley who gave him a smile. It was a smile of love and encouragement and Sean allowed it to fan his flames within.

Christian sat down feeling very pleased with himself. He knew that Sean, son or not, Nephilim or not, could not argue with any point he had raised. When Mr Reeshon supported his case, he would have no choice but to remove Rucelle and allow Christian to oversee mankind and when the time was right he knew that Sean would eventually be by his side.

His daydream came to a halt with an echoing snap of a lone clapper in the Curia. He looked in the direction of where the sound was coming from and he could see Sean walking towards the centre of the Curia, slowly clapping. Christian could feel the smile slowly dropping from his face at this surprising and disrespectful action.

'What a performance!' shouted Sean to the angels and souls that were seated higher and higher. 'Come on ladies and gentlemen, give the man a big hand!' There was a small ripple of clapping from various parts of the Curia and even Mr Reeshon looked around to see where they were coming from. They soon died down with less enthusiasm than they started.

'Tough crowd,' Sean said in Crowley's direction who failed to supress a laugh. 'What a load of crap!' Sean shot a look towards Christian. 'Where do I start? I'll tell you, let's start with the fact that Christian may be under the illusion that he is serving mankind, but he omitted to say he is also serving himself, to huge portions of egotistical self-satisfaction. Did one of us hear how all of this will be done? No, but I am sure he has his own ideas about that because let's face it, he is full of them. He probably has more ideas than a creative five-year-old who's just been given a new box of Crayola's.' Sean spotted Crowley whispering to Rucelle, clearly explaining what a crayon was. 'And no doubt, in his brightly colourful plan, he has placed himself right at the top to make sure that all goes exactly where he wants and how he wants. And I have no doubt in his teachings, as he likes to call them, that he will make sure that every man on Earth knows his name and they should all be thankful and pray to him. I may be wrong, but I doubt it,' he smirked.

'I agree, we do not know if the natural balance of Heaven and Earth will ultimately be affected in a detrimental way. But there are some things, thank goodness, that even Heaven cannot map. So, let's look at his understanding of man, shall we? He says that man makes poor decisions. Yes, we do, but to say we do not learn is not true. On Earth we have a saying, "we learn from our mistakes". Man must make a mistake to not only experience the consequences but to learn from them. Christian says that man is indecisive which is also true, but does that not mean that they never understand the far-reaching implications of their decision? Men do not agonise over trivial matters, they are indecisive over matters that will affect those around him, and in turn, are naturally trying to balance between good and bad.

'Christian talks a lot about luck and fate. What's so bad about mankind revelling in these things? Some people put their faith in family or friends or religion and some yes, hope for luck or fate to be on their side. At the core of all men and women is a need, a want, or a hope. Even babies know when they decide to cry there is a consequence whether it's Mum or Dad bringing a bottle or simply being given a cuddle to make them quiet. By continuing with what was started on the Day of Revelations may not tip the balance initially, but what will the far-reaching consequences be? Well, let me tell you. You now have a husband that does not need to pray when his wife is sick. He can simply ask the angel sat right next to him in plain sight. And the angel will explain that according to his calculations his wife is about to die in exactly six months' time, at home after breakfast but before Homes Under the Hammer starts on BBC1. So, now we have stripped a man of prayer, luck, fate and ultimately hope, all the things that would have kept him and his lovely wife fighting on for six months and when she did die, he could have some peace knowing that he did all he could for her. How is that better for man?' Sean paused for a moment to allow them to digest before moving on.

'What about the man that decides to go out one night, his mind all twisted about the abuse he endured as a child and how the world should pay. And he decides the best way to make himself feel better is by killing a young woman who was on her way to pick up her baby from nursery. What does he feel after he has killed? Well, he could simply say to the angel next to him that it was her destiny and his mapping said that he should kill her, so it was all the birth angel's fault. No remorse, because he can blame something that was totally out of his control from the moment an angel breathed into his soul. You have not only taken away their assessment of consequences, you have also taken away the acceptance of their actions.

'Now I am only talking about two people here. One good and one bad. Which one ultimately benefited mankind and how did the presence of an angel help? Christian is planning on changing the attitudes and beliefs of millions of people; think about that. I know you angels out there feel that this is the superior place and no doubt it's written on one of those dusty scrolls in Nazriel's study. But is it the superior plane?

'For a moment, and I am sure you all did too, I thought that my birth angel blundered mapping my life force because I am half angel. What you all have failed to realise is that I am half man as well.' Sean looked over at Rucelle who sat transfixed, clearly hanging onto his every word.

'My destiny is written, but it simply states that Christian and I will stand on the Day of Revelations. But that didn't mean together! You have all forgotten that at the core of every man is free will, something you angels do not possess. I believe that while the angel inside of me rejected the map of me supporting this abhorrent plan, it was my free will that gave it strength and spurned the absurdity of me wanting to stand with an angel that brought nothing but confusion and misery. It was my human soul that knew the difference between right and wrong. I may have a father that is an angel, but I also have a mother that has a soul, a kind soul and a patient soul and it was that part that gave Nazriel the time he needed to change the most important part of my destiny.

'I apologise to Nazriel; I said to him that all he did was change the date of my death. But in those few months that I gained, I saw the fragility of man and the weakness of man, but I also saw strength, desire, acceptance and above all faith. And because of that I can see clearly the consequences of taking that away from man. An angel showing and removing the decision-making from a man takes away his free will. So, let me take you back to the angel law of serving humanity,' Sean took his one last breath, 'to take away the free will of man, removes his humanity.'

It started with one clap. The clap from Crowley's hands and like a virus it spread and spread throughout the Curia. Mr Reeshon leaned back in his chair and continued to look at Sean, who didn't notice the slight twitch from his lips but if Sean was paying attention he would have seen it in his eyes: pride.

Sean was looking at Crowley. He was now on his feet and clapping enthusiastically only stopping to wipe the tears rolling down his face. Mr Reeshon allowed the applause to continue; occasionally he looked around and quietly enjoyed the spectacle. After a few minutes he raised his hand until the clapping ceased. Sean was still stood in the middle of the Curia. He was aware of his breathing and was surprised to note he was out of breath.

'Please sit down, Mr Allister,' said Mr Reeshon.

Sean walked back to his table and with each step his jubilation was replaced by fear. What if the judgement went Christian's way? Had he said enough? Just because he had support from angels and souls did not mean that Mr Reeshon agreed. *"Who thought OJ would get off?"* he thought.

Mr Reeshon then stood, walked down the few steps to the side of his glass table and made his way to the centre of the Curia to address everyone.

'It's been a long time since I last stood on this spot and most of you were here then when I did,' he smiled and looked as far as he could see. 'The decision I made then I felt was the right one. But let's not fool ourselves into thinking it was the best one.'

Mr Reeshon placed his worn black hands behind his back and began to walk. He stared at the floor as he recalled. 'We had to create a place that no man would want to go to, never mind an angel. We thought at the time that this would make the world a better place.' He stopped and stared at the audience. 'We thought that man would be good knowing this place existed, but it didn't happen as we thought.' He started to walk again in a slow and aimless circle and his speech was slow and steady.' We sent an angel there because he would not serve humanity, and we thought that was the right thing to do. But it turns out, it might not have been the best thing to do. There are some on Earth that worship this fallen angel and call on him and his followers and as I understand the consequences of that are not pretty. Maybe, we should have kept Lucifer in the realms of Heaven where we could have kept an eye on him, contained all that hate and rage. But we were frightened of the shift in the balance of our own world. So, like I said, we made the right decision, but can we be sure it was the best?'

Mr Reeshon stopped, he was back in the middle of the Curia. He raised his head and his voice again, 'I feel the lesson I have learned today is about balance, and just how important that is. So, I will not agonise whether I should make the right decision or the best decision, I have decided it has to be both.'

Sean could feel a sense of dread creeping over him. What did this mean? Was he going to let this happen but maybe let Rucelle run the show?

'Christian,' Mr Reeshon turned to look at him, 'please stand.' He then turned to Sean. 'Sean, please stand.' Both men in unison did as they were bid, their gaze fixed on the deep brown eyes of Adam.

'When man was formed he was made in our image except for the one difference that Mr Allister pointed out. Man must have free will and we cannot serve humanity if this is taken. To take away free will takes away the man. However, you have shown a degree of passion in wanting to serve humanity. I therefore feel the right and best decision is to remove you from Heaven and allow you and your followers to walk the Earth with the people you so desire to help.' Christian began to smile. 'In order to do this, and keep the balance of Heaven and Earth, you will no longer be an angel and your vessel will be replaced with a human soul.'

'What?! You can't do that!' Christian screamed.

'No, I can't,' he then turned to Sean, 'but a Nephilim can.' Mr Reeshon smirked at Sean.

'You sly old dog,' said Sean as he started to smile.

'Judgement has been made,' shouted Mr Reeshon.

And as Crowley would say, whenever he regaled the story, the applause could probably be heard as far as Lanson.

CHAPTER 37

Sean and Rucelle were making the last few changes to the office.

'I prefer the yellow, I think,' and Rucelle waved his hand with exasperation. 'Don't get all huffy! If it was up to you it would be all white like yours. Your office is a cross between an Ikea set and Narnia.'

'I don't know why you make all these references Sean, when you know I don't understand,' moped Rucelle.

'Your office is boring, understand that? I want mine to be fun and inviting and homely. When I work, I want it to be somewhere I want to be not somewhere that people think it should look like.'

'I designed my office myself!' Rucelle pouted. Nazriel walked into Sean's office with a smile on his face.

'All done,' said Nazriel. Sean spun on the spot, smiling from ear to ear.

'Really, Nazriel? So, whenever someone dies they will walk in here and only see a place that they have loved from their life, yeah?' Sean squealed.

'Yes, would you like to test it?' Nazriel beamed. Sean,

full of excitement, skipped out of his new office into the stark white corridor beyond and closed the door behind him and then turned to face the door again. He was full of anticipation to see if his proposed design had worked.

As he opened the door he could see the stairs in front of him and he smiled. Down the hall he could see the kitchen and beyond that the garden with Charlie's vegetable patch growing in abundance. He turned to his right and walked into the living room. The TV and radio were switched off and were in the correct place and the remote controls were scattered haphazardly on the coffee table. Charlie's armchair had the familiar sag where it had been cushioning his weight for a number of years and the slight Rum and Coke stain on the arm of the couch could still be seen. He slowly walked over to the bookshelf in the alcove and spied the thing he wanted to look at the most. It was a picture of him with his mum and Charlie at his twenty-first birthday party. The picture became blurry and with a sniff and a rub of his eyes the picture became focused again. 'Love you two', he heard the memory. 'Love us three,' Sean whispered. He sniffed, wiped his eyes again and turned to see Rucelle and Nazriel standing by the dining table.

'It's not too late, Sean. You can go back. The perks of being a Nephilim,' offered Rucelle. 'And you can still change the things that have been. If I had that power...' Rucelle started to daydream.

'If you had the power to change the past, would you have told me?' Sean asked softly. Rucelle continued to daydream as he stared at Maggie's pea green lounge carpet. He then raised his head and looked at Sean.

'I don't know,' he confessed. Sean walked over to Rucelle.

'And that's the right answer. Just because it was hurtful

at the time or sad, no one should have the power to keep correcting something that maybe was right in the first place,' said Sean.

'How very wise,' Nazriel said in approval.

'Have faith in humanity and allow them to become what they choose to become.' Rucelle smiled and looked proud. Then Sean gave a huge sniff, scanned the room and began to smile again.

'Okay, it works,' Sean said to Nazriel. Nazriel then waved his arm and they were all stood in the same spot but in Sean's office.

'I have to say Sean, I like the yellow,' Nazriel looked around in approval.

'Well, then tell John Lennon here.' Rucelle looked at Nazriel for an explanation who could only offer a shrug. 'So, I think we should call Crowley now and maybe get ready for the interviews.'

'Interviews?' asked Nazriel.

'Sean is insisting he interviews people for their new assistant,' explained Rucelle.

'Assistant?' questioned Nazriel.

'Look, I know Magda did all the transitioning on her own but I'm doing things differently. I'm not just plonking people into any old Division simply because they are short of resource. Reading human souls takes time and Crowley and I want to be sure that we are moving them to the correct Divisions in the first place. We can't have the same mistakes that were made when he arrived. Protector one minute, then spiritual guide the next.'

'Who said it was a mistake?' said Rucelle. Sean stopped shuffling the few bits of paper that he had on his desk and looked at Rucelle. 'You know enough now, surely?'

'Know enough of what?' Crowley came bounding in behind them with a huge grin on his face and an opened bottle of 1998 Krug champagne in his hand. Sean stood for a moment and tried to puzzle the pieces together.

'Was Crowley always supposed to be with me?'

Rucelle nodded. 'Since the day you were born.' Rucelle then turned and looked at Crowley. 'Grace.' Crowley began to smile.

'What? My Grace?' stuttered Sean, 'My New York Grace?' Crowley stepped forward toward Sean who was stood behind his desk.

'I was Grace's Crowley. For me to ascend to Heaven I helped our friend Grace.' The twelve months of Grace finding a new life that ended up with her in New York was one of the happiest and saddest times of Sean's life and he remembered she talked of a Crowley.

'Why did I think you lived in Wales?' he mumbled.

'Because you're stupid!' Crowley quipped. Sean turned and looked at Rucelle.

'Who came first? Grace or me?'

'It was only ever about you, Sean,' smiled Rucelle.

Sean sat down on his new chair. It was the comfiest chair he had ever sat in. He gently swished it from side to side as he stared into space. Rucelle, Nazriel and Crowley all stood on the same spot waiting for him to speak. He eventually looked up and smiled.

'She'll be pissed when she dies and hears this!' They began to laugh, and Sean jumped to his feet, ran around the table and threw an arm over Crowley's shoulder.

'So, me and you are intertwined forever it seems. We'll have to make sure that we get an assistant who's got balls bigger than both of us to sort us out when we start with our carrying on.' Sean turned to Rucelle. 'We've had some right ding dongs, some of them have turned into a massacre, isn't that right Crowley?' Crowley rolled his eyes at the memories of tantrums and tears.

'Well, I think you will find that your first interviewee may fit the bill to perfection,' bragged Rucelle.

Rucelle turned and looked at the door and a lady walked through. She was small with fine brown wavy hair. She wore a crisp, white shirt and wide-leg trousers to match. She was aged about thirty-five, but her eyes were wise which suggested she had died much, much older. Sean squinted at her; he recognised her from somewhere, but he couldn't quite place her. She looked around the room and turned her nose up slightly. She then looked at all the men and eventually rested her gaze on Sean and Crowley.

'I got three rules,' she started in a broad New York accent. 'No camomile tea, unless you're fucking hippies. You're not hippies, are you?' she snapped. Sean and Crowley shook their heads. 'Number two. I got plenty of framed photographs that I like a certain way, so you don't touch them. Okay?!' Again, the men nodded, and Crowley began to smile. 'And my last is, I'll only work for you if my dog can come too.' She turned, and a small dog came bounding into the office. Crowley dropped into a squat to receive his four-legged friend.

'Benji! How are you, old boy?' Crowley vigorously scratched the top of an appreciative Benji's head.

'You know this dog?' stammered Sean, 'you know this woman?' Crowley stood back up with a huge grin.

'Sean, may I introduce Kate Mortimer. Kate Mortimer, Sean Allister.'

It was her. She was the lady in the picture from Grace's exhibition. It was the exhibition of Kate Mortimer's work after she had died.

'You're Mrs Mortimer? Grace's Mrs Mortimer?' he asked with an incredulous tone.

'What? Don't you recognise me without my camera?' she smiled. 'Now close your mouth before you catch a goddamn disease. There's a queue of dead people outside!' She moved to the side of the office, waved a hand in which a desk appeared complete with pens, paper and a plethora of framed photographs. Sean looked at Crowley in disbelief.

'Do we need to get her to sign a contract…or something?' Sean stuttered as Crowley shrugged with a grin.

'What's a girl gotta do to get a goddamn drink around here.'

'We'll leave you to it,' whispered Rucelle.

Nazriel gave them both a goodbye nod and walked out into the corridor with Rucelle at his side. They both noted the large queue of recently deceased souls already forming outside the office door that was labelled:

OFFICE OF TRANSITION
Sean Allister
(NEPPYPIN)

CHAPTER 38

Nazriel drained the last drop of his tea from his cup and placed it on Rucelle's white desk.

'I'm sure they will make a formidable team,' said Nazriel.

'A human soul that can measure the love within. Another that could artistically expose a soul through a photograph and a Nephilim who struggles to resist a leather jacket.' He too took the last gulp of his tea and placed the cup back on its saucer. 'Magda didn't stand a chance.' They both laughed, and as it died down Rucelle caught Nazriel studying him. 'What?'

'You seem more human than angel as of late,' Nazriel smiled.

'Really?' Rucelle tried to suppress that he was flattered by the comment. He failed with his blushes.

'It suits you,' said Nazriel as he began to stand. Rucelle looked up at his fine friend and hoped what he was to say next was received in the way it was truly meant.

'Thank you.' Nazriel bowed his head and Rucelle felt he understood what he was grateful for. He watched as

Nazriel left to return to his study which prompted Rucelle to think of it. He thought of Nazriel surrounded by his books, tea cups and worn-down couches and realised he had never noticed before just how much people's environments told so much about them. He looked around his own. It felt better now the Carcerem had gone. It felt like it was back to normal. But did it reflect who he was?

He turned and waved his hand over the table behind his desk and a record player appeared with an LP already spinning. He placed the arm at the edge of the disc and as the opening beats of music began with the introduction "Morning! Today's forecast calls for blue skies", Rucelle sat back in his chair with a large grin on his face. He continued to look around his office and as the music of Mr Blue Sky by ELO filled the room his eyes rested on his plain white desk. He again waved his hand and smiled at his creation and the new addition to his office.

A box of new Crayola crayons.

THE END

ABOUT THE AUTHOR

Estelle Maher was born in the heart of Liverpool, England. After spending her teens in rural Dorset, she returned to the North of England and now resides in Wirral with her husband, 2 children and 2 dogs.

Her career has been varied, working in shipping, insurance and finance. But in her spare time, she's quite at home with a paint brush upcycling furniture. She also writes a blog, 'The Secret Diary of a Middle-Aged Woman', a humorous snapshot of random thoughts.

Estelle has been writing on and off for several years and her best-selling debut novel Grace & The Ghost won the Soul & Spirit Magazine award for Best Spiritual Fiction 2018.

For more information on books by Estelle Maher:

www.estellemaher.com

T: @EstelleMaher

FB: @EstelleMaherAuthor

Winner of the Soul & Spirit Magazine's award for **Best Spiritual Fiction 2018**

Praise for Grace & The Ghost

This is a brilliant, self-assured debut novel.

It's so beautifully written; from the laugh out loud and really heart-warming moments, to the somewhat sad and very thought-provoking moments.

Definitely a five-star read.

At times I felt as though I was right in the middle of it all standing alongside Grace.

http://bit.ly/GraceGhost2

Printed in Poland
by Amazon Fulfillment
Poland Sp. z o.o., Wrocław